ALSO BY P. C. CAST AND KRISTIN CAST

House of Night
Marked
Betrayed
Chosen
Untamed
Hunted
Tempted
Burned
Awakened
Destined
Hidden
Revealed
Redeemed
The Fledgling Handbook 101
Dragon's Oath
Lenobia's Vow
Neferet's Curse
Kalona's Fall

THE DYSASTERS

P. C. CAST

AND

KRISTIN CAST

WEDNESDAY BOOKS
NEW YORK

THE DYSASTERS. Copyright © 2019 by P. C. Cast and Kristin Cast. All rights reserved. Printed in the United States of America. For information, address St. Martin's Press, 175 Fifth Avenue, New York, N.Y. 10010.

www.wednesdaybooks.com
www.stmartins.com

Designed by Omar Chapa

The Library of Congress Cataloging-in-Publication Data is available upon request.

ISBN 978-1-250-14104-0 (hardcover)
ISBN 978-1-250-22515-3 (international, sold outside the U.S.,
subject to rights availability)
ISBN 978-1-250-14107-1 (ebook)

Our books may be purchased in bulk for promotional, educational, or business use. Please contact your local bookseller or the Macmillan Corporate and Premium Sales Department at 1-800-221-7945, extension 5442, or by email at MacmillanSpecialMarkets@macmillan.com.

First U.S. Edition: February 2019
First International Edition: February 2019

10 9 8 7 6 5 4 3 2 1

This book is for all of us who have secretly (and not so secretly) wanted to control the elements, save the world, and maybe even fly!

ACKNOWLEDGMENTS

As always we would like to thank our amazing agent and friend, Meredith Bernstein. We heart our Meredith!

A big thank-you to Macmillan's Team Cast, most especially Jen Enderlin, Anne Marie Tallberg, Monique Patterson, and the harried production and design staff who have worked so hard to be sure this book is beautiful.

A sincere thank-you to my friend and trans consultant, Liv. Thank you, girlfriend! You are wonderful to work with. It has been a true pleasure getting to know you and being educated by you. Any mistakes made with Charlotte are mine.

—P. C.

THE DYSASTERS

1

FOSTER

"Cora, why are we here? This has got to be the definition of the middle of nowhere." Frowning at the stains on the bedspread, Foster plopped down on the lumpy mattress. "And this has to be the skeeziest motel we've been to in the past year." She tucked her arms into her flannel sleeves and tried not to stare at the layers of grime covering every surface.

"You hush, and be grateful to have a roof over your head. Some people aren't that lucky." Air hissed out of the chair cushion as Cora sat and scooted her seat up to the small table under the small window of the very small room.

"And some people don't have to spend their birthday weekend in *misery*," Foster groaned.

"Missouri," Cora corrected, pulling her laptop from the beat-up leather bag she was never without. "Homer, Missouri, to be precise."

"After we find this guy, do you think things will go back to normal?" Foster paused, chewing the inside of her cheek. Since her adoptive father, Doctor Rick, had died in a boating accident five years before, she and Cora had developed their own little routine at home in Portland. Oregon, not Maine. Who wanted to go to Maine? But Foster's opinion that the West Coast was in fact the best coast wasn't the point, the point was that her life had been an unending, stressful, semi-dirty (though not in the good, sexy way) road trip ever since Cora had sold Doctor Rick's fertility clinic one long, long year ago. Since then, not one single thing had been normal. And Foster desperately wanted her life back. Her *home* back.

Foster felt Cora's knowing eyes on her and she met her adoptive mother's worried gaze, adding hastily, "Or as normal as they can be?"

"We'll see. Now quit fussin'! I need to concentrate and you're giving me a headache." Mumbling to herself about bothersome children, Cora refocused on her laptop and massaged her jaw absentmindedly.

"You really should go see a dentist. With all the chocolate you eat, you probably have a cavity the size of some giant moon crater. Or maybe it's your wisdom teeth." Contemplatively, Foster drummed her fingers against her knee. "No, I guess you're too old for wisdom teeth. What about—"

"Foster, hush!"

Foster obliged, holding her breath, willing silent the questions surging behind her closed lips. But she couldn't hold. Not for long. Not with Cora. With the rest of the world not talking was no problem. Actually, she preferred it that way, and she was pretty sure it made her come off a wee bit bitchy. Well, probably a lot bitchy, but that was only if she went off of what other people told her about herself, and she tried never to care about that.

Before she even realized she was speaking the levee had broken and words rushed out of her mouth. "Why are we here, anyway? No one stops in Tornado Alley unless they have a death wish." Thunder cracked, rattling the thin glass of the cheap wall sconces. "See! I told you. I mean, that would have been perfect right on cue like that if it wasn't so freaking ominous," Foster said, slinging her backpack over her shoulder as she headed toward the door. "Let's get out of here."

"Calm down, child." Cora's tight dreads skimmed her shoulders as she shook her head. "There's a hospital just up the road a ways. Saw it when we drove in." She took a deep breath and kneaded her left shoulder in the same automatic way in which she massaged her jaw, almost like the action was as necessary yet thoughtless as brushing your teeth. "I know they'll have a basement, and if this storm whips up a tornado, we'll head over there. Until then, sit down. Your teenage angst isn't helping me get through this any faster."

"It's not angst," Foster murmured, picking at the plastic faux wood finish of the table. "I just thought we'd be doing something cooler for my birthday. I only turn eighteen once. I kind of, I don't know, wanted it to be special." She pooched out her bottom lip and batted her impossibly long eyelashes.

Cora glanced up at her and snorted. "Try again." She turned her attention back to the computer, her deep-henna eyes reflecting the brightly lit screen.

"What if we can't get to the hospital in time because of the wind and the hail and the rain and whatever?"

Cora sighed. "Every thunderstorm does not produce a tornado. If it did, there'd be nothing left of the middle of the country."

"Like there's anything here now. And look," she tossed her backpack onto the table and dug through its unorganized contents. "Storms have been changing, especially major storms. And I can prove it. Check this out." Peeling off a crusty ketchup packet, she handed Cora a wad of crinkled papers.

"And what am I supposed to do with that?" Her thick eyebrow lifted with the question.

"It's research. For that science project you gave me. I chose weather patterns. All the other options were ridiculous, like breeding gnats. I'm not some insect sex voyeur, and no one wants more of those."

"So you've been doing schoolwork?" Cora peered over each of her broad shoulders. "What did you do with my Foster? About this high," she held up her hand until it encompassed Foster's five-and-a-half-foot frame. "Bright red hair, and skin like a snowman's. You seen her?" Her pearly teeth gleamed as she laughed.

"Very funny." Foster flipped through the papers she'd printed at their last library stop. Red and orange blotches covered the Midwest's weather map along with alarming statistics for the month's tornado touchdowns and sightings. "I'm serious though. Weather.com says some pretty scary stuff about the likelihood of a thunderstorm causing a tornado. Guess global warming is finally biting us in the ass." A clap of thunder raised goose bumps on Foster's arms. "Right on cue. Again. You can't tell me that wasn't totally freaky." She shoved the papers into her bag and slung it over her arm. "We should go."

Cora's plump fingers feverishly worked over the keyboard.

"I heard thunder. Again. We need to leave. Come on." Foster's pleas remained unanswered. "Cora!" She stomped her foot, and a ring of dust sprayed out of the carpet, making her sneeze violently.

"Dammit! What, Foster? What do you want?" Cora's bark intensified as thunder rolled overhead.

Foster sucked in a sharp breath, her demeanor hardening as she fought off the lump forming in the back of her throat. "Nothing." Her voice was quieter than she wanted it to be. She cleared her throat before saying, "Never mind."

Cora softened, and leaned across the table to grab Foster's hand. She squeezed it gently before dropping it to rub the side of her neck. "I'm sorry. I'm stressed, and real tired of this ache in my neck. These motel pillows are wreaking havoc . . ." she trailed off, an expression passing over her features that Foster couldn't quite read. "But I shouldn't have yelled at you," Cora continued, the spicy calmness returning to her voice, creamy and rich with a little kick, like Mexican hot chocolate. "You're not from around here, and I understand you're nervous. I grew up in Tornado Alley. Storms happen. Plus, it's the end of August. Tornadoes in Missouri like spring and early summer more than late summer and fall. We're safe."

"Promise?"

"Cross my heart. You know you're my baby, and I'd never put you in danger."

"Cora, I'm eighteen. You've got to stop calling me your baby."

"Child, I don't care if you're eighty. You'll always be my little strawberry baby."

"Oh, god. Fine, call me baby, just don't call me 'little strawberry baby.'"

"We'll see," Cora muttered, already distracted by her computer again.

"I guess we'll see's better than 'Child, I'll call you my little strawberry baby till they put one of us in the grave.'" She mimicked Cora perfectly. "I'll take what I can get." Foster's unease quieted and she slipped into the chair opposite the stout woman. Even though her gut was roiling in time with the approaching storm, Cora's words soothed her. Her adoptive mother had never gone back on a promise. She'd been there for her since the day Foster was born, premature and on life support in the Neonatal Intensive Care Unit. Her birth parents had told her stories about her "aunt" Cora, the selfless nurse and hero who'd been there every day making sure she'd grow up healthy and strong. Foster's heart squeezed with the memory of her parents. "Hang on, you said stressed. Why are you stressed?" she blurted, not wanting to think about the past any longer.

"Because if I'm right about who we're meeting tonight, our whole world will change."

"Wait, is this the guy? The one we've been searching for for the past year? You didn't tell me you'd found him. Who is he? What's his name?"

Ignoring the questions, Cora pointed to her suitcase. "Go over there and grab those two maroon sweatshirts."

Foster trudged to the rusted luggage rack and unzipped the suitcase. She held up the thick sweatshirt and pointed to the gold lettering: HOMER HIGH SCHOOL PANTHERS. "I thought homeschooling was going fine. And I can learn a lot more from you than from a crappy backwoods public school. And I graduate this year."

"Give it here." Foster tossed Cora the sweatshirt, and she pulled it on before explaining. "You're not going there. You're just going there. Now put that one on. I don't want to be late."

Foster zipped the baggy sweatshirt up over her flannel and rolled up the bottom a few inches until the frayed edges of her shorts stuck out and she no longer looked half naked. "I look like a plum," she grumbled, frowning at her reflection in the dusty mirror. "But at least I don't have to go back to high school." Not having to go back to a traditional school had been the only positive outcome of Doctor Rick's untimely death. Cora wanted to finish his research and keep Foster close—something about the healing process that one of Cora's doctor friends had told her. Whatever the reason, Foster didn't care as long as she didn't have to return to the mind-numbing day care they called public school.

Frizzy strands of fiery red hair flopped against her forehead, and she smoothed them back into her messy topknot. "So this person we're meeting," she began as she smeared ChapStick over her lips, "is he one of Doctor Rick's former lab assistants who's now a washed-up old science teacher or something?"

Cora slung her satchel over her shoulder and checked her phone. "Let's go. It's starting soon."

Foster slipped the ChapStick tube into her pocket and turned to Cora. "Has anyone ever told you that you look like Kerry Washington?" She rubbed her lips together and smiled her most innocent smile.

"No, because I don't." The front door creaked as Cora opened it, and the room filled with sticky, cool air. "Now get your skinny white butt into the car."

Foster sauntered to the door, pausing in front of the stocky woman, her cinnamon and cedar scents tickling Foster's nose. "Who are we meeting?" A familiar tingle pulsed within her as she spoke.

Cora rested her hands on her hips. "When I see fit to tell you, you will know. And we've talked about that little trick of yours, Foster. Be careful how you use it."

"I still don't get how you know about my Jedi mind trick." She hopped out onto the sidewalk and drew an imaginary lightsaber.

"There's no such thing as Jedis, and I'm too damn smart to fall prey to your neuro-linguistic BS."

"No such thing as Jedis?" Foster powered down her lightsaber and hooked it on her belt loop. "Broken my heart, you have. Ruining my childhood fantasies, you are."

Cora pursed her lips. "Mmm, mmm, mmm. Strange, you are. Dorky you shall always be."

"Was that Yoda-speak? Your training is coming along nicely, young Padawan. And speaking of training, are you going to drive to wherever it is we're going?"

"No." Cora unlocked the car and Foster slid into the driver's seat. "And I don't need training. I know how to drive. You're just better at it than I am—all Evel Knievel–like."

"You know I don't know who all these old people are that you talk about." Foster started the car and waited for Cora to punch the address into the GPS. "But unlike some people, I've been practicing."

"Yes, I'd say you practice driving every day and I practice sleeping right here in this seat every day."

"No, not driving. My Jedi mind trick. I made a whole rose bloom outside of that restaurant in Pennsylvania." Foster pulled out of the parking lot,

catching Cora's suspicious glance as her gaze swept from her adoptive mom to the navigation screen.

"Okay," Foster conceded, watching the vast, cow-dotted fields fade into the distance as they drove closer to town. "Maybe it just grew a tiny bit before it stopped listening. Oh, but I did get those clouds in West Virginia to look like giant Peeps. I was trying to make it rain, but shapes were all I could get. Remember that?"

"I remember the car's air conditioner going out and us cooking in here. You could've swam in this car I was sweating so much."

"Yeah," she laughed. "That was pretty nasty." Thunder rumbled overhead, and Foster let it pass before continuing. "I know there's something out there that will listen one hundred percent of the time. Maybe not people, or flowers, or the clouds, but there's something. I just have to find it."

The car jostled as Foster flipped on the turn signal and pulled into a large field. She parked behind a giant Ford truck and turned off the car. "We're here."

Tall grass tickled Foster's bare ankles as she stepped out of the car and onto the makeshift parking lot. "Wherever *here* is."

"Go Panthers! Woo!" A gaggle of maroon-clad girls squealed as they jogged past.

Foster craned her neck to peer around the monstrous truck. "You've got to be kidding me." She shot an annoyed glance at Cora. "A football game. Seriously?"

"Seriously." Cora pulled her bag out of the backseat before locking the doors. "Now, kill the attitude. I'd like to try and make a good first impression."

"Ugh," Foster groaned, trudging behind her as she tugged at the ridiculous sweatshirt. "But it's going to rain." She tilted her chin toward the sky and studied the swollen, charcoal clouds. "And quite possibly tornado. The sky's all sick-looking and green."

"I'll get you whatever you want from the snack bar," Cora offered.

"Snack bar? Well, why didn't you say there'd be food?" With a little more pep, Foster looped her arm through Cora's and headed toward the stadium entrance.

Pockets stuffed with boxes of sour candy and an extra-large bag of popcorn in hand, Foster stood on the sidelines and studied the bleacher's section signs.

"One fifteen, no. One twenty, no. Ah, there it is! One twenty-five." She tipped the bag to her lips and shook a few kernels into her mouth. "Ouch!" A sharp shove spun her around, knocking a box of candy and the bag from her grip. Popcorn spilled around her feet like salty snow. "Damn! You made me ruin the best thing about coming to this barbaric display of testosterone."

"I'm the best thing about this barbaric display of testosterone."

Foster looked up, and then up some more at Mr. Stereotypical Jock towering above her. He was, of course, perfect. Dark hair, ridiculously blue eyes, cheekbones for days, and lots of long, lean muscles—though he would've been way cuter if he'd had on jeans and a T-shirt and had been carrying a book, instead of wearing that stupid plum and gold jersey and carrying a football.

He grinned, displaying perfectly straight, white teeth—of course—and handed her the box of Sour Patch Kids she'd dropped. "Call me Tate Nighthawk Taylor."

Foster rolled her eyes so hard she almost lost her balance. "Wait, I'm sorry," she said with mock innocence. "Did you say Night Douche?" She shook her head. "No," she cringed. "That sounds too much like some kind of medical procedure. My mistake. You must have said Douchehawk. Yeah, that's what it was."

"What? No. That makes me sound like an ass, and I'm not. Seriously. Ask anyone. I am not an ass."

"I see anatomy is not your strong suit."

A column of uniforms jogged by, their cleats crunching on the track ringing the football field. "Nighthawk! Let's go, bro! Coach will shit if we're not huddled up soon."

"Yeah, I'm coming!" Tate called to the players as he started jogging slowly backward, following the rear of the pack. "Hey, Strawberry, let me show you how not an ass I am."

"Jesus! Don't call me Strawberry."

"Then tell me your name!"

She sighed. "Foster."

"Well, Foster, there's always a party after we win. And as long as I'm out there, we're winning. How 'bout I give you my number, so you can find out where it's at, and so I can show you how much of a non-ass, nice guy I am?"

"Answer a question first."

"Shoot, Strawberry!"

"What's your favorite book?"

"*Sports Illustrated*!" He winked.

"Yep, exactly what I thought."

Pink bloomed in his cheeks.

I'd be embarrassed, too. Maybe he realized he sounded like a total douche—hawk or not.

Then he started to speak again, and she decided it was probably sun and not sense coloring his cheeks.

"My number's really easy to remember. It's just—"

Foster held up her hand. "No. Just no. Not if my life depended on it. But good luck out there, Douchehawk." She gave him a salute, spun on her heels, and headed to section one twenty-five, her feet clomping noisily as she trudged up the aluminum bleachers.

Cora was examining the flimsy little one-page program as Foster slid in next to her. "You will not believe what just happened," Foster said around a mouthful of sour Skittles. "I met the most stereotypical jock douchebag. He asked me out. Sorta."

"On a date?" Cora's brow hit her hairline.

Foster snorted, sounding a lot like her adoptive mom. "Not the kind you used to get asked out on to the disco back in the eighties or whenever. This is one of those, 'show up at this place, and if I feel like hanging out with you, I will, but if not, I never officially asked you to go with me, so you can't get mad' things. Total guy garbage logic." Annoyed, she popped another Skittle into her mouth and chewed sharply. "And I'm sure it was really just about him showing me how awesome he, and everyone in Podunk, Misery, thinks he is."

"For the last time, it's Missouri, not misery," Cora said. "And the disco? In the eighties? Really? Baby girl, you gotta stop watching so many sci-fi shows and start with those history programs that are on your schedule. If you want to graduate, that is."

"I know a lot about World War Two. You can quiz me, which should get me at least a few extra points toward my history homework." Foster paused, waiting hopefully for Cora to give her a break on the boring documentaries.

"You don't get extra points for learning about something that's not in this semester's curriculum. You should be doing that regardless."

"Fine," Foster huffed. "But back to my interaction with the native Missourian, the guy introduced himself as Tate Nighthawk Taylor. Nighthawk! I swear, I can't make this crap up. Isn't that like the most ridiculous dudebro thing you've ever heard?"

"Tate Taylor?" Cora asked.

"Yeah, Tate *Douchehawk* Taylor. Can't forget that part."

Cora sighed.

"What?" Foster asked, taking a swig out of Cora's water bottle.

"The person we're here to meet, his name is—"

"No," Foster interrupted. "Don't do this to me, Cora."

"Tate Taylor."

TATE

Tate inhaled deeply as he jogged into the locker room. The scent of Icy Hot and sweat said he was where he belonged—home. Guys he'd been playing with since peewee football milled around, popping towels and smacking shoulder pads as they tried to harness pregame nerves and psyche themselves up for Homer High School's version of *Friday Night Lights*. Tate didn't need to psyche himself up. His two favorite things were brewing just outside the locker room—a big storm, and a big game.

His least favorite thing, though, had him staring blankly into his locker as he considered bashing his forehead against its metal sides. Tate *Nighthawk* Taylor sucked at talking to girls. And if the girl was pretty . . .

His shoulders slumped.

I actually told her Sports Illustrated *was my favorite book. After I already made myself sound like a deluded superhero wannabe by introducing myself as Nighthawk—to a total stranger—a hot, disinterested, total stranger.*

"Shit. Maybe I am a douche."

"Yo, Nighthawk, who was that ginge you was talkin' to? She ain't from here, that's for sure." Kyle Case bumped Tate with his shoulder. "If you're gettin' in on that St. Joe action, you're gonna be in major trouble with our women. Especially Emma."

"Emma and I broke up. I can talk to whoever I want."

"Not if they're from St. Joe you can't. She's a Spartan. We're Panthers. The two do *not* fraternize," said Kyle.

"Fraternize? You been studying your vocab words again, Ky-kee?" Tate waggled his brows at his best friend.

"Dude." Kyle lowered his voice. "We talked about this. Like, a million times. You cannot use my baby sister's nickname for me. Ever."

"Oh, I can. I definitely can."

"Nope. It's not cool."

"Hey, you call me a nickname all the time," Tate said.

"Nighthawk is cool. Ky-kee is not. End of discussion. Get back to the ginge with the big boobs."

"Big boobs? What? No." Tate shook his head. "I wasn't talking to her because of that." He'd been so caught by Strawberry's big green eyes, amazing red hair, and that skin that looked like she could have been carved from marble—smoking hot, flawless marble—that he hadn't noticed anything else about her. Well, except that she didn't like football and, more specifically, she didn't like him.

"Did you say big boobs?" asked Ryan. "Whose?" The linebacker's head turned in Tate's direction, along with half the team, making them look like mutant baby birds. "I thought you and Emma broke up."

"We did. Kyle's just being an—"

"Nighthawk got his hands on some boobs. Again!" Ryan, who had never been a genius, talked over him, knocking kids aside as he tunneled his six-foot-two, three-hundred-fifty-pound way through the team to get to Tate. "I gotta get me some details."

"No details!" Tate said. "I was talking to a girl. That's all."

"She's a Spartan," Kyle said.

"I didn't say that!" Tate said. "I don't know what she is, except not real friendly."

"Definitely a Spartan," Ryan said. "But I think big boobs cancel out the Spartan-ness of her."

Kyle scoffed. "Tell that to Emma and her friends."

"*We broke up!*" Actually, Emma had dumped him. Two weeks ago. No explanation except "Babe, it's not working out." Not working out? What did that even mean? He was still trying to figure out what he'd done wrong.

"Tate! Get your head out of your pants and into the game!" The team parted with biblical reverence as Tate's dad strode toward him.

"My head's totally in the game, Coach!" Tate assured his dad as his teammates snapped to attention.

"Good, because you have your work cut out for you tonight. Do I need to remind you that St. Joe's a four-A school and we're a two-A school?"

"No, Coach!" Tate shouted.

"No, Coach!" the team echoed.

"And do I need to remind you that the weather out there is looking crappy, which means anything can happen when the field turns into a swamp?"

"No, Coach!" the team shouted with Tate.

"Hey, Coach, no worries about the weather," Kyle said. "The darker it gets, the better Nighthawk sees!"

Tate's dad smacked the back of Kyle's head. "Boy, when the entire team can see in the dark like Tate, then the crappy weather's a plus. Can you see like a hawk in the dark?"

"No, sir!" Kyle yelled.

"Like I've told you boys since you were in grade school—nothing, not even great night vision, can replace hard work and focus. Now, huddle up and take a knee."

With the rest of the team, Tate took a knee in the circle of teammates around his dad while everyone bowed their heads and linked hands.

"Keep us safe out there—strong out there—sure out there. Keep us Panthers out there!"

"Go Panthers!" the team chorused.

"Oh, yeah. Almost forgot," his dad said, looking around the team conspiratorially. "Are you ready?"

"Yes, Coach!" the entire team, except Tate, yelled.

"Go!"

"Happy birthday to you! Happy birthday to you! Happy birthday dear Nighthawk! Happy birthday to you!" They all sang—badly, but enthusiastically.

"Sweet eighteen and never been kissed!" Ryan quipped.

"Shit, sweet eighteen and never been *missed*!" Kyle said.

"Okay, okay, you've had your fun. Time to line it up. Captain and co-captain first."

Tate and Kyle took their places at the front of the double column of Panthers. They moved in perfect time to their end zone, where they waited together for the band to start playing the fight song.

"Damn, your dad wasn't kidding about the weather," Kyle said, giving the green sky with its ominous dark clouds a nervous look. "Think they'll call the game?"

"Hell, no!" Tate said. "Well, not unless the lightning starts. And I hope it doesn't." He breathed deeply, loving the scent of rain and the sudden cooling of the air that signaled a storm. He was obsessed with storms! He always had been. It was as if he could feel the power building inside him in time with the distant thunder and the rolling clouds.

"Be careful out there tonight, Son." His dad was beside him, putting a firm, familiar hand on his shoulder. "I know you like your storms, but if that sky opens and starts pouring, watch yourself. That ground'll get slick as pig shit. Break something, and you'll be sidelined. It's early in the season, but you can't mess yourself up or you'll risk losing that Mizzou scholarship."

"Don't worry, Dad. I'll be fine—like always."

His dad patted his shoulder and smiled affectionately at him. "Right. I'll leave the worrying to your mother. Don't forget to wave to her."

"She's out there? But she hates storms."

"Of course she's out there—right on the fifty-yard line as usual. Your mom hates storms, but she loves her *little Nighthawk* more."

"I'm six-one, and eighteen years old as of today. Why does she have to add the *little* part? Jeesh, Dad, only Mom could make that nickname lame." *Well, Mom and that green-eyed strawberry,* he thought.

The first snare drum beats of the fight song drowned out his dad's laughter, and had the home side of the small stadium coming to their feet as Tate sprinted through the tunnel of cheerleaders and pompoms, leading his team onto the field. As they circled to begin their warm-up, Tate waved to his mom. She was easy to find. Her thick blond hair, which Tate had always thought made her look like a Disney princess, was a golden beacon under the bright lights. She waved and blew him a kiss while the rising wind lifted her tresses like a restless spirit.

Tate was calling cadence for their warm-up burpees when a blaze of red in the bleachers above his mom snagged his attention. Red hair, broken free from whatever had held it on top of her head, spilled around her. Damn, that girl had a lot of hair. Tate blinked—and then blinked again. It was *her*! The strawberry! She was sitting next to a big black woman who was studying him like he was a two-headed science fair experiment. But the strawberry? She was busy trying to tame all that wind-crazed ginger hair while she looked every-where *but* the field.

Burpees done, Tate called for the team to change positions and begin jumping jacks. He snuck another look at the girl. Yep, she was still staring everywhere but at him. *No, wait. She's not staring everywhere. She's staring up at the sky.*

The ref's whistle sounded the end of warm-ups, calling team captains to the center of the field for the coin toss. He jogged to meet the Spartan—shaking his hand and trying not to think about the fact that the kid's lack of a neck and full beard made him look thirty instead of seventeen.

"Heads," the Spartan called in a voice so deep and gravelly it sounded like he'd been smoking for decades.

"Tails! Panthers' choice!" the referee announced, shouting to be heard above the wind.

"We'll receive," Tate told them. He jogged quickly off the field, huddling with the rest of the offense as his dad put his hand into the middle of their circle. He had to yell to be heard over the whining wind, but his strong voice rose to the challenge.

"All right, Panthers. Get that damn ball and show those Spartans that big-ger doesn't mean better! On three—one, two, PANTHERS!"

Like the well-practiced machine they were, Tate's team flowed to their positions, standing at the ready as the Spartans lined up for the opening kickoff, but before the ref could blow the whistle to start the clock, the bruised sky opened, spilling ropes of rain down on them. The bright stadium lights flickered along with the scoreboard, and the ref hesitated before blowing the starting whistle.

Tate couldn't help it. He had to glance at the bleachers. He had to get a glimpse of that soggy strawberry. He found her easily. She was the only person standing, one arm raised, pointing up at the sky. As he watched, wide-eyed, she screamed one word so loud and in a voice so filled with raw terror that everyone turned to look up at where she was pointing.

"TORNADO!"

Tate's world exploded.

The whining of the wind shifted, morphing to a scream. From the black clouds above, the hook of a funnel began to descend, heading directly for the field.

"Everyone, get into the school! *Now!*" bellowed the loudspeaker.

Panic had the crowd on their feet as everyone tried to run from the bleachers. Tate felt as if he had been nail-gunned to the ground. His gaze trapped on the descending funnel. He could feel the power of the tornado—feel its anger and its destructive strength pass through him, swirl around him, and build . . . build, until he wanted to lift his arms and embrace it and let his shout join its raging roar.

"Tate! Run!"

His father's bellow broke through the tornado's spell and suddenly Tate was no longer filled with the excitement of the storm. He was just a kid, standing alone in the middle of a football field as death in the shape of a funnel plunged from the sky.

Everyone on the field sprinted for the locker room, but the bleachers were a nightmare of panicked people. Through the wind-slanted rain, he found his mom's blond hair. She was at the edge of the bleachers. He watched in horror as someone shoved her from behind and she fell.

"Mom!" Tate yelled, racing toward the stands.

"Tate! Get to the locker room!" His dad seemed to materialize out of the rain beside him, grabbing his wrist.

"But Mom's—"

"Go! I'll get your mom. You're the captain. Be sure your team's safe!" his dad shouted, hugging his son hard and fast, before shoving him toward the stream of people flooding into the school.

Caught in the tide, Tate was swept along the sidelines with hysterical cheerleaders and panicked parents. He meant to go into the locker room. He meant to do as his dad had told him—to make sure his team was safe. But the closer he got to the concrete building and safety, the more he felt it—the *need* to stay out there, to stay in the heart of the storm, to do something . . . anything . . .

The funnel cloud connected with the earth at the far side of the field, ripping the metal goalposts from the ground and slinging them into the field parking lot and onto the cars and trucks parked there—as well as the helpless people who had chosen to run for their vehicles instead of the school. The screams started in earnest then, mixing with the wind and rain to create a symphony of terror.

The tornado moved down the center of the field in a bizarre parody of the game it had destroyed. From the sidelines, Tate watched it close in on the second goalpost.

A flash of red glinted through the rain and wind. For a strange moment—a moment Tate would never forget—he was able to see the strawberry girl called Foster. Her back was to him. She was on her knees beside the black woman she'd been sitting with. The older woman lay crumpled on her side, clutching her chest as Foster tried futilely to lift her to her feet.

Horrified that the tornado was making its way directly toward them, he ran. He cupped his hands around his mouth and shouted, "Foster! Get out of there!"

Her head whipped around and he saw those big green eyes go wide with shock as she looked over his shoulder at the black funnel bearing down on her.

He thought she would run. She should have run.

But she didn't.

He could see in that instant she wasn't going to. She wasn't going to leave her fallen friend.

And he wasn't going to get to them in time to help. He would be too late.

He slid to a stop, wishing he were dreaming. Wishing he wasn't going to see a beautiful stranger get sucked into the air and killed.

Numb with shock, he watched Foster get to her feet. Instead of running away, she stood straight and strong, and began walking *toward* the roaring funnel. Her lips moved, but he couldn't hear what she was saying until she stopped, planted her feet wide, put her hands on her hips, and shouted directly at the tornado.

"YOU WILL NOT COME THIS WAY!"

Her words sizzled through Tate's body. He felt them in the core of his soul. It was as if her voice was moving inside him, as palpable as the wind and rain, and with it he also felt the power—the pulsing, pounding force that mirrored the whirling maelstrom before them. Her words were a leash, tethering the tornado as if it were as alive as a plunging stallion. Tate could feel that tether, that bind, and his mind, his heart, his soul, followed it.

The girl had somehow pressed a massive pause button. The tornado stopped! Right there in the middle of the fifty-yard line, the funnel quivered, spinning and spinning, straining at its leash, but not moving forward.

Tate stared at Foster. She'd raised her arms so that her palms were pressed forward, stop sign–like, at the whirring funnel of death and air. Her body began to tremble. She staggered back one step, then another, until her legs pressed against her friend's crumpled body. Tears streamed down her face. Her eyes were wide and frantic, and they found his.

"Help me!" She mouthed the words as the tornado broke free.

Tate's body moved with an instinct that felt foreign and familiar at the same time. Pumping his arms, he ran onto the field between Foster and the tornado. He raised his arms and, just as he had been practicing for as long as he could remember, football-like, Tate threw that newly awakened power within him, the power that tethered him to the storm, directly at the funnel, using the same command Foster had given it, *"YOU WILL NOT COME THIS WAY!"*

There was a sound like lightning striking a massive tree, and the tornado shattered, exploding into multiple smaller, but deadly, funnel clouds that scattered, tearing great hunks from the earth and leaving trails of destruction in every direction except toward Foster, her fallen friend, and Tate.

Tate stood frozen, feeling his power splintering with the tornado, unable to move as one of the new funnel clouds—the clouds he had somehow created—tunneled away from him down the sidelines, ripping through the people trying to flee the death trap the bleachers had become.

Tate saw it happen. He saw her bright, Disney princess hair disappear into the maw of the funnel—saw his father's coach's jacket torn from his body just as his wife had been torn from his arms—and the tornado devoured Tate's parents.

3

FOSTER

The sun reappeared briefly, stretching its long, golden fingers through puffy white clouds. As if mocking them, sunlight caressed Cora's fuliginous cheeks, seeming to brighten as her breathing became more labored and the glint dulled from her eyes. Foster knelt beside Cora, wiping rain and mud from her face.

"Cora, what's wrong? Where are you hurt?"

Weakly, Cora snagged one of Foster's hands, pulling her closer.

"Listen to me carefully, baby girl." Her tremulous voice was barely audible over the roar of wind and the screams of people.

"Foster! We need to get off this field!" Tate's voice interrupted.

Foster barely glanced over her shoulder at him. "No. Not without Cora." Then she turned back to the woman who had been mom, dad, and best friend for the past five years. "Where are you hurt?" she repeated.

Cora squeezed her hand with surprising strength. "It's my heart, child. There's nothing you can do."

"Yes, there is something I can do! Cora, come on. I'm taking you to the hospital," Foster said, snaking her arm beneath Cora's shoulders. "We're making it to the hospital."

"No, no child. It's too late for that. Now you have to listen, and listen good." Cora's cold hand pressed Foster's. "She's here."

"She? Cora, you're delirious. It's a bunch of freak tornadoes. We have to get out of here. You need a doctor."

"No. *Listen to me.*" Cora's gaze trapped her as Foster recognized her adoptive mother's tone.

She's not playing. She's completely serious. Oh, god. What's happening to her? To us?

"Okay, okay. I'm listening."

"Foster! *We have to go.*"

Foster's head snapped around. Tate had torn off his uniform shirt and tossed his shoulder pads to the side by his discarded football helmet. He was getting ready to sprint away. Foster's insides roiled. "Then go! No one's making you stay here!" She turned back to Cora. "Tell me."

"The tornadoes aren't accidents. I don't know how she got them to manifest here, but *they are not accidents.*"

"She, who?"

"Eve."

Foster's breath caught in her throat. "Eve? As in Eve of Doctor Rick's Core Four?"

Cora nodded wearily. "I saw her. If the others—Matthew, Mark, and Luke—are here, too, you're in great danger. You and that boy." Cora cut her eyes at Tate, who was wearing a fresh trench in the ground with his pacing, but hadn't gone anywhere.

"Tate? This doesn't make any sense." The pulse hammering behind Foster's ears seemed to skip a beat. "Do they want to kill us? Like they did Doctor Rick."

"Child . . ." Cora paused, gasping for breath as her face twisted in pain.

"Come on! We're getting out of—" Foster began, but Cora's hand, suddenly vise-like, kept her from moving.

"I don't have long. You have to listen to me. They're all in this together. Your father isn't dead. He's gotten . . ." Cora winced, panting for breath. "He's in trouble. Don't know if he's gone mad or if they have something on him. All I know is he's alive."

Shock seized Foster's gut, pinching her stomach until she felt like she'd puke. Staving off the bile and the lump of despair growing suffocatingly large in the back of her throat, she swallowed several times before speaking. "N-not dead?"

"No. And not trustworthy. He's not the man we knew."

"Cora, I don't understand." Foster dug her fingernails into her palm to keep from sobbing.

"Baby girl, there's things about yourself you don't know."

"My Jedi mind trick?"

"More . . . more. You're linked. You and that boy. And others. I—I believe your father and the Core Four are here for the two of you. You and Tate. You can't let them get you, Foster. You can't go to the police. You have to run. Now."

"I don't know what you're talking about, and I'm not going anywhere without you." Tears washed hot down Foster's cheeks.

"You have to. Your life depends on it. So does his. So do others. Baby girl, I've been dying for this past year. There's nothing that can be done, but I can't rest unless you promise me you'll get Tate out of here and go to safety."

Foster swiped the back of her hand against her eyes. "Where are we supposed to go?"

"Sauvie Island. Outside Portland. You know where that is, right?"

Numbly, Foster nodded as Cora tried to pull her satchel from across her shoulder. Foster bent and helped her. Trembling, Cora pressed the leather bag into Foster's arms.

"Good. That's my good girl. Take this." Cora gasped for breath, and then spoke in one long, final burst of energy. "The address is in my bag. So are the codes to the gate and the front door and a letter for you. It'll explain the rest, but don't waste time reading it until you get to Sauvie. All the files are there. You have to go. Go to the address. *Now.* Take Tate and go. *Hurry.* You know how to stay under the radar. Your lives depend on it. Go."

Foster sobbed so hard her words came out in broken, painful strips of breath. "Not without you! I can't go without you!"

Cora's hand shook as it reached up to cup Foster's cheek. "I wanted more time." She grimaced, her face blanching to a frightening gray. "At least I helped you," she gasped. "Helped you find the first one." She drew a labored breath and her gaze shifted to over Foster's shoulder. "Take her now, boy. I'm trusting you to keep her safe for me."

Foster didn't turn, but she felt Tate at her back. Cora's watery eyes went to Foster's face. "I love you, my little strawberry baby girl. Always have. Since the moment I saw you. Always will."

"I love you, too!"

"Promise you'll do as I've told you: Sauvie—the letter—the boy." Cora gasped for breath between words, her voice trembling with effort.

"I promise, Cora! I promise!"

"Thank you, baby girl. Now, finally, I can rest."

Cora's breath hitched, her familiar brown eyes widening as if she'd been surprised by something remarkably, wonderfully amazing and then her hand fell from Foster's face as she released her final breath.

Foster's heart beat so fast and so unbearably loud, she felt like that was all she was—just one raw and bleeding heart in the middle of a football field.

"Cora!" she screamed. "Cora!"

Strong hands captured Foster's shoulders, lifting her and pulling her from Cora's still body. Foster fought—kicked and shrieked for him to let her go—but it was like fighting a brick wall.

"Hey! Stop it!" Tate shouted as he half carried, half dragged her from the football field.

"Get your hands off me! Let me go!"

"No! She's dead, Foster. And she told me to keep you safe. I'm doing what she told me to do."

Foster felt as if her body had suddenly melted, like ice cream splatting against hot concrete, chunks of itself liquefying until it was nothing more than a dark stain—a shadow of what it used to be. But she knew Tate was right. Knew deep in her heart Cora was dead. She stared back at her adoptive mother's crumpled body as she let the football player lead her from the field and from the only family she had left.

She almost gave up then. All she had to do would be to jerk away from this guy and run. People were screaming and stampeding all around them. He'd never find her in this mess. Foster's sharp eyes swept the crowd of hysterically milling people, judging the right time to get away—to go back—to be with Cora.

That's when she saw her.

Eve.

She was striding away from the football field at the opposite end of the destroyed bleachers. Her head swiveling from left to right, right to left, as she searched for someone. For them?

The rain had returned, obscuring Foster's view, but there was no mistaking that it was Eve. Foster would know her anywhere, even though she hadn't seen Eve since she was twelve. The woman was unforgettable with her velvet black skin, her closely shorn hair, and the enormous hoops she always wore through her ears. She was tiny—barely five feet tall—yet she seemed to fill Foster's sight as she studied the panicked people around her with cold, expressionless eyes.

Foster knew Cora had been right. She'd died warning her about Eve. *If I let Eve get me—get us—Cora will have died for nothing.*

Foster planted her feet, throwing Tate off balance, and he stumbled to a halt.

"Not that way. We need to get to the parking lot. Find the car," Foster yelled to him.

Tate nodded. "Over here!"

They ran, dodging debris and fallen people. Foster didn't look at them. She refused to think about them and how broken and bloody and still they were.

The rain began again, and she put her head down against the slanting droplets and followed Tate. They rounded the corner away from the football field and Foster's knees almost buckled as she staggered to a stop, gaping in horror at the scene before her. Half of the parking lot was gone, reset to dark brown newly tilled earth. The other half was a war zone of twisted vehicles, sections of the metal bleachers, and bodies. So, so many bodies.

Not now. Don't think about them now.

Foster adjusted Cora's satchel over her shoulder and charged forward to the section of the parking lot that was relatively undamaged. "We have to find a car. Did you drive here?" she shouted. Blinking against the rain, she scanned the patch of cars the tornado had randomly chosen to skip over. "Did you drive?" Foster repeated, whirling around in irritation when Tate still didn't respond.

Tate stood twenty feet away, round eyes wide and unblinking.

"Tate!" Foster's shoes squelched in the mud as she marched closer. "We have to go."

"M-m-mom?" His chin quivered, and Foster couldn't tell if rain or tears slicked his pale cheeks. "Mom!" He sprinted forward.

Foster clutched the satchel as she raced after him. "Tate!" she shouted, reaching out and snagging the crook of his arm. "Stop!"

"Let go!" Tate growled and tore away from her grasp. "My parents need my help!"

Foster's gaze followed his outstretched hand. Metal entwined with metal to form a macabre sculpture. Long, blond hair swirled out from between two cars. One smashed on top of the other with such force it was almost impossible to decipher where one ended and the next began. Her stomach pitted as her eyes landed on stiff, square fingers reaching out, broken and awkward, from the sleeve of a maroon coach's jacket.

"Dad!" Tate lurched forward as the wind changed direction, and Sleeping Beauty's blond locks tangled around the snarled hand.

"Don't." Foster found Tate's arm, her grip tightened as much to keep him from running to the awful gravesite as to keep her legs from crumpling beneath her. "They're gone. Like my Cora. Gone." Foster shielded her eyes as a sudden gust of wind pelted her with BB-like pieces of gravel.

Tate charged ahead.

"Don't!" Foster shouted, lunging toward him. "Tate, there's nothing you can do to help them!"

Heat licked Foster's face as a rib-rattling boom threw her onto her back. Screams echoed around her as the ground felt as if it were pitching and rolling. Struggling, Foster pushed herself up from the mud, gasping to refill her lungs. Squinting against the flames twisting up from the mound of entwined metal and flesh, Foster searched for Tate's white uniform.

He was sprawled on his back, pieces of wood and metal covering his legs. Foster fell to her knees next to him, her bare shins sinking into the mud as she shook his shoulders. "Tate!" she shouted through the ringing in her ears. "You have to get up! We have to go!"

Tate's eyelids fluttered open. "Wh-what happened?"

"Come on!" Foster pulled him to his feet. Draping his arm across her shoulders, she led him away from the fire, away from the final resting place of his dead parents, and to the last row of undamaged cars in the parking lot.

"Please, please, please, please, please," she whispered, leaning Tate against the side of an early-2000-model pickup. Foster squeezed the door handle. "Oh, thank god," she said, releasing the breath she hadn't realized she'd been holding. "Get in." Foster resumed her place as Tate's crutch and helped heft him into the bright red truck.

As she rounded the front bumper, she unzipped the bag and dug around blindly for Cora's giant wad of keys. Foster threw open the driver's side door before selecting the thickest, strongest key and jamming it into the seam of the piece of hard plastic covering the inner workings of the steering column.

"My m-m-mom and d-d-dad. Th-they, they . . ." Tate sputtered between ragged breaths.

"Put your seat belt on," Foster instructed, the ringing in her ears finally subsiding. Plastic pinched her fingers and she winced as, centimeter by centimeter, she wiggled her fingertips into the slowly growing gap.

"They, they, they . . ." Tate repeated, stuck between what'd he'd seen and what his mind was willing to process.

"Hey!" Foster barked. "I need you to focus or we're going to be as dead as all those other people. Put your seat belt on." Cora had taught her that in times of uncertainty, stress, or panic, the best things to do were to remain calm and take one step at a time.

The lump in Foster's throat returned, and she blinked back the tears pressing hot against her eyes. She needed to do what Cora had taught her, what Cora would have done. She needed to get Tate out of his head, out of his grief, and back in the game. "Nighthawk," she said as evenly as she could while yanking on a piece of bolted-down plastic.

Tate's white compression top, soiled with mud and grime, matched the dirty paleness of his features as he turned to face her. He sucked in a haggard breath. "Yeah?" His voice was small, and, in his dirty, stripped-down uniform and cleats, he looked like a lost little boy.

Foster's stomach clenched. She knew that look, knew exactly how he felt. She wished she could stop and tell him that she understood what he was going through and that the hurt would lessen, though it would never, ever go away—how eventually he'd find a new normal and life would go on, that he'd be okay.

But she couldn't. With Eve so close, it would be a lie.

"Can you put your seat belt on? I can't start the car until you do."

With a blank stare, Tate reached over his shoulder, grabbed his seat belt, and clicked it into place.

Foster gritted her teeth and gave the plastic one final yank. "Yes!" she shouted in a burst of relief, tossing the covering out the door before climbing into the driver's seat. "See what happens when you put safety first?" For an instant, her lips quivered in a nostalgic smile as she repeated the words Cora had said to her so, so many times.

Cora is dead.

The alien thought filled her and her smile slipped back into a sorrowful frown as her eyes swelled with tears. Would she ever be able to genuinely smile again? At that instant, Foster wanted to stop, to curl up and let the anguish overtake her. She'd lost another mother, another home, and she'd never get them back. She was caught up in something bigger than herself like a seed carried too quickly by the gusting wind to ever settle and grow roots.

I can't do this. I can't be like Tate. We both can't be out of it. Do what Cora taught you to do: think—act—one thing at a time.

Mentally shaking herself, she wiped her sweaty palms on the upholstered seat and reached into the guts of the steering column. Foster's fingers fumbled around wires and metal until they found the small rectangular box with the metal pin she saw so clearly in her mind's eye. She pressed on the clutch and shoved the pin to the left. The truck rumbled to life, and Foster silently thanked the Internet gods for the magic of YouTube.

"H-how'd you learn to do that?" Tate asked, the color beginning to return to his cheeks.

"I was homeschooled. I learned a lot of things during my independent study periods that you public kids haven't ever even heard of." Foster slammed on the gas, kicking up gravel as she tore out of the parking lot and onto the main road.

"Ever take a first-aid class?" Tate held out his shaking hand. Blood streaked his fingers, and he quickly returned his hand to the gash in his thigh.

"You're in luck." Tires squealed beneath them as she swerved around tree branches and mangled car parts. "You happen to be sitting next to an American Red Cross first-aid certified—" Air fled her lungs as she slammed on the brakes, the seat belt catching and pinning her against the back of the seat. Silence hummed between them, broken only by the squeak of the windshield wipers and the steady, pleading whine of emergency vehicle sirens.

The parking lot, Tate's stadium—those were nothing in comparison.

The tidy neighborhood flanking the high school had been destroyed—a bomb exploding in the middle of nowhere America.

And the people. The people crawling out of the wreckage and stumbling broken, bleeding and mute looked like zombies, more dead than alive.

Foster turned away, rocked by a wave of sickness and pity. Her eyes found Tate's bleeding leg. She glanced up at his achromatic features, his expression slack with shock and eyes glazed with horror. Slowly, as if moving through mud, Tate lifted his shaky, bloody hand, reaching for the door latch.

She cleared her throat and threw the truck into first. "We'll clean up that cut as soon as we get to the motel," Foster said as the vehicle lurched forward, though she was barely able to press on the gas through the wild shaking of her legs.

"No, we have to stop. We have to help these people," Tate said hoarsely, leaving behind bloody fingerprints as he gripped the dashboard.

"We would if we could, but we can't." To keep her hands from shaking as badly as her legs, Foster squeezed the steering wheel so hard her palms ached. "Listen. I can hear sirens. Help is coming. They'll be fine," she lied, averting her eyes from the survivors tripping over the wreckage like broken automatons.

"But this is my town." Tate's voice was so raw with pain that it made Foster wince. "It's all I've ever known."

Now they were both homeless.

But she didn't stop. She didn't even pause. She just kept driving. *One thing at a time. One thing at a time.* Foster guided the truck down the road, barely able to breathe as toys and clothes and memories became nothing more than speed bumps beneath the heavy tires.

"These are my people. I've known them my whole life."

Still unable to control her shaking, the truck nearly slammed to a complete stop as she pulled into the motel parking lot. "Yeah, I get it, but—"

"Where did you grow up?"

The truck rocked as she ran over a stray piece of debris and guided it into a space a few yards away from her room. "San Francisco originally, then Portland, but Cora and I have been a little bit of everywhere since . . ." she trailed off, her chest aching with grief. She didn't want to talk about her past. Not with Tate. Not with anyone. All she could do was keep charging forward. If she stopped for too long and found that one moment of stillness, her heart might just break into so many pieces she'd never be able to pick them all up.

"Then you don't get it," Tate continued. "I see these people almost every day. The same people. Every day. I couldn't save my parents, but I can do something for them. They're all I have left of my life with Mom and Dad."

Foster put the truck in park, and turned to face him. "Look, I *really do* get it. We both lost people, but—"

"Stop saying that!" Tate shouted over the wind now nudging the pickup from side to side with harsh bursts. "You don't get it at all!" Tate's fist hit the dashboard with a loud thump. "That lady back on the field, she wasn't your mom. My mom *and* dad are dead. You lost a road-trip buddy."

Foster stiffened, her spine straightening like an enraged cobra seconds before delivering a poisonous strike. "Look, *Douchehawk,* let's get something straight right now. You do not know me. You do not know what I've been through. And you do not have the right to *ever* talk about my Cora."

"When I first met you I thought you were pretty. You know what I think about you now? I think—"

Foster held up her hand. "I do not give one solitary shit about what you think. And besides that . . ." Her tirade trailed away as thunderous pounding broke through the torrential rain and her pissed-off-ness, pulling her attention from Tate. The wind calmed, gently whistling through the loose window seals as Foster peered at the motel in front of them where three horribly familiar men moved from one room to another, banging on the cheap, dingy doors.

"Get down!" she hissed, nearly tackling Tate onto the bench seat.

"Shit!" she whispered, her face way too close to his. "How in the hell did they know Cora and I were here?"

Tate's forehead crinkled in annoyance as his blue eyes met hers. "Probably because this is the only hotel in town."

"Seriously? God this town sucks." Foster scowled. "And *that* is not a *ho*tel. It's a *mo*tel. Now keep your voice and your big head down."

Tate frowned. "My head isn't big. Or at least not that big," he whispered back. "Who are we hiding from?"

Foster grimaced. "Them," she peeked above the dash. "Matthew, Mark, and Luke."

4
MARK

"Father isn't going to like this." Mark muttered the words more to himself than to the two men striding at his side. But, as usual, Matthew, who always seemed to hear every damn thing, answered—even though Mark hadn't asked a question.

"It'll be fine. The girl has to be here. Eve said she saw her drive away in a red truck with the boy after Cora died. This is the only place she and Cora could've been staying. We'll just knock on all the doors until we find them, and then we'll grab 'em," Matthew said.

"It's *not* fine," Luke ran his hands nervously through his strange white hair, causing sparks to sizzle and crack dangerously in the air surrounding him. "Those fucking kids screwed up everything. We should've moved the second we spotted Cora and Foster, and since we didn't every damned news station in the Midwest is going to be reporting this newest disaster."

"Calm down, Luke. Lighting shit on fire isn't a smart idea right now," Mark told his brother as he took a step back, out of range of Luke's sparks. "Drink this and cool down." Automatically he reached into the travel pack he carried slung across his shoulders and pulled out a bottle of Gatorade, tossing it to Luke. He brushed his long, dark hair back from his face, enjoying the slick, damp feel of it. *Water—anything that's flooded with water feels good.* Then he

shook himself mentally and took in both men with one gaze. "What happened couldn't be helped," Mark said sternly.

"That's bullshit! We should've grabbed Foster right away and taken Tate after the game," Luke insisted before he upended the Gatorade and chugged it in one long gulp.

"No. Like Eve said. And Father told us. Wait until Tate and Foster meet. To see what happened. Then take them *if* they manifest their element." As usual, Matthew's speech got choppy as he became emotional. "I called the tornado like Father said. I didn't know those two kids would mess it up. Be so powerful!" The air around him swirled, lifting his shaggy, nondescript hair, and his arms begin to flicker in and out of sight, like he was part of a cheap cartoon that had only been half drawn.

Mark stopped and faced the two men he called brothers. He drew a deep breath, aware that he was standing in a pool of water that had nothing to do with the storm that raged behind them. *God, I hate it when Eve leaves me in charge of these two. I swear, someday I'm going to fucking leave. Just walk away. Disappear. Be by myself. Live a normal life.* Just the thought of it calmed him, and his footprints immediately dried. "Settle down. Both of you. Control your elements." He skewered Matthew with his dark gaze. "Air has already screwed enough up today."

"But I didn't—"

"We know." Mark silenced him. "It was the kids. But now this is all you." Mark gestured around them at the wailing wind.

"Okay, okay. You're right. I've got this. I can do this." Matthew closed his eyes, obviously concentrating, and rubbed his arms as if he was cold. Slowly, the roiling clouds and the gusting wind began to dissipate—in time with the color reappearing in his arms.

"And you get a handle on your temper," he told Luke. "The last thing we need is a fire to draw attention away from that mess," Mark jerked his chin in the direction of the distant stadium. "To this mess. Plus, we don't have time to hook you up to an IV. So, handle yourself, Fire."

Luke grunted at him, but he also drew several deep, calming breaths and the sparks that shimmered around his every movement faded into nothingness.

"All right. Let's start knocking on doors," Mark said.

"What are we gonna do when we find them?" Matthew asked.

Mark blew out a long, frustrated breath. "What we were sent here to do. We're going to tell them they have to come with us." He raised his fist and pounded on the first door.

"Who are you and what do you want?" came a reedy old woman's voice from inside the room.

"Sorry, ma'am. I'm just looking for my daughter. She's only fourteen, but she looks twenty-one, if you know what I mean. I think she's here with some scumbag boy."

"Not in this room she ain't! Go on—get!" the old woman shouted. "And take better care of your home business. Women only go bad when men act like fools!"

Mark ignored her as he and his brothers moved to the next door.

"What if they won't?" Luke said.

"Won't what?" Mark knocked on the next door.

Luke shot him an annoyed look. "Won't go with us."

The door opened, but only as wide as the cheap chain would allow. "What?" a man's deep voice bellowed from the crack.

"Sorry, sir. I'm looking for my daughter. She's a runaway," Mark said.

The man slammed the door in Mark's face. Maintaining a tenuous hold on his temper, he moved on to the next room, saying, "They're kids. Barely eighteen. We're adults—older and smarter than them. We do what Eve said, tell Foster her adoptive father is alive, needs her, and sent us to get her. She'll come with us. And Tate's a teenage boy. He'll chase along after Foster. It's just not that damn difficult." Mark spoke grimly, moving to the next crappy-looking door.

"Yeah, I would've said the same thing before they caused a town to be leveled," Luke said. "I'm thinking it might not be so easy to get them to do what we want them to do now."

Mark shook his head. "They don't know how to do any of that. Not really. What happened back there was an accident—an accident we set into motion for them. Period." He knocked and waited. Nothing. He knocked again. Still nothing. "Okay, room twelve is empty. Remember that. We mighta beat her here. That storm's a lot to drive through, especially for a kid." They moved to the next door. "And we have to remember they're scared. They have no real idea about what's happening. As far as we know they think those tornadoes were after *them*. And that's good for us. They need us to teach them how to control their powers. Until then they're a danger to themselves as well as others."

"Yeah, but air would never hurt them. I can feel how tied to the element they are already." Matthew's voice was annoyingly whiney for a man of thirty-six.

"Like they know that, genius?" Luke said sarcastically.

As Mark lifted his hand to bang on the next door, Luke grabbed his shoulder, halting him.

"What color did Eve say that pickup was?"

Mark followed Luke's gaze to the parking lot where it rested on a red Chevy pickup, empty, but idling in what had, just moments before, been a vacant space.

"Red."

Matthew spoke at the same moment a girl's head peeked up just over the dash of the truck. Mark felt a rush of relief as he immediately recognized Foster's mop of bright auburn hair.

"That's her. Follow me, but smile. Let me do the talking." Mark glanced surreptitiously around. No one else was in the parking lot. Everyone seemed to either be rushing toward the stadium or hiding inside, but he didn't want to take any more chances. He concentrated for a moment, gathering himself, listening to the wet, wonderful sound of the blood pumping through his body. He followed that sound—that exquisite feeling—and drew his element to him. "Make it rain," Mark whispered.

The familiar thrill washed through him. It didn't matter how often it happened. Calling the power of his element always filled him with a heady rush of pleasure. Rain began to fall from the gray sky. Mark loved it. Loved how it slid seductively against his skin, caressing him, completing him. It didn't matter that immediately the darkness just beyond the edges of his vision quivered and throbbed, shivered and writhed with the murky things that haunted his power, his life, his waking dreams. The Frill. The creatures that came whenever he called his element, water. The Frill waited at the edge of his eyesight, always present, always lurking.

If Eve were here she would remind him sternly that they were hallucinations—that the only way they could hurt him was if he allowed them to drive him completely mad.

But Eve didn't know everything, and one of the things she *didn't* know was a fact that had lodged itself deep within Mark's troubled mind.

Someday the Frill, with their fluid, bendable bodies and their impossibly large mouths and flat, serrated razor teeth, would swarm and he wouldn't be able to stop them.

Someday the Frill would devour him alive.

"They aren't real." The heat of Luke's hand on his shoulder brought Mark back to himself.

Someday the Frill would engulf him, swarm him, destroy him, but that day was not today.

"Like I said, follow me." Striding through the rain he'd summoned, Mark headed to the truck. He grinned and waved his arm as the girl's head disappeared beneath the dash again. "Lacy Ann! It's Daddy! Girl, your uncles and me, we've been worried sick 'bout you!" Mark added a country twang to his voice. "That dang tornado was a doozy, weren't it?"

He was only a few feet from the truck when Foster's head popped up again—along with the boy, Tate, beside her in the passenger's seat. Mark was in the middle of another big wave, pretending to have to wipe away the rain from his face, as if he couldn't see her clearly, when Foster ground the truck into reverse. The girl spun it backward and around—like the damn kid was a professional stunt driver—throwing gravel all over them, she roared the Chevy onto the road.

"Goddamnit!" Mark swore and sprinted for the Range Rover they'd parked on the other side of the lot—with Matthew and Luke running after him.

5

FOSTER

"What the hell was that about?" Tate chided. "Those guys might've needed our help."

"What makes you think that? The way they were beating on every motel-room door and didn't stop until they saw me? Or maybe the way they're chasing after us?"

"They could've been looking for survivors or . . . I don't know . . ." Tate scrubbed his hand down his cheek, adding blood to the streaks of dirt. "Didn't that guy think you were his daughter? He's probably just a dad worried because of the tornadoes. Why are you going so fast? If Sheriff Jamison—"

"Jesus! Shut up! That guy you think is a sweet, innocent dad and the two creeps with him are following us. I recognize them. They aren't good guys. *That's* why I'm going so fast."

Tate groaned and grabbed his leg as he turned to look out the back window. Foster made a mental note: *Remember, Douchehawk is hurt.* Sadly, she was going to have to stop and get some bandages and something to clean the wound with. *God, Cora, he's a pain in the ass already.*

"Hey, you're right. That's them in the black Range Rover, isn't it?"

"Yeah."

"They're getting closer. You know that thing can outrun this old Chevy, don't you?"

The Chevy's tires squealed as Foster dodged around a fallen tree blocking part of the road.

"Whoa! Careful! You're gonna get us killed!" Tate told her as he hastily rebuckled his seat belt.

"Just shut up and let me drive," Foster snapped at him as her mind whirred. She glanced in her rearview mirror in time to see the Ranger Rover easily navigate around the tree.

"I'll shut up if you tell me your plan and who those men are," Tate said.

"I don't have a plan, and all I know about those men is that they're bad. Cora knows everything else." Sweat slicked Foster's palms as she gripped the steering wheel. Her leg ached from keeping the gas pedal pressed against the floor—and still the Range Rover gained on them.

"Cora's dead."

"I'm aware of that." Foster ground her teeth together and didn't take her eyes off the road. *This guy is why I hate people. They're just plain stupid.*

"So, since she's dead, how are you going to know what those guys want and—"

"Tate! Shut. The. Fuck. Up! I only know they want us, they're dangerous, and Cora told me we needed to run from them. And that's what we're doing—running. God! I wish one of those tornadoes would fall down from the sky and blow them away from us!"

Except for the rattling of the windows and the sound of the overtaxed engine, uncomfortable silence once again unfurled within the cab of the truck. But she could feel Tate staring at her. Feel it almost as if he was touching her . . . running a hand along her skin . . . making her breath deepen and her blood sizzle through her veins as warmth flushed across her body.

"Do you feel that?"

Tate's voice made her jump. "Feel what?" she asked.

Tate shivered like a horse knocking off flies. "That sensation all over my skin. It started as soon as you said you wished a tornado would—"

The roar of a descending funnel cloud cut off Tate's words. Foster's eyes felt cemented to the scene unfolding in her rearview mirror. A stone gray tor-

nado touched down behind them—neatly cutting off the path of the Range Rover, and anyone else who had the bad luck to be following.

"Thank you," Foster whispered automatically, immediately feeling foolish for doing so.

I didn't just make that happen. That wasn't me. Was it?

"You are welcome. You felt it, too, didn't you?" Tate said.

Foster frowned at him. "Okay, first, I wasn't thanking you. I was thanking the, um, universe for that." She pointed her thumb over her shoulder. Tate turned in his seat—again grimacing in pain. Foster glanced down at his leg. A crimson stain soaked his uniform. *That might actually be bad. We have to get something to fix that ASAP.* "And second, what feeling are you talking about?"

Still turned in his seat, gawking behind them, Tate seemed not to hear her. "Daaaaamn. That tornado is not playing. No one's getting past it. Seriously. It's just sitting there, spinning, like a glitching video game."

Foster did a mental eye roll. *Of course he's a gamer.*

Tate finally turned back around. "You can slow down now."

Foster somehow managed to relax her foot enough to let up on the gas.

"All right. Tell me," Tate said.

Foster glanced at him. He stared at her.

"Tell you what?"

"That you felt it, too. It was like on the football field. Something happened to me. To us. I felt it all over my skin. Tell me you felt it, too."

Foster didn't take her eyes off the road. She sighed and said the first thing that came to her mind. "Truthfully, the only thing I want to tell you right now is that I wish you'd do like the picture book says and go the fuck to sleep." Heat needled her skin and Foster held very still, waiting for whatever the hell would happen next.

Inside the window-rattling silence of the truck, Tate's sudden yawn was fantastically loud.

"Man, I can't think straight. My leg hurts. I'm so tired. Everything that happened today just doesn't seem real . . ." He propped his elbow against the window, dropped his head against his fist, and yawned mightily again. "I can't believe Mom and Dad are gone. It's not real, right? Tell me we're stuck in a nightmare and I'll wake up soon in my bed with Mom telling me I'm going to be late if I don't hurry."

"Yeah," she forced her voice to soften. "If calling it a nightmare makes it better then I'm good with that. And thankfully, we're almost out of town."

Because your town is pretty much the size of a super Wal-Mart. She thought that part. It was best not to poke the sleepy bear.

"Wait, what was I saying? My head doesn't feel right."

"Rest while I drive. I remember there's a little store just up the freeway. I'll run in, grab some stuff to fix that cut on your leg, some sustenance, maybe we'll get lucky and they'll even have something to wear that's not covered in mud and"—she glanced down at the grime clinging to her ripped sweatshirt—"whatever else. You'll feel better after you sleep, change, and get something to eat."

"Fine, but when I wake up we gotta get back there and start helping people," Tate grumbled, his eyelids drooping to half-mast and then closing completely.

Foster adjusted the rearview mirror. Behind them the wall cloud continued to maul the sky, and the rain-wrapped tornado was barely visible, and there definitely wasn't any sign of Matthew, Mark, and Luke's Range Rover. But a knot of worry sat in her stomach, heavy and thick like she'd eaten too much cheese.

She'd felt it. She'd definitely felt it—not that she wanted to talk to Tate about it. Why the hell would she? Like she trusted him? A stranger? Plus, then she might have to admit that she'd also felt her Jedi mind trick working. Foster cut her eyes to Tate.

Sure enough, Tate was zonked out—sleeping so deeply that his hands twitched with a dream.

Did I really do that, too?

Lost in her thoughts, the Quickie Mart seemed to pop up out of nowhere and Foster made a sharp turn into the gravel parking lot.

Tate's head shot up and he grunted disapprovingly.

"Sorry." Foster left the truck running and slid out of the cab. "Any requests?"

Half asleep, or possibly half passed out, Tate mumbled something unintelligible and shooed her away.

"Hey, don't be upset when I don't bring you back anything," Foster said, slinging the satchel over her shoulder and scratching the base of her disgustingly matted bun. Her head itched. Her face itched. Hell, any exposed skin grew more and more itchy and uncomfortable as the mud dried, tightened, and turned into gross dirt scabs. Foster reached behind the seat, grabbed a dusty Spartan hat, and smashed it down over her tangled hair. With a sigh, she brushed away the dirt she could from her damp top, closed the door, and trudged toward the Quickie Mart, head down against the endless rain.

Thwack! Foster tensed as she opened the dingy, rain-streaked door. *Thwack! Thwack, thwack!*

"*Dagnabit,* piece a crap television. Work!" He reared back a pale, pudgy hand and smacked the side of the clunky box. *Thwack!*

"Umm," Foster cleared her throat, and let the door swing shut behind her as she wiped water and who knew what else from her face. "Excuse me?"

The attendant hopped from his step stool, wincing when his feet hit the ground. "Caught out in that storm, huh?" He wiped a yellowing handkerchief down his cheeks, pink with exertion. "Not even an umbrella will save you from the rain now. Not no more." He felt behind his ear and pulled out a toothpick. "It's like them storms suddenly got minds of they own." He grunted, shoving the toothpick between his lips while scratching at his bulging stomach.

"Yeah." The air conditioner kicked on and Foster shivered in the cool breeze. "I just need a few things, Band-Aids, water . . ." She bit her bottom lip to keep her teeth from clacking.

"Over by the headache pills and all of them feminine lady things." He winked and motioned to the back of the store.

"Thanks." Foster attempted a polite smile, but felt her lips twist into a disgusted grimace. No matter how hard she tried, being polite didn't come easily, especially not to bumpkin Neanderthals. And, well, maybe she wasn't trying *that* hard.

Foster's shoes squeaked on the sticky tile as she turned down the first aisle, the steady *thwack thwack* echoing behind her. With practiced expertise she plucked her favorite snacks from the shelves as she wound her way to the back of the store. She had made enough stops at enough stores like this to know exactly which, out of all of the gross processed foods, would stay in your stomach and which would leave you sprinting from the car to the nearest roadside ditch. Her stomach grumbled as if in remembrance. She'd made that mistake a few times.

Staying as far away from the cold air of the reach-in as possible, she grabbed enough bottles of water to not only stay hydrated, but also to rinse Tate's wound and some of the grime from her own hands and face.

She tucked a box of large Band-Aids and gauze under her chin, snagged a bottle of hydrogen peroxide and a tube of triple antibiotic goo and waddled, arms full, to the checkout counter.

"And I'll take a couple of these." She pulled two SOMEBODY IN MISSOURI LOVES ME T-shirts off the rack by the register and threw them onto the pile.

The man grunted, taking the chewed toothpick from his mouth and pointing it at the TV. "Always gotta be at least two people out there in them damn storms."

The flickering image cleared, and her pulse quickened.

It was her.

"One idgit out there like this one filming with one of them smart phones," he continued. "And at least one other out there in the thick of it. Dumb ass rednecks."

No, it was *them*. She watched Tate join her as both of them lifted their hands and actually paused the tornado.

"Well I'll be . . ." His hand fell to his side and the toothpick made a hollow *clink* as it bounced off the counter and onto the floor.

Her mouth went dry and she swallowed hard as she watched Tate stretch his arm back and . . . Static swallowed the image.

Foster lowered the cap over her eyes and tried unsuccessfully to hide the rip across the front of her soaked sweatshirt. "Just this stuff." Her hands trembled as she dug through the bag for Cora's wallet.

"Hey, that's you in the middle of that ball field," his gaze swept over her, pausing at her dirt-caked hands, the rip in her shirt, and finally on the long tail of muddy hair draped across her shoulder. "Ain't it?"

"Me?" Her attempt at a casual laugh sounded more like the bray of a stran-gled goat. "Nah," she shrugged. "No way. That's not me. I don't like sports. At all. Football's even at the top of my sports I hate list." She bit the inside of her cheeks to silence her nervous bleating.

"No, no, that was you." His wisps of hair fluttered as he bobbed his head up and down. "Same Panther's sweatshirt. Same red hair. What'd you do to that tornado? I've seen my share of 'em out here, what with 'em poppin' up every other week here in the past few months, and I ain't never seen one stop. Not like that. Not like it was listenin' to you tellin' it to." His twang deepened as his words came out in a rush of excitement. "Oh, man. I gotta call my cousin Bobby. He works up there at the news station. Be willin' to pay at least fifty bucks for a real-life tornado tamin'," he paused, yanking his phone from his pocket. "Whatever you are."

"Wait! You don't want to do that." Foster spoke automatically, willing him to *hear her*. Instantly, energy crackled over her body, a lot like a hot wind had just blown across her naked skin—which made zero sense.

But then the pudgy man spoke, and Foster understood what had happened—what had actually happened for the very first time since she didn't count accidentally putting Tate to sleep.

"Guess I don't," his shoulders lifted and fell in an exhausted sigh. "Do I?"

Foster blinked. "Shit, it worked. I mean, it actually worked."

His thick, sweat-streaked brow wrinkled with confusion.

"Uh, okay, so," Foster glanced at his nametag. "Billy Bob, really?"

"Named after my uncle and my daddy." He grinned proudly.

"I just," she shook her head. "Anyway, I'm going to take these things, and *you're not going to remember that I ever came in here.*"

"I never remember nothin'." He nodded. "Would you like a sack for all that?" he asked, already bagging her goods.

"Um, thank . . . thank you, Billy Bob."

He pulled another toothpick from behind his ear and stuck it between his lips. "Pleasure."

Foster was halfway to the door when guilt washed over her. "Crap." She took out a couple wadded twenties and hurried back to the counter. "For," she made a sweeping motion that took in the bag and the fuzzy television screen. "Everything."

Foster burst out of the Quickie Mart, excitement turning her walk into fervent skips. "Cora is going to pass out when I tell her—" She stopped short of the door to the truck, sorrow slamming into her gut.

She'd never have the chance to tell Cora anything ever again.

Foster doubled over. Chunks spewed from her mouth, coating the wet gravel in mockingly cheerful shades of brightly colored sour candy.

She passed the back of her shaking hand across her lips. "Get it together, Foster. You can't make this guy come with you if you're falling apart, and Cora said he has to come. So . . ." She dug out a bottle of water and rinsed her mouth before squeezing the handle and hefting herself onto the seat. "I got stuff to clean that cut," she announced, swallowing back her despair. "And some beef jerky. It's practically a road-trip requirement."

Tate grunted, his head lolling to the side to rest on the window. Soft snores spilled out of his parted lips and Foster pulled back onto the two-lane road, hot tears silently slipping down her cheeks.

6

FOSTER

The freeway stretched ahead, bordered by flat, dry, brown nothingness. All the middle states looked the same, and Foster couldn't wait to finally be back on the West Coast. She took a swig from her almost empty water bottle, mentally kicking herself for not picking up a few Red Bulls at the Quickie Mart.

God, Cora picked a hell of a time to die, Foster decided, skipping over the in-between stages of grief and landing smack in the middle of anger. *Not an hour before I successfully used my Jedi mind trick—twice! And not for evil either like practically every time I've ever tried to use it before. But, I mean, who could really call trying to get out of doing homework evil? Well, I mean, who besides Cora. Anyway,* Foster shook her head, trying to hold on to her anger, *that's not the point. This time, I used it for good and Cora wasn't even there to see it. And I don't want to think about what would have happened if it didn't work. Tate would have annoyed me to death and that bumpkin could've gotten us captured or killed.* For the umpteenth time, she checked the rearview mirror. *Murdered by Eve and her creepy minions. Just like Doctor Rick.*

She squinted, flipping down the visor to block the sun as it continued its descent below the cloudless horizon.

Wait. No, not dead—missing. *Cora said that Doctor Rick is alive.* Hope clenched her heart, and then fled just as quickly. Doctor Rick was alive, but he was also . . . *not trustworthy.* Cora's words uncurled a memory. *He's not the man we knew.*

As impossible as that sounded, Foster believed in Cora with every fiber of her being.

If she said Doctor Rick was alive. He was.

If she said he'd turned into a bad guy. He had.

Foster believed Cora, but that didn't make her heart hurt any less. She blinked hard, refusing to cry.

Okay, one thing at a time. First, I get us to Sauvie Island safely. Then I read Cora's letter. Cora will have an explanation for this mess. Cora always had—

"Did you abduct me?"

Foster jerked in surprise, almost slamming the truck into the small sedan zooming by. "Uh, no." Hiding her near collision, Foster flipped on the turn signal before drifting slowly, deliberately into the neighboring lane. "You fell asleep about two hours ago."

"*Two hours?*" The tendons in Tate's neck bulged as he scrambled to look out the front, side, and back windows, wincing as the cut in his leg opened and began to weep scarlet. "Ouch! Damn!" He pressed his hand over his thigh and spoke through pain-gritted teeth. "You've been driving for *two hours?*"

"Welcome to Nebraska," Foster said with a flourish of her hand. "Not much better than *Misery* if you ask me."

He ran a hand through his wavy, dark hair. "I can't believe you let me sleep for *two hours!*"

Sighing softly, Foster tilted her head to the side. "And they were the most peaceful hours I've had since we met."

"Stop the car." Tate's glare was almost palpable, filling the cab with thick cords of tension.

"Not until we need gas." She tightened her grip on the wheel. "And it's a truck, actually," she added with forced nonchalance.

"Stop the *truck.*" His neck flamed the same cardinal red as the old pickup.

"Not until we need gas," Foster enunciated.

"Fine." Tate unlatched his seat belt.

"What are you doing?" Foster asked, ping-ponging her attention from the road to him and back again.

He popped the lock. "Getting out of the truck," Tate stated as simply as if he was recounting what he'd had for lunch that day.

Foster let out a bark of laughter. "I'm going, like, seventy."

"Then stop the truck," Tate said with cool determination.

Foster's brow furrowed. "You wouldn't."

With another disinterested shrug, Tate pushed open the door.

Tires screeched as Foster slammed on the brakes and careened onto the shoulder. "What the hell is wrong with you?" she spat, bolting out of the cab to meet him behind the back of the truck. "You almost got out of a moving vehicle. *On the freeway!* They would've been picking up pieces of you for days!" she shouted at him as he limped back in the direction they'd come, his thumb stuck out away from his body. "And now you're, what? Hitchhiking? Oh, sure. That makes sense. It's not like you look crazy or anything, all dirty and *bleeding from the leg.*"

Tate spun around so fast, Foster almost smacked into his chest. "I told you to stop the fucking truck!"

Thunder rumbled overhead, the sky around them darkening.

"And I told you that we need to get as far away from Bugtussle, *Misery,* as possible!" Rain dusted Foster's arms and cooled the sticky hot air swirling between them.

"Why?" Tate threw his hands up. "Because some woman I don't know said some shit I don't understand?"

"It's not a stretch to think that you don't understand a lot of what people say." A sudden gust threw bits of dirt and rock against her bare legs.

"I'm not stupid, Foster!" Tate shouted over a roar of thunder. "My life was fine before I met you. Perfect even."

Foster couldn't keep a wry burst of laughter from shooting from her lips. "Living in the dirty belly button of the U.S. was *perfect*? Your town had two stoplights! If that's perfection, then you're a hell of a lot dumber than I originally thought."

"And you're more of a bitch than I thought, and that takes some damn doing!"

Eyes wide, Foster sucked in a surprised breath. "It's really easy to see why everyone calls you *Douchehawk*!" Plump raindrops splattered her shoulders, painting her new gray tee the same sooty shade as the gusting, churning sky above.

"No one calls me Douchehawk! No one! Except you! If I wanted to take the time, I could figure out a shitty nickname to call you, too! If there's even anything shittier than being called a huge, hateful *bitch*."

There it was again. The *B* word. And he was using it to describe *her*. If her hideous tourist T-shirt had sleeves, she'd roll them up in preparation to rear back and knock him on his ass. "You could figure something out? Really? Could you?" she asked, pitching her voice patronizingly high. "Well, I don't think we have that kind of time." She lowered her brow and balled her hands on her hips. "And I am *not* a huge, hateful bitch!" A blast of wind smacked against her back, and she tensed to keep from stumbling forward.

"My parents are dead," Tate paused, biting his lower lip. "I watched them get sucked up by a tornado and then burned in an explosion. And then you come along and kidnap me so I won't be able to plan their funeral or be there for my g-pa or help fix my town. In one evening my life has been destroyed, and I want to know why and how I can put it back together. I can't do that driving away from my home with you. So, *bitch*! *Move!*" Tate's gaze narrowed as lightning cracked overhead.

"Kidnap you?" Foster's nails dug into her palms as she tightened her fists. "No one would ever kidnap you. You're a dick! You keep saying that your parents died like this is a competition—like Cora isn't important to me, like I didn't just leave her body back there on a field. You don't have to be spewed from someone's vagina or be the result of one lucky sperm to call the people who love you your parents. Cora is a better mom than a lot of bio moms out there, and she's dead. My *mom* died today, too! And thirteen years ago my birth mom and dad died in a car accident. Five years ago my adoptive dad, Cora's husband, died when his boat capsized. So guess what? If this is a competition *I win big time because apparently everyone around me dies*!" Her skin felt hot and tight, like it had suddenly stretched too thin to contain her. Tears stinging her eyes, Foster's anger fueled her as she shoved her open palms hard against his chest. "And stop calling me a bitch!"

Tate stumbled backward, landing flat on his butt in a cloud of dust. She shielded her eyes against the stinging rain. Something was . . . different. Tate

sat on the ground looking dumbfounded as water dripped off of him, staining the parched clay brickred. Foster glanced down at her feet as the wailing wind lifted her dank, red hair. Muddy earth bubbled around her Vans as heavy rain pummeled the inch of standing water. But dust had plumed where Tate landed. *His* hair wasn't flying around in the wind. There wasn't any wind where he was, and the earth was dry and . . .

"Tate!"

He blinked up at her, his chin bobbing as if words would come if he only continued to move his mouth.

No, he wasn't staring at *her*. He was staring at the rain-wrapped windstorm she stood in the center of.

Foster took a hesitant step toward him. Beneath her feet, the fresh section of cracked, dry earth swallowed the steadily falling rain.

"I think I know what's happening!" She rushed to Tate, shrouding him in her cloak of rain and wind. Taking his hands in hers, she guided him to his feet.

"I'm glad one of us does." Tate squinted, looking up at their patch of swirling gray sky.

"Breathe with me," Foster said, releasing some of her anger with a long exhale.

"I'm always breathing." Black hair flopped in wet clumps against his forehead as he shook his head. "If not, I'd be dead."

"Can you, just for a second, try not to be so—" Foster caught herself before releasing another insult.

"Confused? Freaked? Worried? Pissed?" Water slid down Tate's face like errant tears.

"Douchey," she corrected.

Tate stiffened, recoiling slightly as if she'd pushed him . . . again.

"Relax. Don't be so, I don't know, *squishy*. Just listen to me. Now, inhale," silently, Foster counted to five before instructing them to exhale. The raindrops slowed, turning from dive-bombing water warriors to a gentle, caressing mist. "It's working!" Excitement lifted Foster to her tiptoes. So far, she was three for three. "Inhale again."

Tate's compression top stretched across his broad chest with another slow inhale.

"And exhale." Foster tilted her chin to the sky. The wind and rain ceased, the sky clearing to its dusky orange glow. "It's gone."

"Whoa," he paused, surveying the dissipating clouds. "That was amazing and *we did it*. We made it stop." The corner of Tate's lip quirked up in a half smile as he squeezed her hands.

Foster nodded her head and, realizing he still held her hands in his, yanked them away and stuffed them into her pockets. "Yep. We sure did."

"Damn," Tate groaned. "This means that this—all of this—has something to do with us."

Foster couldn't roll her eyes hard enough. "Jesus, god! Yes! That's what I've been trying to tell you this entire time."

"Ah, ah, ah. You can't get mad at me." He waggled his finger before pointing up at the sky. "'Cause, well, you know what'll happen."

With yet another deep inhale, Foster retied her matted, wet hair on top of her head and trudged back to the truck. "By the time this is all over, I'll deserve some kind of deep-breathing award."

"Yeah, well, what exactly is *all of this*?" Tate opened the door and, with a painful groan, slid onto the upholstered bench seat that they'd officially ruined. "I mean, whatever's going on with us, the rain, the storms, the tornadoes. You have answers, right?"

Foster chewed the inside of her cheek. "Well, kind of. I mean, I have some, but I need help to figure the rest out."

Tate fished the dry T-shirt out of the bag and wiped his face. "If we figure out how this is happening and stop it from happening to anyone else's family, I'm in. Totally."

"Okay," Foster wrung out the bottom of her shirt one last time before joining him in the cab. "But that means no more freaking out on me or trying to jump out of the car."

"Truck." He winked. "Got it. And, hey"—Tate sobered—"I'm really sorry about your mom. I shouldn't have acted like she wasn't important to you. And, um, about your other parents and your adoptive dad, too. That really sucks."

"Yeah," Foster's chest tightened. "Thanks. And I'm sure you're sorry about calling me a bitch as well."

"Actually," Tate stuck a wad of beef jerky in his mouth and flopped back against the seat. "I still stand by that one."

Clenching her teeth, Foster took yet another deep inhale. "And Douche-hawk strikes again."

7

EVE

"Let me get this straight. Not one. Not two. But three—*three* adults—grown men who have the ability to control wind, water, and fire somehow couldn't manage to control two teenagers? Do I have that right, Eve?"

Holding to calmness and serenity, Eve had hung back when they entered the beach home on Sunset Key, just a short boat ride from the private airport on Key West where their jet lived, always ready to take them to the mainland. She continued to keep her thoughts to herself, as she had on the quick trip from Missouri to the research island. Eve didn't respond to the question, but remained very still in the shadows watching the man who was the center of her world pace back and forth in front of the three men she called brothers. *Just let him talk,* Eve prayed silently, hoping her brothers would've learned by now. *Let him vent his anger and be rid of it—then we can try to reason with him.*

"Father, there was more to it than that."

Mark spoke up immediately, proving to Eve once again that prayers were never answered. There was nobody "up there" listening. The only religion in the room was science, and Doctor Rick Stewart was their only god.

Stewart rounded on Mark, focusing the full weight of his sharp-eyed glare on him—tall, handsome, *broken* Mark. Her water brother. Out of the three of them, he was the one she counted on the most. Which is why she'd put him in charge—insisted he go to the motel when she couldn't because . . . because . . . because she was broken, too, and had been fighting her demons, unable to help her brothers.

"Really?" Stewart spoke sarcastically. "*More* to it than that? You mean *more* like the fact that because of you Foster and Tate are together out there somewhere causing unimaginable harm—maybe to themselves, maybe to others?" Stewart had stopped in front of Mark; with each question the doctor fired, he moved closer and closer until he stood almost nose to nose with the younger man.

"Father, it wasn't his fault."

Slowly, with a grace that belied his age and always reminded Eve of one of his pet snakes stalking a feeder mouse, Stewart turned from Mark to approach Matthew.

"Wasn't his fault? Then whose fault was it? You and your brothers—men who are thirty-six years old—failed to do the one thing I asked of you? Failed to bring me two teenagers. Explain it to me. I want to know."

Eve closed her eyes. *No, Matthew! Just stay silent!*

"I . . . I called the tornado like Eve said I should. But then we had to wait, like you told us to, and see how the kids would react. Father, if, uh, if we'd, um, grabbed them before the game—or at least one of them—things would've been different." Matthew seemed to shrink as he fidgeted. He couldn't meet Stewart's eyes, and instead sent his father apologetic, nervous glances.

Stewart's voice was deceptively soft. "Are you blaming your sister for your shortcomings?"

Matthew's throat swallowed convulsively. "No," he corrected hastily. "I'm not blaming Eve."

"Then you must be blaming me."

Eve held her breath, wondering which Rick Stewart they were dealing with: the one she worshipped or the one she feared. Unconsciously Eve rubbed the place on her forearm hidden by the long sleeves of her shirt. The instant she realized what she was doing she dropped her arms to her side, fisting her hands so they would not be tempted to stray again.

"Nobody blames you, Father," Luke spoke up.

Stewart's gaze went from Matthew to Luke, and then rested on Mark. He blew out a long breath and put his hand on Mark's shoulder, causing the man to flinch.

"Of course you don't blame me. You're my sons. You have more loyalty than that, don't you, Mark?"

"Yes, Father."

Along with the three brothers, Eve released the breath she'd been holding as she moved from the shadows at the side of the room to Rick Stewart. She slid her hand in his and looked up into his intelligent brown eyes.

"It was my fault, Father. I let things get out of control. At first I only saw Cora, and when Foster finally joined her, the wall cloud was forming the tornado. I thought they'd react more normally—run for the school like almost everyone else. By the time I realized I was wrong it was too late. Foster and Tate had joined and fully manifested air, *and* caused a major splintering of the tornado. It was like a war zone, Father. I'm so, so sorry."

Stewart pulled her into the circle of his arm, his gaze fond—his touch gentle and fatherly.

"Sweet Eve, you are not to blame, though I do not understand why you weren't at the motel with your brothers."

"I would have been. I meant to be with them, but I lost control." Her eyes beseeched him to understand.

"We've talked about this. Over and over. Until I find the cure for your hallucinations . . . and for the symptoms of your manifested elements," Stewart paused and included the brothers in his gaze. "You *must* keep reminding yourselves that what you see is simply *not of this reality* and learn to push through the discomfort your elements cause."

"Father, I tried. I was handling it. But . . . but then I found Cora. She was dead and I lost control." Eve blurted the last part and then froze, waiting for Stewart's reaction.

Slowly, he took his arm from around her shoulders. He moved several steps away from the four of them and leaned against the sleek glass desk that sat before the wall of state-of-the-art laboratory equipment that dominated the room. Stewart ignored the brothers and spoke only to Eve.

"Tell me."

"It was her heart. You read the report we found last year when Luke hacked the clinic's records—right before it sold and she and Foster went off the grid. The cardiologist advised surgery and a total lifestyle change to try to repair the damage to her heart, but she disappeared instead. You said it then—Cora Stewart has a time bomb ticking inside her chest. Father, you were right. You are always right."

"Mark, Matthew, Luke . . . leave us," Stewart said. But before the brothers could hastily exit, Stewart's deep voice bellowed, "Mark—a moment, please."

Mark paused as his brothers threw relieved looks over their shoulders as they bolted from the room.

"I know you, Mark. I see you, truly see you."

"Yes, Father. I know you do. And I am sorry I disappointed you today."

Stewart made a sharp, dismissive gesture. "That is a mistake you will correct—I have no doubt. Tell me, Son, what would happen to you if you left us and went out on your own?"

"Father, I wouldn't think of—"

"Do *not* lie to me!" Stewart's voice had Eve cringing, and she was glad his back was to her and he didn't notice. "I said *I see you*. Do you think I don't know you better than you know yourself? I created you. I raised you. I am your family. And still you dream of walking away from me—from your brothers—from your sister—*from your family*." Stewart shook his head in disgust. "Answer my question. What would happen to you if you went out on your own?"

Eve watched emotions flicker over Mark's handsome, expressive face. She saw anger and fear, guilt and love battle just behind his eyes. Then his broad shoulders slumped and his gaze dropped to the floor.

"I would lose control. People would see what I can do—that I can control water, which means I can control the rain, the tides, lakes, rivers, and all the rest. When they realized what I could do, they would take me. Capture me. Treat me like a science experiment." Mark's voice was filled with resignation.

"They would dissect you." Stewart spoke the words in a calm, rational voice that made them all the more horrible. "But you probably wouldn't even be aware of what they were doing because the Frill would have devoured your mind by then."

"I—I know."

"Then you also know why it is so important that we find Foster and Tate now that their eighteenth birthday has passed and their powers have manifested, don't you?"

"Yes, Father."

"Say it!" Stewart demanded.

"We have to find them so that people don't discover what they can do—that they can control air. Because if we don't find them what would happen to me will happen to them. They'll be studied and dissected and driven mad."

"Yes. And the rest of it? Perhaps the most important part?" Stewart prodded.

Mark deflated even more. "You can use the new kids to figure out how to save us from the madness that comes with our hallucinations."

Mark wiped a trembling hand across his face. Eve couldn't stand it for one more moment. Pushing aside her own fear, she went to him and slid her arm around his waist, putting on a brave smile, which she beamed at Stewart.

"But no one is going to go mad because we are going to find the teenagers and bring them here and protect them. That's why Father created them in pairs—so that they can share the element—share the power—and avoid the madness that threatens the four of us. And while we're teaching them to understand their connections to the elements, Father is going to study them and find a way to save us as well." She tiptoed and kissed the man she called brother on the cheek. "Don't worry. Father has it all figured out, and we'll bring Foster and Tate here—just like we'll bring the other three pairs here."

"But only *if* they manifest their element. You see, Son, why we must wait until each pair turns eighteen and is drawn together, don't you? No matter what you and your brothers think, I am no monster. I wouldn't tear children from their families and their lives unless it was completely necessary. So, perhaps you were right after all. What happened at the stadium was my fault."

"The boys would *never* call you monster, Father!" Eve exclaimed. "And they do understand. We all understand."

She unwrapped her arm from around Mark and gave him an almost imperceptible push toward the half-opened door, speaking under her breath quickly as she turned her body so that Stewart would have a hard time overhearing.

"Open the files on Cora and Foster. Go over everywhere they were before they disappeared last year. Get our P.I.s in those regions on the phone. Tell them whoever finds the kids will get a one-hundred-thousand-dollar bonus. Make Luke activate that program he created to track credit card uses. Cora's dead. Foster might slip and use a card. We need to find them before the water kids turn eighteen next month."

"Yes, Eve," Mark murmured.

As her brother slipped from the room, Eve went to Stewart. She held her head high, knowing how much he appreciated her strength. *Don't let him guess. Don't let him see how tired I am—how I wish we could rewind the clock eighteen years and be a real family again.*

"I know Cora's death hurts you. It hurts me, too. Let me grieve with you." She stopped before him and gently touched his arm.

His hand covered hers. "My little Nubian princess. You know me so much better than your brothers do."

"Well, as you've been saying for years—one woman is worth three men."

"Actually, Cora said that," her father corrected.

His smile made his lined face look much younger than his seventy-two years, and Eve was hit by a wave of nostalgia as Cora's big, happy voice lifted from the deep memories of her past. *Rick Stewart, I do declare you are taller and more handsome than Laurence Fishburne.*

"I know. I remember," Eve said softly. "Even though she didn't know it, I loved her. Even though she didn't know it, she was my mother."

Stewart's dark eyes flashed dangerously. "I told you never to speak of that!"

Eve recoiled. "I-I'm sorry, Father. It's just the two of us."

Stewart sighed and patted her shoulder gently. "No, I'm sorry. It's just that the truth of your parentage must be our secret. Think of how wounded your brothers would be if they discovered you are my biological child—the only true child of my love with Cora. I believe it would wound them. They already claim that you are my favorite."

"Yes, you're right of course, Father," was what Eve said, but her thoughts were much darker: *It also would be very bad for anyone to know that you stole your wife's eggs, fertilized them yourself, then mutated and grew a child.* But Eve couldn't say that. Eve could never say that. Instead she smiled sadly at her father.

"Would you like to walk on the beach? The ocean always makes you feel better, and it's after sunset. No one from the mainland will see you."

"Yes, I would, sweet Eve," he said.

Hand in hand, Eve and the only father she'd ever known left the building that looked from the outside like any other Florida beach cottage. Eve kicked off her shoes as they reached the sand. The muggy August air was thick and hot and damp, and there was almost no breeze. Eve wished she had on a tank top, but the wish was fleeting. It was more important that her arm was covered. She wanted to keep what was hidden there to herself—if only for a day or two.

They walked along the beach, letting their feet dig into the warm sand, inhaling the breath of the ocean until the beach curved around the far side of the island that looked out onto open waters. There Stewart stopped to stare out at the star-filled sky and the fat, risen moon.

Eve concentrated on her element—earth. Finding her connection without evoking the element, she embraced the calm she had already called to her during that terrible time at the stadium when she saw her mother, crumpled and dead in the middle of that horrid, muddy field, and felt peace and protection spread from the painful spot hidden under her sleeve throughout her body—though she was careful to hold it to herself—careful not to let any energy leak from her hand joined with his. And then slowly, carefully, she began asking the questions that had begun to take over her mind.

"Father, I didn't want to say anything in front of the boys, but I'm worried about how tired you've been looking lately."

Stewart shook his head slightly, pulled his hand from hers, and waved it dismissively. "All is well, sweet Eve."

"But Father, forgive me if I'm overstepping, but you have always told us that we have to take care of each other, and it's not just that you're tired."

His gaze left the night sky and found her eyes. "What are you getting at, Eve?"

Eve clung to the earth's calmness. "Well, you weren't like this before."

"Before? By *before* do you mean *before* the scientific community sneered at me and ruined me? Yes, you're quite right. I have changed. *We* all must change."

She cleared her throat and tried again. "I understand things are different, have been different since your research was shut down, and I don't mean any disrespect, but Father, you seem completely obsessed with these teenagers."

"Of course I am. I've been obsessed with them for eighteen years—waiting for all four pairs to mature. The time is now, and my plan to bring the first pair here has already failed. It seems I should have been *more* obsessed. Perhaps then today would have ended differently."

"You're brilliant. You created us. Why do you need those kids? Surely you can find a way to cure us if you just keep researching?"

"There are things you do not understand, Eve. Things I haven't wanted to bother you or your brothers with. Just trust me."

"I do! But can't you trust me, too? What *things* do you mean?"

Eve saw anger harden her father's expression, but it faded quickly as she smiled up at him. He touched her cheek and then made a sweeping gesture around them, taking in their private island. "My princess, how do you think I've kept all this going for the past two decades?"

"Your fertility clinics made a fortune and rich men paid you a lot of money for your research."

"They did indeed. And then the scientific community shunned me for that very research. I invested wisely, but even the vast amount of money I had eventually runs out."

Eve felt chilled. "Are we broke?"

Stewart's smile was sly. "Not quite. And not for long."

"What does that mean?"

"Bring me those teenagers and you will understand—you *and* the scientific community that scoffed at my research."

"I wish you would trust me enough to tell me everything," Eve said.

"Really? Do you? And yet you hide yourself from me."

"F-Father, I don't know what you—"

"Show me. I know it's there. It must be. It's why you didn't go to the motel with the boys." Into the companionable silence, Stewart's words were like a physical blow.

"It's nothing. Not important at all right now. *You're* what's important right now."

"Show me!" His voice hardened as he turned to face her.

Resigned, Eve bowed her head and brushed the sleeve of her top up over her elbow. Smooth skin, the color of a fertile field, was marred only by a purple crystal the size of an egg that was growing, tumor-like, from the middle of her forearm. The jewel caught the light of the moon, changing silver to deep purple and shimmering from within its faceted surface.

"Never hide this from me. You know better," Stewart said as his fingers skimmed lightly over the amethyst jewel. "This one is big. You must have been terribly upset."

Eve forced herself not to flinch at the pain his touch caused.

"But you were not supposed to manifest earth. You must save your power and only use it when absolutely necessary. You're stronger than the boys, but you are not immortal."

"I didn't mean for it to happen, but when I saw Cora—when I realized she was dead—I lost control. An earthquake manifested. It's what created that explosion in the parking lot. Father, I had to calm it. I had to or it would have swallowed Foster and Tate and the entire town."

"And called much more attention to what happened there than a rogue tornado or two. So, to protect your family you calmed the earth, knowing what the price would be—knowing the agony it would cause you."

"It's only amethyst, Father. It isn't difficult to bear, and really only painful here." She touched the raw jewel gently. "The rest of it helps me. Calms me. Protects me. Just as it does the earth." Her voice sounded small and she was ashamed of herself—ashamed of the unasked question her words held.

"We've discussed this for almost two decades, Eve." Stewart's voice flattened and took on the emotionless tone of a lecturing biology professor, though Eve saw the desire in his gaze and how he couldn't stop staring at the tumor-like jewel. "You have to disperse the energy and remove the stone. If you don't what does our hypothesis tell us?"

"That the energy will build until I can't control it, and the jewel will spread over my skin, eventually encasing me." She spoke the words by rote, sounding as emotionless as he pretended to be.

"And?" he prompted.

"And it would kill me," she finished. "All right. Do it. I'm ready." Eve held her arm out to him.

He finally managed to pull his hot gaze from the jewel to meet her eyes. "I only do this to help you. You understand that, don't you?"

"Yes, Father."

"If it weren't dangerous you could keep it. Keep all of them."

"Yes, Father. I know. Go ahead." Eve lifted her arm higher, offering it to him and bracing herself for what must come next.

With a sigh that held so much need that it sickened Eve, Stewart pressed the palm of his hand against the hunk of amethyst. Quickly Eve covered his hand with her own and closed her eyes. She reached through her body—through her feet that connected her to the sandy skin of the earth—and found just a small piece of her element. Focusing that power she pulled it up, up through the soles of her feet . . . up her legs . . . her core . . . up her spine to rush over her shoulder and build in intensity until that raw earth energy blasted into the amethyst jewel—and from the jewel directly into Doctor Rick Stewart.

The older man gasped and his body went rigid like an electrical shock was jolting him, but Eve knew different. She watched with emotionless eyes as Stewart gasped in pleasure before his hand fell from her arm and he dropped softly to his knees in the sand. His breathing deepened and when he looked up at Eve his pupils were fully dilated and his expression was unfocused. Stewart's face was filled with such calm—such serenity—that he appeared to have youthened several decades.

"Oh, Eve! You were right. It is sublime. Leave me now and let me grieve for Cora and for all that was lost today by myself . . ." His words faded as Stewart lay against the sand. Eyes wide and fixed, he no longer saw her—no longer saw anything as the power of Eve's jewel surged within him, filling him with a high that no drug could ever hope to replicate—a high to which he was completely, irrevocably addicted.

Silently, Eve turned from him. Her steps were heavy as she traced their tracks in the sand. Absently, her hand brushed at the jewel in her arm and it shattered, raining colorless specks that reminded Eve of smashed eggshells.

As always after Father drained one of her crystals, Eve felt tired and empty, as well as ravenous. The sense of calm with which the amethyst had gifted her

was gone, leaving an absent, aching place, but she couldn't indulge in the luxury of longing, of wishing she would, just once, be allowed to keep her power. Father would spend the night on the beach, riding the high he'd siphoned from her.

The jewel was big. He'll be out for at least eight hours. I have to help my brothers find some trace of Foster and Tate before he wakes—before he takes out his anger on one of them. Again. And what was he insinuating tonight? That those kids will somehow make him money? Somehow fix his relationship with the scientific community, which means he's planning on going public—showing he's not dead and forgotten. That has to be good, doesn't it?

"Those kids—those four pairs of air, fire, water, and earth—they must be our only hope. Through them Father can discover how to fix us, and he has to . . . he has to start researching and experimenting again." Eve spoke to the sandy island, feeling her connection with earth in her every step. "He has to fix us. He is the only one who can. It was Father who created us, and Father who broke us."

Eve trudged toward the cottage her brothers shared. As she walked, her own words echoed around and around her mind, *the energy will build until I can't control it, and the jewel will spread over my skin, eventually encasing me . . .*

And for the first time, Eve let herself wonder for just a moment if becoming a living jewel of the earth would be more terrible than being a living drug for an addict.

8

TATE

"Okay, slow down. The left turn should be just around the next bend in the road," Tate said, raising his hand and squinting against the setting sun. "Yeah, that's it." He pointed across the dash of the truck at a gravel-covered lane securely blocked by a wide, high iron gate. A fence fed into the gate—one of those big, black metal privacy fences. Tate estimated it must be at least eight feet high and it looked like it enclosed the property on the other side of the gate, too. *That would be a bitch to climb over,* he thought, noting the pointed black tops of the fence and imagining them snagging pants and flesh if anyone was stupid enough to try it.

Foster wearily put the truck into park. She stretched, yawning loudly, and then rubbed the back of her neck as she silently stared at the gate.

Tate's gaze went from the barricade to Foster, and back to the barricade.

"Um, I know there's no house number." Tate paused and squinted, trying unsuccessfully to see down the shady little road. "Or even a house, but I swear this is the right place."

"I believe you." She turned and looked at him as she reached back behind the bench seat for the satchel she'd said had been her mom's. "You're the best navigator I've known. Way better than I am."

"Hey, thanks! I'm good at directions. Real good. I don't think I could get lost if I tried." Tate smiled, though it felt odd—strained. Then he realized it was the first time he'd really smiled and felt, just for an instant, happy since the day before when a tornado and this girl had torn his life apart. *Mom and Dad are dead.* The thought caused him physical pain. His expression instantly sobered, which Foster, of course, didn't notice.

"You're welcome. And I'm serious." She kept talking as she felt around in the bottom of the big satchel. "I'm crap at navigating. It would've been awful to try to find this place by myself, especially with cell service being out the entire trip." Foster closed her eyes and smacked herself on her forehead. "Balls! I can't believe I forgot. Where's my phone?"

Tate glanced around the messy cab of the truck, kicking burger wrappers and empty cups aside. "Here it is." He leaned down and pulled it from the sticky napkin sandwich that had formed around it.

"Thanks," Foster said absently as she snatched the phone from him, working her sparkly cover off as she spoke quickly. "Good. Still no service. Okay, look through that glove box for something small and sharp—like a paper clip or a thumbtack."

"Okay, no problem." Tate popped open the glove box and pawed through the papers and old, discarded crap, trying to ignore how hot and sore the cut on his leg felt.

"Will this work?" He offered her the rusty paper clip that held the truck's insurance paperwork together.

"Yep, it should." Foster took it, stretched it open, and stuck the little end into a tiny hole along the side of her iPhone. A thing popped out, which she grabbed and then shoved in her pocket before she tossed the phone into the satchel and went back to searching the bottom of it.

"What's that thing? The guts of the phone or whatever?"

She gave him a look like he'd asked her the stupidest question in the universe—but Tate was beginning to think that's just pretty much how Foster looked all the time.

"It's a SIM card, genius. Where have you been for, I don't know, since 2000?"

"Hey, I have a phone. Well, I used to. It's in my gym locker. I use it. I just don't take it apart."

"The failures of the public education system never cease to amaze me." Foster shook her head. "Ah, here it is!"

Without saying anything else to him, Foster got out of the cab and went to the gate. With a resigned sigh, Tate followed her. She was holding a little leather pouch she'd finally found at the bottom of that satchel. It reminded Tate of what his g-pa called a coin purse, and he figured the key to the gate was inside. But instead of unlocking the gate Foster studied the ground around it until she found a fist-sized rock, which she picked up and carried to the stone pillar to the right of the gate. She reached into her pocket, took out the SIM card, held it against the pillar, and then with impressive dexterity, she smashed the rock against the card without also smashing her fingers.

Then she turned to face him.

"No cell phones unless we buy burners, and even then we need to be careful," she said.

"But how are we supposed to call people?"

"We aren't. You aren't. Ever." She turned her back to him and then went to a keypad he'd just noticed that was recessed into the brick column. She opened the coin purse–looking thing and pulled out a piece of paper, punching the numbers written there into the pad. There was the click sound of a release and the gate swung open.

"Good. That means we have electricity." She spun around and headed back to the truck, but Tate didn't move. "Hey," she called as she opened the driver's door. "Come on. This is the place."

"I have someone I need to call."

Foster frowned. "No. It's not safe."

"Why?"

"Because Cora said it's not safe, and I trust her. Completely. Even though she's dead. All of this"—she made a sweeping gesture at the land behind them— "was set up by Cora for me." Foster hesitated and then corrected herself. "For us, actually. To keep us safe from the people who are chasing us."

"But *why* are they chasing us?" Tate insisted. When she didn't answer— again—he started to get pissed. "Look, I need answers. I've come with you, even though the only place I want to be is home trying to figure out how I'm supposed to go on without my mom and dad, but I'm here—mostly because there is obviously something bizarre going on with us and the weather, and I need to understand what."

"And men are chasing us," Foster added.

"That, too," he admitted. "But I have a grandpa—my mom's dad—he's all that's left of my family. He lives in Texas and he's going to be devastated when he finds out what happened." Tate paused and felt himself deflate as he realized the rest of it. "G-pa's gonna think I'm dead, too. Oh, god, I just thought of that. Foster, I *have to* call him."

"Okay, I get it. But let's talk about this at the house."

"I don't see a house," Tate said stubbornly.

"I'm pretty sure that's the point—that you can't see it from the road. Come on, get in. We've come all this way, you might as well see where we were going," Foster said.

Tate gave a sharp nod and went back to the truck, climbing into the passenger's side. "I need answers."

"Tate, so do I. That's why we're here. Just trust me a little while longer," she said as she drove through the gate, which closed silently behind them.

"Do you trust me?" Tate swiveled in the seat to look at her.

She glanced at him briefly and he could see her hesitation, and also see her decide to tell him the truth. "No, I don't. But don't take that the wrong way. I've only trusted one person in the past five years, and she's dead."

"You do seem like the kind of girl who has trust issues," Tate said.

"That sounds like misogynist bullshit. I'm not a *girl* with trust issues. I'm a *person* who has learned through hard life lessons that people suck."

"I don't know why you think I should trust you if you won't trust me," Tate said.

"It's simple. I don't suck."

Tate snorted, but his attention was pulled from her by the neat farm that appeared at the end of the long entrance drive. There was a big, gray, two-storied house that had a giant wraparound porch sitting back from a much smaller building that reminded Tate of something that could have been a storefront in one of the old John Wayne movies his g-pa liked to watch. Over the top of the store in what looked like freshly painted red letters was the cheery logo: STRAWBERRY FIELDS. Pastures stretched on either side of the driveway, and

a barn that matched the house sat near one of them. Behind the house Tate saw several produce-filled fields that ended at a thick line of trees. Just peeking out from around the rear of the house was part of what must be a giant garden. He could also see the edge of something that looked like a chicken coop. Nothing stirred except for the lazy breeze and a bevy of chipmunks that scampered from the little storefront and disappeared into the waving grass.

"It's pretty. Who lives here?"

When Foster didn't say anything he looked at her, automatically annoyed at her typical silence, and then he felt like a total turd when he saw tears dripping down her cheeks.

"Hey, what's wrong?"

"It says Strawberry Fields." She smiled through her tears and wiped her cheeks with the dirty sleeve of her shirt.

"Yeah, like I said, it's pretty. Why are you crying?"

She shook her head. "I'm okay. It's nothing. You asked who lives here? We do. Come on, let's go check it out." Foster slung the satchel over her shoulder and left the truck, heading for the front door of the tidy-looking farmhouse.

"Is this where you lived with Cora?" Tate limped up the front stairs just behind Foster.

"No. I've never been to Sauvie Island before. Cora and I used to have a brownstone in Portland—right in the Pearl District." Tate heard her voice soften with nostalgia. "Man, I loved that place. It had the coolest rooftop ever. Cora and I used to sit up there and gawk at people all the time. There was a game we used to play where we guessed how many dogs we could count walking by. The loser had to do the dishes."

"Dogs?" Tate asked softly. He was hesitant to say anything. He didn't want to mess up this version of Foster. She seemed so much nicer than the girl he'd just spent twenty plus hours with in the cab of that truck.

She'd pulled the piece of paper from the leather coin purse again and was punching numbers into the keypad on the front door.

"Yeah, dogs. Portland is majorly dog friendly. We were going to get a dog. I wanted a mastiff. Cora wanted a Scottie. We were arguing about it when everything changed a year ago."

Foster opened the door and they both stood there, peering inside. Tate immediately thought it was a nice house. Not mansion nice. Not even rich nice. Homey nice, with a big fireplace, comfy couch, a couple of recliners, and even a beanbag chair plopped in front of the big-screen TV. From the front door he could see the dining room table and got a peek into the cheery kitchen painted a happy yellow.

He was just going to ask why they were still on the porch when Foster unfroze and walked into the living room, heading straight to the wide stone fireplace mantel and the row of framed family pictures there. He followed her more slowly, taking in the nice details—there were pretty pictures, mostly of landscapes and city scenes—plus lots of bridges.

A small, choked sound returned his attention to Foster, who had stopped in front of the fireplace. Her hand was lifted toward one of the framed pictures, as if she wanted to touch it, but couldn't make herself. He knew she was crying, but only because she kept wiping at her face with short, angry swipes, and when he looked at the picture, he understood why.

It was of a younger, smiley-er version of Foster. She was sitting on the stoop of a two-story brownstone town house beside a big black woman Tate had no difficulty recognizing as Cora. Cora had her arm around Foster and was kissing her cheek while Foster cheesed for what was obviously a selfie. Tate scanned the rest of the pictures on the mantel. They were all of Foster and Cora—younger versions of the two of them. The joy that filled their faces reminded Tate of his family, and he felt his own eyes fill with tears.

"She did all of this for me," Foster's voice shook as she spoke through her tears. "These pictures—the paintings—even the furniture. They're all from our house."

"Foster, did you lose your house last year?"

She turned liquid eyes to him. "No. We *left* our house last year."

"What do you mean 'left'?"

He could see her struggling to hold on to her temper. She wiped her eyes again and squared her shoulders. "Exactly one year ago yesterday, on my seventeenth birthday—Cora packed two bags. Locked our house. We got in our car. And we left—left our life, our credit cards, our everything. Since then we've never stayed in one place more than a week."

"You've been homeless for a year? On purpose?"

"We weren't homeless. We were flying under the radar," Foster said.

"Why? You gotta explain."

"The truth? All I know is that Cora said I was in danger, and that we had to leave before they took me, and now I have to keep you safe, too."

Then Tate processed all of what Foster had told him. "Hey! Our birthdays are on the same day."

Foster sighed sadly, still staring at the pictures. "Happy birthday to us," she said unconvincingly.

Tate opened his mouth to ask one more of the zillion questions spilling from his overwhelmed mind, but Foster spoke before he could.

"Look, I have to get cleaned up. And I want some real food—like more than nasty drive-through. Something green and alive. And you look like crap. I mean, worse than me, and that's bad."

Tate glanced down at himself. He had on the stained T-shirt Foster had got in Missouri, a pair of baggy gray sweatpants they'd bought at a truck stop somewhere in Utah, and a pair of dad slippers that had IDAHO? NO YOU DA HO written across the top of them. They'd found them outside Boise. Foster was right. He looked like crap.

"A shower sounds good," he said. "Then food."

"Agreed. Let's shower then forage. Then talk."

"Okay," he said.

The bathrooms were big and all three of them were stocked with necessities. Tate stood under a fat stream of water as hot as he could stand and tried to wash away his pain—his homesickness—his shock, along with the dirt and blood. But all he actually wanted to do was to bolt for the front door and start driving west. Toward home.

He couldn't, though. Not yet. Tate had to find out how those tornadoes had been caused—and how to stop them from ever happening again.

He decided that the shower did make him feel a little better, and towel dried his hair then put his pieced-together outfit back on. The cut on his leg was sore, but it didn't look infected, which was at least a small relief.

Foster wasn't in the living room, so Tate made his way to the kitchen and scavenged through the empty fridge. The kitchen cabinets were filled with dishes and pots and pans and such, and there were even some canned foods in the pantry, but there was definitely nothing "green" anywhere.

Tate made his way back to the stairway that Foster had taken to the upstairs bathroom she'd claimed. He was trying to decide whether he should go up there and knock on the door—or if he should just call out her name—when he heard it. Somewhere just down the hallway in front of him a girl was sobbing as if her heart was shattered.

Tate followed the sound until he came to a little room that was obviously an office. The door was partially open. Foster's back was to him. She was holding something in both of her hands, and was bent around it like someone had gut punched her while she sobbed.

His mom hadn't been a crier, so the times when she did cry it always made Tate's heart hurt. He heard his mom's voice as if she were standing beside him, *Tate, you're a smart, educated, white man. Don't be an entitled jerk. Be unexpectedly kind—you'll never go wrong if you err on the side of kindness. Oh, and also be a feminist—that'll really baffle them.*

Tate moved on an instinct that had been drilled into him by his kind, woke mother. Foster was a bitchy pain in the ass, but Tate had been raised right. So, he went to her. Later, he wasn't sure exactly what he'd been intending to do. Not only was Foster not the crying kind, but she also didn't seem like the "give me a hug and make me feel better" kind. He didn't get the opportunity to find out for sure because the picture she was holding snagged his attention. Over her shoulder he saw that it showed a group of five people. Four looked like they were in their late twenties–early thirties. They surrounded a tall, older man who looked distinguished and serious. They were in front of a medium-sized boat that was docked, but was obviously ready to go out to sea.

There was something about the picture . . . Tate sucked in a surprised breath, which caused Foster to spin around and glare at him.

"What do you think you're doing sneaking up on me like that?"

"I wasn't sneaking. I just walked in here. The door was open." He pointed at the picture she still clutched. "Those men. Three of them are the guys who came after us."

"This is Cora's office—Cora's stuff. Don't ever come in here again." Foster's voice was hard and angry. All signs of the sobbing, broken girl evaporated before his eyes.

And Tate snapped, "Look, I've been trying to be nice to you, even though you've made it pretty damn hard. But I'm done with that. My parents died because of something going on with the two of us. You owe me an explanation. Now!"

Foster held up the picture, and for a second Tate thought she was going to hit him with it. Instead she pointed at it, and in a voice filled with fury said, "Owe you an explanation? I don't owe you shit! Cora and I saved your life when we showed up at that football game and got you out of there. You're right. These three men *are* the ones who came after us. That woman was with them. I saw her at the edge of the field right after Cora died. And this man, Doctor Rick"— her finger poked the glass of the picture so hard Tate was surprised it didn't crack. "He was my adoptive father, Cora's husband. This was the last picture of him. It was taken before they killed him. Only on the football field Cora told me they *didn't* kill him. That he's working *with* them and that they're after me and they're after you. No, I don't know why, but if you could manage to quit whining and leave me alone I might be able to figure it out!" Thunder cracked overhead in time with her shout. She threw up her arms. "Great. Now look what you've done."

"Foster, you are a bitch. Worse than that—you're a mean, insensitive bitch." He said the words slowly, deliberately, before he spun on his heel and stalked from the room.

"Where are you going?" she called after him.

Tate turned in the doorway. "I'm going to get food. Then I'm going to eat. Then I'm going to sleep. And *then* I'm going to figure out how to go home."

"Fine. Do what you want."

"Fine." He paused and hated the next words that he had to speak. "I need money."

Foster reached into the satchel she seemed to always have with her and pulled out a wad of cash, tossing it at him. "Get something green. The code to the gate's 9662. Close the door on your way out."

Tate slammed the door to the office and stomped from the farmhouse.

The sky looked ominous, pregnant with rain that had just started to change from drizzle to downpour. Wind wailed around him, lifting his hair and making him shiver. He scanned the darkening sky for a wall cloud. Fog obscured the green ridge of distant mountains and he couldn't see shit. *Ah, to hell with it! I got rid of a tornado once—I can do it again.* Head tucked against the wind and rain, Tate ran to the pickup.

He started the truck easily. Foster had made him do it over and over again on their trip. He floored it, getting spiteful pleasure from hearing the gravel spray the porch. He paused at the gate, but it sensed the truck and opened soundlessly.

It wasn't until he got all the way back to the little store that sat beside the bridge that led to the mainland that Tate's temper cooled. He parked the truck and sighed, rubbing his face and trying to get his thoughts together. What was he doing here? He should've stayed in Homer, no matter what crazy-ass Foster had said.

Then, as if he was watching a movie replay from his memory, Tate saw the two of them—Foster and him—standing side by side as that tornado plowed down the football field. He heard his shout again, *YOU WILL NOT COME THIS WAY!* He felt the rush of electricity that swept over him as he literally hurled that huge twister away from them.

"That's why I'm here," Tate muttered to himself. "We did that. I have to figure out how, and I can't go home until I do."

Tate rubbed his face again, thinking he'd never felt this tired in his life as he stared blankly into the distance . . . until he realized what it was he was staring at.

"Yes! Things might just be looking up for me!"

Tate hurried from the truck, taking the stairs to the little clapboard-sided store two at a time. Moving quickly, he filled his arms with food—remembering to grab some green stuff—then he piled everything up before the only cash register.

"Looks like you're camping this weekend," said the old guy who sported a long, scraggly beard and a man bun as he rang up and bagged Tate's groceries.

"Yes, sir," Tate said automatically.

"Well, I hope the weather gets better for you. It's been a mess lately."

"Me too. Hey, does that pay phone out there work?" Tate jerked his thumb toward the side of the parking lot where the old aluminum and glass booth sat like something out of a seventies movie.

"Well, yes son, it sure does. It's probably the last one in this part of the country that works. It even takes quarters."

"Cool. Could you give me a bunch of quarters with my change, please?"

"Sure, kid." The guy handed him a handful of quarters with his change. "Hey, you're not going to turn into Superman or anything, are you?"

"No, sir. I'm a different kind of superhero."

Tate left the store in a wash of the man's chuckles. He put the groceries in the cab of the truck and went to the phone booth. Feeling like he'd stepped back in time, Tate dialed the number he'd memorized when he was five years old. The gruff old voice answered on the third ring.

"Hello?"

"G-pa it's me, Tate. I'm not dead." And then Tate Nighthawk Taylor began to sob.

9

TATE

"Look, before you yell at me, I'm not technically in the room. I also brought you something green." Tate extended a grocery bag. "Truce?"

"I found something. Put the bags down and come here," Foster said, barely glancing up at him from the papers she'd been studying on the desk.

Tate grunted, "So, am I allowed in or what?"

"Look, Tate, this is me trucing. If you think I'm going to offer some apology, I'm not because I'm not sorry. People shouldn't apologize if they don't mean it. So take it or leave it." Pulling her damp, freshly washed hair off her shoulders, she did look up at him then. "Or you can eat and leave. Like you said you would. Just make up your mind."

Tate put the grocery bags down and went to stand before the desk. "I made up my mind. I'm staying, but I'm going to be as honest about it as you. I'm only staying because I have to find out what we are. I have to know if I caused that tornado and my parents' death. When I figure this weird crap out I'm going to leave and do whatever I can to make sure this doesn't happen to anyone else's family, whether you want to stay here with your head stuck in the sand or not. Deal?"

Foster shrugged. "Sounds fair."

"One more thing."

Her sigh was long-suffering as she brushed curling scarlet hair from her face. "Yes?"

"Stop being so hateful. I know you hurt. So do I, but being mean to me—the *only* person who's in this with you, is just stupid."

"Are you calling me stupid?"

"If you keep being hateful, yes, I am. Because it'd be true. And I agree with you—I won't apologize for saying that because I wouldn't mean it." Tate's gaze locked with hers.

"What if what you consider being hateful is what I consider being honest?" she said.

"Well, as my mom would say, then you need to do better."

"And what about you?"

Tate tilted his head to the side, considering. "I'll try not to bait you, even though you're damn easy to bait. I'll also work as hard as you to figure out what's going on. So, real truce?" He offered his hand to her.

Foster hesitated. Tate could see her mind working and had no clue if she was going to react like a rational person or a lunatic. So he waited, hand extended, practicing that kindness his mom would be proud of him for.

Finally, Foster stood and took his hand, shaking it with a firm grip. "Deal. Follow me." She moved from behind the desk to the near side of the office and the wall of bookshelves there. "Here," Foster pointed to one of the shelves.

"You found books. In an office." He wondered, not for the first time, if Foster might be more than a little crazy. Like, seriously and literally in need of meds and counseling.

"No," Foster's lips pursed. "I found this." She pressed the left edge of the middle bookshelf and stepped back as it swung open.

"Narnia," Tate breathed.

"What? No. It's not Narnia. It's where Cora kept all of her . . . stuff."

"No, Cora kept all of her stuff in the rest of the house where people's stuff belongs." He peered into what was obviously a well-built, expertly stocked safe room lined with metal file cabinets. "*This* is a Batcave. Why did Cora need a Batcave?"

"Gah, Tate, I'm trying not to be mean. Really, I am, but you make it difficult. Cora needed a Batcave *because we're in danger.*" Foster walked back to

the desk, motioning for Tate to follow her. She pointed at three soggy yellow legal pages filled with neat cursive writing that had bled blue ink all over. "And, sadly, being on this island isn't enough to keep us safe."

"What's this letter?" Tate bent over the desk, trying to decipher the washed-out writing on the soaked pages.

"It's from Cora."

"What happened to it?"

"My fault." Foster sighed and sounded truly miserable. "It was in her satchel. Before she died she told me to come here and that she'd written a letter explaining everything, but that I should wait until we got here to read it." She shook her head, clearly pissed at herself. "I should've known better. I should've checked to be sure it was safe and dry. I found it in the outside pocket, totally soaked."

"Hey, it's okay. There's a lot of it that we can read." Tate squinted, reading between the soggy lines.

"Who's Molly?" he asked.

Dear Foster,

If you're reading this it means that I'm dead and you made it safely to Sauvie Island.. First, I'm so sorry didn't tell you I was sick, but baby girl, that was my choice. My heart disease was bad. Terminal. I chose to spend my remaining time with you and not in a hospital. It was my choice, Foster, and I don't regret so don't you blame yourself. Not for one instant. I won't have it.

Next – Molly you in danger girl!

Go ahead, Strawberry. Let yourself laugh like you and I would if we were reading this together. Don't ever forget to smile that beautiful smile and have fun. And then get to work. I know how you like your bulleted points, so to begin:

• You're already in my office at Strawberry Fields (Named after you, my little strawberry baby girl!). If you're sitting at my desk look to your left. Go to the bookshelf where it meets the wall. Run your fingers under the edge of the middle shelf to find the hidden button. Press it and then step back. It's going to swing open to reveal a safe room. Yes, it's very Kingsman-like. No, I'm not hiding Colin Firth in there, though girl, I know you know I wish!

Look around the safe room. Be sure you keep the supplies current,

- In the rear left corner a square of the wood floor can be lifted if you use the letter opener on my desk. It's another trap door. You can drop down into the crawl space under the house and get out. The safe is important. The combo is the same as the front gate. Change that ASAP. Inside the safe you'll find:
- Documents for your new identity, Foster Fields, as well as documents for Tate's new identity, Tate Johnson.

- You have money. Quite a lot of it, actually. Spend it, but be careful. Foster, the plastic is there for emergencies. Try not to use it. You know how to stay off the grid. We've been practicing for the past year. Keep it up.
- Oh, yes, I was sure Tate was the kid you and I have been looking for. I should have told you sooner. I thought you and I would have more time. Forgive me, baby girl.

- Study them. You must know your enemy.

Foster snorted, pulling his gaze to her. She was actually giggling a little!

"That's a quote from *Ghost*. It was Cora's favorite movie. She loved her some Whoopi Goldberg almost as much as she loved her some Patrick Swayze."

Tate smiled. "Cora seems nice. And funny."

Foster's eyes went liquid. "She was," she said softly, touching the damp paper gently.

Tate cleared his throat. "Okay, well, I can read most of these bulleted points." He paused, scanning the page quickly. "Wow, the Batcave even has an escape hatch."

"Cora was good at planning," Foster said wistfully.

Tate met her gaze, thinking that her unshed tears made her green eyes shine like emeralds. "So is my mom." He shook his head quickly and corrected himself. "So *was* my mom."

"I know. It's hard for me to believe Cora's gone, too. I—I keep expecting her to come through the door and yell at me about how messy my hair is."

"Mom would tell me mine needs to be trimmed. She was always on me about that," Tate said.

"Moms always seem to focus on weird hair things," Foster stated.

"We can definitely agree about that," Tate said.

"It's a start. Right?"

Tate thought Foster suddenly looked younger, like a little girl who was actually trying hard to be good. He forced the corners of his lips up and nodded. "Right." Then he refocused on the soggy pages. "Tate Johnson? Did she really have new identity papers made up for me?"

Foster hurried into the Batcave and came out with a manila envelope, spilling the contents onto the desk. He picked up the Oregon driver's license and stared at the picture beside the name, TATE JOHNSON, and some kind of phony address in a town called Ashland.

"She really did," Foster said, flicking a finger at her own new license that said she was FOSTER FIELDS.

"Damn, you got my superhero alliteration," Tate said. "And how the hell did Cora get my junior yearbook photo?"

"I told you. She was a genius at planning." Then she added, "Superhero alliteration?"

"Yeah, I was Tate Taylor—like Clark Kent, Peter Parker, and Bruce Banner."

"Huh. I never thought about that before. So I guess that means I get to be the superhero. Cool. I'll be Wonder Woman."

Tate snorted. "Fine by me. We definitely need Wonder Woman." He went back to studying the letter. "This is serious. No one would go through all the trouble Cora did to set all of this up without a major reason. We're really in trouble."

"Yep. Us and the others."

"Others?"

"Keep reading."

He moved to the next page, which was wetter and harder to decipher.

You know your stepfather used to believe he could halt climate change and save the earth by genetically engineering fetuses so that *experimented on four fetuses, born about thirty-six years ago.* *the Core*

Four: Eve, Mark, Matthew, and Luke. You also remember that they were why your father's experiments on Sunset Island were shut down. He told me that the Core Four were complete failures and that they were living normal lives on their own after the island facility was closed five years ago, just before his "death." I didn't question him. I wanted to believe him. Then he died in that boating accident, and I thought the subject moot.

Until I sold his Portland clinic four years ago. I was cleaning out the basement and I found a stash of hidden files – the twelve in the safe. As I read through them I realized I had been wrong .

wrong to believe he died five years ago. Most importantly, I had been wrong to believe he did not experiment on you.

Okay, now, don't you be scared. This is all going to be okay. There is nothing wrong with you. You are perfect exactly as you are. Oh, baby girl, I wish I could be with you now, but I want you to know that my strength is still with you – my love is still with you – my heart will always be with you. You can do this, but you're going to have to open yourself to help.

Sorry. I digress. This is more difficult than I thought it would be.

Read the files. Look through the newspaper clippings and internet stories I collected. You'll see what I did. Those Core Four – they've popped up in the news over the past five years whenever there were major natural disasters. Study the pictures. Do you see him in the crowd?

Doctor Rick Stewart is not dead.

Foster, we talked about that final picture – the one he took with the Core Four right before his fatal "accident." We thought they had something to do with his death, but the more research I did, the more I've come to believe Rick faked his death with the help of the Core Four and he's waiting until turn eighteen. That's when the Core Four began to manifest their abilities. I believe that's when you

abilities

Core Four are going to come after you.

find the others.

I do not know why he created eight of you this time instead of four. I do not know who the other six kids *are; I only know their birthdates*

his unusually good night vision – the same as your night vision.

connect the dots to the others. You always have been good at puzzles. I have faith in that beautiful, unique brain of yours.

Tate finished reading as much as he could make out, and then looked up at Foster, who had started pacing back and forth in front of Cora's desk. "There are more like us."

"Yeah. Freaks like us. In danger like us. Being hunted like us."

"But this Doctor Stewart guy, he's your dad."

"Yeah, well, Jim Jones had kids, too."

"Man, this is bad." Carefully, Tate picked up the last page of the letter, which was soaked. Half of it was illegible, but even that half was enough to send skitters of fear up his spine.

? I'll tell you Strawberry:

- *You and Tate are linked*
- *Your stepfather needs you and the other children t*

- *Rick Stewart and the Core Four cannot be trusted*

se the man who was my husband for thirty years – the man who was your father – he couldn't have done these terrible things. He couldn't have faked his death. He couldn't be trying to manipulate the earth's climate. He couldn't be after my sweet strawberry girl. But, Foster, I truly believe he is, and if you see any of the Core Four you will know he is.

Do not ever underestimate him. And if he has become as ruthless as he is brilliant, it isn't just you and seven other kids who are in danger – the world is in danger.

You can't risk going to the authorities.

They'd make you science experiments – or worse. And they can't keep you safe. Rick's a lot smarter than they are.

I have to close this now, baby girl. Strawberry Fields is your future - you can be safe on that fertile little island, I truly believe it. create a sanctuary for you and the others, and this was the best I could do. I planned on being there with you. Forgive me for dying too soon – but you know how I like to be early rather than late.

I want you to understand one thing beyond everything else. The greatest joy in my life has been being your mother. You brought love and light, laughter and happiness to me, and you have made me so, so proud. Trust your heart. It's beautiful. I know I've taught you to hold tight to your feelings. I did that to keep you safe, but now that I'm gone you're going to have to allow yourself to trust others. You'll be smart about it. I know you will.

I love you, Strawberry, more than I've ever loved anyone. Be kind to yourself, baby. You're doing the best you can, and that's all I've ever asked of you.

Your Mama,
Cora

"It's hard to make out, but does that really say this Dr. Stewart guy experimented on us genetically?" Tate realized his hand was shaking and he put the paper down.

"It does."

"Damn, that's creepy."

"Right?" Foster rubbed her arms like she was cold. "Makes me feel all crawly inside."

"Hey, no. We're not gonna do that," Tate said firmly.

"Do what?"

"We're not gonna start thinking we're freaks."

"Uh, Nighthawk, we are freaks. Why do you think you can see so well at night? Why do you think you threw around a tornado like a gigantic, deadly football? We. Are. Freaks. Doctor Rick did something to us. On a genetic level. Your public school education obviously isn't allowing the gravity of that biology to sink in, so let me educate you. *We might not even be human.*"

"First, I'm good at biology—public school or not. And I do get how bizarre this is, but tell me this, what good does it do to wallow in pity and call ourselves freaks?"

She stopped pacing and fisted her hands on her hips. "I don't wallow."

"I thought you said you were honest."

Foster frowned. "I'm wallowing?"

"Totally."

She cocked her head to the side, studying him. "Why aren't you wallowing?"

He shrugged. "I'm a 'glass half full' kind of guy. Sure, we're science experiments, but I've always loved my night vision. Maybe once we figure out all these blurry, water-damaged parts we'll love being, uh"—Tate looked down at the letter. Finding the right part, he read aloud—"'linked.'"

"You really think so?"

"Yep. Why didn't you tell me you have the night vision thing, too?"

Foster lifted a shoulder. "I don't, um . . ."

"Trust people because they suck," Tate finished for her.

She flashed him a hint of a real smile. "Ten points for the brunette."

"Could we make another deal?"

Her smile faded like a snuffed candle. "Depends."

"How about you stop keeping things from me and I promise anything you say to me goes into the vault."

Foster furrowed her brow as her green-eyed gaze went to the Batcave. "Vault?"

"Not a literal vault. It's what my g-pa and I always say when we tell each other a secret. It goes into the vault and it doesn't come out unless the person who put it in there, which would be you, says it's okay to tell someone else."

"What if it's never okay to tell someone else?"

"Then it stays in the vault," he said.

"You're serious?"

"G-pa and I never joke about the vault. It's for real."

Foster blew out a long breath. "All right. Deal. But if you mess that up, even once—I'll never—"

"I won't," Tate interrupted. "I swear on the memory of my mom and dad."

Foster's eyes widened. "I believe you." She drew another deep breath, like she was getting ready to dive into a pool, and then blurted. "I have this Jedi mind trick thing I can do."

"What does that mean?"

"It means if I concentrate, or maybe want it bad enough, I can make people do what I want them to do."

"Like Yoda? Seriously?"

"Like Yoda. Seriously." She picked at her fingernails. "I used it on you accidentally when I told you to go the fuck to sleep in the truck. But I didn't know it would work. It never did before—not really. Then while you were asleep I went into the Quickie Mart and there was this bubba in there. He was watching the news and we were on it."

"What!"

"Yeah, someone must have recorded us. It was when you tossed the tornado away. He recognized me and was going to call some news guy he knew. I panicked and used my Jedi mind trick. On purpose. And it worked. I told him to forget he'd ever seen me, and he did."

"Holy crap. You Obi-Wan Kenobi–ed him! And me!"

She kept picking at her fingernails. "Well, I didn't mean to Obi-Wan you. Only him. But, yeah, I did."

"That's freaking awesome!"

Foster blinked. "You actually think so?"

"Are you kidding? That's a super helpful power to have! Of course I've gotta watch that you don't go over to the Dark Side, but still. Super helpful."

"I wouldn't go to the Dark Side."

"Said Anakin Skywalker, like, a bunch of times before he went over to the Dark Side." Tate felt a rush of excitement. "Hey! What if all we have to do is find this Doctor Rick guy and have you use your Jedi mind trick on him and make him tell us everything?"

All the color drained from Foster's face. "No. I don't want to see him again. Ever."

"But Foster, he could—"

"He pretended to die. He left Cora and me. *He fucked with our genetics when we were fetuses and then he sent his goons to capture us.* Who cares if he's telling us everything if he's also trying to use us or destroy us? No, Tate.

Let's figure out how to find the other kids. Bring them here. And then decide what the hell we're going to do *without that crazy bastard having any part of it.* Okay?" Her green eyes beseeched him.

Slowly, Tate nodded. "Okay. I get it. I hear you." He ran a hand through his hair and sighed. "So, where do we begin?"

Foster headed into the Batcave, calling back over her shoulder at him. "I started making piles on top of the file cabinets in here. One stack of stuff I thought might help us find these other people, and the other is full of stuff so sciency and confusing that I can't figure out if it'll help us or not."

"Okay, well, I got some ramen. We can make a few bags and figure out where to go from here."

"We don't have time to stop and have some fancy dinner."

"It's ramen. Not all that fancy."

Foster continued as if she hadn't heard him. "There are crazy people out there who are hell-bent on capturing not only us, but six other people who may or may not know that they're complete freaks. You might not give a shit about me, but think about them."

"I give a shit about you."

Foster turned and met his gaze, her emerald eyes inscrutable.

"I mean, I care about people, and you're a person, so . . ." When she just stood there staring at him, Tate went to the entrance to the safe room and spoke in his most rational voice. "Look, we'll work a lot better if we eat. We can even take some of those files into the kitchen with us. One of us can cook and the other can read aloud and make notes."

"I suppose you want me to do the cooking."

"Nope. I'm an excellent cook. And ramen is my specialty. Plus, providing you sustenance is part of me helping to keep you from turning to the Dark Side."

Foster rolled her eyes at him, but marched past him out of the Batcave, and picked up one of the bags of groceries. "Nighthawk, try not to be such a dork."

"Do or do not, there is no try," he said automatically. Foster was walking ahead of him, so Tate couldn't be sure, but he thought he heard, just for a moment, her laughter.

10

FOSTER

Sunlight streamed into the room, bathing Foster in its delicious warmth. She stretched her arms above her head, curling and uncurling her fingers like she did every morning. And this morning was exactly like all her other mornings. It had to be. Everything that had happened—Tate, the tornado, *everything*— it had all been a bad dream.

Foster tucked her arms against her chest and nestled into her pillow. Definitely a bad dream. There was no other explanation. She would *never* go to a football game, and it was just silly to think that she could control people or tornadoes *with her words.*

And then there was Cora. *Her* Cora. She wouldn't leave Foster. She *couldn't* leave.

A small sob of realization clenched the back of Foster's throat, and she squeezed her eyes shut even tighter.

Maybe if I don't wake up, if I stay like this forever, it won't be true. Cora will still be here, and it will all go back to the way it was.

Tate yawned, sneezed, and yawned again, reminding Foster for a brief moment of the fat orange tabby she'd had as a child when she'd still had her biological parents.

Why does everyone around me have to leave?

But everyone hadn't. Doctor Rick was still out there somewhere, and so were the six other innocent kids he'd used as guinea pigs for his bullshit experiment. She needed answers. Foster bolted upright, the papers strewn around her fluttering with the sudden burst of movement.

She was in Cora's office at Strawberry Fields. Cora was dead. None of it was a dream.

"You're awake," Tate smiled at her sleepily while stretching his arms overhead, clenching and unclenching his thick fingers in a way so similar to her own that it made her cringe.

"Did you . . ." Foster studied his makeshift blanket mattress. "Sleep in here? I thought you went to bed."

Tate hiked his shoulders. "I did. Real late. Then I woke up sometime after three a.m. I dunno. I just couldn't sleep. I saw you passed out in here on the floor. I didn't think you'd want to be alone." He fiddled with the corner of the comforter he must've dragged in from his room. "*I* didn't want to be alone." His whisper seemed to press through her and disappear into the hollow ache in her chest.

They were connected through more than their abilities, whatever those might be. She and Tate were connected through their pain. She wanted so badly to close the distance between them, to hug him the way Cora had hugged her, and she needed that embrace in return. They both needed kind words and assurance that they weren't in this world alone. But she couldn't will her body to move or her mouth to speak.

Foster sat frozen in the sunlight.

She didn't know him, and could barely trust him. The risk of getting hurt and creating new wounds far outweighed any momentary release of anguish.

"You snore, by the way." He stood, brushing crumbs from his sweatpants. "Big Heffalump sounding, 'nail down the furniture because you're going to suck it all in' type of snores." He tilted back his head, grumbling and snorting in demonstration.

Before she could stop herself, Foster threw her pillow at him. "I do not!" she exclaimed, stifling a chuckle. She couldn't laugh. Not today. Maybe not ever again. Not when Cora had just . . . "So, I didn't really find anything new last night," she gathered the papers scattered around her blanket. "But I think if we—"

"*I think* you should eat something." Tate crammed a half-eaten sleeve of graham crackers back into its box.

"Those are for s'mores," Foster blurted, rising to her feet. "You don't eat them by themselves." She dropped the papers onto the desk and swiped the box from Tate. "We only eat them with s'mores, and when we're at home."

And this isn't home. Yours or mine. It's just the shell of one, she added silently.

Tate's jaw flexed and his eyes narrowed. "Okay," he took a deep breath and combed his fingers through one of his many sleep-caused cowlicks. "You want s'mores for breakfast?"

Foster frowned. She expected a fight. She *needed* a fight. Arguing was a hell of a lot easier to deal with than whatever was happening now. "No, I just . . ." She gnawed on her bottom lip, pressing back the memories of Cora and their late-night s'more-making, people-watching, dog-counting sessions around their rooftop fire pit. And how Cora thought graham crackers tasted like old cardboard if they weren't coated in dark chocolate and marshmallows.

"Even though they're sort of my favorite, I won't eat naked graham crackers again. I'll wait for s'mores," Tate continued. "But Foster, you have to eat something. Take a second. Then I promise we can come back and I'll keep helping you figure this out. My dad always said that you have to feed your body to feed your brain." Tate's eyes misted, and he shifted his gaze from her to the window. He quickly wiped his eyes and cleared his throat, saying, "Plus, it's sunny outside, and doesn't that, like, never happen here?"

Foster opened her mouth to object, but paused as her stomach released a low rumble. Maybe he had a point, although she would never let him know that he was right. "People think it rains here twenty-four/seven, and we let them think that so they're less likely to move here, but that's really more of a Seattle thing."

"Guess I have a lot to learn about the Northwest."

"*Pacific* Northwest," Foster corrected.

"You're proving my point. So, are you going to be my everything Pacific Northwest teacher?" Mischief rested in his smile.

Three swift knocks echoed from the front door down the hallway, saving Foster from answering.

"Are you expecting someone?"

"No," Foster swiped the letter opener off the desk and silently tiptoed toward the front door.

Tate shuffled down the hallway behind her. "What are you planning to do with that?"

"Do you not remember those guys from yesterday? The ones who chased us?" Foster said in harsh, clipped whispers.

"You think it's them? Would they knock?"

"Jesus, Tate, I don't know. I'm not some deranged psycho killer." His brow wrinkled as she sliced the letter opener through the air with each gesture. "Just stay behind me."

"That doesn't make any sense."

"Why? Because you're a guy and I'm a girl?"

"Well, yes. But no. But . . . I don't know, kind of. Hey, get your Jedi mind trick ready, just in case."

"And you get ready to tackle someone in case it doesn't work."

"I got your back, young Padawan."

Three knocks came again. Foster halted mid–eye roll, tightening her grip on the hilt of the dull blade.

"Hello? Ms. Cora? It's me, Finn."

Finn? Foster mouthed over her shoulder to Tate.

"Be right there!" Tate called.

With her free hand, Foster hit Tate's shoulder as he passed her on his way to the front door. "What are you doing?"

"Being hospitable. Try to unclench."

"Unclench?" *Unclench?*

Had he actually told her to try and unclench? Like he hadn't seen first-hand why she needed to stay a little bit *clenched.* They both needed to if they wanted to remain free long enough to figure out everything Cora had left for them. And anyone else who was part of their group of freaks would have to stay clenched, too.

Foster nodded stiffly to herself, gripped the letter opener tightly behind her back, and stomped after Tate for the second time in as many days.

"I swear to God, Tate, if it's any of the Core Four, I'm pushing you out the door and locking it behind you," she snapped as Tate unlocked the dead-bolt and twisted the handle.

"Hey!"

Foster lifted onto her tiptoes and peered over Tate's shoulder at the owner of the cheery, unfamiliar voice.

"There you are!" He angled his crooked smile at Foster. "I'd recognize you anywhere. Man, she said it was strawberry red, and she was not lying. The pictures don't do it justice, though."

"What?" Foster asked, nudging Tate over as she claimed a space next to him in the doorway.

"Your hair. It's *really* red. Strawberry red. Just how Ms. Cora said it was. Where is she anyway?"

"Wait," Foster slid the letter opener into the back pocket of her sweats before crossing her arms over her chest. "Who are you?"

"Finn," Tate answered.

"My man!"

Tate and Finn leaned forward simultaneously, each extending their right hand to slap, grip, and then shake before effortlessly half-hugging.

"No, no, no. You can't just 'my man' someone and instantly become best friends. You don't even know his name," Foster said, pointing at Tate.

"Sounds like you don't understand the power of a good 'my man,'" Finn punctuated with a wink.

"It's Tate, by the way," Tate added, looking truly relaxed for the first time since the storm.

Foster huffed, "What are you doing here, Finn?"

"I work here." Finn hooked his thumbs around the front belt loops of his grass-stained jeans. "Just came by to let out my girls and check on the fields when I saw the truck in the driveway. Figured you and Ms. Cora were finally ready to settle in. Thought I'd come down and welcome you back."

"You work here? For how long? Did Cora hire you?" Foster fired off the questions, her tone more demanding with each one.

"Hey, take it easy. You're going to give yourself a stroke." Tate stepped between them, mouthing *unclench* as he signaled for a time-out. "How about this, Finn, you hungry?"

Finn's softly angled eyebrows shot up at the mention of food. "I can always eat."

Foster blew out a short puff of air as Tate and Finn once again did that slapping, gripping, shaking hands hug thing.

"Foster and I were just about to make breakfast. Come have some food. Then at least you'll get something out of being interrogated."

"I never turn down a free meal."

Foster readied herself to ground out a witty insult when Tate caught her eye. He had that little-kid "please, please, please will you let Finn come over and play" look in his big blue, puppy dog–sweet eyes. Foster sighed. She might not need friends, actually, the thought of having to go make any made her skin feel all hivey, but Tate wasn't cut from the same icy blue loner cloth she was. If anything, he was from the pastel-colored, squishy baby elephant print variety.

Foster made sure to lock the deadbolt before following the boys into the kitchen. "Did you get eggs when you went to the store?" she asked, surprising herself by how semi-happy and normal she sounded—like this was a regular day in her regular life and not the first day of the horrible, shit-show, freaka-zoid nightmare that would be her new norm.

"If you didn't, we can go out back and grab some. They're better straight from the coop anyway. No pesticides, GMO corn, none of that crap. Just simple, speckled eggs as nature intended."

"There are chickens here? We have chickens?" Tate fluttered around the kitchen with so much excitement, Foster thought he might take flight. *For a big, jocky guy he can sure act like a little kid.*

"And a pig, two cats, one burro, three goats, one cow, a sheep, and two horses."

"It's a zoo," Foster grunted, hunting through each of the yellow cabinets for pots and pans.

"Oh, and a duck and a goose. Did I mention them? I lose track sometimes when I'm not calling them each by name."

"Because it's a zoo," she reiterated, pulling out a skillet and setting it on the stovetop.

"Horses?" Wistfully, Tate set down a carton of orange juice and a few glasses in front of Finn. "Oh, man, I love horses."

"If you're ever out in the pasture," Finn motioned to the window above the kitchen sink. "Just bring them some carrots and they'll love you right back."

"My grandpa raised running quarter horses. What kind are they?"

"They're not horses," Foster remarked, staring out at the pasture at the two almost identical, dapple-gray Hulk-sized creatures. "They're dinosaurs. Big, hairy dinosaurs."

"Close. They're Percherons."

Foster shivered. Horses were pretty much gigantic cars with minds of their own, and Percherons looked like the monster truck version. Why would anyone drive a car that had its own brain?

"No way," Tate breathed as he stared through the window at the beasts. "I can't wait to get out there with them. I've never been up close and personal with a draft horse that size. Are they broke?" he asked, absentmindedly pressing the carton of eggs against Foster's stomach as he slid into the breakfast nook.

"Oh, yeah. And sweet as can be," Finn said.

"Umm, excuse me. What exactly am I supposed to do with these?"

Tate shrugged. "We'll eat 'em any way you make 'em."

Foster didn't conceal her scoff. "I'm sorry. I must have heard you incorrectly."

"Uh-oh," Finn said, resting his scruffy chin on his knuckles. "You're in trouble now."

"Yeah, so, I'm just going to set these right here. You want eggs, you make them yourself."

"No, wait. I didn't mean that since you're a woman that—"

Foster shoved her hands on her hips, waiting for him to finish.

"I—I mean," Tate stammered, "that you should cook because—"

Foster clenched her jaw so tight her teeth might shatter.

"I just . . ." Tate looked at Finn who simply smiled at him with that silly crooked grin. "I think I'm going to make us some eggs."

"I think that's for the best," Foster said.

"You are so much like Ms. Cora," Finn said with a deep, appreciative chuckle.

Anguish squeezed Foster's chest so tightly her inhale sounded more like a labored squeak than a drawing of breath. "She's dead." Foster numbly lowered herself into the chair opposite Finn. "Her heart. She, uh . . . she's dead. You're the first person I've told, actually. The very first. Wasn't that hard. Ripped it off like a Band-Aid."

"Foster," slowly, Finn reached across the table and covered her hand in his. "I'm so sorry." His deep umber skin against her pale, freckled hands reminded her of Cora.

She jerked her hands back, balling them into fists in her lap. "I'm fine. Really." She slathered on her best attempt at a smile. "Thank you, though. I appreciate it."

Tate squeezed her shoulder as he slid a steaming plate of scrambled eggs in front of her, his eyes glistening. There it was again. That bond, that pull that made her want to stand up and bury her head in his chest and tell him that she was losing faith that this time it would all turn out okay. That she was actually starting to think that maybe she couldn't fight all of this alone. That maybe she had already had her allotted amount of people who would love her and that she had gone through all of them already.

"These are great, Tate. Thanks, man," Finn said around a mouthful of fluffy yellow. "You had some questions, Foster. Did you want ask now or—"

"No." The word came out a whisper and Foster cleared her throat and reapplied her smile. "Some other time. I, uh, my stomach is feeling kind of wonky, so . . ."

Finn's phone chimed. "Sorry to cut this short, but I have to go pick up the Gator from the shop."

"There are alligators out here, too?" Foster asked, thankful for the distraction.

Finn laughed. "It's a UTV."

Foster blinked up at him.

"A utility vehicle. It's like a golf cart, but built to handle farm life," Tate said. "Guess being homeschooled didn't teach you everything, huh?"

"Actually, I could use some help if you don't mind, Tate," Finn said.

"Sure! I'll just go put on . . ." He glanced down at his sweatpants and slippers. "Well, I guess this is all I have."

"Okay, we can fix that while we're out, if you want," Finn offered as if Tate's lack of clothing wasn't weird at all.

"But we have to go do, *you know*," Foster said.

Finn scrubbed his hand across his lips to hide a knowing smile.

"Gross!" Foster's face pinched. "Not *that*."

"Finn needs my help, too. Plus, I have to get something else to wear if I'm going to be here for the rest of my life. I have some cash left over from what you gave me yesterday, and I won't be gone long. It's guys shopping, not girls."

"I'll have your man back ASAP," Finn called from the foyer.

"But—" Foster's thoughts were an unorganized whirlwind of snarky retorts. There were so many shitty stereotypes and assumptions happening that she didn't know where to begin. Not to mention the fact that they needed to find out what the hell was going on. Cora did all of this to keep them safe. Figuring out who the other people were, what those four crazies were up to, and whether or not Doctor Rick was as nuts as Cora thought he might be was the least they could do.

"He's not my man" was all Foster could manage as the front door slammed shut.

Without Tate there to distract, no, scratch that, *annoy* her, Foster deflated into her chair, resting her forehead on her hands. "I don't know if I can do this, Cora. I don't know if I can do this by myself." Tears slid off her nose, spotting the powder blue place mat. "What good are these stupid freak powers if I'm sad and lonely and without you? I need you. If you were here, we could figure out how to do it together, but you're not here and I'm all alone. I need help, and I just . . ." Her throat ached with sobs. "I just want to go home."

Warm air tickled her cheek and twirled through the waves of hair resting on her shoulders. Sniffling, Foster lifted her head. She and Tate hadn't opened any windows, and he'd closed the door when he left. But he hadn't locked it. Foster wiped her cheeks dry as she trudged to the front door to latch the deadbolt. Did he not understand the kind of danger they were in?

The refreshing breeze returned, reaching around her with such a soothing, comforting embrace that she couldn't help but relax.

With it, each gentle gust carried the deep, velvety scent of chicory and coffee. "Cora?" Foster's voice broke, her eyes once again swelling with tears.

Gentle ribbons of wind nudged against her back as playful gusts caressed her arms, offering the familiar scent as they drew her forward.

Cora.

The rich, dark aroma of Cora's favorite coffee enveloped her as she followed the ghostly threads of scent down the hall. Fingers of air cupped her cheeks, and Foster closed her eyes as she thought of Cora and how the stocky woman swished and sang around the kitchen every morning as she made a pot of the only coffee she ever drank. She'd discovered it at Café Du Monde while on their family vacation in New Orleans and had it shipped to her every month since. Foster inhaled deeply, remembering that trip when they were still a family. She could almost hear the syrupy sweet notes dripping from saxophones, could almost taste the pillowy dough of plump, warm beignets, and could almost feel Cora and Doctor Rick's hands in hers.

Rustling papers drew Foster from her memories and from the aroma of chicory and coffee and home.

"Cora?" She tentatively stepped into the office, every cell in her body humming with the hope that her Cora would be around the corner. A gust pushed open one of the folders Foster had piled on Cora's desk, blowing its contents onto the floor. Foster gripped the doorjamb as a mini cyclone of papers spun in the middle of the room.

Oh, my little strawberry baby girl. I'll never be too far from you.

Foster's heart squeezed as Cora's words brushed against her ears on a gust of chicory.

We can do this together.

The papers settled in a mess on the floor. All but one. A wrinkled, coffee-stained piece fluttered just in front of Foster, resting at her feet.

"Cora," she choked out, plucking the page off the hardwood. "I'm sorry."

The breeze returned, drying the tears from her cheeks, and pressing warm against her aching chest.

"I love you," Foster whispered as the scents of chicory and home melted into the air and disappeared.

Foster willed herself to stop crying and her hands to cease trembling as she blinked through the remaining tears at the wrinkled page. "Doctor

Rick's handwriting." Foster traced the first line of numbers and letters with her finger. "And Cora's."

In her sweeping cursive, Cora had drawn circles and arrows and written annotations around Doctor Rick's notes.

Foster blindly shuffled to Cora's chair, almost tripping over one of the boxes she'd had Tate haul out of the Batcave.

"One A," Foster read aloud, following Cora's arrow to her first comment. "Air." Breath fled Foster's lungs as she read the date written next to it. "August twenty-fifth." Her hands shook so hard she had to set down the paper. "My birthday."

11

FOSTER

"Okay, August twenty-fifth. My birthday *and* Tate's birthday, but what do eighteen fifty and eighteen twenty-one have to do with anything? What am I missing? What am I missing?" She sat back, tapping the end of the pen against her chin. "Maybe it's math. Maybe if I add up the four numbers, it'll . . ." she trailed off, dropping her head into her hands. "It'll what, Foster? Equal some number that'll magically answer all of your questions? No," she sighed. "It'll just lead you right back to where you are now—hungry and frustrated. But I can fix one of those things, and maybe that will help. Maybe getting something to eat will refuel my brain as Tate's dad would've said." She massaged the nape of her neck. "First I hear Cora and now I can't stop talking to myself. God," she groaned, her slippered feet shuffling out of the office on her way to the kitchen, "I'm some kind of crazy ghost-whispering freak."

"Storms! Come to me!"

Foster paused, her head swiveling to take in the empty living room and hallway. "Tate?" She listened. Nothing. "Nope, not a ghost whisperer. Just a crazy person who hears people who aren't actually here." She shrugged and continued into the kitchen. "Guess I'll add it to the list of crap I don't know how to deal with." She opened the frosted-glass pantry door and immediately found what she was looking for. Three red and black boxes of Kind bars sat on the shelf at eye level, and Foster had to fight back another wave of sadness. Cora had thought of everything.

Foster unwrapped a granola bar and nibbled at a chunk of chocolate the same way she did every time she ate one. She paused, her mouth going dry as she waited to hear Cora's ghost (if that's what it was) say something about being glad Foster was actually eating something vaguely healthy for a change—the same way Cora always had. To which Foster would reply, "I only eat them for the chocolate." She almost choked on a bubble of laughter. How ridiculous was it that she was standing in the kitchen talking to a person that wasn't even there?

"I call upon the powers of the rain and the lightning and . . . other stormy things."

Foster stopped chewing, spinning around to look out through the kitchen window at the pasture. "Tate?"

He had changed into real clothes, but it was definitely him, his cowboy-boot clad feet planted firmly in the grass as he stretched his arms overhead. "The power of Christ compels you!"

No, she definitely wasn't the crazy one.

Foster shuffled out of her slippers and stuffed her feet into the tennis shoes waiting for her by the back door, refusing to acknowledge that their placement was yet another thing her Cora had done to make sure she felt like Strawberry Fields was her forever home. No matter how badly she wanted one, she couldn't have a home without a family.

"Aren't you supposed to be with Finn?" Foster called as she clomped over to Tate, the dewy grass moistening the toes of her shoes.

Tate's arms snapped down to his sides where his hands fidgeted with the cuffs of his plaid shirt. "I was, but then he offered to let me have some of his stuff so I decided to come back." He stopped fidgeting and crossed his arms over his chest. "And now I'm back."

"I see that." Foster took a bite of her granola bar. "So, what were you doing?" she asked, unable to keep the laughter from her voice.

"Oh," Tate's cheeks blazed pink. "You saw that, huh?"

"Yeah, I saw that." Foster passed the back of her hand over her mouth to hide her grin.

Tate chewed his bottom lip before lifting his chin proudly. "Practicing."

"Practicing?" Foster's brow wrinkled with the question.

"Yeah," he nodded. "I know it sounds crazy." He shifted uncomfortably and blew out a short burst of air. "Look, everything that's happened, *is happening* . . . it fucking sucks. And even though I have to force myself every second not to jump in that truck and speed back home, I don't know what I'd do if I had to live in a house full of stuff that reminded me of my parents and the fact that they're never coming back." His swallow was audible. "But, uh, whenever my mom was upset, my dad and I would find little ways to cheer her up. And I thought that if I showed you that I figured out how to channel my powers, that maybe it would cheer you up."

"Oh," Foster fought the urge to back away from the very sweet, and, now that he was dressed in real clothes, possibly very cute boy. (Well, minus the cowboy boots.) In Foster's experience, strangers weren't nice for no reason, and Tate was still a stranger.

Wasn't he?

"So you're practicing your *powers*?"

He nodded again. "I've decided that we're not freaks."

"Oh, yeah?" Foster took another bite.

"Yeah. We're superheroes."

If she wasn't mid-chew, Foster's mouth would've flopped open.

"Think about it," Tate continued. "Cora's letter said that there's a huge possibility that we were genetically engineered, like Captain America. Well, except that he was given a shot and we were, well, you know, changed when we were like embryos or something." Tate scratched the top of his head, making Foster wonder whether or not he knew anything at all about how babies were made.

Public school for the win, Foster thought before tuning back into Tate's explanation.

"And this," he proudly motioned toward the house. "Is our Fortress of Sauvietude."

Foster had no words. No words at all.

"Superman has his Fortress of Solitude, and we have our Fortress of Sauvietude."

Foster coughed around a mouthful of granola, trying hard not to gag.

"Can you stop making fun of me for a few minutes? Just long enough to try it?"

"What? No. You look stupid."

"So what? Who's going to see us?" Tate's gesture took in the huge hedgerow of evergreens that framed the entire rectangular-shaped farm. "I'm surprised. I thought you didn't get embarrassed."

Foster swallowed the last bit of chocolaty granola and stuffed the wrapper into her pocket. "I don't."

"Then give it your best shot. Plus, you're the one with the superhero alliteration name now, not me. That gives you an edge."

Heavy, earth-trembling clomps echoed behind her and Foster froze.

"Oh, hey there, Calliope. No, I don't have any more carrots for you. There was just that one I got from Finn."

A husky snort swirled against the top of Foster's head, and she whirled around with a sharp squeal, reminding herself of the terribly annoying, screaming blond girl from the original *Jurassic Park*. And Foster wasn't far off. The enormous Percheron dinosaur bristled, snorted, and lunged backward as she shrieked again.

"Get away!" Foster flapped her arms at the giant beast, barely recognizing the terrified scream that tore out of her throat.

Ears pinned, Calliope snorted as if she was confused as to why Foster was freaking, then turned, swished her braided tail, and trotted heavily away.

"Guess we found your Achilles," Tate groaned, climbing out of the hedgerow and picking green sticky needles from his clothes.

"Oh my god, she got you." She helped him from the bushes, her hands still shaking from the close encounter.

"No," he rubbed his chest. "You shot me," he said with a cough. "You spun around and shot me with your hands. Your air cannon hands."

"What?" Foster looked down at her hands. "Wait a second." She held them, palms out. "Horses are monster trucks with brains!" she shouted, invoking the same terrified feeling she'd had only moments before.

Tate stumbled backward, a burst of air blowing his shirt tight against his chest.

"It's not storms or tornadoes," Foster realized with a sharp clap. "It's air. We're controlling air! That's what she meant." She grabbed the crook of his arm and pulled him behind her as she jogged back to the house. "I found this paper. Actually, Cora and air helped me find this paper, but that's not the point."

"Cora and air found a paper?" Tate asked, nearly tripping up the stairs as she practically dragged him behind her.

"Yes, but that's not the point," she reiterated. "The point is, that part makes sense."

"That part of what?"

"The paper! Jeez, would you keep up?"

"I could if I understood even for a second what the hell you're babbling about."

Foster released Tate's arm as she ran into the office. "Babbling? I'm not babbling. I'm just trying to tell you this very exciting, very amazing, very crazy, extremely life-changing thing that I found that you have to look at because I think that maybe, just maybe, we might have accidentally figured a part of it out," she blurted in a rush of adrenaline.

Okay. Foster took a deep breath and sorted though the papers strewn across the desk. *Maybe she was babbling.*

Tate leaned against the doorframe. "Is this you excited?"

Foster held the paper out to him, pointing at the circle Cora had drawn with the arrow pointing to the word *Air.*

"It's cute." His lips ticked with a smile as he went to her and plucked the page from her fingertips. "So is this the exciting, amazing, crazy, life-changing thing you just had to show me?"

Foster's chin bobbed, but no words came out. And her cheeks felt all warm from him calling her cute.

Gross. He's Douchehawk, remember?

Foster cleared her throat. "Yes. Yes it is." She brushed back the wild section of hair that kept falling into her face. "August twenty-fifth, one A, two A—that's us. And Cora, she already figured the A part out. I just didn't get it until now."

"We're air," Tate breathed, scrubbing his palms down his cheeks. "Not storms. Not tornadoes. We're air. We can control air? So I wasn't out there talking to the sky like a complete ass?" He glanced over at Foster who hid her smirk behind the wall of hair that kept obscuring her vision. "On second thought, don't answer that. We can control air. This is fucking nuts!"

Foster couldn't help but join in as Tate hopped up and down. "We're superheroes!" she squealed, happiness stretching her lips into a smile—a brief, but genuinely happiness-filled smile.

"Wait," they stopped bouncing as Tate pointed at the page. "The other pairs, they each have different abilities."

Foster nodded. "Water, fire, and earth."

"The Planeteers. We're the Planeteers!" Tate's eyes were so wide Foster half expected them to pop in and out of his head like in a cartoon.

Foster cocked her head. "You lost me."

"Captain Planet," Tate said matter-of-factly.

Foster clicked her tongue. "Nope, still lost."

"It was a huge thing in the early nineties."

"Hello, I'm only eighteen."

"Yeah, so am I. That's not an excuse for not knowing anything about classic cartoons." With an extraordinarily dramatic sigh, Tate fished the laptop out from under a stack of papers and set it in front of Foster. "Google it, Miss Millennial."

"You are such a nerd," Foster mumbled, typing in the password to Cora's laptop.

"That's the nicest thing you've ever said to me. You're gettin' soft." Tate jabbed her shoulder playfully.

"You wish," she grumbled, her cheeks getting obnoxiously warm once again.

So gross.

She opened the browser. The small, colorful circle spun momentarily as the last page Cora had looked at automatically reloaded, playing a live meteorological broadcast.

"And now, as you can see, Krista, the wind has picked up considerably since we first arrived. The gusts are," the rain jacket–clad reporter paused, squinting as ropes of water lashed his face, "extremely strong." An icy white burst filled the screen followed by the crackling boom and fiery archs of what looked like fireworks.

The picture went dark before returning to the studio.

"Justin?" The meteorologist tucked her hair behind her ear and pressed her fingertips against her earpiece. "Justin, are you still with us?" She folded and unfolded her hands before clearing her throat. "We're receiving reports that a transformer blew near Justin and his team. We hope they stay safe out there in this unprecedented storm." She took a deep breath and pointed at her green screen. "If you are in any of the areas you can see here on the map—any of them at all—please, take cover immediately. I repeat, take cover immediately. As Justin was saying, tornadoes, at least three," again she pressed her fingers against her earpiece. *"Five?"* Her calm demeanor faltered. "At least five F-four tornadoes have been confirmed and are heading in your direction. Again, take shelter immediately. It is confirmed that at least five tornadoes have touched down. Please—"

The video froze.

"Vermont," Foster whispered as she read the headline. "That can't be right. Five tornadoes don't just touch down in Vermont on a Sunday afternoon." She clicked the refresh button, and the page reloaded. "Have five tornadoes *ever* touched down in Vermont?" she asked rhetorically.

White letters glared at her from the empty black rectangle where the video had been only moments before. *This station is no longer streaming live. Check back soon for more from WCAX.*

"Jesus, Foster! It's happening there, too. Just like it did back home. But it's not supposed to. Not outside of Tornado Alley. Not usually even *in* Tornado Alley. Not until recently." Tate sagged down onto the stack of boxes next to the desk. "Those poor people. They didn't see it coming. Someone needs to help them."

Foster snorted. "Someone? Tate, *we* are that someone."

"But how? We suck as superheroes."

"Oh, so you're already giving up? Seriously?" Hands on hips, she pinned him with her narrowed gaze.

Then it happened. Again. A warm, comforting breeze swirled around her, caressing her heated face, before it swooped down to lift the papers they'd left haphazardly scattered on the desk, allowing all of them to fall back into place except for one—the one with the strange dates written on it. Tate's defeated eyes found that one piece of paper the same time hers did and they reached for it as they spoke together.

"There's something about this," Foster said.

"Hey, I think I get this!" Tate said.

Tate lurched up from his seat on the boxes, grabbing the still fluttering paper as Foster stared at it.

"Check this out. Eighteen twenty-one is the year Missouri became a state! And that's where I was born," Tate said.

"How do you know that?"

Tate's handsome face broke into a wide grin, making him look boyish again. "Public education, Strawberry."

Foster frowned at him and sucked in air. *Strawberry? No one calls me that but Cora!*

"Where were you born?"

"Huh?"

He jutted out his chin and released an exasperated puff of air. "Where. Were. You. Born? As in, what state?"

"California."

"And what year did that become a state?"

She wasn't sure. And why was that so harped on in school that even Tate remembered it? Wasn't it more important to know how to grow your own food or file taxes or change a tire?

Tate pointed at the open laptop on Cora's desk.

"Fine," she grunted. "I'll Google it." Her fingers flew across the keys and, sure enough, eighteen fifty popped up after the question: When did CA become a state? "Shit! You're right."

"Google the rest of the dates!" Tate craned his neck to look over her shoulder. "I think we're on to something Foster, but we need to find the others, and we need to find them now."

"Of course we are. Cora left the breadcrumbs and we're birding them. We can help," Foster said, her voice holding a lot more confidence than she felt. "We *will* help. We have to. No one else can. After all," she gave him a sassy sideways smile. "We *are* the Planeteers."

12

EVE

Eve smiled as she approached Mark, who was sitting on the sunlit beach, his loose linen pants rolled up and his feet submerged in water and sand. He was bare chested and his long, dark hair floated free around his broad shoulders. Mark was a grown man, but what Eve saw when she looked at him, especially when he was on this beach, was the sweet, sensitive boy he used to be.

"I thought I'd find you here."

He didn't even look up at her, but patted the sand next to him as if offering a seat. "It's pretty easy to find any of us on this island, which is no accident—as we all know."

Eve sat beside him, delicately crossing her legs under her so that not even her feet touched the salty water.

"You still don't like the ocean?" His tone was light and teasing. It was a family joke between them. If they were in the middle of the country—as they just had been—Mark continually asked, "Are we there yet?" Meaning, are they back on the coast yet, echoing the whining he used to do as a child whenever Father took them off island. Eve had, of course, been the opposite, and only felt truly at peace when miles and miles and miles of ocean-free land surrounded her.

"Never have. Never will," Eve said firmly. "You are the only water I like."

As if in petulant response to her statement, an errant wave washed too close to her feet. With a quick, slight motion of his hand, Mark directed his element to stay back.

"Better?" he asked.

"Of course. And thanks."

"Of course. And you're welcome." Mark sighed, his gaze resting on the turquoise waves. "Where is he?"

"In his laboratory staring at nothing, as usual. Did Matthew have any luck picking up credit card usage for either of the kids?" Eve asked, even though she knew the answer. Had her brothers found even a hint of anything she would have been the first to know.

"Nothing. The boy's parents were killed at the stadium. He's listed as missing and presumed dead, with a couple dozen or so other teenagers. A bunch of them were stupid enough to run to their cars instead of into the school, which was a designated disaster shelter. One of the funnels sucked up the cars and after it spit them out they exploded, making it tough to identify the remains." Mark shook his head. "Idiot teenagers."

"But you're sure it was him with Foster in that truck, right?"

"I'm positive." Mark picked up a broken shell and heaved it into the ocean. "I'm so pissed that none of us got the license plate number on that damn truck."

"Hey, don't beat yourself up. You would've caught them if they hadn't invoked another tornado. And there's no way any of us—not even Father—would have believed they could have shown that much control over air that soon."

"How bad is he today?"

Eve worried her bottom lip between her teeth before answering in one clipped word. "Bad."

"Damn, I'm sorry, Eve. Is there anything I can do?"

"Find those kids. He's as obsessed with them as he is with my crystals. I'll handle Father."

"He's getting worse and worse. All of us can see that," Mark said. "Isn't there some way you can stop him? Wean him off or something?"

"You think I haven't tried?" She hurled the question at him. He winced at the harshness in her voice, making her instantly contrite. *I don't ever want my brothers to fear me as they do Father.* She touched his arm gently. "Hey, I'm sorry. I didn't mean to snap at you like that."

Mark met her gaze. Not for the first time Eve thought how very beautiful this strong, gifted brother of hers was. *If only he wasn't also so very haunted . . .*

"Eve?"

"Oh, sorry. What did you say?"

"I said that maybe you should overdose him."

Eve blinked at Mark in shock, pressing her finger against her lips to shush him, and then looking quickly behind them. She saw nothing but palm trees and grass that had once been meticulously maintained but had gone to seed more than a decade ago. Like everything else on their island—it used to be sweet and beautiful, but was now wild and neglected. Ever cautious, Eve closed her eyes, rested her hands on the sandy ground, and concentrated, reaching into the earth and listening with the grass, swaying and seeing with the palms . . .

She opened her eyes and slid closer to Mark, lowering her voice to a whisper. "You can't just blurt out something like that."

"I get tired of hiding how I feel, Eve." The waves mimicked Mark's frustration by swirling and rippling around his ankles erratically.

"It won't help if he hears you say something like that."

"But he isn't here. He's inside messing around with his lab equipment and not actually accomplishing anything because he's a fucking junky obsessed with his next fix. So, I'm saying it again. Maybe you should overdose him."

"Keep your voice down," Eve whispered at him. "Mark, what do you think would happen then, after he ODs?"

"If we're lucky he dies. Or falls into a vegetative state. If he's dead I'll bury him at sea. If he's a turnip we'll use part of those billions he stashed away to put him in a nice facility until his body gives out."

"Lucky?" Eve practically hissed the word. "How would it be *lucky* that the only person on earth who can fix us dies or becomes a vegetable?" She didn't mention anything about the billions they apparently didn't have. There was just no point in giving Mark anything else to be pissed about.

Mark turned so that he faced her and spoke slowly, clearly. "Eve, he cannot fix us."

"Of course he can!"

"Then why hasn't he?"

"He needs those kids. He needs to study them and use his findings to create a vaccine that will fix us. You know this. He's talked about it over and over again," Eve said, trying not to sound as exasperated as she felt. Mark was the strongest of the brothers—the sanest. But that didn't mean he wasn't damaged. They were all damaged.

"What if he's lying?"

"He's not."

"How do you know that?" He held up his hand as she started to answer. "No, don't talk. Just listen for a change. What if Father has been lying to us? Maybe not all along. Maybe there was a time when he believed he could fix us. Then years passed. *Almost two decades passed.* And he realized he can't fix us. Nobody can. What if he wants us to bring those kids here not as our salvation but as our replacement?"

Eve felt a shudder begin deep inside her and move outward, like an earthquake. She fisted her hands in the sand to stop their trembling.

"Then that would make him a monster." She stared into Mark's eyes. "Do you think he's a monster, truly? Do you think our father, the man who created us—cared for us—loved us our entire lives is a monster?" When Mark remained mute Eve thought everything within her might shrivel and die. She wouldn't be earth anymore, dark and fertile and rich. She would be desert. Eve didn't think she could bear to be shriveled, dry, and cracked inside. In despair she asked her brother, "Don't you love him at all anymore?"

Mark's dark gaze had returned to the water, but at her last question his eyes found hers again. "I love him. He's my father. I'll always love him. But Eve, that doesn't make him any less a monster. What you have to ask yourself is when will it be time to slay the monster?"

"Oh, god, Mark . . . I don't know!"

"I hope you do know before he destroys us all."

Eve deflated. Her shoulders sagged. She filtered sand through her fingers, trying to let the warmth of the sunbaked granules soothe her. "Okay, I hear you. And I suppose Matthew and Luke feel the same way?"

"It's getting harder and harder to tell with those two. If I try to push them into talking about Father, Luke starts to heat up. I can't tell if that's because he's as pissed as I am, or because he's scared or still in denial."

"Or maybe because he's on Father's side. You have to consider that, Mark."

Mark sighed and splashed salt water on his face and chest. "I'm aware of that. It's one reason I quit questioning him."

"What's the other?"

"I'm pretty sure Father would know something was going on if Luke lit our cottage on fire."

"That'd be pretty obvious," Eve agreed. "What about Matthew?"

Mark shook his head. "I think he feels the same as I do, but it's even harder to tell with him."

"He's disappearing more and more?"

"Well, yes and no. He starts to fade away when he's stressed, but that's how he's been for years. What's changed with him started a decade ago."

Eve nodded. "Yeah, when he realized his connection with the Internet."

"It's his thing, that's for sure, and we all thought it was a great outlet and a damn convenient talent, but it's changing him, especially this past year when we've been relying on him more and more to try to track Foster and Cora and the others." Mark met her gaze again. "I swear, Eve, someday he's going to disappear inside one of those damn computer programs of his."

"I should spend more time with the three of you. I knew Matthew was struggling, but I've been so wrapped up in myself I haven't wanted to face it. I'm sorry, Mark."

"Eve, let's be honest. You're only wrapped up in yourself because our father is using you as a living drug for his addiction. When was his last fix?" Mark shot the question at her.

"The night we got back from Missouri."

"That was three days ago. *Three days.* I saw him this morning, Eve. He looked like he was ready to crawl out of his skin. Do you remember when he used to only syphon your jewels when you'd manifested one because you invoked your element?"

"Yes." Eve drew her knees up and hugged them tight, resting her chin against them. "How could I not remember? It wasn't bad then. Father was only helping me."

Mark snorted. "I think that's more of his bullshit manipulation, but I know that's an argument I'm not going to win. So, how long did he used to go between crystals?"

Eve raised her head from her knees and narrowed her eyes at her brother. "You know that answer as well as I do."

"Yeah, I do. But *as well as you*? I don't think so. I think you're so mired in Father's addiction that you can't see how bad it is."

"That's bullshit. No one knows how bad it is with Father *except* me. I'm the one he uses! Me, Mark! Not you—not Matthew—not Luke. It's always been me!" Eve's voice broke as tears spilled down her smooth, ebony cheeks.

"Sssh, don't cry, little sis. I didn't mean to make you cry." Mark reached out and caught a tear on his finger. The drop of water balanced there, perfectly preserved through his bond with the element. Then he opened his mouth and dropped it onto his tongue, making Eve shake her head as she wiped her eyes.

"It's disgusting when you do that," she said.

"But you stopped crying. Eve, I'm just trying to get you to think. You love him too much. You're too loyal to him."

"How can you be too loyal to someone who has raised you?" Eve said.

He answered her question with a question. "How long can he go between fixes?"

"It used to be a month or so."

"But now?"

"Since we lost Cora and Foster a year ago he's gotten a lot worse." Eve felt smaller and smaller as she spoke, but the words seemed to pour out of her, her brother's questions setting her free from the dam of loyalty that usually kept them contained. "At first I understood. He was upset. He loves Foster and Cora. When they disappeared I thought it was going to destroy him."

"So you invoked your element, knowing the crystal that appeared would need to be syphoned by him, and he would get the benefit of whatever properties that crystal contained."

Eve nodded sadly, dropping her head to rest on her knees again. "It's my fault, Mark. I insisted. And I only invoked crystals that would calm and soothe him. I thought . . . I thought I was helping."

"Little sis, it's not your fault he's an addict. That's like blaming the bar-tender for pouring an alcoholic a shot of whiskey."

"It feels like it's my fault."

"How many days can he go between fixes now?" Mark repeated the question gently.

"Three. At the most."

"Damn. I knew it was getting worse. I didn't realize it was that bad." He took her hand in his. "You have to start telling me these things. We have to work together."

"To what end, Mark? Do you really think I could ever harm Father?"

"I think you won't let anyone hurt your brothers—not even Father."

Instead of responding, Eve's gaze went to the horizon, which was when she noticed the blue August sky had begun to change to a watercolor pallet of yellows and oranges as the sun descended into the ocean. She squeezed Mark's hand before dropping it and standing, brushing sand from her shorts.

"I have to go. I've left him alone too long."

"You're going to conjure a crystal."

Mark hadn't phrased it as a question, but Eve answered anyway. "Yes. I have to, Mark."

"Okay . . . okay. I get that, but can I make a suggestion?"

"Of course."

"Think about what *you* need instead of what he needs," Mark said.

Eve's dark eyes widened. "You mean stop using amethyst all the time like I have been."

"What are amethyst's properties?"

Eve answered by rote. She knew the properties of every crystal, stone, jewel, and rock that rested in the bosom of earth so well that her response was as easy as breathing. "Amethyst is a stone of spirituality and contentment. It focuses ener-gies on calming and soothing. It also facilitates stability, strength, and true peace."

"I can see why you choose that crystal for him. But if I told you that along with being soothed I need help focusing on my analytical reasoning and pro-tection against fear, envy, rage, as well as a mental boost—something that would help get rid of my sadness so that I could think more clearly—what crys-tal would you conjure from earth if I needed *those* things?"

Eve chewed her bottom lip thoughtfully and then said, "Well, there are a few that would work, but my instinct says carnelian would be best." She studied her brother. "Mark, I would let you syphon from me. You know that, don't you?"

"Oh, little sis! No, no, no. I struggle with my own demons enough. I don't need anything added to them. There's a reason Father's addicted. He's not bonded to earth. He wasn't meant to share the element with you. But you *are* earth. Conjure carnelian and hold it close to you for as long as you can. He can last another few hours." Mark stood, also brushing sand from his tall, lean body. "I'll go to him now, buy you some time."

Eve hugged Mark tightly. "Thank you," she whispered into his shoulder.

"We're in this together. Don't ever forget that," Mark said.

Eve found the true center of the island easily. She had, of course, been there countless times over the past thirty years. She'd been the first to move to the island—several years before her brothers joined her. Unlike her, each of the boys had had parents, though they had been eager to grant the great Dr. Rick Stewart full custody of their children after the boys began showing signs of what was diagnosed as acute early onset schizophrenia.

Eve had never known any other father except Rick Stewart, and the closest thing to a mother she'd had was Cora Stewart, but she'd only had her for a few years and Cora had never known the truth about Eve. Not about her bond with earth, nor about her conception.

Eve shook herself mentally. It served no purpose to allow the past to torment her. It couldn't be changed. It could only be endured.

But how much longer could Eve endure?

The centermost spot of the island used to be marked by a cluster of poinciana trees and a small park that held a wisteria-covered gazebo and a fountain that was a replica of the mermaid mother and child fountain in San Francisco's Ghirardelli Square. The poincianas were in full flower, filling the abandoned park with the scent of caramel. The fountain had been dry for five years and wisteria had devoured the gazebo—though Eve thought that made it charming and magical.

Ducking inside the curtain of green vines and fragrant, grape-like clusters of purple flowers, Eve felt as much at peace as she was able to on an island.

There was a long metal box under the dilapidated bench seat that ran along the inside circle of the gazebo, and from it Eve took a thick meditation pillow. She went to the center of the gazebo, placed the pillow on the wood floor, and sat on it cross-legged. Then she closed her eyes and spread her arms wide as if she was expecting to wrap someone within her embrace.

And Eve was embracing someone—she embraced Earth.

It was an understatement to say that she reached with her mind to find the thick curtain of vines that covered the gazebo. It was more accurate, and yet incomplete, to say that she reached with her mind, her spirit, *and* her body to join her essence with the growing plants. She felt them and her full lips lifted in a contented smile. Wisteria might look like a delicate blooming vine, but there was nothing delicate in its nature. She could feel the plant's strength and tenacity. Eve joined with it and followed it down . . . down . . . down . . . As deep as she could go before hitting the water table.

Eve rested there a moment, surrounded by the fecund earth, drawing comfort from its beautiful mysteries. When she felt ready, Eve sent out her call. With every fiber of her spirit and the altered DNA that bound her to earth, Eve focused on what she sought. When she spoke her mouth did not open, yet her voice echoed eerily all around her from the leaves of the wisteria as the vines swayed with the weight of her need.

"Come to me, carnelian.
I need your protection against
Envy
Fear
Rage
I need your clarity. Stimulate my
Intelligence
Inquisitiveness
Instinct
I need you to dispel
Apathy and passivity
In return I give you my body, for you are mine and I am yours.
Come to me, carnelian!"

Eve welcomed the rush of sensation that opened within her like a flower bursting into bloom. She was filled with a sudden clarity that had her intelligent mind whirring with possibilities, and though there was pain—the pain of the perfect russet crystal that instantly began to swell just beneath the skin of her right shoulder—Eve welcomed it, accepted it, and appreciated it. The power of the earth was balm to her harried body and soul and she wished desperately that she could remain there, communing with her element, being filled with protection and clarity.

She could not remain there, though. What would happen to her brothers? To her father? *To her world?*

Eve's eyes opened and she stood quickly, shoving the pillow back into the box and hurrying from the gazebo.

Why hadn't she thought of it before? It was simple, really.

They shouldn't be searching for Foster. That was a dead end. Cora had made certain the girl could hide from them.

They shouldn't be searching for Tate, either. That he hadn't surfaced—not to bury his parents—not to return home to what was left of his life—meant that Foster had convinced him to remain hidden with her. If that's how the boy wants to play this, then they should accommodate him. Tate should have to *stay* off the grid. If he wants to act like he doesn't exist, perhaps he *shouldn't* exist, or at least not legally. Tate is following Foster's lead, but he's just following. He's not like Foster. He wasn't raised by smart, savvy Cora Stewart. Up until a few days ago he was a normal kid. Now he has no parents and no home.

"He won't want to lose his entire world," Eve spoke aloud to the waving palms and the swaying grasses. "And he won't want to lose anyone left in his world. So, let's turn up the heat on good-boy Tate, and keep an eye on any family he has left. He's going to break. He's going to contact them, and when he does—we'll have Tate and Foster—two for the price of one!"

Filled with the clarity of carnelian, Eve continued speaking to the waving grasses and swaying palms.

"We can't make the same mistake with the water kids. They need to be drawn together. One's already in the Gulf. The second should be on his way there, but Matthew needs to be sure of that. He needs to follow those credit card trails. And Mark—my water brother—needs to brew up something that will be impossible for them to resist . . ."

Smiling with satisfaction, Eve headed to her brothers' cottage with re-newed energy and determination. Perhaps it was the sudden insight she'd gained, or maybe it was the stone's protective properties, but as her steps light-ened, so, too, did the pain in her shoulder where the carnelian crystal emerged from her skin. Eve touched it gently, thankfully.

Mark was right. I needed this.

As if in response a soft rain began to fall, baptizing Eve in the warmth of its gentle touch.

13

CHARLOTTE

August in the Deep South was many things: hot, muggy, green, magnolia-scented, mosquito-compromised, tick-filled, gator-friendly, and hot. Really, *really* hot.

Charlotte Davis hated everything about it except the magnolia-scented part. That she liked. Well, and she didn't hate the heat too much, but only because heat meant sweat and sweat was salty and wet like the ocean. She loved the ocean most of all.

I-85 South was a conundrum. When it passed through cities it was a non-descript superhighway of boredom, but when it cut through mile after mile of what looked like uninhabited forestlands, Charlotte thought it was almost pretty.

She rolled down the window of her very used Ford Focus, put her hand out of the driver's window, and let the hot, moist air surround her skin like one of those warm towels aestheticians used during facials.

"Oh my, what I wouldn't give for a lovely facial right now," Charlotte spoke on a sigh, the soft Southern drawl that colored her words always more pronounced when she was alone. In Charlotte's life, she only truly relaxed when she was alone. When she was six she'd learned that sharing too much about herself with too many people was a mistake. A big, bad mistake.

Window still down, Charlotte breathed deeply of the humid air and just then passed a sign that blazed WELCOME TO SOUTH CAROLINA THE PALMETTO STATE. Her lips, glossed with the perfect tint of pink, lifted and, purposefully exaggerating her North Carolina drawl, Charlotte said, "Well, bless your heart, Palmetto State, but are you talkin' 'bout the trees or the bugs?"

Her musical laughter filled the car as she rolled up the window and turned up the volume as Etta James hit the first notes of the bluesy "At Last." Charlotte's smooth alto was harmonizing with Etta when her "Under the Sea" ringtone interrupted, but she didn't mind. It was her favorite person in the world. She punched ACCEPT.

"I did it, Grandma Myrtie! I've officially departed the state of North Carolina. For evah!" she said, sounding a lot like Scarlet O'Hara.

"Oh, Charlotte, my dear! Well done! Where are you now?" Her grandma's voice would always evoke the sweetness of the homemade caramels she would be eternally famous for making—and famous for guarding her secret recipe from the world.

"I believe I am somewhere outside Spartanburg, South Carolina. Why do towns in South Carolina all sound so much like battle stations?"

"Because, my dear, too many Southern menfolk think life *is* a battle station. Which is the only reason you're fleeing the South."

"But is fleeing to Texas actually an escape?"

"You're not simply fleeing to Galveston. You're going to Texas A&M to set down your water-loving roots and become who you will be for the rest of your life," Grandma Myrtie said firmly.

"I feel like I need to say thank you again, Grandma Myrtie."

"Charlotte, there is no need, but as always I appreciate your politeness."

"And I'll always appreciate you blackmailing my parents so that they were forced to let me be me."

"Charlotte! I did *not* blackmail them. I just explained to your mother if she didn't give you what you need, I would refuse to give her what she needs."

"Her trust fund check," said Charlotte with an eye roll.

"Exactly. Most of the time it's a royal pain in my rear end to be in control of the family money, but sometimes it's spectacularly satisfying. Using that control to force your mother to do the right thing is one of those times. To be honest, I am often thankful your parents turned out to be such dolts. Were they the people they should be, you and I might not have become—how do you put it again—*besties?*"

Charlotte giggled softly. "Yes, Grandma Myrtie. We are definitely besties. But, thank you. You saved me, you know."

"My dear, we saved one another. You are, after all, my favorite granddaughter."

"I'm your only granddaughter."

"Just so. When did you say fall semester officially begins?"

"August twenty-ninth."

"Perfect! You'll have plenty of time to settle in and find your way around. Just remember, there's more to the city than the Gulf."

"Don't worry, Grandma Myrtie. I'll get good grades and make you proud. No one will ever be able to say you wasted your money on me."

"Charlotte Myrtle Davis, how could I *ever* waste money on you? You, my dear, are priceless."

"Did Mama call you? Did she say anything after she saw me?" Charlotte hated that she still wanted her mother's approval after all this time, especially because she knew she would never get it.

"Now, you know I'm too polite to repeat any nonsense your mama spouts, bless her mistaken heart. My dear, you just focus on yourself and that bright, beautiful future that stretches before you," said Grandma Myrtie.

"You're right. You're always right. Thank you for reminding me."

"That's why I'm here—to remind you of how special you are."

Charlotte's blue eyes began to fill with tears, but she straightened her spine and lifted her chin. This was the first day of her new life. She was not going to let her mama spoil it.

"I love you, Grandma Myrtie."

"I love you, too, my dearest one."

A roadside sign announced that a truck stop was a mile ahead. Charlotte glanced at her almost-empty gas gauge and merged into the right lane.

"Hey, Grandma Myrtie, there's a truck stop comin' and I need to get gas. I'm going to go, okay?"

"You stay safe, Charlotte. You have your pepper spray gun, don't you?"

"Yes, Grandma."

"And your police whistle?"

"Yes, Grandma."

"And you'll lock your car."

"Yes, Grandma. I promise. I'll take care," Charlotte said as she took the exit to the rest stop.

Grandma Myrtie sighed. "That bathroom situation. It frightens me."

Charlotte wanted to say "me too," but she hated the worry that made her beloved Grandma's voice sound suddenly old and tremulous. "It doesn't scare me at all. I'm just going to go in, get gas, and then get back in my car."

"After you check to be sure no one's in the backseat?"

"Grandma Myrtie, if I have to leave my car, I promise I'll lock my doors. I have to go. I'll call you when I get back on the road so you know I'm okay," Charlotte said as she pulled up to a gas pump marked by a faded number seven.

"That would give me peace. Thank you."

"Bye-bye, Grandma Myrtie. I love you!"

"And I you," Grandma Myrtie said, followed by two soft kissy sounds, which was how she always said good-bye to Charlotte, whether she was kissing her cheeks or kissing the air at the other end of a telephone.

Charlotte quickly checked herself in her rearview mirror, fluffed her blond bangs, and straightened the spaghetti straps on her little sundress, taking a moment to appreciate the way the blue embroidered flowers on the bodice brought out the turquoise in her ocean-colored eyes. She was checking to be sure her pepper spray gun was easily accessible in the side pocket of her red Kate Spade purse when there were two sharp raps on the car's window. Charlotte jumped and turned to see a youngish guy in a faded uniform. She rolled her window partway down.

"Fill 'er up?"

"Y-yes. Please," she said.

"Okay, but ya gotta go inside and pay."

Charlotte's stomach felt suddenly queasy. "All right. Yes. I can do that," she babbled. Then she drew a deep breath, steadied herself, and opened the door. She smoothed her sundress and nodded to the attendant, who was already undoing her gas cap, before hurrying toward the door of the little truck stop.

"Tell Floyd it's pump seven," he called after her.

"Thank you. Will do," she said.

The door chimed as Charlotte opened it. She was instantly overwhelmed by the scents of overcooked hotdogs and underwashed humans. Taking shallow breaths she went to the island that held the cash register. Behind it was one of the underwashed humans whose nametag read FLOYD.

Floyd was tall, somewhere south of middle age, and his gut said he liked beer and disliked exercise. A lot.

"Hey there, missy. What can I do you for?" he drawled as his small eyes scanned up and down her body, without once stopping at her face.

"Please fill it up. Pump seven." Charlotte opened her baby blue wallet and handed him her credit card.

He took it, and finally looked at her face. Floyd grinned, showing dirty yellow teeth. But instead of running the card he twirled it through his fingers.

"Haven't seen your pretty face 'round here before. Where you from, sis?"

"North Carolina. Um, is that the key to the ladies' room?"

He glanced to his left at a key on a block of wood stained with peeling pink paint. "Well, it sure 'nuff is." He took it off the hook and held it out to Charlotte, but as she reached for it he jerked it back. "Not so fast there, sis. How 'bout a smile first? You're pretty—I'll give you that. But you'd be lots prettier if you'd smile."

Charlotte's stomach roiled. She wanted to tell him to keep his damn key, and she'd keep her smile, but she knew she couldn't. The stupidest thing she could do was to make a scene—or piss off this bubba. So, she steeled herself and smiled, saying, "I'll take that key now, sir. And my credit card, too."

But he didn't give her the key. Instead he glanced down at her card. "See, I knew your smile would be pretty, and it sure is. So, let's see if your name is as pretty as your smile." He paused, staring at the name on the card. When he looked up at her, his expression had hardened. "You don't look much like a Charles, sis. I'm gonna need to see your driver's license."

Charlotte tried to keep her hands from shaking as she held her license up for him to see.

"What the hell? That picture do look like you. Kinda. And it says your name is Charles Mason Davis, but that there's a boy. And you don't look like no boy to me. You're gonna have to explain yourself."

"Charles was the name I was given at birth. This is who I am today. That's all there is to explain. May I have my card now, sir, and the key to the ladies' room?"

"You can have your card back, *sis*." This time he sneered the word. "But you don't need no key. The *boy's* room ain't locked. It's the dirty one, just to the left outside there." He flicked the card at her and it fell to the grimy floor.

"Thank you," Charlotte retrieved the card from the floor. When she stood she saw that the man had obviously been trying to look up her dress when she bent over.

His smile was cruel as he rubbed the bulge in his crotch. "I'll bet you give one hell of a b.j."

Charlotte fled with his mocking laughter following her. She didn't want to go to the men's room, but she was certain she was going to be sick. She rushed inside, closing the door after her. The stench of the urinal hit her and she doubled over, puking into the full trash can. With hands that shook, she went to the sink, running cold water so she could rinse her mouth and as she straightened, Charlotte caught her reflection in the mirror.

Her makeup was perfect. Her hair was perfect. Her dress was perfect. Everything, *everything* about her was perfect. Everything except that name on that card, and that name did *not* define her.

"Don't let them win, Charlotte," she told her reflection. "Don't let them break you. You're on your way to the rest of your life. You're going to be Charlotte by the Sea, not the butt of someone's joke." She smiled through her tears—a *real* smile. One meant for herself and no one else. "Remember, you're *priceless,* Charlotte Myrtle Davis."

Bastien

"Hey! You can't sleep here."

Bastien's eyelids snapped open and he grimaced at the sand being kicked onto his naked back.

"Move it along!"

Bastien instinctually felt around the beach for the leash of his board before sitting up and scrubbing off the snow white, salty ghosts of the waves that had washed up his shins and lulled him to sleep. For as long as he could remember Bastien had felt at home in the water. His elementary school self had even begged his parents for a waterbed. But that was in the before. All of his happiness was in the before.

"I have ears, me," he said, freeing the sand from his inky black hair with a few swift shakes of his head.

"Then use 'em and listen to me when I tell you to get outta here."

Bastien stood and took his time patting down his empty pockets before lifting each of his feet and peering down at the golden granules like he'd lost something. Truth was, he didn't own anything except the clothes on his back and the board at his feet. Everything else he'd left back in Louisiana.

"I haven't got all day." The young man sneered, wrinkles forming across the bridge of his thin nose.

"There you are!" The cheerful voice wiped the sneer from his face—most of it anyway. Bastien wasn't sure the guy could get rid of it completely. He'd just walk around the world with that "I smell shit" look wrinkling his narrow features. "You'll have to excuse my little brother." She brushed her hand through his sunbleached hair, mussing the gelled strands much to his disapproval. "He fell out of the dick tree and hit every floppy limb on the way down." She elbowed him in the ribs a bit too hard for a simple joke.

Bastien just might like this girl, whoever she was.

"Haven't I seen you around?" She glanced at his board, at the majestic phoenix stretching its wings from the glowing embers of its past. "Yeah," she bobbed her head like she'd just received an answer to a question she'd long been wondering. "I've definitely seen you out there. You were here when all those waves started. That was like a week ago, wasn't it, Richie?"

Richie. Well that just about figured, didn't it? Wasn't Dick the nickname for Richard?

"I guess," Richie grumbled.

"Well, anywho, we're looking for help. A bunch of our staff was seasonal and is headed back to college. How would you like a job?"

"Josie!"

The corner of Bastien's mouth ticked up in a faint half smile. Little Dickie might just have a heart attack and start Bastien's day off right.

Josie held up her hand. "Daddy gave this location to me, Richie, *to me*. Plus"—her long mermaid blue braid slid off her shoulder as she hiked it up toward her ear—"I can tell stuff about people, their auras I guess you could call it, and I can tell that you need a little help. Not that this is charity or anything."

Richie snorted, and Bastien just might agree with him.

"It's not," Josie continued, shooting a narrowed side eye at her brother. "There's work involved. A lot of work. It's minimum wage plus tips paid in cash all off the books. Plus, there's a bed in the back where—"

"A cot," Richie interrupted.

Josie pushed on. "Where you can stay as long as you're okay with closing up the place each night."

Bastien mulled over the proposition. He didn't particularly like the idea that he'd be accountable to someone, someone who was keeping him away from the sweet Galveston waves, but he'd also be on the beach every day, which was no different from how he was living currently, but he currently didn't have to be somewhere every night to close up shop. However, and this was a big however, a monumental however, he'd have his own money.

"Who'd I be workin' for?" His eyes never left Josie's, not wanting for one second for Richie to think he had any kind of power over him.

"You'd be working for me as a Seas the Day Team Member," she pointed to the logo on her brother's T-shirt that matched her own. "Just like Richie. We'll be good to you if you're good to us."

Bastien nodded. He figured he could manage if he worked for Josie and not good ol' Dickie. "Sounds fine." But it was more than fine. It was a relief. Now he wouldn't have to go back to that house his mother forced him to call home. He could stay away, *far away*, forever.

"Great!" Josie chirped, her face brightening. Bastien knew what she thought. Knew she saw him as a troubled, homeless boy who needed a handout. But that was only half true. He picked up his shirt from the beach where he'd rolled it up as a pillow, shook it out as best he could, though you never could really free yourself from the tiny grains that seeped like lazy stowaways into even the smallest nook.

But Bastien wasn't homeless—not by the true definition of the word. He'd chosen to leave. And all that money and fine food and the fancy cars and grand estate—they were all waiting back there behind him, stretched out like a shadow.

"Richie will get you an official Team Member shirt and will show you the ropes." She turned to Richie and, lowering her voice, said, "I'm going to go open up. Don't be . . ." she sighed. "Just give him a chance. We really need the help." She jogged back to the straw-roofed hut and disappeared inside the open doorway.

As soon as Josie slipped inside, Richie crossed his arms over his chest. "My sister has this thing about strays. A few times a year, she'll pick one up, give it some food, shelter, a place to work, but it never lasts. They always fuck it up." He buried his foot in the sand as if to say, *I'm here to stay, and you're only temporary.* Part of Bastien wondered if he'd whip it out and piss all over the side of the hut just to prove his point. "And you're no different, just another beach bum preying on good, sweet-hearted people like my sister."

Bastien's stomach swelled with anger, and he did what years of hearing accusations and insults much more cutting than any skinny Dickie could hurl his way had trained him to do: he affixed his gaze on a point just to the side of Dickie's right ear. Any farther and the person he was trying not to hear would notice, and quick. A slap in the face had taught him that. It had branded the message along with so many others along his left cheek. He absentmindedly rubbed his cheek, sand scraping across his face as his eyes settled on the ocean. The waves seemed to surge in time with the anger churning in his gut. He breathed deeply. He couldn't release his anger, not on this fool. It'd been with him, simmering for so long, that if he let it erupt now, he'd probably send Dickie to the hospital.

A seagull braved the roiling waves, splashing into the water, disappearing for a moment, and then reemerging, soaring up, up, up triumphantly.

The truth of it was, all that anger scared him. That's why he'd left. At first he thought putting distance between himself and his parents would be enough

to quell the heat building in his belly, but he'd discovered after only a few hours outside of Acadiana that he was just running from himself.

And all that running only made him tired.

"You don't have to worry about me, no," Bastien said, unsure whether or not Dickie had finished proving the point he seemed to so enjoy making.

"God, you talk funny."

Bastien nodded, tucking his board under his arm. "That's for true," he said, leaving Dickie behind him, cross-armed and pinch-faced, as he walked to the hut.

TATE

"Tate! Damn, boy, it's good to hear your voice again. How's it going up there at your, wait, what are you calling it?"

"Our Fortress of Sauvietude!" Tate said, laughing at his own joke.

"That's it. Damn queer name if you ask me, but if you and Foster like it, that's all that counts," grumbled Tate's grandpa.

"G-pa, queer doesn't mean weird anymore. You know that, right?" Tate said, leaning against the cool glass side of the phone booth and grinning into the ancient black rotary dial dinosaur.

"Old dog. No new tricks," G-pa said. "But we're not talkin' 'bout me. How's the air wrangling goin'?"

Tate blew out a long, frustrated breath. "We've been working on it for two weeks now, and let me tell ya, G-pa, Foster's a lot better at it than I am."

"Well, boy, get used to that. Women are better at everything that counts. All we can do is hitch ourselves to a good one and try to keep up. Your mama was the best of the best, and your daddy had the good sense to hitch himself to her." G-pa had to pause and clear his throat before he could go on. "Your Foster sounds like she's a good one, too."

"She is. Or at least she is sometimes. It's hard to get close to her, G-pa."

"From what you tell me she rightfully has trust issues. Give it time, son. You'll win her over—if that's what you want to do. Is it?"

Tate shuffled his feet, kicking at the pea gravel that littered the little concrete slab on which the phone booth sat. "Yes. No. I dunno."

"Better make up your mind. The good ones don't have much patience for yes, no, and maybes."

"She'd freak if she knew I call you," Tate admitted.

"Boy! You haven't told her?"

"No, sir."

"Tell Foster. And fast. Didn't you say she has air cannon hands?"

Tate grinned into the phone again. "Yes, sir. She sure does."

"Sounds like something you need to remember next time you think about lying to her," G-pa said.

"I didn't lie to her! I just didn't tell her, that's all."

"An evasion is little different from a lie. You want my advice?"

"Always, sir," Tate said.

"Come clean. Tell her the truth, and explain that the two of you are still safe. You're calling me from a pay phone to my landline—a number that's not published and is registered in the name of a trust that's buried under mounds of corporate paperwork and red tape meant to keep people from knowing it's me. It's safe to call me. And not because I knew you'd need to hide from a mad scientist and his evil minions."

"Yeah, it's buried so no one knows the retired biology teacher and coach is filthy rich," Tate added.

"Yep, yep, yep. I realized years ago, when they discovered oil on my land, that folks act stupid when they find out you have money. So I decided way back when that folks just don't need to find out."

"I'll tell her, G-pa. When the time is right," Tate said.

"You know when's the right time to tell the truth?" G-pa asked.

"When?"

"Always, boy."

"I hear ya, G-pa." Tate sighed heavily. "Want to know the whole truth?"

"'Course."

"What I want more than anything is to figure out exactly what caused those tornadoes and how to stop it from happening again. Did you find out anything for me?" Tate neatly changed the subject to a stranger, though more comfortable one.

"I did! Well, first I found out that I hadn't completely forgotten the biology I taught too many years ago for me to admit. Guess the old dog still has it." G-pa chuckled.

"G-pa, of course you still know your stuff. You taught for, like, six decades."

"Well, not quite, but it sure felt like it. There's nothin' like high school kids to keep you feelin' young while they're really makin' ya old. I have a theory that teenagers are really energy vampires, but we'll discuss that another time." G-pa paused. "Where the hell was I?"

"You said you found something—something about what was done to us?" Tate prompted.

"Yes and no. Those equations you read to me—they're really somethin'. Lucky I still know my way around the Texas A&M MSL."

"MSL?"

"Medical Science Library, boy," G-pa muttered. "Get with the program. It's also lucky I know my way around the Dewey Decimal System and can research by looking through actual books and journals instead of the goddamned internetathon."

"G-pa, you know it's really not called that, right?"

"Don't make one lick of difference what it's called, especially when the damn thing doesn't work for shit."

"It's bad down there in Galveston, too?" Tate said.

"The weather is crazy as a bedbug, especially the wind. Keeps knocking out cell towers and what the hell ever makes the internetathon work. And I've never seen the waves in the Gulf look like they do now. Do you know they're drawing surfers? Actual professional surfers! Have you ever heard of such a thing?"

"Nope, G-pa, I haven't." When his g-pa didn't continue, Tate nudged, "Um, you were talking about not using the Internet and finding stuff out anyway?"

"Yep, yep, that's the truth. Good thing I'm used to picking shit with the chickens. I can research without it."

"What did you find?"

"Doctor Stewart might be evil, but he's undeniably brilliant," G-pa said.

"Yeah, that's what Foster keeps saying."

"Well, the girl's right. Tate, you might need to sit down for this."

"G-pa, I'm in an old-timey phone booth. The best I can do is lean against the side of it."

"Then lean, boy, and listen up. I believe you and Foster and the rest of those kids were altered on a genetic level. I can't figure out the whole thing—wish I'd finished my damn doctorate. I might know more. But, from what I can piece together, during the gastrulation phase of in vitro fertilization Stewart inserted organic material directly into your cells and then he used gamma rays to irradiate that material *and* your cells."

"Gastrulation, that's the early phase of an embryo, when it's still a blastula. When a bunch of important stuff happens, right?" Tate focused on accessing the science file in his brain, rather than panicking about what had been done to him.

"Yes, boy. *Very* important, as in setting a foundation for who or what the embryo becomes. My working hypothesis is that your DNA has been joined with organic material and altered."

"I'm trying not to freak out here, G-pa."

"Does it help if I compare you to Peter Parker?"

"Don't kid around. This isn't science fiction. This is science fact—*fact* that happened to Foster and me and probably six other kids," Tate said.

"I'm not kidding around, Tate. Listen, I think the only place we can find clues about what was done to you *is* in science fiction. At one time flying machines and submarines and anything resembling the internetathon were the stuff of sci-fi. Sometimes reality takes a while to catch up with fiction." G-pa's voice gentled, "Hey, you did name your place the Fortress of Sauvietude. Seems to make sense that you're actually a superhero."

"G-pa, I'm eighteen. I'm nothing but scared and alone."

"Boy, don't you ever say that! Don't even think it. You have me. You'll always have me. Foster's there for you, too. She's in this with you, as are six other young people. You can be scared, but you'll never be alone. I give you my word on that," G-pa finished firmly.

"You're right. Sorry, G-pa."

"Not one damn thing to be sorry about. I'm proud of you, son. Real proud of how you're handling this."

Tate had to fight back tears. "Thanks, G-pa. I—I wish you were here with us!"

"Yep, yep, yep—me too. But I need to be here for the time being. I gotta keep researching. If I can figure out exactly what he did to each of you, it might help you learn to control your powers. Or at least you can figure out the extent of your powers. For instance, I believe the organic material he irradiated and joined with your and Foster's DNA is basically O-two."

"Oxygen!"

"Yep. Good ol' air. And the organic material he joined to the next two is hydrogen with oxygen."

"Water!"

"Exactly."

"So, what Foster and I thought might be the truth, really *is* the truth! The next two kids will be bonded to the element water!" Tate felt a rush of excitement.

"As far as I can tell."

"G-pa! I wonder if the crazy waves going on down there by you have anything to do with the next two kids being bonded to water?"

"Well, before the football game there certainly was an increase in tornado activity—and that increase has remained the only consistent thing about this damn weather, so I'm thinkin' you could be right, son." The old man paused and added, "And if you're right, it's going to be damn awful when we get to the kids bonded to fire."

"Which is why we need all the information we can get ASAP," Tate said. "Foster and I think we've figured out a code Stewart used for the state where each kid was born."

"Good! Keep at that. It'll be easier if we can narrow it down by even a little where the kids might be," said G-pa. "I'm goin' back to the MSL every day and doin' more research. And every day I'm deciphering Stewart's formulas a little—but honestly, Tate, when I say *a little* that's exactly what I mean. It's like trying to learn a language without a Rosetta Stone." He paused before adding, "Are you certain you don't want me to take this to one of the genetics professors? They're a lot better at this than I am."

"No, G-pa! You promised to keep this to yourself!"

"Hey, don't get your feathers ruffled. I always keep my word, and if you say no outside help, then that's that. I was just double checkin'."

"Cora told Foster we had to stay off the grid. G-pa, Cora even had fake identity papers made for me and Foster. She changed our last names and everything. Foster totally trusted Cora, and Cora was married to Stewart, so she knew the guy better than anyone, and if she was this scared I have to agree with her. We're in danger and we need to lay low."

"Okay, boy. I get it. Lockin' my mouth and throwin' away the key." G-pa cleared his throat before continuing, "Got somethin' else to tell you. It's good and bad news."

"How about the good first?"

"I'm pretty certain no one outside Stewart and his four goons are going to be lookin' for you," G-pa said.

"That is good, but why would you say that?" Tate said.

"That brings me to the bad. Son, you've been declared dead."

Tate didn't say anything for several breaths. It was tough for him to think past the sudden humming in his ears. Finally, after clearing his throat much as his g-pa had just done, he managed to say, "How? I'm alive."

"The official story I got from the cop who notified me is that your remains were identified through your dental records."

"But that's impossible. I'm standing right here."

"Yep, yep, yep—which is why I asked a lot of questions. What I found out is that your dental records from Dr. Theobald's small-town dental office were all computerized. And because it's a little mom-and-pop office they don't have much security. Even to an old dog like me it seems that it'd be damn easy for one of those computer geeks to hack into your records and make some changes. And it stands to reason that a mad scientist would have access to a computer geek."

"So I'm seriously legally dead?" Tate couldn't seem to wrap his brain around the idea.

"Legally, officially, and seriously. They even shipped what they called your remains to the cemetery here where I put your mama and daddy to rest. I pretend buried you beside them."

Tate had to clear his throat again, but still his voice broke. "Thanks, G-pa. That musta been awful for you."

"Nah, it wasn't bad. Thanks to you findin' a pay phone I knew you were just fine. It was a lot different burying my little girl and your daddy."

Neither man said anything for a little while. They just listened to the very alive sound of each other's breath. Finally Tate made himself speak. "I'm sorry I wasn't there with you, G-pa. You shouldn't have had to deal with that by yourself."

"A parent should never bury a child. It's not the way nature intended. I wish you'd been here, too, son, but it would've put you in danger, and I don't believe I'd survive *really* burying you, too."

"I promise you won't have to, G-pa. And you won't be alone, either. I'll keep calling, just like I have been, and when we get this mess figured out we'll be together," Tate continued, lifting his voice because he hated the sadness that had crept into his g-pa's tone. "Hey, you'd really like it up here. It's super green and there're lots of plants and stuff—biology is practically everywhere you look."

"How're you outfitted for dogs? You know I don't go anywhere without my Bugs-a-Million."

Tate grinned. Bugs-a-Million was G-pa's enormous, shaggy Irish wolfhound who was attached to him at the hip. "Strawberry Fields is about twenty-five acres. Perfect for Bugsy. Hey, G-pa, what number is this one?" G-pa always had an Irish wolfhound, and he always named her Bugs-a-Million, after his favorite bookstore that had been letting him bring the giant canines into their store for more years than Tate had been alive.

"This is Bugs-a-Million number five, and I do believe she's the smartest one yet. Just weighed her yesterday and she's comin' in at a slim one hundred thirty-five."

"G-pa, that's not a dog. That's a person." Tate laughed.

"Nope. Dogs are always better than people."

"I'm not gonna argue that, G-pa. Hey, I gotta go. If I'm gone too long Foster will worry."

"Boy, you gotta tell her the truth," G-pa said.

"I hear you, G-pa. I will. I'll call you again as soon as I can. Love you."

"Love you, too, son. Stay safe. Promise?"

"Absolutely."

15

TATE

"Foster? I'm back from the store! Hey, I stopped at that Bella Organic winery place on the way back and got a major haul of those little flying saucer–looking squash things you like so much. If you cook them in that coconut oil and salt concoction that makes them so good, I'll light the grill and slap on that plank of salmon I found at the grocery, and I'll bet I can find some ripe tomatoes and peppers in the garden, too." Tate paused as he put away the last of the perishables in the fridge to peer back through the kitchen and down the hallway. "Foster!" he shouted.

Is she in the Batcave? Even then she usually comes running when I get home from the store. Not for me, of course, but for food. Foster does love her luncheon, which is what she calls every single meal. At first Tate thought that was weird. Now he thought it was cute, and *he* was starting to call breakfast "first luncheon."

When there was still no sound from Foster, worry began to niggle at Tate's mind. Ignoring the stuff that wouldn't go bad if it was left out, he started toward the hallway, but a movement outside the breakfast nook window caught his attention. Tate stopped to move aside the lacy half curtain and his breath hitched as he caught sight of Foster.

She was in the back pasture—the one behind the house that adjoined the little creek they'd discovered running through the rear of the property. Foster was standing in front of what looked like a wall of willows. Her arms were raised as if she was a conductor. The trees were her symphony. And they were playing beautiful air music for her.

Tate hurried out the back door, crossed the porch, and skipped all the stairs. He sprinted to the back pasture gate, which he climbed quietly and easily. Then he slowed so that he didn't startle Foster, under the pretense of not wanting her hands to blast him with another air cannon. But the truth was closer to his heart. Tate liked watching her, especially when she was air weaving.

That's what Foster had started calling what she was doing with air. They both realized that they could see air currents. It was crazy, but there were highways of different currents of air all around and in the sky above. When he and Foster concentrated and called to their element, they became visible. Sorta.

Tate drew a deep breath and with that breath he began to think about air ... wind ... breezes ...

And it happened! Suddenly he could see more than Foster moving her hands like a graceful maestro while the long, veil-like branches followed her, mimicked her. He could see the shimmering thermals of currents that flowed up, down, and around the trees, Foster, the waving grasses—the entire world.

Tate breathed deeply again. "Air." He said the word softly, reverently, like a small, secret prayer and a slight ribbon of glistening current shifted direction and sweetly came to him, bringing with it Foster's voice.

She was singing! Well, no. More accurately Foster was humming and air was moving the wall of willow branches in time to her song. What he could catch of the melody was familiar, and Tate was trying to place the song when Foster started trilling,

"*Tweetly-tweetly-dee, tweetly-dee-dee!*
Tweetly-tweetly-dee, tweetly-dee-dee!"

Tate's eyes widened and he held his breath as he listened. Her voice was sweet and strong and filled with a lightness he'd never heard in her words before. *Man, Foster can sing!*

She played around with the melody that Tate was still trying to place as air followed her direction. And then Foster started singing. Softly, at first.

"He rocks in the treetops all day long
Hoppin and a-boppin' and singing his song
All the little birdies on Jaybird Street
Love to hear the robin go tweet tweet tweet!"

Holy crap! Foster's singing a Jackson 5 song!
As she got more and more into the song Foster began to dance, making sliding steps left and right in time to the words. Magically, magnificently, the boughs of the willows whispered the chorus with her.

"Rockin' robin, rock rock
Rockin' robin
Blow rockin' robin
'Cause we're really gonna rock tonight!"

Foster's strong, beautiful voice grew more and more confident as she danced and sang with wind and willows.

Tate thought she was the coolest thing he'd ever seen. He said a silent thank-you to his g-ma (God rest her) for being a Motown fan—and to his g-pa for forcing him to take dorky swing dance lessons when all he'd wanted to do was play football. But G-pa had told him as a young boy that in order to *properly woo a woman*—seriously his G-pa used words like *woo*—he had to learn to dance. And as the old man had said, *Really dance—not that air-humping crap that passes as dance moves today.*

So, Tate wiped his sweaty palms on his jeans, took a deep breath—and then, trying to channel the suaveness for which G-pa claimed to be famous, Tate started walking to Foster while he harmonized with her on the next verse.

"Every little swallow, every chick-a-dee
Every little bird in the tall oak tree . . ."

Foster's breath hitched and her song sputtered as she whirled around to face him, her face blazing red, but Tate just grinned and held out one hand to her. "Come on! Dance with me!"

She stared at his hand as the air seemed to hold its breath.

"Unless you're worried about what other people—like me—think of you," he said with a sly smile.

"Not for one second!" She took his hand and sang loud and strong.

"*. . . The wise old owl, the big black crow*
Flappin' their wings singing go bird go!"

Tate picked up the beat easily. Of course he knew the old song, but it was more than that. As he spun Foster around, the air filled with her song and it seemed the leaves of the surrounding trees caught, held, and then began playing the melody with them.

Foster's green eyes widened and he held her close, leading her in a swing so perfect he could almost see his G-pa's nod of approval.

"Can you hear that?" she whispered.

"Yeah! Keep singing!" Tate twirled her around as he sang the chorus again with her.

"*Rockin' robin, rock rock!*
Rockin' robin
Blow rockin' robin
'Cause we're really gonna rock tonight!"

The air around them was filled with music. It was like someone had plugged nature into one of those electric keyboards that could make a zillion different musical sounds—only it wasn't electric—it wasn't man-made at all—it was their element, air, playing around them.

"Look, Foster! Look around us!"

Foster whistled the melody in time with the air orchestra as she danced in his arms. She tilted her head back and together they stared at the amazing currents of twirling, trilling air that glowed wisps of music in all the colors of a rainbow.

"It's unbelievable!" Foster said, and when she began singing the last stanza the world was her accompaniment.

> *"Pretty little raven at the bird-band stand*
> *Told them how to do the bob and it was grand*
> *They started going steady and bless my soul*
> *He out-bopped the buzzard and the oriole!"*

Tate guided Foster through one of his favorite swing moves, the pretzel. Her grin blazed as they sang the chorus together again,

> *"Rockin' robin, rock rock*
> *Rockin' robin*
> *Blow rockin' robin*
> *'Cause we're really gonna rock tonight!"*

And then he tried to do a classic hip lift with her, which failed epically as he tripped over an unfortunately placed rock and fell on his butt with Foster flopped over his legs, giggling hysterically as the wind around them stilled and then faded to the normal sound of swishing through willow leaves.

Wiping her eyes, she stood and held out a hand to help him up, which he took, brushing grass and dirt off his butt.

"How in the hell do you know that old song?" she said between giggles.

He grinned back at her. "Who *doesn't* know Motown?"

"Um, lots of people. Well, *young* people. The same people who don't know how to dance like that."

"Well, I have a grandpa who insisted I learn how to *really* dance."

"Your grandpa made you take dance lessons?"

"Not just any dance lessons—swing dance. And, yep, twice a week for years. I used to love/hate it. A lot."

"And now?" she asked, her eyes still shining with humor.

"I got to dance you around *and* make you laugh, so I'd say I'm feeling pretty good about G-pa's weird obsession. Who got you into Motown?"

"Cora, of course. She loved Motown. And the Rat Pack. And what she called *real deal blues*. I don't think she liked anything that wasn't recorded last century. She was pretty stuck up when it came to music."

"You can really sing," Tate said.

"You're not so bad yourself."

When the silence threatened to get awkward, Tate shook himself mentally and reminded himself to do more than stare at her eyes, because for some reason he suddenly remembered how he'd felt the first time he'd looked into them—totally shell-shocked by their deep green beauty.

"Hey, that thing you were doing with the air and the trees—it was awesome."

"Oh, thanks. I did it by accident. You heard it and saw it, too, didn't you? The air music?"

"Yeah, I did. It was—it was *incredible*. Like the earth was playing music for us."

"Not the earth—the air. It started before you joined me, but then when we were dancing and singing, and I was, well, distracted." She paused and he saw her cheeks go very pink. "Anyway, I think I just figured something important out. The less I think about trying to get air to do what I want it to do, and just relax and let the feelings sweep through me, the easier it is. I'm realizing that it's the *feel* part that's most important."

"What do you mean?"

"Well, like the time you almost maimed yourself by bailing out of the truck, and the time I smacked you with my hand air cannons—I was feeling negative things. First I was pissed. Then I was scared by the dinosaur."

"Percheron," Tate corrected.

"Whatever. The point is when my feelings are negative I invoke the bad qualities of air. But when I'm relaxed, or happy, I invoke good things. Like, today it was just so pretty out here, and sunny without being too hot or cold—*and* amazingly enough it wasn't raining—and for a second I thought I heard music in the wind, so I started playing around with it. Then you were here, too, twirling me around and singing with me, and I was having fun—*not think-*

ing, just feeling happy—and you see what happened, my tree music." She shrugged her shoulders, obviously struggling with whether she should be embarrassed or not. "I guess it's not very helpful to be able to make trees accompany me like a band. I mean, it's not like that'll stop the next tornado or protect us from the Core Four or anything like that."

"Don't be so sure. It's about control, and you were showing great control. Way more than me, that's for sure. Foster, you're getting better and better with air. All I'm getting better and better with is grocery shopping," he said.

"That's an excellent skill, and one I do not have. I hate grocery shopping. I've, uh, been meaning to tell you how much I appreciate you going to the store as often as you do. It's giving me time to feel at home. So, thanks."

Tate had to force himself not to hang his head in shame. He knew the dirty truth. He didn't do the grocery shopping to help Foster. He did it so that he was free to call his g-pa. Feeling awful, he heard himself blurt, "Hey, I think I figured out what some of Stewart's equations might mean."

Foster's happy, open look flattened and then closed off. "Riiiiight. The jock deciphered the brilliant mad scientist's equations."

Tate felt his cheeks flush. "That's a real bitchy thing to say."

"Bitchy or true? Why do men always assume when a woman tells it like it is that she's being a bitch? Can't she just be telling the truth?"

"Not when it's *not* the truth. I'm *not* a dumb jock, and I'm tired of you stereotyping me. I thought we'd gotten past that."

Foster sighed dramatically. "Not if the stereotype is true."

"It's not!"

"Really? Let me remind you that your answer to my question, What is your favorite book, was *Sports Illustrated. Sports Illustrated,* Tate. You actually said that. And that is a classic dudebro dumb jock answer."

"I only said that because I thought you were so beautiful that I blurted stupid shit. I turn into a moron around a pretty girl," he said, glaring at her.

"Wait. Back up. You said *thought* and *were*." Foster's green eyes skewered him.

"Huh?" Why were girls so damn difficult to understand, and what the hell was she talking about?

"You said it in past tense. Like you *used* to think I'm pretty. What? I'm not so pretty now?"

Tate grinned, finally getting it. "Hum . . . I guess not because I can answer you for real now." Ignoring her frown, he rolled on. "Choosing my favorite book is tough because there are so many of them, but if you want my top five I'll try to narrow it down for you. Gotta give a shout out to my favorite horror writer, Ray Bradbury, and *Fahrenheit 451*. Man, that book is like a song. Bradbury's figurative language is unbelievable. 'The magic is only in what books say, how they stitched the patches of the universe together into one garment for us,'" Tate quoted. "Fantastic, right? And then there's Richard Preston. I love science, biology, physics, chemistry—all those things. Preston's books are super gross, but great. I liked *The Hot Zone*, but *Demon in the Freezer* is even better."

"Uh . . ." Foster began, but Tate was on a roll and he kept on rolling.

"But just so you don't think I'm one of those guys who only reads 'guy books,'" Tate air quoted, "I'll round out my top five with three women authors. I don't like genre labels, but YA authors are killing it right now with their awesomeness. Last year I read Laini Taylor's *Daughter of Smoke and Bone* trilogy. Damn, those books rocked! But I'm not counting them as three. So . . ." he tapped his chin, thinking. "I know! S. E. Hinton's *The Outsiders* is a classic. I even made my dad take me to Tulsa one spring break so I could check it out." He paused again and gave the very silent Foster a raised-brow look. "The city wasn't anything like the book, but I did visit the center of the universe there. Anyway, one more. It's gotta be Renee Ahdieh's retelling of the Shahrzad story, *The Wrath and the Dawn,* and its sequel, *The Rose and the Dagger*. My mom turned me on to them, and they were just flat-out cool. So, there you have it. My real top five favorite books. For right now. I've been checking out those thrillers in Cora's library, though. Would you mind if I borrowed some of them?"

When he stopped talking he realized Foster was staring at him as if she'd never really seen him before.

"Yeah, you can borrow any book you want." Foster cleared her throat. "Well, I admit it when I'm wrong, and I was wrong. You're not a dumb jock cliché." Foster's lips twitched again as the beginnings of a smile formed on her surprised face. "You do a great impression of one, though."

He felt himself relax. She actually admitted she was wrong! And she was almost smiling at him. Tate shrugged. "Yeah, well, I am planning on using a football scholarship as well as an academic scholarship to get me through college so I won't be stuck in debt forever. It takes a lot of education to become a doctor."

"A doctor?"

Tate nodded and tried not to sound too gleeful. "I'm good at science. Really good, as in scholarship-level good. I want to be a neurologist. My g-ma died of Alzheimer's. It was awful. I'm going to find the cure."

"Seriously?"

"Seriously."

"Why in the hell have you let me believe you're just a dumb pigskin thrower?" she asked.

He shrugged. "I guess I didn't want to tell you who I am. I wanted you to get to know me and find out for yourself. Like, when I first saw you I thought you were probably a cheerleader."

Foster looked like she'd bitten into a lemon. "A cheerleader!"

"Well, yeah, until you opened your mouth," he said with a totally straight face.

"What!"

"Yeah," he went on nonchalantly, pretending that she wasn't giving him her "I'm going to knock you on your ass with my air cannon hands" look. "Then I got to know you better and I decided that if you were a cheerleader by day, by night you'd for sure run some kind of underground political school paper where you'd probably uncover a major human trafficking ring and were on your way to being the youngest journalist to win a Pulitzer in the history of Pulitzers."

Foster just kept staring and staring at him, until finally she started to giggle, and the giggle turned into honest-to-god laughter. "I thought you were a dumb, can't grow hair and chew gum at the same time, football guy," she gasped, still giggling. "And you were making up the coolest story ever about me. Tate, I owe you a major apology. I absolutely misjudged you. You're not a douche. You're an onion."

"Is that better than being a douche?"

"Of course it's better! You look like one thing, but if your surface is

scratched just a little, there are layers and layers of *stuff* waiting to be discovered. You're an onion, Tate. Embrace the onion."

Then, Foster Stewart Fields smiled at Tate—*really smiled*—and in that moment a wonderful, terrible feeling sizzled through his body.

When she looks at me like that she makes me feel as if I could do anything. And I can do anything; I will do anything, to keep her looking at me like that.

Suddenly Foster's green eyes widened in shock, and that beautiful smile that radiated from them somehow, impossibly, grew brighter.

"Tate, I just found my story for you, and you're not just an onion. You're The Hawk. By day you're the star quarterback leading his team to victory, but by night . . . by night you're a superhero."

Tate's stomach felt filled with the light of her smile and he laughed. "Okay, Hawk is better than being an onion, but a superhero? You're only saying that because I call this place our Fortress of Sauvietude."

"Nope, I'm only saying that because it's true. Tate, look down."

He did.

He was floating about five feet off the ground.

"Fuck!" he shouted.

Then he dropped from the sky like a stone—or, as his g-pa would say—like a good ol' dog turd.

"Tate! Shit! Foster! What the hell is going on here?" From behind them came the sound of Finn's panicked voice as he and a young woman sprinted across the pasture toward them.

16

FOSTER

"Shut up! Shut up! Shut up! Just everyone shut up!" Foster shouted over Finn's questions, Tate's stammering, and the constant *you can't be serious* coming from the young woman standing too close to Finn to simply be a casual acquaintance.

"What the hell is going on?" Finn asked for the zillionth time.

"I said shut up!" Foster barked.

"Don't yell at him like that." Purple-streaked braids sliced the sky as the young woman whipped her attention from Tate to Foster. "He's freaked out. We're both freaked out. We just saw someone—"

"I just need it to be quiet!" Foster ran her hands through her hair. "For, like, two seconds. This won't work if I can't focus." She could fix this. She *had* to fix this or . . . or what? There was no alternative. To save Tate and herself, Foster would erase this moment from existence.

Tate eyed her suspiciously. "You're not going to—"

"Yes," Foster surprised herself with her calm collectedness. "Yes, I am."

"Not going to what?" Finn's panicked gaze bounced from Tate to Foster and back again.

"Oh, god, Finn. I'm not going to hurt you." Foster let out a grunt of annoyance. She had passed panic and was well on her way to frustration—at Tate for Superman-ing all out in the open, at Finn and the beautiful girl standing next to him for showing up when they did, and at herself for not using her Jedi mind trick the second she heard Finn's voice. "Just look at me."

"Look at you?" Finn's dark eyes were completely rimmed in white. "I haven't been able to look anywhere else since I saw," his motion took in Tate and a few feet of air above him. "Whatever *that* was."

"Flying! A human being flying in the air!" Finn's counterpart added emphatically.

"Yeah, but . . . well, it was just . . . I didn't really . . ." Tate scratched the top of his head and cast his gaze up to the sky.

Foster totally got it. It had to be rough—flying, falling, and then immediately being confronted by the only friend he'd made since losing his family. So Foster wouldn't erase their memories only because Finn and his lady friend might run away screaming to anyone who would listen about the flying science experiment living out at Strawberry Fields, which would be like waving a giant *Hello! Here we are!* flag at Doctor Rick and the Core Four. She would erase their memories for Tate, so that he could keep his friend.

Foster cleared her throat, took a deep breath, and focused on channeling her ability with far more concentration than she ever had before. *"You didn't see Tate fly."* She paused. She expected *something*—the prickling heat she'd felt at the Quickie Mart or even a gentle sigh of acknowledgment from her element. But she felt . . . nothing. She squinted, intensifying her level of concentration, and tried again. *"Nothing out of the ordinary happened here. You only saw Tate and me standing with our feet on the ground looking at the trees."*

The young woman looped her rich Tiger Moth–brown arm around Finn's and drew him against her protectively. "You just tried to *Men in Black* him."

"What? Like with that flashy memory wiping thing?" Tate inched closer to Foster, waves of nervous heat thickening the air around her. "No. No way. That's not real."

"Well, neither are flying white boys," she countered.

Foster would have commended her on her levelheaded retort had she not been caught off guard by the fact that nothing had happened. Finn still had the same shocked, wide-eyed expression and was still staring at the air above Tate's head like a pulley system would appear if he just waited long enough.

Maybe she'd focused too hard. Since her birthday, her Jedi mind trick had worked each time she'd used it, but she hadn't been trying very hard. She'd just said what she needed and it sort of *happened*.

"Sabine's right. You tried to wipe my memory."

Foster opened her mouth to attempt a more casual approach to erasing what Finn had seen, but stopped at the genuine sadness woven through his words.

"But it didn't work," he continued with a bit more grimness. "I know what I saw."

"What *we* saw," Sabine added.

Tate's gaze was a weight against Foster's profile, and she turned to face him, wincing in apology at the steam practically shooting from his bright red ears.

"So whatever you want to call it, it didn't work," Finn said. "And I'm a little pissed you even made the attempt. I can keep a secret."

"Cora didn't hire him simply because he's good at feeding livestock." Sabine's round cheeks were ruddy with frustration. "If the cats had thumbs, they could do *that*."

"Well, my job is a bit more involved than only feeding animals, and certain ones need certain things, so . . ."

"I know, babe. Sorry," Sabine said through clenched teeth. "Just trying to make a point."

Cora? Foster thought with a shake of her head. *What does any of this have to do with Cora?*

"Wait. What was that about being able to keep a secret?" Tate asked the question perched on Foster's tongue.

"She said some things," Finn said, shoving his hands into his pockets. "That one day there might be people who come out here looking for the two of you and that we couldn't ever say anything about anyone who lived here. Not the truth, anyway."

"We made up a story and I buried this place and your real identities. If anyone looks, everything will lead exactly where we want it to," Sabine said.

"You told her?" Foster clenched her jaw so tightly she could feel her pulse in her teeth.

"No, Cora did." Sabine balled her hands on her hips. "She trusted us. *Both* of us."

"And it wasn't easy. It was a long process, getting this job, Cora's trust." Finn wrapped his arm around Sabine's shoulders. "But Sabine and I, we'd do anything for Cora. She helped us . . ." Eyes misting, he bit his lower lip and inhaled shakily before continuing. "She's a good woman, and we'll keep her secrets to the grave."

Sabine reached up and squeezed his hand. "We'll offer you the same thing we did Cora—our word."

Foster ran her tongue along the inside of her teeth and thought about what Finn and Sabine had said. Cora trusted them. But did Foster really believe that? And *if* Cora trusted them then Foster should, too, right? But without asking any questions? This wasn't like the letter Cora had left that, what they could read of it, detailed, at the very least, something way too suspicious to overlook and at the opposite end something that could end up getting her, Tate, and six other people killed. This was a guy Cora hired and his maybe girlfriend possibly using Cora's name to gain her trust.

Foster crossed her arms over her chest. "Sabine, I need to talk to you. Alone."

Sabine's braids brushed her triceps as she nodded stiffly.

"We'll be back," Foster called over her shoulder to Tate and Finn as she led Sabine closer to the tree line.

"We'll, uh, be here." She didn't have to look back to know that the two of them were still standing there awkwardly staring at each other.

Out of earshot from the guys, Foster asked, "What happened between you and Cora? How did she help you?"

Now it was Sabine's turn to cross her arms over her chest. "You don't waste any time, do you?"

"This is too important, and I'm not the sugarcoating type."

"Neither was Cora."

Foster swallowed.

"I was pregnant," Sabine blurted after a long pause. "Now I'm not."

Foster shook her head, confused. "Isn't that usually how it goes?"

"In this country, the babies usually survive."

There was another long, stomach-clenching pause.

"But Cora . . . she . . ." Sabine's voice didn't waver as tears shined against her cheeks. "She made sure our baby had a fighting chance. And Cora was there with us in the end—holding her with us—helping us say good-bye."

"I'm sorry . . ." Foster trailed off, the words seeming meaningless and hollow as an offering to ease such despair.

"Me too," Sabine whispered. "And about Cora. I loved her."

"I loved her too" wasn't big enough to contain the way Foster felt about her mother, so she said nothing and let the tears fall.

There was a whole part of Cora's story that Foster didn't know. That she would never know. But Foster had figured out one part—that her Cora truly did care about and trust Sabine and Finn the same way she had with Foster's biological parents and all the other parents she'd sat awake with and comforted as their babies fought for life, and sometimes lost that fight.

Cora had witnessed the hardest and worst part of Sabine and Finn's life. A time that could have infected them, growing as dark and toxic as black mold. Instead, Cora had trusted them with Foster's life and Tate's. In Foster's eyes, that was the highest stamp of approval a person could ever obtain.

She dabbed her cheeks with the sleeves of her shirt and stepped closer to Sabine. "Would you like a s'more? They're the peace food of my people."

Sabine's purple-painted lips parted in the beginnings of a smile. "And what people would those be?" she asked, brushing tears from under her eyes.

Foster sniffled away the last remnants of her current sadness. Cora would be proud of her for making such a grand attempt at acquiring a friend. "Red-headed introverts who might sometimes be mistaken for being semi-bitchy."

"Hmm." Sabine's full smile was dazzling. "Can't say I've ever had a fellow introvert invite me to do anything in real life, but there's a first time for everything."

And Sabine couldn't be more correct. About both points. Foster couldn't think of the last time she'd asked someone who wasn't Cora to do something. She'd asked a lot of people to go away or stop talking or leave her alone, but she was pretty positive that wasn't the same thing. And this wasn't just a regular *Hey want to grab a coffee? Or go to Powell's? Or go silently judge people in yoga?* No. This was huge. This was *s'mores*. She'd yelled at Tate for eating naked graham crackers and couldn't even bring herself to open the bag of marshmallows much less roast one and make it into a dessert sandwich, but Sabine and Finn and Foster and Tate had been through so much—had lost so much. Maybe this new friendship, this new family, could be the silver lining of all that pain.

"Then let our s'mores be in honor of new beginnings," Foster paused. "And telling new friends the truth instead of erasing their memories."

17

FOSTER

Between her fingers, Sabine twirled and untwirled one of her long, thick braids while narrowing her upturned eyes at Foster. "You're avoiding."

"I'm not avoiding." Foster piled a bag of chocolate chips atop an unopened bag of flour before closing the pantry door. "Can't a woman just want some cookies?" she asked, setting the items on the kitchen counter.

Sabine remained silent and Foster's defenses rose as Sabine's deep fall leaf–brown gaze continued to bore into her. "You can't still be mad at me for try-ing, unsuccessfully I might add, to Jedi mind trick Finn. For one, that was all the way in yesterday, and two, when you got out of class today you immedi-ately came over with Finn and brought me scones. That doesn't scream *I'm still mad at you*. That says, *Hey, we can totally be friends*. Plus, I'm making cookies. Friendship pastries galore!"

"I know." Sabine pursed her plump lips. "And that last point was two things."

Foster pawed through the Tupperware cabinet until she found a large mix-ing bowl. She set it on the counter and tried to remember in which drawer she'd seen the measuring cups.

Sabine was still looking at her. She could feel it. Sabine's gaze of judgment clung to her, hanging suffocatingly heavy in the air around her like humidity. "Then what?" Foster said, no longer able to ignore Judgy McJudgerson.

Sabine's braids rested on the table as she tilted her head. "What?"

"You keep looking at me like you have something to say, so just say it." Foster opened the spice cabinet a little too forcefully.

Sabine flipped her hair over her shoulder and shrugged. "Nothing."

"Okay, but if you don't stop staring at me like I'm an alien, you're not getting any cookies. I'm hoarding them all for myself." Foster turned the bag of chocolate chips over so the recipe was faceup. She read the instructions five times and still hadn't registered what the short, numbered sentences wanted her to do. Was this what it would be like with anyone who found out what she was capable of? She shook her head. Maybe if she just carried on like nothing major had happened, Sabine would, too.

"This says baking soda," Foster lifted onto her tiptoes and peered into the cabinet. "But we only have baking *powder*." She removed the tin from the shelf, popped the lid, and jiggled the round canister. "They look the same." She offered it to Sabine. "Do you think there's really a difference?"

"Foster, I don't think you're an alien, but I'm starting to think that you might be blind."

Foster squinted at the can. "They seriously look the same. They're both white powders."

Sabine sighed. "Not *that*. But yes, you can use baking powder instead of baking soda. The texture might be a little different but—" she sighed again. "God, girl, now you've got me talking about cookies." Yet another sigh, this one far more annoyed sounding than the first two. "You do realize that he's cute, right?"

Foster set the baking powder next to the bowl and closed the cabinet. "Who?"

"*Who?*" Sabine's eyebrows practically rocketed into her hairline. "Tate! That's *who*."

Tate? Foster thought, tearing open the corner of the bag of chocolate chips. *No way.* He was goofy and tall and sort of reminded her of Clark Kent, who just happened to be the boy-next-door version of her favorite superhero of all time, what with his dark hair and strong bone structure and Midwesternness—*oh my god.* She crammed a handful of chocolate into her mouth. "I guess," she said, around the melting sugary mass.

"*You guess?*"

Foster swallowed. "Yes, Polly, I guess."

Sabine blinked up at her.

"She's a parrot," Foster offered.

Sabine's perfectly manicured brow wrinkled. "Now that's one bird Finn does not own."

"No, because you keep repeating me," Foster sighed. "Never mind. My point is that *I guess* I noticed that *maybe* Tate is a *little* on the cute side."

If a little cute means that last night I might have accidentally on purpose positioned myself to see him come out of the bathroom right after he finished showering, then yes, he's definitely a little cute. Her cheeks heated with the memory of his muscular wet torso, towel-clad waist, and that silly, smiley wave he'd given her while blushing himself.

But Foster kept that part to herself. After all, it was only that one time.

Sabine snorted.

"What?" Foster tensed, afraid that she might have admitted aloud her vaguely pervy, stalker-like behavior.

It was just the one time! she practically shouted at herself.

"You know that boy is fine." Foster opened her mouth to object, but Sabine held up her slender, perfectly manicured finger, shushing Foster until she'd finished. "And I can tell you know how fine he is," she continued with a tilt of her head. "Because, right now, your cheeks are as red as your hair."

Foster clapped her hands over her traitorous cheeks. "They are not!" she exclaimed, trying to keep from spilling chocolate chips all over the floor.

"You are *lying.*" The last word came out more in song than statement.

"Am not." Foster poured another mound of chocolate into her hand before dumping it into her mouth. At this rate, her cookies would just be batter.

"You can lie to yourself, but you can't lie to me."

Foster sank into the chair opposite Sabine. If she was being honest, Foster spent quite a bit of time thinking about Tate and his stupid, gorgeous face and how nice he was even when she was being horrible. She'd even sighed *aloud* on more than one occasion when she'd innocently, accidentally, in no way on purpose stared at him while he was out shirtless in the pasture. "Apparently I can't lie to myself, either."

"I knew it," Sabine said with a clap. "I just knew it!"

"Wait. You set me up? You didn't actually know how I felt about Tate. You were fishing."

Sabine held up her hands. "Before you spin off into one of your defensive, 'I don't need anybody I can do this by myself' tantrum things, I have a plan."

"I don't have tantrums."

"I have heard many a story." Arching her brow, Sabine blinked slowly. "Self-reflection isn't really your thing, is it?"

"Shut up!" Foster exclaimed in a burst of laughter.

"So, you want to hear my idea?"

Foster nodded listlessly before eyeing the opened bag of chocolates and wishing she'd never put them down.

"There's this place, Bella Farms, just down the main street from here, and every Friday night they have dancing and food and general jubilance." Her pointed fingernails clicked against the table in an unidentifiable rhythm. "And today happens to be Friday, so we should go."

Click, click.

"All of us."

Click, click. Click, click, click.

"On a double date."

Click. Click, click.

"Ask Tate to go with you."

"Ask Tate to go out with me? On a date?"

"A double date. That way you can more easily explore this uncharted territory."

Easy? Nothing about going on a date sounded easy. Foster had only been on one. With Ronald Watson at space camp when she was fifteen, and, yes, it was absolutely as horrible as it sounded. It was at that same camp with that same boy that she'd lost her virginity. And yes, that was also as horrible as it sounded.

Foster cringed.

"A date?" She felt like her stomach was dangerously close to falling out of her butt. "We . . . we can't go out tonight."

"Oh, because you have to wake up so early to get to class. Or is it work, maybe? The two of you are so busy with all of your extracurriculars it's hard to keep your schedules straight."

Defeated, Foster leaned back in her chair and crossed her arms over her chest. "You know, this is why I usually don't have any friends."

Sabine resumed twirling her braids. "You're welcome."

Foster was ready. She'd even done her hair. Okay, that was a lie. She'd sprayed a considerable amount (half a bottle) of dry shampoo into her hair before brushing it. But she was wearing a clean, she paused to sniff the armpits of her top, yes, a *clean* flannel over the sunflower yellow cotton dress she'd found shoved into the back of her closet.

"Wear something that shows your legs and isn't frayed or torn or wrinkled." Sabine had paused on the porch with further instructions before leaving to collect Finn and force him to shower before their impromptu double date.

Mentally, Foster scanned her closet. "So, pretty much tear down the drapes and make a brand-new wardrobe in the next hour."

Sabine had poked her head back into the foyer, craning her neck to eye the kitchen's checkered window treatments, a deep dimple appearing beneath her right cheek as she smiled. "You better get to sewing."

Foster almost had to until she'd found the dress that Cora had obviously bought for her since it was girly and pretty and not flannel.

Maybe she should go all the way, try something completely different and get out of the security blanket disguised as a long-sleeve button-down. She shrugged out of the top and let it pool around her feet. "I actually have arms." She chuckled nervously before smoothing her palms down the wrinkleless, unmarred cotton. "And this is way better than curtains." She rose onto her tiptoes and turned her back to the mirror. Looking over her shoulder, she narrowed her gaze to her butt and stretched the flowing skirt firmly against her very large and very comfortable leopard-spotted panties.

She nodded to herself. *Giant underpants completely hidden.*

Even though it was their first date, *gulp,* and Foster had shaved her legs for the first time in . . . she squinted up at the ceiling as if her memories were packed away in the attic. She shrugged. Well, she'd shaved for the first time in far too long, but that didn't mean that she wanted Tate to see her panties through her dress as if she was luring him out of the friend zone with her jungle cat–spotted ass.

Goose bumps popped to life across her arms and her heart fluttered a little too quickly within her chest. What if Tate *only* wanted to be friends? He was good at that—being friends—but what if that was as far as their relationship would ever go? And what if he had a girlfriend back in Missouri? Had she even thought to ask? No. Foster hardly ever asked him anything about how his life was before she'd spun into it and sucked him up and away to Oregon. Sure, they talked, but was she ever really saying anything or was she just going on and on about stuff that didn't really matter in order to avoid talking about anything that did actually matter? And what if she asked him out and he said yes and they had a horrible time and ended up ruining their friendship forever?

Oh, god. Oh, god. Oh, god. This is a mistake. A gigantic mistake.

Worry pitted Foster's stomach.

I bet if I ripped off this dress and ran downstairs in nothing but my leopard boy shorts and T-shirt bra that Tate would just look at me with those obnoxiously gorgeous blue eyes and smile with those stupid perfect teeth and then just go on talking about how much he likes to listen to the chickens cluck or something else really sickeningly charming.

This was one of those times when Foster really hated not having a phone. She wanted nothing more than to text Sabine in all caps to let her know how mad she was that Sabine, her only friend, made her realize that she had some ridiculous tweenie crush on the guy she had to spend the foreseeable future with.

Thanks a lot, friend.

"Foster?"

Tate! When had he gotten home?

Heavy footsteps clomped on the stairs leading up to her room.

And he's coming up here. Oh, god. Okay. Just breathe. She fluffed the ends of her hair and gave her armpits a final sniff. *Of course he wants to go out with me. I mean, look at me. I'm pretty positive I'm attractive. And I'm nice enough.*

She shook her head. *Okay, maybe I'm not super nice, but I'm nicer to Tate than I am to any other guy. Is that a redeeming quality?*

Tate knocked lightly against the door. "You in there?"

Foster's legs carried her to the door before her mind finished building a case as to why she should slip back into her sweatpants and pretend this whole date idea never happened.

"Hi." She opened the door, a gentle gust dancing in the soft waves of her hair as it wrapped around her chest and ever so gracefully twirled and lifted the ends of her skirt. Man, was she learning how to make an entrance.

"Whoa. I— You—" Tate tugged at the neck of his shirt. "A dress."

Foster tilted her chin. "Thanks." She grinned, deciding that *a dress* had to be short for *you are amazing, and I don't have a girlfriend back in Nowheresville, and I'd be honored to be your best friend and boyfriend.*

"So, are you busy, like," Foster glanced at her wrist as if her freckles could somehow show her the time. "Nowish?"

"No, no, definitely not. Finn said something about seeing me later, but I can tell him that I'm doing something else. I mean, if you want to, you know," he coughed before clearing his throat. "Do something, or something."

Foster couldn't help but blush. He was tripping all over himself, and not in his normal Tate-ish way. This was different. He was nervous. And that made two of them.

"Actually, Sabine told me about this place just down the road. The same one where you get those spaceship squashes. I guess they have food and there's a live band and they set up a dance floor. They were going to come by and get us so we could go on a—"

"Double date!" Tate's cheeks flushed bubblegum pink.

Foster smiled. "So you want to?"

"Yes!" His cheeks were blazing now, and Foster felt a little foolish for ever turning this whole double date invite into such a huge thing.

Foster crossed her legs, uncrossed them, and then finally settled on placing her hands in her lap as she sat at the picnic table with Sabine while they waited for Finn and Tate to return with glasses of what Sabine called the world's best marionberry lemonade.

The small crowd's spirited laughter drifted over to them on the backs of fluttering monarchs as they flitted between the tables on their way to fresh sprigs of bright purple flowers that were potted around the edges of the dance floor. Foster closed her eyes for a brief moment, listening to the gently tinkling wind chimes hanging around the red barn's storefront, all lit up with sparkling strands of lights.

A soft gust swirled up from under the wooden table, and Foster pressed her hands more firmly against her thighs. She wasn't used to having to be so vigilant about keeping her goodies hidden from the outside world. That's what pants were for.

"See, you look like a girl. A pretty girl. Especially when you don't do that." Sabine waggled her finger across the table at Foster's face. "Frown all annoyed and pee pantsy like that."

"I'm not frowning," Foster huffed, realizing she was indeed frowning. "And I don't have to wear a dress to look pretty or like a girl."

"That's not what I'm saying. Look at me," Sabine stood, did a sassy little twirl, the fringed edges of her crop top lifting from her jeans to join in her spin, and sat back down. "I'm not wearing a dress and I look good enough to eat. I only meant that a change in clothes can make you feel like a completely different woman. So can a good wig or a pair of thigh-high faux leather boots, but I don't think you're ready for either of those things."

"Not ready for what?" Finn asked as he and Tate set down the drinks and he took a seat on the bench next to Sabine.

"For these moves!" Sabine grabbed Finn's hand and practically pulled him onto the dance floor. "See you two out there." She winked before galloping over to where Finn was standing, snapping and tapping the toe of his boot to the beat.

"So, what do you think?" Tate shoved his hands into his pockets and removed them just as quickly. "Would you like to dance? Again?"

"Well, yeah, but this is a slow song, not a swing-me-around song."

"Hey, no worries. I can do slow, just follow me. I got ya. Again."

"You won't drop me this time?"

"Never."

Foster felt kind of drunk as Tate offered her his hand and guided her to the makeshift dance floor. Bubbles of excitement popped throughout her body, making her dizzy and fizzy and giddy. The only other time she'd felt like this was after half a bottle of cheap champagne in at, well, space camp.

"Fucking space camp," she mumbled.

"What was that?" Tate's eyes were the same endless blue as the sky, and Foster thought, for a moment, that if he never looked at her again she might just die.

"I'm having a great time. It's wonderful, really." If Past Foster could see her now, she'd smack her and tell her that the world was unraveling and people needed saving and she hadn't spent nearly enough time being depressed. But Present Foster didn't much care for her former prickly, grumpy self. She wanted to bottle this girl, this moment, this feeling, and be this new person forever. Foster lifted her hand from Tate's broad shoulder, flipped her hair, and giggled.

"You're laughing."

"I am."

Tate moved her slowly, confidently around the dance floor. His hand lowered to the small of her back as his thick fingers spread wide and he held her more firmly, pressing her to him, squeezing the air out of the space keeping them apart.

And she let him.

Foster never thought she wanted to be that girl, the one who melted into someone else and called him happiness, but if this is how it started, it sure felt damn good.

The music changed to a dreamy, jazzy melody and Foster's eyelids hung heavy as she closed out the world around them and reveled in Tate's earthy scents of hay and horses and the way each muscle of his chest firmed against hers as he maneuvered them around the dance floor.

"You're okay?" It was less a question, and more a release of tension, but Foster answered anyway.

"Yeah, why?"

"You seem . . . different."

She was. She could feel it. It was as if she'd been living inside someone else this whole time, waiting, incubating, until the space around her was safe enough to occupy—safe enough to call home. Her entire world might not be safe, but Tate was. *Her* Tate.

Foster's nerves fizzed with warmth.

Could he actually be hers?

"Tate—"

"Foster—" they blurted simultaneously.

Tate brushed a stray hair from her cheek, tucking it behind her ear as he guided them to an empty corner of the dance floor. "Go ahead."

"Right now, with you . . . This is the only place I want to be."

And then his breath was all she knew, like he'd peeled the air from the clouds, stored it in his lungs, and brought it to her as a gift. His mouth covered hers, searching for answers and releasing soft, patient prayers with each flick of his tongue.

The earth beneath Foster's feet stilled as if she and Tate controlled the entire planet, and at this moment each of them poured their energy into the other and there was nothing left to keep it spinning.

Then someone screamed.

Not a bloodcurdling shriek. More of a confused and frightened squeal for attention.

The music stopped.

And then there were gasps followed by chairs scraping the pavement and rushed footsteps beating into the gravel in sharp, staccato crunches.

Foster didn't want to pull away, didn't want to stop the sweet exchange that had her nerves alight with the promise of their future. But she had to. Something was wrong. She could hear it in the way the people ran through the parking lot and the yells coming from behind them—coming from Sabine and Finn.

Keeping her tucked against his side with his arm snuggly around her shoulder, he turned them to face the fields behind the barn-like store. And there, descending on them against an angry red setting sun, was a wall cloud spewing the hollow point of a deadly funnel—a funnel that was coming directly at them.

18

TATE

"Fuck! No no no no no. This shit is *not* happening again!" Tate's voice was strong and serious, and didn't shake at all—even though his insides were spinning around in a weird rush of *ohmygod I just kissed Foster* and *fucking tornado is going to kill us all!*

"Tate! Foster! You gotta do something!" Finn spoke fast and low.

"Get out of here. Now," Tate told their friends.

"Okay, yeah. Let's get back in the truck. I'm sure we can outrun it," Sabine panted, looking wide-eyed and truly terrified.

In his imagination Tate could see the two of them crushed in the middle of a mound of vehicles . . . just before they exploded . . .

"Tate!"

Foster's voice brought Tate's mind back to the present. He met her haunted gaze.

"There isn't time to run," she said.

"Hey, wake up you two! We need to get out of here!" Sabine cried.

"No. Not by driving," Tate said. "The parking lot's already a traffic jam. None of them are going to make it out of here."

"Listen up!" a man's voice boomed over the band's loudspeaker system.

"The Bennett Farm across the street has a root cellar! Everyone over there! Hurry!"

The panicked tide of people shifted direction, and instead of bottling up the parking lot, people climbed over Bella's fence, crowded through the gate, and poured across the little two-lane road as the sky opened and rain began to pelt them along with the whipping wind.

"Go!" Foster told Sabine and Finn. "Get to the cellar!"

Finn and Sabine nodded and, holding tight to each other's hand, started to rush off, but Sabine pulled them to a stop to shout over the wind. "What about you two? You stay out here you're going to get killed!"

Tate and Foster shared a long look. He nodded, understanding the wisdom in Foster's serious green eyes, and then he told Sabine, "We're going to stop this tornado from killing anyone."

"But how can—" Finn began, but Foster cut him off.

"Don't worry about that. Just get out of here. Tate and I can handle this."

Then, very deliberately, Foster took Tate's hand, and squeezed it before looking up at him with those eyes and that beautiful, honest face. "We can do this. We can save these people."

And suddenly Tate believed they could do it—they could save them. "Together," he said. "We'll save 'em, like we couldn't save our parents."

Holding hands, Tate and Foster walked in the opposite direction everyone else was running. They walked around the rear of the store and directly for the diving funnel.

"Okay, tell me again about how you got the willows to be your air orchestra," Tate said. His voice was calm, but he and Foster were clinging to each other's hand as if they were living lifelines.

Foster didn't look at him. She stared at the funnel. He could feel the trembling of her body through their joined hands.

"Hey," he pulled her so that she had to look at him. Her green eyes were wide and a little glassy. Her face was almost completely drained of color, and her pretty yellow dress had wilted against her skin like the long, dank strands of her muted hair. He thought she looked as terrified as he felt, and Tate knew that was bad. Real bad. So, he touched her cheek and spoke softly to her, like they had all the time in the world to chat and not like they were standing in lashing rain directly in the path of a descending tornado.

"Hey," he repeated. "We've got this. I flew. You played an air symphony. We've been practicing for two weeks. So, remind me. What did you say about the willow music?"

"I—uh—I said it's a-a-b-bout how I'm feeling," she stuttered at first because her teeth were chattering from cold and fear, but as she spoke Foster steadied herself and got stronger. "If I'm negative, things don't go so well, but when I'm relaxed and not really trying—or just having fun—then air is almost easy to control."

"Okay. So. Let's have a good time." Suddenly, Tate grinned. "Hey! You said Cora liked the Rat Pack. Do you know the words to Sinatra's 'Luck Be a Lady'?"

In typical Foster fashion, she frowned and then rolled her eyes at him. "Seriously? You want to sing right now?"

He waggled his eyebrows at her. "Seriously. And dance. And make beautiful air music. If it's about how we feel, it could work." Then, not caring that he definitely looked like a crazy person—after all, the only person who could see him was Foster, and she already knew his kind of crazy—he started snapping his fingers to the rhythm of the old Sinatra tune. He crooned the first line.

"Luck be a lady tonight."

And then nudged Foster expectantly.

"Luck be a lady tonight," Foster repeated, speaking more than singing the line.

But Tate nodded reassuringly, picking up the tempo and starting to walk forward, doing a little sliding dance step, while he snapped his fingers.

From beside him, Foster's strong, pretty voice picked up the next line.

"Luck if you've been a lady to begin with . . ."

Tate took both of her hands and began guiding her into a swing as he joined her singing *"Luck be a lady tonight!"*

They'd made their way to the beginning of the fields, all filled with ripening pumpkins and squashes, and Tate saw Foster's eyes get huge as she stared over his shoulder at the the whining, rain-wrapped wall of wind and destruction.

"Sing it with me, Foster!" Tate shouted over the storm. Together their voices raised in harmony.

> *"Luck be a lady tonight!*
> *Luck if you've been a lady to begin with . . ."*

That's when Tate heard it. The air around them quieted and stopped screaming in anger. Instead it picked up the melody and began to wrap it around them in shades of yellow and pink and blue.

"It's working, Foster! Don't look, just sing and dance with me!"

Foster's green eyes found his, and he smiled at her, trying to show her with his touch and his expression how much faith he had in her.

And she did it. Foster nodded and sang as he moved her around the soggy, pumpkin-filled field while the air around them was colored by happiness and filled with music.

> *"Luck be a lady tonight!"*

As they paused before the next lyrics, Tate met Foster's gaze and dropped her hand. "Now, air! Sing with us!" He lifted his hands then, just like he'd seen her doing earlier that day, making little upturned, flicking motions with his fingers as he sang the next lines.

> *"Luck be a lady tonight!"*

Tate could hardly believe it. He wasn't even really thinking about the tornado, just about the song and how cool it would be if air played along with him—and as he flicked his fingers up, the funnel stopped descending. He heard Foster's gasp from beside him, then her hands were raised, once again maestro-like, and she, too, was moving her fingers in time with the melody as she sang with him.

"Yeah, Foster! We're doing it!"

She sang the finale notes with the lyrical timing of a perfect Sinatra swagger. He lifted her, spinning her around with him while the music began to fade. Then, breathing heavily, they finally looked up at the sky . . . *and the funnel, in perfect time to the end of the air music, disappeared into the roiling wall of clouds.*

Tate laughed joyously. "Foster! It's working!"

"It's fantastic! But it'd really be nice if the wind dried up this rain and sent it to, uh, Seattle," Foster quipped, grinning up at the sky as she squinted her eyes against the droplets.

As if she'd pressed a mute button, the rain shut completely off.

"That's perfect!" Foster giggled. "Thank you, wind!"

"And I think it'd be great if that wall cloud cleared off, so the sky could be like it was earlier today—super clear and super pretty." As Tate spoke he made motions in the air, kind of like he was wiping off the whiteboard where his dad used to draw the team's plays.

The clouds began dissipating immediately.

Then Foster wasn't shivering anymore as the air around them settled, softened, and warmed.

"That's awesome!" Tate said. "But there're still more clouds back there that need to clear up." Tate lifted his arms higher, focusing on the bruise-colored cumulous mountains of water and dust particles that billowed ominously in the distance. "Hey, there's no need to be so pissed off," he told the clouds. "Be chill like the Rat Pack. Everything's okay." As those distant clouds began to flatten and fade away, Tate could hardly contain his joy. *They were doing it! They were controlling this disaster!* As his happy thought formed, Tate felt himself being cradled by air and, ever so gently, he lifted—going up, up, up like he might join the last of the clouds playing across the sunset sky.

He lifted higher, and then higher, until he was hovering just beneath the roofline of the barn-like store.

"Tate! Be careful!" Foster was looking up at him with a mixed expression of worry and delight.

"It's fine! This is cool!" Tate wasn't afraid, and he was shocked that he wasn't because he'd thought about it, a lot actually, since the day air had dropped him on his butt. And his thought was that he was definitely *not* Superman, and any flying should be left to Superman.

Yet there he was, hovering a good twenty feet or more in the clearing air, and loving every moment of it. He spread his arms wide, as if to embrace the glistening strands of the air superhighway that was all around him, which is when it happened.

First, he felt it. It was a sensation he'd never had before, and it started in his hands—his widely outstretched hands. The only thing that came close to what was happening to them was how his foot felt if he sat on it too long and it went to sleep, but the sensation wasn't an awful one. It wasn't painful, though it was weirdly numbing. Not understanding what he was feeling, Tate glanced at his right hand.

It wasn't there!

It was gone!

Tate fisted his fingers, squeezing hard. He could feel his hand responding—squeezing, but he saw *nothing there* but air and sky.

Tate's gaze flew to this other hand. It, too, was missing—as well as a part of his left forearm.

A terrible foreboding skittered down Tate's spine.

"Tate?"

He looked down at Foster and found his voice. "Something's happening to me! I'm—I'm disappearing."

He saw her eyes widen and her brows shoot up to her auburn hairline as she looked from one side of his body to the other . . . from one disappearing hand to the disappearing arm attached to it . . . to the other.

Tate's breath was coming fast. His hands felt cold. Really, really cold. *Need to get down . . . need to get down . . . need to get down . . .* The words were a silent litany in his mind, but his body didn't move. The air didn't obey him, and his right forearm began to disappear.

"Tate."

He heard her voice, but he couldn't take his eyes from his disappearing arm. He was afraid if he looked down, the next time he glanced back at himself he'd have no arm . . . no arm at all.

"They're not there, but I can feel them," Tate shouted, hoping Foster could hear him. "They're there—I promise! But I . . . but I . . ."

"Tate!" Her voice coming from directly beside him jolted Tate enough that he was able to tear his gaze from his disappearing limbs.

Foster floated in the air next him. Her hair was lifting gently around her, and he saw that she had to use one hand to hold her dress down. He almost smiled at that, but realized it was hard to make his voice work.

"Tate, pull it together! I'm right here!" Foster reached out, flailed through the air a little, and then her hand connected with Tate's cold, invisible hand. "Hey, look in my eyes!"

Tate did as she said, and the cold, empty feeling in his hands changed. He could feel her pulse against his skin, and her warmth. He could also feel how tightly she was gripping his hand.

And he was able to draw a long, deep breath.

"Look," Foster said softly, cutting her eyes to their joined hands.

Hesitantly, Tate peeked at them . . .

"It's visible! I can see me again!"

"Yeah, Tate! We're doing it!" Foster echoed his words.

They hung in the air while Tate breathed deeply and gripped Foster's hand.

"Okay, wind, don't play with my dress, please," Foster spoke nonchalantly, like she was asking Sabine if she'd stop tapping her fingernails on the table.

Tate was wondering what she was up to when she lifted her hand from her dress and gracefully floated around so that she was facing him. Smiling a little shyly, Foster felt along his right arm until she found his invisible hand. She wove her fingers with his, and he breathed even easier as his right hand filled with warmth and became visible.

"Whew, that's good. I can see both your hands now. How are you feeling?" she asked.

"Amazing. I think. Maybe a little light-headed, but better. *A lot* better with you up here, too." Tate glanced down. "Uh, any idea what we should do now?"

"Well, maybe. It's just a guess, but how about we think about drifting slowly, *real* slowly, back to the ground?" Foster said. "Like to the tempo of a lullaby, um . . ." she paused, thinking, then a quick grin turned up the corners of her lips. 'Moon River'! Cora used to sing it to me at bedtime. Do you know it?"

"I don't think so," he said.

"No worries. It's from one of Cora's favorite old movies, *Breakfast at Tiffany's*. It's a sweet, sleepy little song. I'll sing. You just think about the melody and drifting slowly down with it."

"Okay, I can do that, but don't let go of my hands," he said.

"I've got you. Promise." She gave his hands a reassuring squeeze and drifted a little closer to him as she started singing a sweet, soft lullaby.

> *"Moon river, wider than a mile*
> *I'm crossing you in style some day."*

Foster's voice wrapped around him and the warm, gentle breeze picked up the melody of the lullaby, making the air glow in

wisps of peach and tangerine. Tate knew he was supposed to be thinking about drifting with the song, but all he could think about was how close she was, and how beautiful she was, and how much he wanted to kiss Foster.

Kiss her again, that is.

And again.

And again.

Without conscious thought, Tate guided Foster into his arms, wrapping her in his embrace. He bent, holding her carefully, gently, like the precious gift she was, and he kissed her—long, and deep, and like he never, ever wanted to stop kissing her.

Their feet touched the ground together. They didn't move apart. Foster's arms lifted, wrapping around his shoulders, and she kissed him back with a passion that had his head feeling dizzy again.

"Oh. My. Freaking. God! We think they're dead, and what are they doing? *Making out!*" Sabine sputtered as she and Finn rushed around the barn and almost ran into them.

Foster reluctantly broke the kiss. Her eyes smiled up at Tate and she whispered, "I think we need to train our minions better."

19
TATE

The night was perfectly clear. Perfectly warm. Perfectly starry. Tate, Foster, Finn, and Sabine had taken up seats that were rapidly becoming "their" places around the Strawberry Fields fire pit while Foster stuck fat, cloudlike marshmallows through the ends of shish-kebab sticks. On a platter next to her were graham crackers and flat hunks of dark chocolate.

Foster sighed and held two sticks near the fire, turning them so they didn't burn. Finally, she said to Sabine, "Okay, *now* ask your zillions of questions."

"Jesus! It's about time. So, let's see if I have this straight, and I realize this is an oversimplification, but basically you and Tate serenaded a gigantic, descending tornado—"

"It's called a funnel cloud until it touches the ground," Tate interrupted Sabine.

Sabine narrowed her dark eyes at him. "Semantics are not important at this moment."

"Be careful," Finn said in an exaggerated whisper. "She's getting the crazy eye. When she gets the crazy eye, you're in trouble."

"Finn, do you truly want to see crazy?" Sabine's voice was entirely too innocent.

"Oh, no no no no. I do not. Been there. Don't want to return."

"Here, have a s'more," Foster passed Sabine a warm, gooey, cracker mess on a paper plate.

"The peace offering of your people?" Sabine's eyes sparkled mischievously.

"You have an excellent memory," Foster said. "Dark chocolate makes everything better."

"I hear ya on that," Sabine agreed. She nibbled at one very hot edge before continuing. "Where was I? Oh, yeah. You serenaded a *funnel cloud* with a Sinatra song."

"Not just any Sinatra song—"Luck Be a Lady," Tate said.

"Is what song they sang important?" Finn asked.

"Actually, I'm starting to think it might be," Sabine said. "So, you sang to it and the funnel cloud went back up with the rest of the wall clouds. But then you somehow stopped the rain and made *all* of the clouds disappear. I mean, look up there." Sabine pointed at the star-dusted sky. "Not one cloud. Did you sing another song for that?"

"Nope, we just—uh . . ." Tate began and then his words trailed away as he turned to Foster. "How the hell did we do it?"

Foster lifted her slim shoulder. "I'm not sure, because we really just asked it to go. I said something about wishing the rain would go away—to Seattle, I think. I mean, after the air music stopped and the funnel cloud was gone, the rest was pretty easy."

"Yeah, and then I pretended like I was wiping off a whiteboard while I asked the clouds to go away," Tate said.

"No singing, so the song's not what's important. Do you think it's the— what do you call it—*air music* that's important?" Finn said, taking a s'more from Foster.

"I think the air music is something that happens when we're doing the right thing," Foster said.

"Yeah, once the music starts and we can see the air currents that's when everything seems to fall into place."

"Wait, you can hear music in the air?" Sabine asked, s'more paused half-way to her mouth.

"Yep, we can hear *and* see it," Tate said.

Sabine said quickly, "How were you two feeling when you heard music and saw the air currents?"

Tate and Foster exchanged a look, and it was Tate's turn to shrug. "Good, I guess. Well, at first it was pretty scary, but then Foster reminded me that when she was playing with air earlier it was about how she was feeling—relaxed and happy. Right, Foster?"

Foster nodded. "Yeah, because when I've been pissed and wind shows up things don't go so well."

"That's exactly what I mean! Okay, okay! You tamed the tornado and the wall cloud, then Tate, you started to fly. How were you feeling when you did that?" Sabine scooted forward, staring at Tate, s'more forgotten.

"Super happy and relieved. Last time we tried to stop a tornado things went bad. Real bad. Tonight no one died. No one was even hurt, so I was feeling pretty great."

"But then you said you felt weird and started to disappear?" Finn said.

"Yeah, I didn't feel weird *until* I saw that my hands weren't there. Then everything got confusing. My head felt like it was full of cotton. Foster had to save me." His eyes caught Foster's. His smile was slow and intimate. "Not that I minded. At all."

"Yeah, yeah, we saw," Sabine said. "And then Foster flew, too. Right?"

"Well, I think float is a better description, but yeah, I did."

"How?" Sabine asked.

Foster thought about it as she chewed a bite of s'more and then answered simply, "I just thought that Tate needed me and I should get up there, and there I was. Up there with Tate."

"How did you *feel*?" Sabine prodded.

"I was worried about Tate, but mostly I just wanted to get up there and calm him down. He was definitely freaking out."

"And then she was there, and as soon as she touched my hand I felt better. Then she started singing that nice little lullaby and everything just felt good. I calmed down right away. Basically, I was happy she was there with me. It made everything right again." Tate answered Sabine's question, but he didn't take his eyes from Foster, whose cheeks were blazing so red that even by the soft light of the fire he could see her blush. But she didn't look away and she didn't make some kind of dismissive comment. She just gazed right back at him—and smiled.

"What was the song?" Sabine asked.

When neither Tate nor Foster answered, Sabine stretched out her long leg and gave Foster's foot a kick.

"Oh, uh, what?"

"Girl, try to pay attention. We're having a major discussion here and I think I might have figured something out. What song did you sing to get Tate down safely?" Sabine said.

"'Moon River,' from—" Foster began, but Sabine finished the sentence with her. *"Breakfast at Tiffany's."*

"See! People still know that song," Foster told Tate.

"Hey, I'm pretty sure I was Holly Golightly in another life," Sabine said.

"Wasn't she a prostitute?" Finn said.

"She was an escort!" Foster and Sabine yelled together, frowning at Finn.

"Okeydokey then." Finn retreated behind a bite of s'more.

"So, you floated down and then you started making out. Do I have that right?" Sabine continued.

"Almost," Tate said. Then he pressed his lips shut, hearing his mom's voice in his head: *A gentleman does not kiss and tell. Locker room talk should be about the game and not about women's body parts.*

"Almost?" Sabine lifted one brow and sent Foster a *look*.

Tate stayed as silent as Finn.

Through a big bite of s'more Foster muttered, "The kissing started in the air."

"Yes!" Sabine cried, causing everyone to jump. "I'm right. I know I am. Okay, one more thing: when you two are hooked into air—really hooked into it like when you can hear the music and see the air currents—do you ever sense anything from it?"

"Anything like what?" Tate said.

"Like feelings," Sabine said.

Instead of scoffing at the idea, Foster sat forward in her chair. "I'm not sure if this counts, but Tate and I can feel it when we're invoking air. It's hard to describe, but it's a feeling that starts over our skin. It's kind of like static electricity. Right, Tate?"

He nodded. "Yeah, but the feeling changes. On the football field that first time it was crazy. It felt like my skin and even my blood was sizzling, but when Foster was playing the willow orchestra—you know, when you guys saw me flying—the feeling wasn't the same."

"No, it's softer." Foster blew out a long breath in frustration. "That's not it, either. But yes, we do sense something from air."

"That fits my theory. Get this—what if air is pissed? I don't blame it. Look at all the pollution and crap people have poured into it. It's awful. So, what if air—and the rest of the elements—are pissed, and what you two can do is calm it, but only if you're calm. If you're not, then terrible stuff happens, maybe stuff that's even more terrible than what would happen if you *weren't* around."

Tate sat up straighter. "Foster, what if she's right? What if we didn't cause the tornado to appear at the football game, but once it was there it reacted to us? I don't know about you, but I was fucking scared."

"I was scared until Cora fell. Then I was pissed. Really pissed," Foster said.

"Just like you were in the truck when the tornado formed and smashed down on the highway blocking the Core Four from following us," Tate was speaking as quickly as Foster.

"Yeah! And then you and I were super pissed when we had that fight, and I was wrapped in a crazy, almost tornado, but nothing actually formed because we calmed down and breathed," Foster said. Her gaze went from Tate to Sabine. "You are definitely on to something. Air does react to how we feel. So, it's not a stretch to believe air has a type of sentience."

"It wasn't our fault. That tornado—we didn't cause it." Tate felt a great release, as if a rubber band had suddenly been unwrapped from around his chest.

"You couldn't have," Sabine said. "The way you two were sucking face, there's no way you were pissed."

"Not just that," Foster spoke slowly, staring at Tate. "I wasn't pissed at the football game. Not before Cora collapsed. I'll admit to not wanting to be there, but I did have popcorn and Skittles, and it was my birthday. I felt fine."

"And I was happy. I was playing a game I love surrounded by my friends and family. We didn't cause it to happen, Foster." Tate was blinking fast, trying to keep the tears from spilling from his eyes.

"*They* did it," Sabine said.

Everyone turned to her.

"Who did what?" Foster said.

Sabine practically bounced out of her chair with excitement. "Them! Those three men and that woman who are after you. You call them the Core Four. Foster, you said Cora kept you off the grid for the past year because of them, but Tate didn't know anything about them, right?"

"Right," Tate said.

"But *they* knew about Tate because: one, they were there that night." Sabine held up her fingers, ticking off points. "Two, Cora had fake ID's made for *both* of you, so she had to at least have had the suspicion that the Core Four knew where to find Tate. Three, Cora bought this secret place for you *and the other kids you're trying to find.*"

"Four," Foster added. "The Core Four are working with my adopted dad—the man responsible for altering our DNA. He created the records. He must know where each kid lives."

"Each kid except you," Tate said pointedly. "Which is why he had to draw you out."

"Foster, oh my god, what if the Core Four are attached to the elements, too? What if *they* called a tornado?" Sabine said.

"In a terrible way that makes perfect sense," Foster agreed.

"Core Four, hell. I'm calling those assholes the Fucktastic Four from here on out," Finn said.

"I like it," Foster said.

"Me too, babe," Sabine made a kissy face at Finn.

"But why would the Fucktastic Four do that?" Tate asked. "People died!"

"To draw me out." Foster's voice had flattened. "They couldn't find Cora and me, but they knew where you were, Tate. And they also knew something was going to kick in on our eighteenth birthday—something that binds us to air."

"You're right. The Fucktastic Four would definitely know that whatever Dr. Stewart did to us manifests on our eighteenth birthday," Tate said. "So, what? They hang out at the football game and call a *tornado* down on my hometown because they have a hunch you might be there?"

"What if it was more than a hunch? More than *might be there*?" Sabine asked with dread shadowing her voice.

"You mean like whatever it is inside those two that binds them to air also draws them together?" Finn said.

"I guess that might be true," Foster said.

"But you didn't feel drawn to Missouri?" Sabine asked.

Foster snorted. "Uh, no. Never." Then she paused and added. "But I didn't need to *feel* drawn to Tate. Cora was doing that for me. She found Tate. She brought me there to him."

"Right! But what might have happened if Cora hadn't found me? Maybe you would've ended up at that football game anyway," Tate said.

"Well, I think we're going to find out. From the files Cora left us we've figured out that there are three other pairs who will be having their eighteenth birthdays in the next three months," Foster said. "We only have what we think are the states where each of them was born, and none of them are in the same state. If we're right about the pairs being drawn together on their eighteenth birthdays, then the next two will be coming together in the next three days."

"But wait, what if it's not just these other people who are drawn to each other? What if you have to add the disaster to amp up the attraction and to make their connection with the element manifest?" Sabine said. "Did either of you do anything with air *before* that football game?"

"Never," Tate said.

"No. I tried to use my Jedi mind trick, but it never worked well until after the first tornado. Not that it works one hundred percent of the time now, as you two already know. But doing anything else—like with the weather or air—never entered my mind," Foster said.

"So, we have three days and then two more kids are turning eighteen and probably facing another major disaster," Sabine said.

"Water is next," Tate said. When everyone gawked at him, he added. "I figured it out from Stewart's equations. He bonded Foster and me with oxygen molecules when we were barely embryos, and then bombarded us with gamma rays. The next two he bonded with H2O—water."

"We have to find those next two kids, like now," Sabine said.

"We've been trying to, but those files are crazy hard to understand," Foster said.

"Show us," Sabine said. "Hey, Finn and I have already been sworn to secrecy, and I'm a sophomore pre-med student. I'm damn good at research. We can help. Let us help."

Foster met his gaze and Tate shrugged. "It's Cora's stuff, so it's up to you."

"Let's do this," Foster said. "Come on. I'll show you the Batcave. Bring the s'mores."

"Okay, seriously. Your crazy daddy is brilliant," Sabine said, glancing up from a thick file of equations and graphs and medical records. She was sitting on the floor of Cora's office next to Foster with files spread all around them.

"He's not my dad," Foster said.

"Hey, sorry. This has to be really hard for you," Sabine said.

"No. Yes." Foster sighed and swept back her thick fall of red hair, retying her ponytail. "It's hard, but I shouldn't take it out on you." She paused and looked from Sabine to Tate and Finn, who were sprawled on the floor beside them. "I shouldn't take it out on any of you. I just . . . How about we don't call him my dad ever again?"

"Done," Tate said.

"Fine by me. The guy's an ass," Finn said.

"Anyone who could hurt Cora and you isn't worth being called dad," Sabine said.

"Thanks. So. We've been going over this stuff for three hours. I got nothing. How about you?" Foster asked the group.

"This crap is worse than a foreign language," Finn held up a yellow legal-sized sheet of paper that was filled, front and back, with equation after equation. "It's an alien language."

"Tate? Any more revelations?" Foster asked him.

Tate tried not to jump guiltily and was unable to meet her eyes. "Um. No. I need more time, and some, um, biology books."

"We could go to the library tomorrow," Finn said. "After I feed. I need to run into Portland anyway. Want to come with me?"

"Yeah, thanks," Tate said.

"Well, I have an idea, but it doesn't have anything to do with all this stuff." Sabine's sweeping gesture took in the papers spread out on the floor as well as the Batcave, which was filled with more files. "Of the next two kids whose birthdays are in three days we know one of them was born in Louisiana and one was born in North Carolina, right?"

"Yeah, or at least that's what we think we know," Tate said.

"What if instead of tracking people we track weather and the state?" Sabine said.

"Explain," Foster said.

"Tate says the next pair are bonded to water. So let's watch the weather off the coast of North Carolina and in the Gulf. If the point is to draw the pair together and get them to manifest their element bond, then it seems logical that they would be drawn to one of those two states. Or at least that's all we have to go on regarding their locations. Both states are on a coast. My guess is in three days one of those states is going to be the site of a major water disaster," Sabine said.

"Damn, girl! Have I told you lately how sexy it is that you're so smart?" Finn leaned forward and kissed the back of Sabine's neck, making her giggle.

"Okay, but what then?" Everyone looked at Tate. "Let's say that tomorrow we hear that there's a weird hurricane forming off the coast of North Carolina. What do we do? Do we get in a plane and go . . . where exactly to do what exactly?"

"I think all we can do is watch and wait," Foster said.

"And let those two water kids walk into something terrible like what happened to us? To our families?" Tate said.

"I don't know, Tate. I wish I did, but right now all I know is that you and I are safe here, and there are six other kids who aren't safe, whose families aren't safe. I want to figure out how to save them, or at the very least how to get to them before the Fucktastic Four grabs them, but I have no clue how to do that. Do any of you?" Foster's emerald gaze swept the group.

"Do you know where Stewart would take them if he caught them?" Sabine asked.

Foster nodded. "He'd go to his island. It's just off the coast of Key West. Billionaire patrons bought it for Doctor Rick more than two decades ago. It's where he was doing human genetic research as well as supposedly figuring out how to genetically alter seaweed to break down plastic and absorb pollution. When I was about . . ." she paused, thinking back. "Um, eight, I think, the government shut down the human branch of his research. They said he deviated from his declared study and moved to unapproved human trials, so the scientific community basically shunned him. Cora said it was a big deal, but I was too young to really understand much, and he refused to talk about it. All I know is after that he was still conducting the seaweed experiments up until five years ago, when he 'died.'" She air quoted.

"Who's on the island now?" Finn asked.

"No one. It's abandoned and quarantined. There was supposedly some kind of toxic leak from his lab right after Doctor Rick's fake death," Foster said.

"But you don't believe that," Sabine said.

Foster shook her head. "That's probably where he's been all this time."

"So shouldn't we go there? Confront him?" Finn said.

"No!" Foster shouted. Then, with obvious effort, she calmed herself before continuing. "At least not until we know more about our powers—and the Fucktastic Four. Right now I can see us walking in there . . . and never walking out."

Tate nodded. "I have to agree with Foster. As much as I'd like to face that old man and ask him what the hell's wrong with him, I know that Cora was scared—of him and of the Fucktastic Four. Scared enough to spend an entire year setting up a safe house for us and teaching Foster how to live under the radar. I didn't know Cora, but from everything you three have told me, she wasn't someone who spooked easily. We need to remember that and stay well away from Stewart until we're sure we can handle him and his Fucktastic Four."

Foster sent him a look filled with appreciation, which had Tate's heart skipping happily around inside his chest.

"Okay, I get it," Sabine said. "So, tomorrow, when I'm at my mind-numbingly boring work-study job in the provost's office at PU, I'm going to hope that the Internet actually functions. I'll watch the weather off the coast of North Carolina and Louisiana. Better yet, I'll head over to the Environmental Studies building. They offer a minor in Water Resources, and I'm almost positive that includes a weather study section. I'll check with one of the PA's over there about tracking unusual water weather patterns."

"Don't tell anyone why!" Foster said.

"Girl, please. I'm sitting outside your Batcave. I am in league with superheroes. I'm not saying shit," Sabine said.

"Thank you," Foster said earnestly. "I really appreciate you."

"And you trust me?" Sabine prodded, raising one perfectly shaped brow.

"And I trust you," Foster said firmly.

"Good." Sabine held up her hand. "Finn, help me up. It's time to go."

"Oh, okay babe." Finn stood and pulled Sabine up beside him.

"Hey, there's no rush. You two want another s'more or anything for the road?" Tate asked, helping Foster up and using that as an excuse to thread his fingers with hers and hold her hand.

"We live ten minutes from here. We're fine. And we're not rushing. We're just clearing out so that you two can figure out your sleeping arrangements." Sabine shot Foster a mischievous look. "Which I want to hear all about tomorrow when I stop by for scones before class."

Tate and Foster walked them to the door and waved good-bye. After Finn's truck finished bumping down the road and disappeared into the night, they stood out on the porch staring up at the big, starry sky while they held hands.

"Um, so, about our sleeping arrangements?" Foster spoke hesitantly.

Tate looked from the sky to her. Foster was still holding his hand, but she was obviously uncomfortable—nervous even. He gave a little tug on her hand so that she had to turn to face him.

"Hey, there's nothing wrong with our sleeping arrangements. I like my room. Do you like yours?" he asked gently, trying to be careful not to spook her.

He saw surprise flash through her eyes, and heard the relief in her voice. "Yes! I love my room. Cora made sure everything from our brownstone was moved here."

Tate already knew that—knew that Cora had made sure Foster's room would feel like a sanctuary, and there was no way he was going to trespass there until or unless Foster was *more than* ready to invite him in—and he didn't think Foster was the "one date and we jump into bed" type of girl. "Well, good. Then I have no clue what Sabine was talking about, but I'm really tired." He paused to yawn widely. "You, too?"

"Yeah, I guess I didn't realize it until you mentioned it."

"I'm gonna go to bed. Finn and Sabine are always here super early." He dropped her hand and rested his gently on her shoulders. "Thank you for an amazing date. And thank you for not letting me disappear or crash to the ground."

"You helped," she said.

"That's because we make a great team." Slowly, Tate bent and kissed Foster—softly, gently, with only a little bit of heat. When he pulled away from her, Tate was pleased to see that she leaned toward him and seemed reluctant to let him go. "Good night, Foster. See you in the morning." Tate grinned at her and kissed the end of her cute, freckled nose before he retreated into the house, with his mother's advice echoing from his memory.

The most important thing a woman can give you is her trust. Earn that first and then you'll earn a love that will last. Trust is based on respect. And if you don't treat her with respect, you have no business being with her.

"Mom, I think you'd be proud of me," Tate whispered to the wind as he climbed the stairs up to his room on the second floor of the farmhouse. Somewhere between the porch and his bedroom Tate realized that he felt good—really good—for the first time since that awful night just a couple of weeks ago when his world was torn apart, and the reason for his good feeling wasn't the memory of Foster's lips against his or the tantalizing thought that there was a chance that someday in the future he might be doing a lot more than just kissing Foster. The *really* good feeling came from the way she'd smiled at him when she'd realized he wasn't going to try to pressure her into something—that she could actually relax around him and trust him to treat her with the respect and common courtesy she deserved.

And for a moment, Tate was sure he heard his mother's voice whisper back, *Oh, I am proud of you, Son . . . I am . . .*

20

EVE

Eve tried to calm her excitement as she rushed into her brothers' cottage. "I got your text. What did you find?"

Matthew looked up from the computer screen and grinned at her. "I found Tate's grandfather."

Eve almost collapsed with relief into the chair beside her brother while Mark and Luke emerged from the kitchen, cracking open bottles of IPA and handing one to her as they pulled up dining room chairs, sat, and studied Matthew's computer screen with him.

"There!" Matthew pointed at a grainy digital newspaper image from *The Daily News*. "That old guy in the middle. That's the boy's grandfather."

Eve read aloud. "Linus Bowen, retired high school coach and biology teacher, led the charge to save Galveston's Corner Café from demolition and have it declared a National Historic Landmark. But don't call Coach Bowen a hero. He'd be quick to correct you. *'Nope, nope—I'm no hero. I'm just an old dog who doesn't want to learn a new breakfast spot. Been coming here Monday through Friday for decades. I have no intention of stopping until you plant me in the ground.'*" Eve glanced up at her brothers, a relieved smile shimmering in her dark eyes. "This is good work, guys! Really good work. So, Tate's grandfather lives in Galveston. Nice coincidence that we have to be there in a few days anyway. How about we go early and pay Mr. Bowen a little visit?"

"We'll have to visit him at this café. The old guy is like a ghost. It's why it took forever to find him, and it was really just a lucky Google accident that I did. He's retired, but I can't find property listed under his name—or any name even vaguely like his. As far as I can tell old man Bowen doesn't own a computer or a cell phone or a home—or even a damn car. He does have a driver's license, but it's expired and the address on it is the same as the café's."

"I wonder what this old man's hiding," Mark said. "It's strange that he's so tough to find."

"Or he's just a grumpy old hermit. Guys, let's not start making up conspiracy theories," Eve said.

"Yeah, you're right. We should leave that crazy bullshit to Father," Mark grumbled.

Eve shot him a "be quiet" look before continuing. "Okay, I'm going to give Father this good news and have him get the jet ready. I'm going to ask for wheels up in just a couple of hours. Mark, how's the weather coming?"

"I've been increasing the waves in the Gulf every day—focusing on the Galveston area because we know Charlotte is enrolled in Texas A&M this semester. Surfers are flocking to the Gulf, and since Bastien left home *without* one damn credit card or cell phone, we can only hope that the waves are calling him there, too."

"They are," Matthew said firmly. "Tate and Foster were drawn together by my manipulation of air in Missouri. It's going to be the same for the water, fire, and earth kids."

"It better be."

The four of them jumped in guilty surprise as Dr. Stewart soundlessly entered the cottage. Eve studied him as he moved toward them. He looked rough—thin and ashy-skinned. His usually meticulously trimmed goatee was scraggly and his linen pants and flowered button-down shirt were stained and wrinkled.

It had been two days since he'd last drained crystal power from her, but it looked like he hadn't had a fix in weeks.

He's getting worse . . . so much worse, she thought.

"Father!" Eve rose gracefully and hurried to his side. "I was just going to come to you and tell you the wonderful news. Our Matthew found Tate Taylor's grandfather!"

The mean, haunted look in Stewart's gaze softened slightly. "Matthew, well done my boy, well done. Where is he, and are Tate and Foster with him?"

"Linus Bowen is in Galveston, Texas, which is a happy coincidence! It's going to be like killing two birds with one stone." Matthew beamed under his father's rarely given praise.

Stewart dismissed Matthew with barely a nod and turned to Eve. "Which means Tate and Foster aren't in Galveston."

"Father, it means we're not sure about Tate and Foster, but we are sure about Charlotte and Bastien," Eve said.

"Charlotte? The kid I altered's name is *Charlie*. Charlie Davis. You have the wrong teenager."

"Charlotte used to be Charlie. She's transitioning from male to female and hasn't used her birth name for years, remember? Or are you having memory problems?" Mark said. Eve tried to catch his eye—tried to tell Mark with a look that now was not the time to test Father—but her brother had locked his gaze with his father's and didn't even glance her way.

"No, Mark. I did not remember. And why? Not because I'm having memory problems as you call it, but because his or her gender preference is irrelevant. His, her, or *its* bond with water is all that should be important to me or to you."

Mark had been sitting beside Luke. Slowly, resolutely, he stood—squared his broad shoulders—and faced Rick Stewart.

"They're kids," Mark spoke quietly, but there was no denying the anger that colored his voice. "Barely eighteen. Not even adults yet. But we're tracking them and setting traps to draw them out like they're animals. For what, Father? For the *chance* that *maybe* you can create an antidote to my hallucinations, Matthew's disappearing body, Luke's burnout, and Eve's crystal tumors?"

Eyes glittering with rage, Stewart opened his mouth to retort. Eve sucked in a shocked breath as Mark barreled on, speaking over his brilliant, mad, and quite dangerous father.

"We caused that disaster in Missouri. *We* did! It's because of us that Tate

Taylor's parents and a lot of innocent people are dead. It's because of us Tate and Foster's worlds have been ripped apart, and before we tear up anyone else's world—cause anyone else's death—I want you to tell me how the *possibility* of helping the four of us is worth that, especially to you."

"What do you mean by *especially to me?*"

"Father, I think what Mark means—" Eve began, but Mark cut her off.

"No, Eve. This time I'm going to speak for myself."

"Hey, just so you know, Mark is speaking for *himself,* and only himself," Luke said, after he took a long swig of beer. "I'm cool with there just being a chance that those kids can help us."

"At the price of people's lives?" Mark asked Luke.

Luke shrugged. "I don't know them. Why should it matter to me?"

Mark looked from Luke to Matthew. "What about you?"

"Hey, all I did was call that wall cloud to Missouri. How was I to know air was so pissed it caused a tornado—and then those two kids threw the damn thing and it splintered? As far as I'm concerned, *they're* responsible for those deaths, not me. Not us."

"But it could happen again. I'm calling waves and altering currents and tides. I'm creating the perfect situation for a major hurricane. Charlotte and Bastien are going to be drawn to this change in water weather, and they could affect it like Tate and Foster did air. Those kids have no experience and no understanding of what's happening. People could die. A lot of people," Mark said.

"And I could disappear forever someday if we don't bring Tate and Foster here," Matthew said, turning back to his computer. "I'm with Luke. I'm not going to try to hurt a bunch of people, but if people get hurt, or even killed, because we're trying to save ourselves—so be it. They're strangers. We're not."

Mark faced Eve, obviously waiting for her input, which usually balanced whatever nonsense Matthew and Luke spouted.

"Leave Eve out of it." Stewart's voice was like death. "And I'll answer your question, even though you didn't answer mine."

"Oh, I'll answer yours. When I asked why this is all worth it, especially to you, I meant that you don't seem to care much about anything anymore except Eve's crystals. Are you even up to the work you'll have to do if we wrench

these kids from their lives and imprison them here, with us, on this goddamned island jail?"

Eve took a step away from Father and reached down deep, invoking her element. She did as Mark recommended—as she had been doing for the past couple of weeks. Eve didn't call what Father would want to syphon from her. Eve called what *she* needed to ground herself, to think clearly and powerfully. *Come, calming, cooling rose quartz. Take away negativity and reinstate love . . .* When she felt the swell of pain under her right shoulder blade, and the wonderful infilling of sweet, soothing calmness and self-love, Eve moved quietly back to her father's side, willing quartz's essence to share itself, just a little, with him as her father squared off with her favorite brother.

Eve saw Stewart's shoulders relax an almost imperceptible amount, and the reasonable tone in his voice had her feeling waves of relief.

"I'll ignore that you slandered your sister. You're not yourself, Son. Your brothers would tell you that if you let them. You want assurance that the new children—the young pairs I've bonded with the elements—are going to help me create an antidote to your Frill?" Stewart chuckled low. "There is no such assurance because there is no such antidote. I never intended to create one. But the children . . . they are your salvation. They are all of our salvation."

"As usual, you're not making any sense," Mark said.

"As usual, you're not smart enough to keep up with me," Stewart flung at him. "Listen with your mind, like a man. Not with your emotions, like a child. I created the new elementals in pairs. They are meant to work as a team—to control their element together. Because of how I fashioned them, I know they won't have the same problems you four do. They *share* their powers. Now, imagine this—the water pair comes here and meets their benevolent Uncle Mark. You teach them how to call their element, and in return every time they manipulate water, they stabilize you, much like they do for each other. The malevolent Frill fade back into the abyss of your imagination from which they came. But you're stronger than the two kids, older than them—supposedly wiser than them. You will control the element *through* them, and there will be nothing they can do about it."

Eve watched Mark blink in confused surprise. "Wait, that's all there is to it?"

"No, of course that's not all there is to it," Stewart said. "Once you're stabilized, there is nothing stopping you from using your water bond. Think of it, Mark. With the help of those teenagers stabilizing you, water could transform the Mojave Desert into a fertile basin. Or let's say a farmer in Oklahoma needs rain so his alfalfa crop won't fail—he calls us and water comes to his rescue." Stewart's eyes were bright, almost feverish when he turned his gaze to Luke and Matthew. "Napa Valley's grapes are threatened by a frost? No problem. Fire works with air and the harvest is saved."

"What's in it for you?" Mark said.

"My children don't go mad," Stewart said.

Mark's gaze didn't falter as he repeated the question. "What's in it for *you?*"

Stewart's sigh was long-suffering. "Much of the same thing that's in it for you. It's only right that people pay for our services. We are, after all, saving them."

"And if they don't want to pay and instead arrest us and perform those experiments on us you've been insisting we need to hide from for all these years?" Mark pressed.

"Oh, well, after we have complete control of the elements, *without* the threat of the four of you going mad, we will have complete control of the world's weather. Trying to take any action against us would prove to be as unwise as it is dangerous. You know, Mark, natural disasters can happen anywhere."

Eve stared from Mark to their father. Her stomach felt sick. *Mark tried to tell me. Tried to get me to see how cruel and power-hungry Father has become, and he was right. I think Father is mad.*

But that didn't change the fact that his idea was brilliant and that Eve could imagine all sorts of possibilities for their future—opulent, wonderful possibilities filled with freedom.

Eve moved from Father's side to Mark. She touched her brother's arm gently. "Hey, you'll have what you've always wanted."

"No, I won't. I'll be a pawn. Like we all are now," Mark said.

"No, you won't." Eve met her father's gaze. "Tell him, Father. Tell him what he'll have."

Rick Stewart's expression went from manic to slyly manipulative. He smiled smoothly. "With the money the world will be forced to pay us, you can buy your yacht and live on the ocean like you've dreamed since you were a little boy."

Eve saw Mark's start of surprise. He looked down at her. She smiled and nodded. "See, it's been Father's plan all along for us to have our dreams come true. Luke can live on Hawaii, surrounded by volcanoes."

"Yes, Father! Yes!" Luke exclaimed, downing his beer in one big gulp.

"Matthew can move to Oklahoma City and live directly in Tornado Alley," Eve continued.

"That's more like it!" Matthew said, though he barely looked up from his computer.

"And me. I'm moving to Manitou Springs, Colorado, and buying a mansion on the side of Pike's Peak. It'll have an Olympic-sized freshwater pool so you can be comfortable whenever you visit," Eve finished happily.

"That's a great pipe dream," Mark said. "But how are we going to scatter and still control the weather?"

"Oh, that's simple," Stewart said. "The four of you can go anywhere you want, *after* you bring the eight new elementals here to me. They stay. You go. Everyone wins."

"Everyone? What about the kids? I don't think they're going to believe it's a win for them," Mark said.

"Father will fix up the island," Eve said quickly. "They're kids, Mark. They're going to love living on a private island with their own cottages and— no bedtimes—no curfews—no rules."

"Well, no rules except that they have to remain here, for their safety, and they must do a little weather tweaking when we need them to," Stewart finished for her. "So, is that answer enough to your question, Son?"

Mark's gaze grabbed and held Eve's. She knew what he was searching for in her eyes. He wanted to see that she was still on his side and willing to stand up to Father with him, but she couldn't, *wouldn't* give him what he needed. Not when her freedom was so close.

"Everything is going to be okay, Mark. I promise," Eve told him.

Mark blew out a long, sad breath and said, "For us, maybe. But for those eight kids and the rest of the world?" He shook his head and pushed past them, slamming the cottage door behind him.

When Eve started to go after him, Stewart snagged her wrist. "Let him go. You know he's always been soft. You're going to have to watch him, Eve." Then Stewart's hard gaze included Matthew and Luke. "You're all going to have to watch him. Or he'll spoil this for all of us—for all of you."

"We understand, Father," Luke said. "We'll watch him."

"Yeah, he won't mess this up for us," Matthew said.

"Eve?" Stewart turned to her.

"Father, you know I'll always take care of Mark."

"Yes, but taking care of him and being sure he doesn't self-destruct and take all of us down with him are two very different things," Stewart said.

"Like I told Mark, everything is going to be okay. Now, I'm going to do as you asked and go to him and be sure he isn't self-destructing." Eve began to walk past Stewart, but he didn't release her wrist.

"I'll walk a little with you, my Nubian princess."

Eve looked into her father's eyes and saw there his insatiable need. "Yes, Father," she answered obediently, allowing him to lead her from the cottage and away from Luke and Matthew and Mark so that he could drain the crystal she had just conjured and get his fix.

Someday I will be free of Father, and if that means eight teenagers must take our places here—then so be it.

21

CHARLOTTE

Charlotte could barely contain her excitement. Today, in her Intro to Marine Ecology class, she was going to be able to get out on the Gulf for the first time since she'd arrived at the Texas A&M's campus. She studied herself carefully—oh, so carefully—in the full-length mirror in her dorm room.

Her hair was good tied neatly back in a high ponytail and woven through the rear opening of her Wildfang cap that declared FEMINIST on the brim. Her makeup was perfect—not too much, but also enough to cover her imperfections and bring out her long, thick eyelashes. She was wearing a long-sleeved swim shirt over her sports bra. The fit was almost as flattering as the turquoise color that reflected her eyes so well.

The class had been told to wear swim shirts and swimsuit bottoms. They'd be on and in the water all day. But Charlotte couldn't make herself wear a bikini bottom. All day. In front of strangers. So, she'd opted for one of the oversized swim shirts she always wore and a tasteful pair of pink boy shorts. Still, she studied herself—front, back, side. And had to stifle the urge to cut class.

"No, you will not cut class, especially a class that is held on the ocean!" Charlotte spoke sternly to herself in the mirror. Then she read aloud from the postcard Grandma Myrtie had sent her. Charlotte had taped it to her mirror so she would see it every single day. It was her grandma's favorite quote by the timeless Eleanor Roosevelt:

". . . the purpose of life is to live it, to taste experience to the utmost, to reach out eagerly and without fear for newer and richer experience."

Charlotte kissed her fingertips and then pressed them to the postcard. "Thank you, Grandma Myrtie. That is exactly what I'm going to do."

Her phone alarm bleeped, signaling she was out of time, and she grabbed her backpack and sunglasses and hurried from the private apartment her grandma had secured for her on campus. It was a fantastic luxury, especially as her apartment looked directly out on the Gulf. Charlotte was still trying to figure out how to show Grandma Myrtie her appreciation for her love and belief and support—financial and emotional—and she'd pretty much decided that she was going to have to discover a new species of marine life and insist it be called a Myrtie!

Charlotte giggled musically at the thought as she followed the directions in her syllabus. A half-hour walk down the beach would take her to a dock where her professor and a marine biologist from the Turtle Island Restoration Network would be waiting for their class to join them. Today's mission—that Charlotte could hardly wait to embark upon—was to count, study, and document the remains of Kemp's ridley turtle and loggerhead sea turtle nests. And, hopefully, to get a glimpse of some actual sea turtles while they were at it.

Charlotte took off her swim shoes and walked into the waterline, loving how the warm waves crashed against her calves and swirled sand around her toes. She squinted, staring out at the Gulf, and her happy expression shifted to a frown.

The waves were insane! Not that that bothered Charlotte. She *adored* the passionate, wild, untamed waves! She ached to be out there with them—free, without one single care. But most people weren't like her about the ocean, or at least about heavy waves on the ocean.

Charlotte picked up her pace, almost jogging, until she got within sight of the dock, where she saw a triangular-shaped red flag snapping in the gusting wind.

"Well, shoot!" A red flag was a warning. It meant that the surf is high and the currents are dangerous—too dangerous to take a small boat out on.

She walked the rest of the way to the dock slowly, already knowing what she'd find when she got there, and sure enough, tacked to the cork notice board at the entrance to the dock was a Sharpie-written note that stated: INTRO TO MARINE ECO'S TURTLE STUDY TRIP HAS BEEN POSTPONED—MEET IN CLASSROOM 128 AT 0900.

Charlotte sighed and glanced at the pretty, waterproof watch Grandma Myrtie had given her last Christmas. It was only 0730. She was early. Very early. "Well, that's a good thing," she told herself as she left the empty dock and began to wander along the beach. "Gives me time to relax before class."

Relax?

Charlotte's frown changed to a slow smile. She had a towel and a change of clothes in her backpack. And she had plenty of time to get to class. There was no reason why she couldn't swim a few laps, change, and still make it to class on time.

Feeling lighter just at the thought of being surrounded by water, Charlotte hurried down the beach to a little cove-like indention that was littered with big, black rocks. She tucked her backpack behind one of them and skipped into the water, wading quickly out to where the waves were surging around her waist.

Charlotte drew a deep breath of damp, salty air into her lungs, and let it slowly out. Then she closed her eyes and listened.

She didn't have to wait long, which surprised her. Usually she had to spend most of the day in the water before she began to hear them, but this day—*this* magical, windy, wavy day—Charlotte heard them right away.

Within the waves, lifting from deep under the water, the singing voices drifted to her.

The first time Charlotte had heard them she'd been six. She'd told her parents that she didn't want to be called Charles or Charlie anymore because she wasn't going to cut her hair ever again. Instead, she wanted it to be long like Mother's. And she also wanted to wear pink bows in it and a matching pink dress.

At first her father had laughed, and six-year-old Charlotte had laughed with him, not understanding he was laughing *at* her, not *with* her.

Her mother hadn't laughed, but that was no surprise. Caroline Marie Meriwether Davis only laughed when she was at her club with the other members of the United Daughters of the Confederacy—and then only after her second very dry vodka martini.

Charlotte's mother had tried to shut her daughter up by slapping the sass out of her mouth.

It hadn't worked.

But that day Charlotte had run to the beach and cried herself to sleep. She'd awakened to find half of her body being gently held by the encroaching tide and the sound of beautiful, harmonizing women's voices filling her ears.

She'd stayed there, sitting half in, half out of the water, listening to the ocean's orchestra for the rest of the day.

They'd found her at sunset. Charlotte had tried to tell her parents and the rescue team that she hadn't heard anyone calling her because she'd been listening to the mermaids singing under the water.

They all said she was lying because no one heard the singing except Charlotte. No one ever heard the singing except Charlotte.

And now the mermaid chorus lifted alluringly from the turbulent waves, reflecting the passion that filled the ocean as it entered hurricane season.

Eyes still closed, Charlotte began humming with the ethereal voices, trying to catch words as she always did—and as always, she could hear melodies, but when she tried to isolate voices and words, they slid away from her like waves returning to the ocean.

"Bastien, dude! I'm bailing! It's a bomb. No way I can handle that!"

The rough male voice intruded, first fragmenting and then destroying the mermaid voices. Annoyed, Charlotte opened her eyes to see a young guy trudging to shore not far from her. Tethered to his wrist was a long surfboard that bobbed along behind him. He wasn't paying any attention to Charlotte. All of his attention was focused out on the water.

Charlotte followed his gaze to see that an enormous wave had formed and was growing, gaining momentum and height, as it roared toward shore. From the center of that wave, in the pretty, curling part that Charlotte thought looked like a lovely water tunnel, a surfer shot into view. He was balancing like a dancer, making it look effortless. His dark hair was blowing behind him. He was tall and his muscular chest glistened with water and sweat—and he was grinning as if he was having the best time in his life.

"Whoo-hoo! It's a double overhead, dude! Bastien, you're killing it!" The second guy had made it to the beach and was shouting at the surfer through cupped hands.

Charlotte didn't even glance at him. She couldn't take her eyes from the surfer. He kept riding and riding the huge wave as it got closer and closer to shore. She could see his eyes now, and was shocked by their brilliant turquoise color—a color that reminded her strangely of her own.

The wave kept coming and coming . . . until finally the surfer gracefully stepped off his board and onto the beach as his friend clapped and hooted for him. The surfer turned then, and bowed to the ocean, as if he was thanking it for the ride.

When he straightened he turned, and his eyes met Charlotte's.

She saw him hesitate and even stumble for a second as another wave smacked against him, but he righted himself quickly and nodded to her in a very Southern, very gentlemanly way—something Grandma Myrtie would definitely have approved of.

"Hello, *cher*."

His voice was deep and rich. And Charlotte thought his accent was the sexiest thing she'd ever heard.

"Good mornin'," Charlotte spoke automatically.

"Aren't you sweet. *Douces comme du miel*. I'm Bastien. And this here's my *podna*, Dickie."

Charlotte almost blurted her name. Part of her wanted to tell him her name, phone number, Social Security number, *and* her address. Anything and everything she could tell him so that he'd call her and talk to her more in that gorgeous voice. But she couldn't tell him *everything*. He wouldn't want to hear her *everything*, and because of that she would tell him nothing.

But he was looking at her. Really *looking* from her long, bare legs to her boy shorts, to the swim shirt that was soaked and painted to her skin. He wasn't exactly leering, but his eyes were intense and they reflected his very obvious interest, which sent an all too familiar shiver of fear down Charlotte's spine.

She schooled her face into what her mother would call "acceptable politeness, but not an invitation" and in her best Southern belle accent said, "I am pleased to make your acquaintance, Bastien. Have a lovely day."

As the very sexy, very handsome Bastien opened his mouth to say more, Charlotte gave him a dismissive wave, quickly turned her back on him, retrieved her backpack, and without one glance over her shoulder she hurried away from him, retracing her steps down the beach.

Maybe someday . . . Charlotte thought wistfully. *Maybe someday I can talk to a handsome young man like Bastien without being afraid, but today is not that day* . . .

Bastien

"Didn't know all we had to do was get you in front of a beautiful piece to get the words to roll right out of ya." Dickie clapped his arm around Bastien's shoulders. "What'd you say back there, anyway?"

Bastien shrugged away from the brotherly embrace. That young woman hadn't been some *piece*. She was an *ange*. An angel. Her hair and the way the salt-licked breeze had twirled it around her head had been her halo. And those arms, long and delicate and goose-down white, would at any moment reveal the wings he knew were tucked up inside her, waiting to lift her from this cruel world. She'd landed right in front of him and he'd talked to her in the only way he knew how.

"Douces comme du miel." Dickie's attempt at Bastien's line tumbled around his mouth and came out battered and broken. "I'll have to remember that one and use it sometime. You probably just rake 'em in with that accent and all that foreign-sounding shit. Why the fuck couldn't I have grown up in Arcada?"

"Acadiana," Bastien corrected, promising himself that this would be the last time he did so without using his fists. Dickie was all right, once you got used to the dick part of his personality. Unfortunately, Bastien had discovered, this was 99.9 percent of ol' Dickster, but he'd decided that having the boss's little brother mad at him all the time wasn't how he wanted to live this part of his life, however brief it was before he got too restless and the sea called him away.

"Yeah, Acadiana. What'd I say?"

Bastien ran his tongue along his teeth to keep from grinding them into paste. How many times did he have to explain it to this boy? His sister had even given him an article about the origin of the Cajun people and the parishes making up the Acadiana region, but nothing stuck.

"You gonna tell me what it means, *douces comme—*"

"*Couillon,*" Bastien grumbled, unwilling to listen to Dickie butcher his language again.

"Say, what?"

"Sweet as honey."

"Damn, that's slick."

Slick was right. Slick like oil. Slick like sludge. Slick like all the things dumped and leaked into the great big abyss named ocean, coating and suffocating and poisoning until there's nothing left—only silence, only stillness.

Board under his arm, Bastien charged back to the sea. He waded out until the rough waves licked his bare chest and drowned out Dickie's shouts and questions. He needed to see them, his ocean creatures, to feel them beneath and all around him to remind him of who he was.

He was not the slick before the silence.

That had been his father.

That had been the way the rich Mr. Tibadeau had lured young women into his marital bed. He'd wrap them in satiny words and silky promises. Who cared if he got caught?

Money made everything go away.

Everything except Bastien's mother.

Money kept her glued in place with foul liquid in her glass and hate stitched to her lips. But Mr. Tibadeau could hardly notice. He'd sweep in and out, sweet nothings spilling into his wife's outstretched hands. And then, like a dream, like a nightmare, he'd be gone again, returning coated in glitter and smelling of vanilla, of sweetness, of lust and secrets. And the silence would cloak their home in its funeral shroud.

This family is dead.

May they rest in pieces.

Belly pressed against the glowing phoenix, Bastien paddled toward the break and its barreling waves. He gripped the edge of his board and, with surprising ease, punched through the rippling, tourmaline blue, glass-like center of the wave. He took a deep breath and he cut under as another wave surged overhead.

It has to calm if I'm going to see them, he thought, taking a quick inhale before another wave could crash against him. But it didn't come. The ocean mellowed, absorbing the treacherous conditions as if a whole day had passed while Bastien was busy blinking. He sat up, wiggling his toes in the water as his legs draped over the sides of his board.

They would be here soon to ground him, reassure him that although he was of his father, he was *not* his father.

Bastien felt them before he saw them. The water cooled and thickened, but only for a moment as three majestic, shadowy creatures rose from the depths to greet him. They should have scared him, giant beasts surging close to the surface, their huge, whale-like bodies encircling him as he sat alone, on a surfboard, bobbing in the Gulf. It was the beginning of so many shark attack movies, but he could never bring himself to leave. He'd first seen them on one of their family trips to the Gulf, sitting, much like he was now, on a paddleboard atop the ocean while his parents snorkeled around him. He'd asked if they could see them, feel the cold thickness of the water, but they'd laughed and splashed and told him to stop trying to scare them, for the ocean was a vast and frightening place.

But that had been in the before.

Before the slick and the silence.

And Bastien didn't like to linger in the past.

Although, he'd never really understood what they meant about the vastness or the scariness of the sea. As he got older, it became more and more apparent that this was a real thing, thalassophobia, fear of the sea. Dickie had even said that he didn't like to go out too far without a boat. That the ocean was like Jupiter or Saturn, "a whole 'nother planet that we'll never completely explore or understand." It had been the smartest thing that Dickie'd ever said. But if that was the case, if the ocean was like an unexplored planet, then Bastien was Neil Armstrong.

Submerged, he could feel all the slopes and edges, caves and lightless depths, ebbs and flows.

The ocean was not unknown. It was misunderstood.

The water cooled again as another creature appeared and joined its brethren as they continued to circle Bastien.

"Tell me," he dipped his fingers into the water, "how to wash clean of *mon père*." My father.

They were always silent, his creatures, and, for the first time, Bastien wondered if someone out there could hear them.

22

FOSTER

Foster was going to kill the chickens. All of them. Dead. With a groan she rolled onto her belly and covered her head with her pillow. It felt like all she'd done was collapse into bed, close her eyes, take a deep breath, and then it was morning. And she knew it was morning not because of the sun. Oh, no. Foster had blackout curtains to keep that early-rising bastard firmly on the *outside* of the house. She knew it was morning because of the squawking, or crowing, or whatever word described the god-awful noise that had woken her up.

"Fucking chickens," she moaned, tossing her pillow onto the floor and sitting up. With a yawn, she stretched her arms overhead and squinted at the glowing red numbers on her alarm clock. Eight twenty-three. It wasn't *that* early. At least, not now that she'd adjusted her schedule so that she and Sabine could hang out before Sabine went off to class while Finn fed the menagerie, which would be in about thirty minutes.

Foster flipped off her alarm clock before it started blaring at her, and shuffled out her door and around the corner to her bathroom. She squirted a blob of toothpaste onto her toothbrush, weighing whether or not thirty minutes was enough time to get rid of toothpaste mouth. Toothpaste mouth ruined vegan scones, and they were really the best part of Sabine coming over nearly every morning.

No, she wasn't being honest. *Sabine* was the best part of Sabine coming over. She liked their new routine. It pushed her one step closer to feeling like she was truly at home and part of a family. And that's all she wanted. It was simple, really, just wanting to belong. But so much time had passed and so many bad things had happened since she'd truly felt at home on her rooftop or having s'more nights with Cora that Foster had begun to wonder if it had all been an illusion. That maybe she'd made the feeling up. Maybe she'd only convinced herself that she belonged. But all the days at Strawberry Fields with Tate and now Sabine and Finn had brought with them that fuzzy warm rush of comfort and home, like she'd just been on a long trip and was only a few miles away from her front door.

Foster stuck the toothbrush into her mouth.

September was a month of Foster firsts: first best friend, who she refused to call bestie no matter how many times Sabine insisted; first "boyfriend-ish dating guy" type person; first time float flying; first time living without someone over the age of twenty-one; and first time having to possibly save the lives of two people who were also mutant freaks and who had some kind of water ability.

She spit, gargled, and then spit again.

She'd leave that last first until the very final possible moment. Those two wouldn't be eighteen for another two days, and maybe there wouldn't be any freak water event and there would be no reason to go around saving two fellow teenagers. Yep, she'd let it go. Remove it from her mind. Poof. Gone. A problem for Future Foster.

Her stomach grumbled, reminding her that Present Foster couldn't wait half an hour for vegan scones.

She trotted down the hall, peeking into Tate's room before heading downstairs. Sure enough, he was gone. Bed was made and everything neatly in its place like it magically reset itself every morning. If only Foster could get a little bit of that magic. She practically hopped down the stairs, finally feeling energized as the dark of her room slipped off of her like a skin and the sunlight, casting fun house–mirror shapes along the floor and walls, kissed each patch of her bare flesh.

"Eggs," she said with a chipper sort of finality. "I'll make eggs before

Sabine gets here and has a chance to look at me all vegan and disapproving about my life choices." She rushed into the kitchen and grabbed a bowl from the cabinet before stuffing her feet into her tennis shoes. "And this has nothing to do with those chickens who woke me up," she said to whichever deity might be listening. It wasn't spite. It was her stomach.

On her way to the coop Foster paused, flailing her hands, and the bowl, above her head in an attempt to get Tate's attention from across the vast pasture. It was no use. He was out there with those, she cringed, *horses*. Or at least that's what everyone kept calling them. She sighed and continued her short trek to the chickens' living quarters. To Foster, those two mares would always be dinosaurs and the people who rode them would always be crazy.

Foster stopped short of the coop with its pale gray siding, cheery white shutters, and fully fenced-in yard area where the chickens could chicken about without fear of being eaten by some wild animal. It was a perfect playhouse-sized version of the main house, which is exactly what Finn had intended when he'd built it. And it was nice. *Really* nice. Like, nicer than the vast majority of the motels she and Cora had stayed at. But those hadn't been filled with chickens.

"Hi. Hello. Hi," Foster said, bending over and ever so quietly tiptoeing to the small and open front door of the coop. Gingerly, she waved at the hens sitting sleepily in their nesting boxes. "How's it going?" Foster set down the bowl and rubbed her sweaty palms on the butt of her shorts. "So I'm just going to grab this right here maybe." She tentatively reached into the chicken coop.

"Bwak!" The chicken fluttered its wings and seemed to puff to twice its original size.

Foster yanked her hand back before the chicken had the chance to peck her to death. "Sorry, ma'am. Sorry." She tucked her hair behind her ears and crouched into a squat. "It's just that you happen to be sitting on something that I need."

The hen let out a short cluck of protest.

"But, see, that's kind of why you're here—so we can have your eggs. I mean, there's that whole debate about which one came first, the chicken or the egg, but what if neither came first and they both came at the same time and you, being the chicken, were like, *hmm, I guess I should sit on that,* but me, being the human, is telling you that you don't have to. I'll take it for you and . . . sit on it. You know, so you can have a break."

"Are you trying to rationalize to that hen why you're taking her eggs?"

Foster could almost hear Sabine's eyebrow arch sardonically. "No." She picked up the bowl as she rose to her feet. "We were just talking about . . . *things*."

A bee buzzed around one of Sabine's Princess Leia–style buns and she shooed it away with a calm wave of her hand. "Sure you are." Her smooth eyebrow arched even higher, if that was possible.

"So, scones." Foster eyed Sabine's hands, which were empty except for the iPad she clutched against her stomach. "Where are they?"

"The kitchen. I left them in there when I came out here to get you."

Foster's mouth watered. "Are they chocolate chip today? Man, I love it when you make chocolate chip."

"It's starting." Sabine thrust the iPad in Foster's direction. "All morning I've been trying to figure out a better way to tell you, but I guess that's why they say you can't polish a turd."

Foster couldn't force herself to grab the device. She didn't want it to be real. It couldn't be real. Only a few minutes ago she had told herself that she wouldn't think about those other kids, and that there was a chance that everything would be okay—that Doctor Rick, the Fucktastic Four, the entire outside world would leave her and her new family alone.

Sabine moved next to Foster, pressing the triangular button glaring up at them from the darkening screen. Foster stared speechless at the purples and reds and oranges and yellows swirling on the screen.

"Hey, Sabine!" Tate pecked Foster on the cheek before giving Sabine a friendly hug. "Finn's out feeding, but said it was important I—"

"It's happening." Foster wiped a stray tear from her cheek before Tate or Sabine saw that it had fallen. "Heading for Texas," she passed the iPad from Sabine to Tate who was back by her side. "Galveston if I read the map correctly."

"No, no, that can't be right." Tate stretched his fingers across the screen, zooming in.

"Foster's right," Sabine said. "It's not very big, actually it's the opposite—

small, powerful, deadly, and completely focused on its trajectory. It's heading straight for Galveston."

"Foster," Tate's voice was almost a whisper, and he took a deep inhale before continuing. "There's, uh," the way he avoided her gaze made her heart feel like a trapped lightning bug. It knocked wildly against the confines of her chest, only slowing as the realization set in.

"There's something I need to tell you."

There was no place to fly to.

"Something I should have told you . . ."

Her light dimmed then, the way the bug would have after it lost all hope.

"Well, I should never have kept it from you."

Dimming. Dimming. Dimming.

"I shouldn't have lied."

It went out.

23

EVE

"There he is." Eve spoke under her breath as the old man entered the Corner Café. Matthew, Mark, Luke, and Eve had chosen a booth that gave them a clear line of sight to the front door of the little café. The newspaper clipping hadn't specified at what time old man Bowen had breakfast every day, so the four of them had been there since the café opened at six a.m. At first they'd hung out in the parking lot trying not to look conspicuous, and then at about seven-thirty Eve had had enough and they'd gone inside. Happily, they hadn't had to wait long because at eight o'clock sharp, Bowen had entered the café with a book under his arm and an endearing smile on his face.

Eve leaned in and lowered her voice. "Okay, eat slowly. We need to time this so that we leave when the waitress brings him his check. That way we'll be out in the rental car when the old man exits—we follow him."

"Hey, we got it, sis," Luke said, giving her a sassy wink. She sighed. *Of course Luke's in a good mood. He's eating. He's always in a good mood when there's food or fire involved.*

"Yeah, don't worry. This will be a lot easier than dealing with rogue kids and their elements," Matthew said.

"He's an old man," Mark said. "Let's be sure that we keep that in mind and be careful with him."

The four of them ate slowly while they watched Grandpa Bowen's daily café ritual.

After a few minutes Luke snorted. "Mark, your frail old guy is wolfing down three eggs, a rib eye, fruit bowl, short stack of pancakes, and an entire pot of coffee—extra cream and sugar—while he flirts with the waitresses, who seem to like it. I'm not thinking we need to be very careful with him."

"He's seventy-nine. That's old whether he's in good shape or not. Don't be an ass, Luke. We're not here to hurt him. We're only here to get the water kids and find out where Tate and Foster are," Mark said.

"It's okay," Eve said softly, holding the gaze of each of her brothers, one at a time. She was the only mother the boys remembered, and she took full advantage of the soft spot they had for her. "We're going to talk to Mr. Bowen. *Talk.* We aren't criminals. We aren't going to do anything wrong. Can we all please remember that it's for the best that we find Tate and Foster, as well as Charlotte and Bastien. They could hurt themselves and others. That was already proven in Missouri. Once the old man understands that, everything will fall into place."

Mark snorted again, but didn't say anything.

Linus Bowen didn't rush through his breakfast, but he didn't dawdle, either. Less than forty-five minutes had passed when Eve told her brothers, "He just finished the last pancake. Time to pay and get to the car." Then she put enough cash for a decent tip on the bill, and the four of them nonchalantly left the café and waited in their nondescript rental SUV for Bowen to exit.

"Is the old guy really getting into that Miata convertible?" Luke said, craning his neck around so he could watch Bowen.

"Looks like it," Matthew said. "Old dude's got style."

"All right. Here we go," Eve told Mark, who was driving. "Keep him in view, but hang back. He wasn't hard to find by accident. He obviously values his privacy."

Mark nodded and pulled out of the parking lot, following the quick little Miata. And then they drove for almost an hour as the Miata made its way from Galveston Island to the eastern part of the Bolivar Peninsula.

"Good thing traffic is fairly steady each way. I don't like that we're on this one road following this one car," Mark grumbled.

"Mark, some rain would help," Eve said. "Just a little. Just enough to obscure visibility. Matthew, some low-hanging clouds would help with that, too."

Mark nodded silently again and Eve watched his expression flatten, like his mind was suddenly elsewhere, and then a light rain began—a rain that slanted directly across the highway, almost like the Gulf had begun spitting at them. Moments later clouds started to billow overhead. Eve heard Matthew whispering to himself, and the billowing clouds lowered and expanded, changing to fog.

The lights in the SUV came on automatically as they slowed and the Miata put on a right turn signal.

"There!" Eve pointed, though all of them were already watching the sports car. "He's turning down that little side road. There's only one house down there. See! That big yellow one on stilts. He just pulled the car into the garage."

"I'm going to keep going down the highway for a few minutes to give him a chance to get inside and relax," Mark said.

"Smart," Eve smiled encouragingly at her favorite brother. "And he won't think that we followed him."

Mark nodded silently again. Eve suppressed a sigh. He'd been withdrawn on the jet to Galveston, and silent last night at the hotel. This morning he was barely communicating. Was it just because invoking water was wearing on him, or was there so, so much more to it than that?

"Okay, I'm turning around. That'll give him about half an hour to get settled," Mark said.

"Perfect," Eve said.

"Should we send the fog and rain away now?" Matthew asked from the backseat.

"No," Mark answered before Eve could respond. "If we need to force Bowen to come with us, it's better that we have some cover."

"Hey," Eve touched his arm gently. "We're not here to kidnap anyone."

"Okay, Eve, answer me this." Mark studied the road as he spoke in clipped sentences. "What if he *won't* cooperate? What if Tate's warned the old man and he says he doesn't know anything or he refuses to help us? Are we just going to shake his hand and walk away?"

Eve felt herself harden like the crystals she had begun regularly summoning to her. "We're not going to hurt him, but we need information and if that old man has it, we're going to get it from him."

"Which means the fog and rain stay," Mark said.

Eve bit her lip, but didn't say anything more. They retraced their way to old man Bowen's secluded house in silence.

The small, single-lane blacktop that led from the highway to Bowen's property was like the house and the grounds—well lived in and well cared for. They followed the blacktop, which led to a tall privacy fence and an imposing iron gate.

Mark stopped the SUV in front of the gate and turned to Eve. "Now what?"

Eve gave him an exasperated look. "There's an intercom. Press the button. I'll do the talking."

Mark grunted and pressed the button. A tinny voice blasted through the little speaker. "Hello!"

"Hello, Mr. Bowen?" Eve said, leaning over Mark so that she could speak into the console.

"What can I do you for?"

"Mr. Bowen, we're from the FBI and we'd like to speak with you about your grandson, Tate Taylor."

"My grandson is dead." The old man's voice turned to gravel.

"Yes, sir. We have questions about his death," Eve said.

Bowen's answer was a buzzing sound and the gate swinging open.

The house was nice, Eve decided. Unusual, with lots of art—mostly charcoal drawings of gigantic, shaggy dogs like the one that was shadowing Bowen and glaring at them with distrustful yellow eyes. And the location was better than Eve could have hoped for. The old man had already told them that he owned a two-hundred-acre parcel, and he was the only inhabitant. *Perfect.*

"Now, are you sure none of you would like some pie to go with that coffee? I have cherry and apple—just brought them fresh from my favorite café. Only take a sec to heat up. I like to be sure our law enforcement folks are fed and watered," said Bowen.

"No, sir. This is perfect," Eve said. After they'd produced (fake) identification the old man had welcomed them into his home and promptly poured them each a cup of freshly brewed coffee. Eve had tried not to be too obvious, but the books that were scattered around the coffee table and corner desk in the living room already had her curiosity buzzing.

"Looks like you enjoy science," Matthew said, pointing at a thick textbook on human genetics that rested in the center of the coffee table.

"Taught high school biology for more years than I want to admit," said Bowen. "I like to keep my mind sharp, so I keep studying. You know, we stop learning—we die." He motioned to the huge wolfhound at his side and muttered, "Lie down, Bugsy old girl. They aren't gonna bite you, and if they do feel free to bite 'em back." Then, with his coffee mug that said DOGS—BECAUSE PEOPLE SUCK in his hand, he sat in the reclining chair across from the couch where Eve, Matthew, Mark, and Luke were sitting. "So, what information do you need about my Tate?"

"Well, sir," Eve began, speaking earnestly and looking directly into Bowen's surprisingly clear blue eyes. "We have reason to believe that your grandson might still be alive."

Bowen jerked like someone had slapped him. "Why would you say something like that?"

"Because we found evidence that there could have been a mix-up at the dentist's office. The records that were used to identify Tate's body might have been inaccurate," Eve said.

"Sounds like a bunch of hogwash to me!" Bowen said.

"Mr. Bowen, there's something else. At the football field we found the body of a woman who has been the ringleader in a conspiracy theory involving weather and teenagers. She's the widow of a famous geneticist—Dr. Rick Stewart. With your background in the sciences you might have heard of him. He died in a tragic boating accident five years ago," Eve explained.

"Nope, nope. Can't say that I've heard of him. What's all that nonsense have to do with my Tate?"

"Well, it seems this woman, Cora Stewart, has involved her adopted daughter, Foster, in her conspiracy theory. Both of them were seen at the football game before the tornadoes struck. Cora's body has been positively identified, but Foster was spotted afterward. She was driving a stolen truck and she had a passenger who she might have forced to go with her. We believe that passenger was Tate."

Bowen didn't say anything for several long moments. He simply studied Eve. Still silent, he turned his wise gaze to Matthew, Mark, and Luke. Then he shook his head, put his coffee cup on the end table beside his well-worn recliner, and stood.

When he spoke his words were sharp, cut off by anger and grief. "I buried Tate beside his parents—my daughter, my only child, my son-in-law, and my beautiful wife. They're *dead*. And that's the end of it. Now I'm going to have to ask you to leave my home." The big dog stirred, growling deep in her wide chest.

The four of them stood, too.

"Sir, we do apologize and know that this is a difficult subject. We are extremely sorry for your loss. But we need to be very clear. You are saying that you have not heard from Tate. At all?" Eve said.

"Was I not clear enough when I said I'd buried the boy beside his mama and daddy?"

"Yes, sir. You were," Mark spoke up. He took a card from his pocket and held it out to Bowen. When the old man didn't take it, Mark placed it on the coffee table. "But if you think of anything—anything at all you'd like to talk with us about—don't hesitate to call. We won't judge you. And you won't be in any trouble."

"My partner is correct, Mr. Bowen," Eve said. "You aren't in any trouble. Nor would Tate be if he came to us. Actually, if Tate is alive and somehow mixed up with this Foster girl, well, sir, I'm sorry to say that he's in trouble right now. Big trouble."

"I like to be helpful to you law enforcement types *unless* you're up to tomfoolery. Well, young woman, I believe you and your *partners* are up to some serious tomfoolery. And this time I'm not asking. Leave my property. Now." The big dog stood, her back easily reaching Bowen's hip. Her yellow eyes were trained on the four interlopers as her growl deepened.

"Thank you for your time, Mr. Bowen," Eve said as the four of them filed from the living room and headed to the entry foyer. Eve was directly beside an ancient-looking rotary dial phone when it began to ring. She'd been watching Bowen as he murmured in low tones to the dog, so she saw the fear and guilt that flashed across his face when the phone rang. Without looking at the old man she lifted the phone and didn't say a word.

"G-pa! I'm so glad you're home. Okay, I finally told Foster that we've been talking and she's totally freaked. So, she's here with me now. Would you please tell her everything's okay?"

Eve looked up to see Linus Bowen standing directly in front of her. Her smile was feline as she said, "Oh, hello, Tate. This is Eve. I'm sure you know who I am."

"Tate!" Bowen shouted and lunged forward, trying to grab the receiver from her, but Matthew and Luke rushed him, knocking him to the ground and wrestling roughly with him, pinning his arms behind his back as the giant dog went into high gear, barking and growling menacingly while she slowly approached them.

"Bowen! Tell your dog to back down if you ever want to talk to your grandson again!" Eve snapped at him.

"G-pa! G-pa!" Tate's panicked voice echoed through the phone.

"Bugs, down!" Bowen commanded. The dog obeyed, hitting the ground where she stood, but she kept her yellow-eyed gaze on Matthew and Luke, and her growl was a rolling symphony of anger.

Eve smiled. "That's better." She spoke in the phone again. "Tate, your grandpa is right here, but—"

"This is Foster. Let Tate's grandpa go."

Eve's smile widened. "Foster! How good to hear your voice!"

"Cut the crap, Eve. What do you want?"

"Why, only you and Tate. That's all."

"Don't come here!" Bowen shouted as he began to stand up.

"Shut him up," Eve snapped. Matthew and Luke knocked the old man off his feet again and dragged him into the kitchen.

"Eve! Let Tate's grandpa go, and Tate and I will meet you wherever you want."

"No. That's not how we're playing this. Mark, Matthew, Luke, and I are going to stay here—at Tate's grandpa's home—and keep an eye on him. So sad he's way out here by himself on this lonely peninsula, isn't it? It's simply not safe. So, we'll be here. Alone with the old man. Until you and Tate arrive. Oh, and the sooner the better. I get the idea Mr. Bowen doesn't like visitors. Good-bye, Foster. See you soon."

Eve hung up.

24
TATE

"Don't worry!" Sabine hugged Tate and then Foster. "Finn and I will take care of everything while you're gone. Just get on that plane and save Tate's g-pa."

"Remember our plan B," Foster spoke low and quickly as she and Tate backed toward the security line at PDX airport. "If you don't hear from us by this time next week—"

"Take the stuff from the Batcave to the FBI and tell them everything we've figured out. We know—we know," Finn said.

"No, it's not going to come to that," Sabine said sternly. "You'll be back to our Fortress of Sauvietude soon. With G-pa. Don't get all dark and twisted and negative on me. Again."

"We'll be back. With my g-pa. I believe it, and so does Foster," Tate said. But he didn't take Foster's hand. Actually, he hadn't said much *to* her *or* touched her since he'd told her about G-pa. Then they'd all rushed to the pay phone, and . . .

Tate shuddered, remembering Eve's hard, cold voice and G-pa's panicked shouts. And after Foster had let loose a stream of curses that had even impressed Finn, whose father was a Marine, she'd hardly spoken to him.

They moved quickly through the security line with their pristine fake IDs, and hurried to their gate. Tate and Foster paused to check the flight on the monitor: Southwest Airlines red-eye flight 255 to Houston's George Bush International was departing on time at 12:10 a.m.—arriving at 6:20 a.m. Texas time—and it was now boarding.

"This is going to be perfect," Tate talked at Foster as if they were actually conversing. "We'll get a rental and be on the highway by seven. It takes about an hour and a half to get to G-pa's place on the Bolivar Peninsula. G-pa is practically free already."

Foster didn't speak. Instead she picked up the pace and they almost jogged to the gate. Tate was silently thanking the elusive airline gods for still having seats on this late-night flight. When they arrived at the gate, the Southwest agent was announcing that the flight was open seating and open boarding, and they shuffled onto the plane with the rest of the half-asleep sheep.

"No." Foster spoke suddenly as Tate continued to move toward the back of the plane.

He looked over his shoulder at her. "Sorry? Did you say something?"

"I said no. I won't sit in the back of a plane. Right here is fine." She slid into the window seat she'd stopped beside, which was four rows back from the front of the plane, and the only seat that had the companion on the aisle open.

"Oh, okay. No problem." He took the seat beside her, happy that she'd at least made room for him.

To Tate it seemed like only a few minutes had passed—the plane was definitely not full—when the flight attendant was making the announcement that the cabin door was closed and all electronic devices needed to be powered off.

"We have a lot of room on this flight, I mean, imagine that! Only us crazies want to fly toward a hurricane warning in the middle of the night. So odd," the attendant said sarcastically to a smattering of nervous laughter in the cabin. "Once we're in the air and the captain has turned off the 'fasten seat belt' light, feel free to spread out and move around. Make yourselves comfortable and get some sleep. Although when we get close to Houston prepare for a very bumpy descent!"

The plane began taxiing and Foster sighed. She was staring at the boring in-flight magazine and picking her fingernails.

"Hey, are you okay?" he asked.

She didn't look at him. "No. I hate flying. Actually, hate isn't a strong enough word. I loathe it. Despise it. I would rather try to corral those giant evil monster dinosaur horses and get stomped to death than fly."

"You think our horses are evil monsters?"

She did look at him then and he saw a world of misery in her emerald eyes. "They're a lot smarter than we think. Do you realize how much they talk? Clearly, they're planning something. Maybe a Percheron revolt."

"But you'd rather deal with that than fly?"

"Exactly."

"That's why you won't sit in the back of the plane?"

"That's something Cora taught me. She used to tell me that it's impossible to crash if you fly first class." Foster shrugged. "I know it's not logical, but it stuck. Southwest doesn't have a first class, but still."

"Front of the plane?" he said.

"Front of the plane," she agreed.

The captain said something incomprehensible through the loudspeaker, and within a few minutes they were accelerating down the runway. Tate watched Foster. She'd stopped picking her fingernails, but her hands were gripping the armrests so hard her knuckles turned white. She was breathing in short little pants, staring at the back of the seat in front of them.

Tate decided a distraction was in order. He turned his body to face her, and said, "Can we please talk?"

He was relieved when she gave him an annoyed look. "No."

"I said please."

"And I said no."

"Okay, I'll talk and you listen. I'm sorry."

When he didn't say anything else, Foster glared at him. "That's it? That's your 'talk'?" She air quoted.

"No, but it's the basis of my talk. I am sorry, Foster. I should have told you about me calling G-pa. At first I didn't tell you because I knew you'd just disagree with me and be a pain in the ass." When she started to puff up, he hurried on. "But then I actually got to know you, and I didn't tell you because I didn't want to lose your trust."

"So you just kept lying."

"Foster, I didn't technically lie to you."

"Tate, an omission of the truth, when you actually know the truth, *is* a lie."

"Yeah, that was G-pa's point, too." Tate ran a hand through his hair. "I was going to tell you when I came up to find you before our date. But, uh, then you were *so pretty* and sweet and you asked me to go out with you, and I was selfish. I didn't want to mess it up. My mom would be real pissed with me about that. So, I apologize. You were right. I was wrong. I shouldn't have called G-pa, and since I did, I shouldn't have kept that from you."

She breathed a long sigh before speaking, and when she did, Foster sounded utterly defeated. "No. I wasn't right. You said your grandpa's home, landline, car title, basically everything about him is buried under a trust that's almost impossible to lead to him, right?"

"Well, yeah, that's what G-pa said, but it can't be true because the fucking Fucktastic Four found him."

"Sure, but what are the chances that they found him by tracing a landline to a pay phone on Sauvie Island?"

"I—I don't know."

"Well, I do. The chances are almost nonexistent, which means the Fucktastic Four didn't find him by tracing a phone call. They dug up something about where he lives or another of a hundred different things they could've figured out, which also means if you *hadn't* been calling him we wouldn't know that they grabbed him. They'd just have your grandpa, who wouldn't know anything about us at all. And *then* what would they have done with him?" Foster shook her head. "No, this isn't only your fault, Tate. It's mine, too. If I'd really thought this through—really been smart—I would have had you call your grandpa and tell him to get the hell out of there and come to us, where they wouldn't have found him, and he would've been safe." Foster folded her arms across her chest. "So, because of that I'm going to allow you the opportunity to earn my trust back. You know what that means?"

He reached over and pried one of her hands free, holding it gently in his. "That you like me and you're extremely forgiving?"

"No. It means if you mess up and lie to me again I'll never allow you another opportunity. This is a onetime thing. Got it?"

"Got it."

She blew out a long breath and seemed to relax—and even though she'd pulled her hand from his, Foster's voice was soft and more than a little sad. "And I'm sorry, too. I was being a bitch—telling you what to do and what not to do, and not listening or even thinking. I was just reacting. I—I really didn't know what else to do after Cora died." She looked down at her lap and curled in on herself like a wilted flower petal.

"Don't do that." Tate gently touched her chin, turning her face to him. "None of this would be happening if the Fucktastic Four weren't after us. *That* isn't our fault. We didn't ask to be bonded to the elements. We didn't ask to be orphaned."

"But it happened anyway, and I feel like I'm pretty shitty at keeping us safe."

"Are you kidding? You're *great* at keeping us safe! You figured out how to use music to calm our element. You figured out how to stop me from fading away, *and* you figured out how to float us down from, like, twenty feet or more in the air. Foster, I would've smacked into the ground or faded away into nothingness without you. You told me once that you thought I was a superhero. You were wrong, Foster. *You're* the superhero. I'm just your handsome sidekick."

She almost smiled at that. "I thought the sidekicks were super weird or extremely dorky, not handsome. I mean, think about it—Rocket, *a raccoon,* is Peter Quill's sidekick. Super weird. Robin is Batman's sidekick, and he wears his underwear on the outside of his pants. Major dork. And—"

"We're a new kind of superhero, so I'm making up new rules," he interrupted. "But you're talking to me again, which makes everything okay. So if you want to call me your dorky, weird sidekick, I'm cool with it."

Foster's almost smile went away. "But everything isn't okay. I keep hearing him yelling your name. He sounded so upset—so scared. I'm sorry they have your grandpa."

"I know. Me too. But we're superheroes. We're going to rescue him."

"How?" she said miserably.

"By sticking to your brilliant plan," he said.

"By *my* brilliant plan you mean the one Sabine mostly thought of?"

"Yep, that one."

"I don't like it. I don't want you to go in there by yourself."

"I won't be. You'll be there, too. Close by. Waiting for an opening," Tate said. "Plus, Sabine and Finn and you all agreed that it's perfect to say you and I have been living on the streets in Portland."

"There are a lot of homeless people in Portland," Foster agreed reluctantly. "It'd be real hard for the Fucktastic Four to prove that we were, or weren't, there."

"Exactly. I give myself up to them in exchange for letting G-pa go free. I'm going to tell them that you took off—saying something about heading down the coast and crossing over into Mexico with the stash of cash Cora left you."

"Be sure you tell them that you and I are supposed to meet up in Mexico after you get G-pa free," Foster said.

"Yeah, so they'll be searching everywhere but the Portland area," Foster said.

"Which is exactly where G-pa is going to head once he's free," Tate said.

"And you. You're going with him, Tate. Promise me," Foster said urgently.

"Hey, don't worry. Of course I'm going, too. I'm going to pretend to be the perfect kidnap victim. When you look up Stockholm syndrome, my face is going to be the definition."

"Don't let them take you to their island. I can't believe they're driving all over the U.S., not with the kind of money Stewart soaked up from his patrons. They have to be flying, which is great for us. You'll be safe in the airport. As soon as you get there tell airport security you heard them talking about a bomb. That should do it."

"Then I'll take off and call your burner and you'll know I'm on my way back to our Fortress of Sauvietude," Tate said.

"Or get away *before* they do something like drug you so that you can't tell on them at the airport. That's even safer," Foster said.

"Foster, that would be fine, but there's one more little thing. Well, actually, two more little things."

"Those water kids." Foster looked like she'd bitten a lemon.

"Hey, don't be like that. Right now those two are just like we used to be— clueless and getting ready to have their worlds torn apart on their birthdays, which are tomorrow. When we land."

"Tate, save your grandpa. Let the water kids worry about themselves. We figured it out. So will they."

"We figured it out after we lost our parents and got a lot of help from Cora's Batcave. Not to mention Finn and Sabine. We need to help them, Foster. You know that."

Foster deflated. "Yeah, I do. I'm just scared it's going to be them or us."

"What does that mean?"

"It means either we hang around and save them, or we grab your grandpa, retreat to Sauvie, and save ourselves," Foster said.

"It's not going to be like that. Foster, think about this—*they're bonded to water.*"

"Uh, yeah. I know."

He shook his head. "You're not thinking. We join with them and the four of us are stronger together than the two of us alone. With them we have air and water!"

"*If* they really are bonded to water, and *if* they really will join with us."

"You're a cynic," Tate said.

"I am a realist," Foster countered. Then she yawned.

Tate dug into the flap in the seat in front of him and pulled out a plastic-wrapped pillow. He made a grand show of fluffing it, then he reached across Foster and pressed the button to recline first her seat, then his. He placed the pillow on his shoulder, patted it, and smiled invitingly at her.

"How about you sleep for the next four hours?"

She gave him a grateful look and began to curl up, attempting the closest thing to comfort modern air travel could provide. She had almost settled her head on his shoulder when she looked up at him.

"Aren't you going to sleep?"

"Oh, probably. But first I'm going to read. I always read before I go to sleep." He reached into his backpack and brought out a Dean Koontz paperback, *Saint Odd*. "I found this at that little shop where we got those bottles of water. It's the last Odd Thomas book. I can't wait to find out how he ends up with Stormy Llewellyn."

Foster's lips turned up just a little. "You're a strange one, Tate."

"Thanks, Foster." He bent, meaning to kiss the top of her head, but she caught his lips with hers, kissing him back before she lifted the armrest barrier between them and snuggled warmly against him.

And at that moment Tate felt as if everything would truly turn out okay.

25

TATE

Tate jolted awake as the plane seemed to fall out from underneath them.
He shot upright in his seat as passengers around him gasped and carry-ons that
had been semi-shoved under seats spewed into the aisles. His gaze shot to Foster. Unbelievably, she was curled up with the little pillow on top of her backpack, snoring softly.

The intercom beeped and the captain's voice blasted through the cabin—
this time he spoke coherently and quickly—and Tate hated the underlying
somberness in his voice.

"This is your captain. We have begun our descent into Houston, and have
hit some very rough air. The 'fasten seat belt' light will be on for the rest of
the flight. Flight attendants, return to your seats immediately and remain
there until we have landed."

The plane was still bouncing around, but not as badly as whatever had happened that woke Tate. He watched the flight attendants rush up the aisle, studying their faces as they strapped themselves into the jump seats. He was just
thinking that they didn't look too worried when the bottom dropped out of the
plane again. For the first time in his life, Tate understood why flight attendants
constantly harped on wearing seat belts all the time, because his was all that kept
him from flying up and cracking his head against the luggage compartment.

The guy in the seat across the aisle from him wasn't so lucky. He flew out of his seat, slamming against the low ceiling before falling down, half in the aisle, half in his seat. He clutched his head and moaned. Tate saw blood well between his fingers.

"Ohmygod, what's happening?" Foster was wide awake. Her backpack had landed in the seat in front of them, smacking against a woman who was sobbing loudly.

"Do you still have that pillow?" Tate asked quickly.

"Yeah." She held it up, looking scared and confused.

"Thanks." Tate grabbed it and turned to the guy across the aisle. "Hey, sir. Here. Press this against the cut." He handed him the little pillow. Hands shaking, the guy took it and pressed it against his head just as the plane felt like it suddenly stopped in the air before beginning to shake side-to-side, like they were riding waves on an ocean, and not currents in the air.

"Ohgod. Ohgod. No no no. I don't want to die like this," Foster spoke in panicked spurts between chattering teeth.

Tate grabbed her hand. "Look at me! We're not dying. It's just turbulence because of the storm. We're almost in Houston."

Foster opened her mouth to reply and the plane dropped again like the hand of a god had smacked them from above.

Foster screamed and Tate put his arm around her, pulling her against him, trying to keep her safe.

"It's going to be okay!" He had to shout over the screams and sobs of the terrorized passengers. He glanced at the flight attendants and his heart dropped like the plane. They looked scared. Really scared. One of them even had his eyes closed as tears leaked down his cheeks.

"No!" Foster screamed. The plane lurched to the left and yellow plastic oxygen masks released from above them. Foster's huge green eyes found Tate's. "We're going to die," she said through lips blue with fear. "We're going down."

Tate didn't have time to answer. Over the loudspeaker came another voice. "This is your co-captain. Our landing is going to be rough. All passengers need to brace for impact!"

Tate watched a flight attendant with trembling hands reach up and switch on the intercom. "Passengers, the brace-for-impact position is when you bend over, put your hands behind your head and your face between your knees. Do it! Now!"

The plane bucked and tilted as the passengers screamed and cried, and took the brace-for-impact position. All of the passengers except for Tate. He smelled vomit and blood. The plane's nose plunged downward, thrusting him back against his seat and making his stomach roll and pitch as the jet's huge engines whined dangerously.

We're going down. We're really going to crash!

For a moment Tate's mind was numb with panic. He almost buried his face in Foster's hair and just gave in to the end.

But at that moment Foster lost it. She undid her seat belt and tried to stand. "I'm getting the hell out of here!" She fell against Tate as the plane took a dive to the right. Her body shook and her breath came in big, panicked gasps. "Open the fucking door! I want out of here!"

"Foster! We're in the air! You have to sit down and buckle up!" Tate had ahold of her, forcing her to stay in her seat.

She struggled against him. "No! I have to get out! I have to get out! I can fucking fly, and I'm not going to die in this metal coffin!"

And just like that, the panic cleared from his mind and Tate could really think again. Instantly, he knew what he needed to do. No, what *they* needed to do.

"You're right! This isn't happening. Not to us. Not today." Foster didn't seem to hear him, and she kept struggling to get away—to get into the aisle while her shoulders heaved with her hysterical sobs. "Foster! We are *not* going to crash. Not while air is on board!" When she still didn't seem to hear him, he grabbed her shoulders and shook her. Hard. "Foster! Listen to me. We can fix this. *Air can fix this!*"

Foster blinked at him. Her eyes were glassy and her face was so white she looked transparent. "We're going to die." The words trembled from her lips.

"No! Like you said, you can fly! *We* can fly! Snap the hell out of it! You have to help me!" He shook her shoulders again, making her head bob around and her hair fly crazily.

She frowned at him and the glassy look in her eyes cleared. Then the frown changed to a relieved grin. "Air! We can control air! And we *can* fly!"

Foster

"Stand up!" Foster gripped Tate's forearms, stumbling over him as she pulled him into the aisle behind her. "Do what I do." She spread her feet until the sides of her legs braced her between the rows of seats, and watched as Tate followed her lead.

"Sit down!" Foster barely recognized the female flight attendant's voice through her strangled sobs. "And seat belts on!"

Foster's vision blurred with tears as she craned her neck to look back at the woman who clutched tightly to her co-worker's hand.

"Please, God! Please!"

Those last cries weren't meant for her, but Foster felt them bore into her chest and hatch sixty-eight reasons to succeed. That's what she'd seen on the screen as they entered the Jetway. Sixty-eight seats taken. Sixty-eight souls aboard, including her own.

The plane dropped again, and Foster squeezed Tate's arms to keep from falling. This was when her life was supposed to flash before her eyes, but Foster didn't see her end. She saw sixty-seven others. But she could change that. She was powerful. And no one had to die today.

Taking a deep breath, she slid her hands up Tate's shoulders and clasped her fingers around the back of his neck. She blinked the tears from her eyes and forced herself not to cry again as the plane shook and bounced like it was nothing but a toy and they were just made-up people in a child's playtime.

"Hey," she whispered, lifting herself on her tiptoes to press her forehead against Tate's. Her stomach clenched and the muscles in her legs tightened as she struggled to hold herself steady. "How do you feel about saving some people?"

Tate's hands combed through her hair before resting on her lower back. "I think it's what we were born to do."

Shrieks and sobs tumbled through the cabin, bouncing off the walls, deepening the pit in Foster's stomach.

"We have to be calm," Tate whispered, pulling her closer until his breath seeped between her lips. "Be calm."

Foster swallowed the scream clawing at the back of her throat and closed her eyes, focusing on Tate's pulse steadily, calmly beating against her palms. It set the slow, sleepy pace of the melody as Foster began humming the first few lines of the strong, soulful lyrics.

Foster felt Tate's forehead lift with a smile as he sang aloud where she'd left off, his baritone vibrating against her hands.

"It's a new dawn, it's a new day, it's a new life for me, ooooooh,"

Foster took a deep breath, the burbles of panic settling as she swallowed.

"And I'm feelin' good."

"Foster, look!" Foster's eyelids snapped open.

Her breath caught in her throat as she followed Tate's gaze around them, beneath them at the shimmering air currents. But these weren't the panicked, wavy bursts coming from the mouths of the passengers, these were the currents *outside* of the rapidly descending aircraft.

"We can see them through the plane."

Clutching on to Tate's seat, Foster knelt down, extending her hand toward one of the twisted, spiked, plum-colored currents. Pain slapped her fingers and she recoiled, blood welling from small cuts on her fingertips. "They're mad. Rageful, even."

Tate's knuckles whitened as he flattened his hands against the overhead compartments and used them as braces as the plane jerkily barreled toward the earth. "Together! And no stopping this time. Foster, we *can* do this."

Foster held his gaze, those blue eyes anchoring her as they sang together.

"Yeah, it's a new dawn, it's a new day, it's a new life for me,
ooooooh . . .
And I'm feelin' good."

Thunder crashed around them, echoing the boom of trombones Foster heard so clearly in her mind as wind whistled around the plane in time with the molasses drawl of the violins. Hesitantly, Foster reached toward the purple currents beneath her. They bristled and she snapped her hand back before they struck out.

As they continued to sing, Foster poured every bit of herself into the jazzy lyrics.

Her story wouldn't end like this.

Music surged through the plane and pulsed past its aluminum shell to settle the softening spikes of air, lightening from violet to amethyst to lavender. It was magickal, and, for a split second, Foster wished everyone could see the true beauty of her element.

The nose of the plane started to tip back up, up, up until they were level. Foster released her grip on the seat and flexed her aching, stiff fingers.

"It's a new dawn, it's a new day, it's a new life for me"

She reached her arms out by her sides. The shimmering, periwinkle currents rippled around her like a school of fish, each nestling against her palm in silent thanks before twirling around the tips of her fingers and joining the vast openness surrounding them. Foster's hair swirled around her, and Tate spun her into his arms as the music swelled.

"And I'm feelin'... good."

From behind her, seat belts clicked open, shifting Foster's focus from the elation in Tate's blue eyes to the shaking flight attendant closing in on them.

"Seats!" With a trembling hand, she pointed to their chairs. "Now!"

Tate released Foster and, bowing awkwardly, he herded her back to their places. "Just figured that if we were going to die, we might as well go out with a little song and dance."

"Seat belts!" The flight attendant snapped less as she clutched the seat backs and continued her jittery walk toward the back of the plane.

The captain's heavy voice came back over the loudspeaker, announcing something about landing, but Foster couldn't pay attention. If they hadn't got-ten yelled at, she'd still be in the aisle. Only this time, instead of wedging herself between the rows and hoping they wouldn't all die, she'd be running up and down, kissing babies and doing cartwheels. Neither were things she'd ever do normally, but this wasn't a normal situation. They had just saved a whole plane full of people!

She turned in her seat, pressed her palms against Tate's cheeks, and pulled his face to hers. She gave him a big, happy, hooray-we're-not-dead smooch, only releasing him when she needed to breathe.

Foster's stomach flip-flopped as the plane touched down with a jolt.

"Holy shit," Tate said, unbuckling his seat belt and standing robotically. "Holy shit. Holy shit."

Foster avoided the flight attendant's disapproving glare as she followed Tate through the Jetway and into the airport.

"Holy shit."

"Is that all you're going to say?" Foster looped her arm through his and whispered. "We just stopped a fucking plane from crashing."

"Yes!" he exclaimed a little too loudly. "Holy shit!"

"And saw air currents *through* solid objects. Like, what the fuck was that all about?"

"Magic," this time, he joined Foster in whispering, "fucking superhero magic."

"Holy shit!" Foster said, realizing that it did indeed encompass her feelings.

"You were amazing." Shuffling out of the flow of traffic, Tate pulled her into his arms. "And Michael Buble," his breath brushed against her lips. "Who knew he would help save us from dying."

Foster pulled back, shaking her head. "Try Nina Simone, the High Priestess of Soul. Cora used to say that her voice was the closest thing in this world to magic. That her songs could cast spells that would make everything else disappear. I figured we needed a little bit of that. So, thank you, Nina." Foster tipped her chin toward the sky. "For all you went through. You completely saved us."

"Don't forget about us. We had a little something to do with it, too. The Super Sauvies for the win!"

"No," Foster wrinkled her nose as she and Tate joined the rest of the bodies heading to the rental car desk. "I mean, Super Sauvies is horrible, and we also aren't very super. That was almost a total disaster."

"*Inside* a disaster." He waggled his eyebrows. "Is that meta?"

Foster practically saw the lightbulb go off above her head. "We're the Disasters, not the Super Sauvies."

"But it *wasn't* a disaster," Tate said with a sigh. "We're on the ground." He hopped up and down. "See? *And* we're alive. Again, I say total win."

"That's not what I meant." Foster walked on a few paces before realizing Tate wasn't still next to her.

"Holy shit!" Foster turned to face him along with almost everyone else rushing through the terminal. "*We're the Disasters!*"

26
G-PA

Bowen dressed carefully. He wasn't going to let something stupid like a wardrobe malfunction screw up his well-laid plans.

He pulled on his comfortable work jeans and covered a slick, form-fitting wetsuit shirt with an old University of Illinois sweatshirt. He chose his sand shoes, a worn pair of Vibram's that he'd spent the season breaking in. From the top drawer of his dresser he grabbed a stash of cash, his identification, and a razor-sharp pocketknife that had belonged to his father. He stuffed all of that up under his shirt where it hid snugly against his waist.

Bugsy came up to him, wagging her tail expectantly.

"That's right, old girl. Stick close to me. You heard 'em last night. They're up to some nasty shenanigans and they've picked the wrong old man to mess with."

As he shaved, brushed his teeth, and combed his hair, Bowen thought back over the previous day. After Eve hung up on Foster, Bowen had been careful to make it clear that Matthew and Luke had hurt him badly when they'd wrestled him away from the phone.

It was, of course, a big ol' lie. They'd only bruised him a bit. He'd been hurt worse playing with Bugs-a-Million. But those two young assholes didn't know that, and hadn't cared at all that he limped around—that much was obvious. The man named Mark was different. Mark had made sure Bowen had an ice pack to put on the hip he'd pretended pained him, and kept dosing him with ibuprofen. Then Eve had started her interrogation.

"Mr. Bowen, where's Tate?" Eve had asked once Bowen was settled in his recliner with the ice pack and a short glass of whiskey.

"On his way here, I expect."

"No, I mean where has he been these past several weeks?"

"I have no goddamn idea."

"Right. Just like you had no goddamn idea your grandson was alive," Luke said sarcastically.

"I lied about that," Bowen admitted easily. "Wouldn't you? I don't know what exactly is going on with that boy, but I do know you're not family and I have no reason to trust you."

"That's a good point," Mark said, taking a seat across the coffee table from him on the couch. "We're not family, but we do want to help Tate and Foster— and only we can help them."

"What exactly did Tate tell you about what's happened to him and Foster?" Eve asked.

Bowen shrugged. "Well, didn't seem to be much to tell. He said he and Foster are somehow connected to tornadoes. Don't know how—don't know why. But they're scared, I can tell you that."

"You're telling us your scared grandson who you thought was dead has been calling you, and you couldn't even get him to tell you where he is?" Luke scoffed. "That doesn't make any sense."

Bowen frowned at the young man and shook his head. "You have mean eyes. Has anyone ever told you that, boy?"

"I'm not a boy, old man. I'm thirty-six."

"I'm almost eighty, and from where I'm sitting you're a boy. A mean little boy who doesn't seem to have been raised right."

"He might be mean," Mark interrupted, "but his question is valid. You're not a mean man, Mr. Bowen. So it's hard for me to believe Tate wouldn't confide his whereabouts to you."

Bowen sighed and shifted in the chair, being sure to moan painfully before answering. "Yep, yep, yep that surprised me, too. But I didn't take into account the girl."

"Foster?" Eve leaned forward from her seat on the couch beside Mark.

"Yeah." Bowen did his best grumpy old man impression, which was spot-on because sometimes he was truly a grumpy old man. "Girl's got him whipped. Tate did call me without telling her, but I haven't been able to convince the boy to tell me where they are. I've been trying to make him admit to that girl he and I are talking, and then bring her to the damn phone, but before today he's refused. Said Foster would be mad. Seeing as he's gone sweet on her, that'd be a bad thing."

"He's right," Mark said to Eve. "We didn't take into account that Tate would fall for Foster."

"Let me ask you something," Bowen said. "Why are you the only ones who can help my Tate?"

Eve and Mark shared a long look before Mark turned to Bowen. "We're connected to tornadoes, too. Or, rather, Matthew is, and it's not just tornadoes. It's the element air. I'm water. Eve is earth. Luke is fire."

"Figures," Bowen said, sending Luke a dark look. "So, this does have something to do with Foster's adopted father—Rick Stewart, the geneticist."

"It does," Mark said.

"And that's all we're going to say about that," Eve added. "But we are the only people who truly understand what your grandson and Foster are going through, and because of that, we're the only people who can help them control it."

"Then why don't you just do that? Help 'em. Instead of trapping and kidnapping 'em."

"We're not kidnapping anyone," Mark said.

"Sure, boy," Bowen said. "Just like you're not holding me here against my will." He shook his head in disgust. "I don't think you're a bad person, but if you stay with this lot you're going to be forced to do things bad people do."

"Hey, old man," Luke sneered. "If we were really bad guys we'd gag you so that we wouldn't have to listen to your crap."

"Ya see, young pup, the thing is, I believe that's the least of what you'd do to me if Mark wasn't here to stop you."

Luke stood and started to approach Bowen. Waves of heat began to lift from his skin and Bowen could feel the fire that simmered too close to Luke's surface.

"Enough!" Eve snapped. "Luke, go outside in the rain and cool yourself down." She turned to Bowen. "First, stop baiting them. Next, you need to understand that I'm in charge—not Luke, not Matthew, and *not Mark*. So if you want to be saved, you better look to me for that."

Bowen tilted his head and studied Eve. "Well, young lady, instead I think I'll stick with a motto that has served me well for almost eighty years."

"And what's that?" she asked.

"The only person I can truly count on is *myself*. If I need savin', I'll manage it, like I've managed for almost a century."

"Must suck to be so fucking old," halfway out the door, Luke called back nastily over his shoulder.

"No, boy. It's the alternative that sucks. That and having to deal with jackasses like you for such a long damn time."

Matthew's sarcastic laughter filled the room. "The old dude's funny!" he said.

"Matthew, shut up. Luke! Get outside," Eve shouted, eyes flashing. "Bowen, you need to shut your mouth, too."

"Fine with me. Like my dad used to say, there's no sense in arguing with drunks, fools, or mules." Bowen settled back in his recliner and lifted his empty whiskey glass. "Mark, would you help an old man out and refresh this? And hand me the remote. I'm sure there's a game on somewhere."

Bowen had sipped whiskey and watched football into the evening, pretending to get drunk and pass out so that Eve let down her guard. Her whispers to the three men she called brothers, but who obviously were not blood relations, made his stomach clench with fear for Tate and Foster—and the six other kids these four were determined to capture.

Not if I have any say about it, you won't.

A little after dark, Mark "woke" him and helped him up the stairs to his bedroom, where Bowen settled in to get a good night's sleep. He'd need his rest. He'd decided to get the hell out of there first thing in the morning.

Slowly, quietly, carefully, Bowen made his way down the stairs. Bugs-a-Million, as always, was by his side, but the big dog was surprisingly graceful and truly intelligent. She crept with him, making no noise at all. Not far from the bottom of the stairway, the voices that were just susurrus became intelligible, lifting with the tantalizing scents of breakfast and the distant drone of the TV. Bowen and the big dog froze, listening carefully.

"You're cooking? You haven't cooked in years." Bowen recognized the deep voice as that of Mark, the only one of the four of them with troubled eyes.

"I thought it would make the old man feel better. We were pretty rough with him yesterday. I don't want him hurt. Hell, Mark, I don't want *him* at all. Just the kids, and we're not even going to hurt them." Eve's voice carried easily to Bowen, making him suppress a sarcastic snort.

"Nah, we're not going to hurt them. We're just going to completely uproot them from their families and disrupt their lives forever," Mark said.

Bowen nodded in silent agreement with Mark.

"Come on. They'll be fine. Better than fine. They'll have money and their own space on the island, and they'll learn to control their powers without hurting people," Eve said.

"Gilded cage."

"What's that supposed to mean?" she said.

"You know what it means. You've been living in one your entire life, and now you want to be someone else's jailor? It's not right, Eve."

"I'm not going to be anyone's jailor. I'm going to have my freedom. Just like you will," Eve said.

"Oh, that's right. The 'we'll be free and rich but out of Father's reach' pipe dream." Mark's voice was heavy with sarcasm.

"It's not a pipe dream. It's going to be our reality once we get all eight of those kids to Father."

"You sound like you really believe that."

"I don't just believe it, I'm going to make it happen. For all four of us. Now, we need to talk about the hurricane."

Bowen moved a little closer, wanting to be sure he caught every word.

"Nothing to talk about. I've changed its trajectory. It's heading directly for us."

"Oh, well. That's good. That's exactly what I wanted you to do." Even from where Bowen crouched he could hear the surprise in Eve's voice.

"I thought the change was smart. Bolivar Peninsula is less inhabited than Galveston Island."

"Good point, well done," Eve said. But Bowen could tell by her tone that she really didn't give a damn.

"I also made another change. It's not a hurricane. It's a tropical storm."

"Uh-uh, that's not what we agreed to."

"Well, when it's earth's turn you do what you think is best. It's water's turn, and I think it's irresponsible to create a hurricane and then send it to smash into lowlands like this peninsula or Galveston Island. It's already bad out there. And besides that, if there's much more than a tropical storm warning they're going to start evacuating, and then we'll never find Charlotte and Bastien."

"Okay, you're right about that. Actually, you're *very* right." Eve's voice sounded sly and pleased. Very pleased. "You said the eye of the storm is headed directly for us here?"

"Yes. It's about eight-thirty right now. It should come to shore in the next hour."

"Perfect. It'll draw the water kids here. The old man said he owns the two hundred acres surrounding the house, and no one else lives on it. He has a beach that stretches for hundreds of yards—a *private* beach. Those two kids will be simple to grab."

"Then we sit here and wait for Tate and Foster and, eventually, Charlotte and Bastien?"

"Exactly."

"And you think they're really just going to walk into this trap?" Mark asked.

"I know they will, or at least Tate will. We have the only person left in Tate's family. He'll be here. Once we have him it'll just be a matter of time before he gives up his girlfriend," Eve said.

Bowen had heard enough. He signaled for Bugsy to follow him back up the stairs. He grabbed the walking stick he'd carved himself and turned to the big dog. Looking her in her bright, intelligent eyes, he said, "All right Ms. Bugsy, we're ready for our close-up," he misquoted *Sunset Boulevard* as the dog's tail wagged enthusiastically. "Let's do this."

When Linus Bowen started down the stairs the second time, it seemed a different man inhabited his skin—an older, sicker, frailer man who could barely hobble without leaning on the cane and the big dog. He was halfway down the stairs when Mark's head appeared. The man was frowning and looking pale and miserable.

"Mr. Bowen, here, let me help you." Mark started up the stairs, but Bugsy's warning growl had him hesitating.

"Nope, nope nope. Can make it down just fine," Bowen said between exaggerated pants and his very best old man moans. "We're used to doing things by ourselves. Don't like people much." He made sure to glare at Mark as the man retreated so that he and Bugsy could limp past him.

"Good morning, Mr. Bowen! I have fresh coffee brewed and I'm making your favorite, steak and eggs with all the fixings," Eve smiled prettily over her shoulder as she stirred what Bowen thought smelled like grits.

"See you made yourself at home," Bowen grumbled. "Even though no one gave you permission to."

"Well, I thought since you couldn't make it to your Corner Café this morning—I'd make the Corner Café come to you. I'll even pour your coffee."

She was doing just that when Bowen caught her gaze with his. "How long have you been following me?"

She laughed. "Oh, not long at all. But you were a hard man to find. Why is that, Mr. Bowen? Hey, may I call you Linus?"

"I'm not hard to find. Not if you're friend or family. And, no, you may not call me Linus. I'll take two sugars and a dollop of cream in my coffee."

"Here you are, Mr. Bowen." Eve handed him the steaming cup of coffee. He raised it to his lips as Bugsy whined pitifully up at him.

"Sorry, old girl. I'm not myself today. Almost forgot." Bowen put the mug down on the kitchen table and slowly began hobbling toward the front door, leaning on his stick and resting his other hand on the wolfhound's strong back.

He'd only gone a shuffling foot out of the kitchen when Luke was suddenly standing in front of him. "I think you need to sit down. You're not moving so good."

Bowen looked up at him wearily. "'Course I'm stiff and hurtin'. You would be too if you were an old man and some young bucks had broken into your house and thrown you around. My hips don't work like they used to."

"My brothers are sorry about that," Mark said, coming up behind Bowen and circling around the slit-eyed dog. "But why don't you have a seat in your recliner? We'll bring your breakfast to you and anything else you need."

"Well, that sounds better than a sharp stick in the eye, but I gotta take Bugsy out first for her morning constitutional." Bowen continued limping slowly, painfully, toward the door.

Matthew stepped up beside Luke. "Can't let you do that, Mr. Bowen."

The old man lifted his head and skewered the two men with his icy eyes. "Boys, you are damn lucky I'm not just a few years younger. Did you know I played football for the U of I? Didn't know that, huh? Well, I did. Back when football players weren't pussies and didn't need titanium helmets and a mound of pads. Too bad you didn't know me then. I would've enjoyed taking you out back and teaching you a thing or two about respect."

"Okay, okay, old dude. We hear you. You used to be the shit. Well, now you're just old, and you're not going outside with that giant thing you call a dog," said Luke.

"Riiiiight," Mark drawled the word. "Because he can obviously run away— in the middle of a tropical storm—over sand and sea grass and whatever else is out there—*when he can barely hobble to the front damn door*. Step aside and let him take his dog out for a crap."

Bowen held his breath as Eve joined them.

"Empty your pockets," she told him.

Slowly, making sure his hands trembled like a frail old man, Bowen emptied his pockets, which held nothing but lint. The money and ID pressed safely against his skin inside his hidden wetsuit shirt.

"Where are your car keys?" she asked.

Bowen pointed to a corkboard by the front door where a set of keys dangled.

"You can take the dog out. But leave her out there," Eve said.

"Storms make Bugsy nervous," Bowen said.

"Put her in the garage," Eve said.

"Would you want to sit out a storm in the garage?" Bowen grumbled at her.

"No, but I'm not a dog, either. And that's the deal. You can take her out. Do whatever you want with her, but she doesn't come back in with you. Got it?"

Bowen stared down at Bugsy, fixing his face before he looked at Eve. When he did he made sure his voice sounded tired and sad, and he bowed his shoulders even more. "I've got it. I'll put her in the garage."

"Excellent. Don't be long. I'd hate for your breakfast to get cold."

Bowen said nothing. He continued to limp slowly toward the door, but before he could get there Mark had it open.

"Do you need help? Want me to bring blankets for Bugsy? A water dish or something?"

"No, son," Bowen said, not unkindly. "There're old work blankets in the garage, and I keep extra bowls out there. She'll have water from the hose and her dry food."

"There's nothing I can do to help?"

Bowen looked into Mark's eyes and saw the utter lack of hope that filled the space between his quiet demeanor and his obvious concern. Bowen recognized that hopelessness. He'd lived it as he watched his beloved wife slip away from him and leave behind the shell in which she used to reside, and then even that shell faded into dust. For a moment the recognition of hopelessness made him feel bad for the young man, and he used that moment. Bowen rested a trembling hand on Mark's shoulder. "There is something you can do. Can you let me have a few minutes with Bugsy? Eve wants me to hurry, but I need to let the old girl know everything's okay. I—I just don't want her to be afraid. Do you understand?"

"I do." Mark nodded. "Take all the time you need, sir. I'll be sure Eve doesn't bother you." He paused, and Bowen waited. Then he added, "And I'll also make the rain hold off until you come back inside. No sense in you and Bugsy getting soaked out there."

"Thank you, son. Thank you." Bowen squeezed Mark's shoulder. Then he shuffled out onto the wide porch that framed his house. Slowly, carefully, he hobbled down the front stairs, making a show of stopping when he reached the ground and leaning against the railing like he was having a hard time catching his breath. Finally, he shambled around the side of the house, heading in the direction of the garage.

Bugsy stayed close beside him, watching Bowen with wise, yellow eyes.

About halfway to the garage Bowen dropped his cane so that he had to stop and bend painfully to pick it up, and as he did he glanced up under his arm at the house.

Mark was standing on the porch watching him. Bowen straightened like he was the Tin Man needing oil and before he continued on his slow, doddering progress he gave Mark a thumbs-up. Mark waved and then disappeared inside the house. Bowen stood for another moment, pretending he needed to catch his breath. He saw no one watching. No one came out on the porch. No one was looking out any window.

He could hardly contain his excitement, but Bowen kept in character—actually, he was enjoying his frail old man act. When he reached the garage he leaned against it, coughing like his lungs had suddenly gone old and feeble, too. Then he shuffled around the side of the building where the door was located—and where the garage blocked the view of him and Bugsy from the house.

Bowen dropped the cane and then began to do several warm-up stretches as Bugsy started to wag and jump happily around him.

"That's right, Bugsy old girl. Did I tell you about the time I scrimmaged against Notre Dame with a broken arm? Back before football was for pussies? And those dumbasses inside our house think knocking me around a little actually *stopped* me? Hell, I was offered scholarships in track *and* football by a Big Ten university. I still go to the gym five times a week, and every morning, rain, shine, or hurricane, you and I jog up and down this beach in the sand. Let's show 'em how real athletes age!"

Then Linus Bowen, who was almost eighty years young, *ran*. Arms pumping, but upper body relaxed, he still had the form of the track star whose hundred-yard-dash record stood at his high school for almost forty years after he graduated. Beside him the huge wolfhound kept perfect pace.

In no time he'd made it to the sand dunes and the tall sea grass that he'd let grow wild on his property because the old biology teacher in him loved nothing more than providing a natural habitat for what he considered after all these years *his* seabirds and *his* coastal flora and fauna. There he had some cover, and was able to slow to a jog, weaving his way easily between mounds of sand and scraggly bushes.

"Steady old girl, steady," he spoke to Bugsy between deep, even breaths as he stripped off his sweatshirt and tied it around his waist. "The Chevron station is two miles this way, on the other side of Cobb's Cove. That's where we're headed. Then I'll call *real* Texas law enforcement and they'll be on those four like stink on shit." Chuckling, Bowen jogged on, with the big dog at his side.

27

CHARLOTTE

Charlotte's phone blared the melody of Ursula the sea witch's "Poor Un-fortunate Souls" from *The Little Mermaid,* forcing her awake. She picked up the phone, sighing at the time. Eight a.m. sharp. At least her mother was a creature of habit. Too bad she hadn't remembered that the night before and silenced her phone.

But because she had forgotten, and she'd never been good at ignoring this particular person, Charlotte cleared her throat and answered with her perkiest voice. "Good morning, Mother!"

"Happy birthday, Charles."

Charlotte's eyes went heavenward. "Mother, we've talked about this. Please respect the fact that my name is Charlotte."

Her mother's voice was hard and cold, which was only intensified by her perfect Southern-belle accent. "It is the name your father and I gave you eighteen years ago, and that is the only name I will ever call you."

"Then I don't understand why you call at all. Mother, I'm an adult now. I am no longer your responsibility."

"Thanks to that meddling old woman who calls herself my mother."

"I've told you before, if you speak badly of Grandma Myrtie I will *not* talk to you," Charlotte said.

One of her mother's dramatic Southern sighs floated up from the phone, trying to smother Charlotte in a blanket of old guilt and wasted dreams. "You've always preferred her over me—your own mother!"

But Charlotte was done being bullied by her mother. "Because Grandma Myrtie has always accepted me and loved me for who I am."

"Don't you mean she indulged and spoiled you?"

"No. I said exactly what I meant. Mother, I'm going to go now. I don't think this call was about wishing me happy birthday. Sadly, I think this call was about trying to make me feel guilty for being myself."

"I cannot believe I gave birth to a child who would grow up to be so heartless to his mother." Emotion intensified her accent so that Charlotte thought she sounded more like a caricature than a real person.

Not that that thought was a surprise. The truth was Charlotte often thought of her mother as a caricature of the perfect antebellum Southerner—stuck purposefully in a rose-colored-glasses version of an ignorant, racist, and homophobic past.

"I realize you're incapable of understanding who I am. I stopped trying to get you to see my side of this years ago. I only wish you would learn to respect my decisions."

"Why, when you clearly do not respect your father and me."

"Mother, I respect you. That's one reason I chose to leave North Carolina. I simply don't agree with you. You can respect me, too, without agreeing with me."

"That's ridiculous. Why should I respect your homosexual desires? God doesn't!"

"Mother, I've told you over and over. I am not gay. I'm a woman. Liking boys has nothing to do with it."

"Tell that to someone who didn't change your diapers." Charlotte's mother gasped before continuing in a hissing whisper, "Now look what you've done! You made me stoop to using vulgarity."

"I didn't *make* you do anything. You chose to stoop. Just like you chose narrow-minded cruelness over compassion and understanding when I came to you with my truth."

"Because it was all a bunch of hooey instigated by your wretched grand-mother."

"Good-bye, Mother. We won't talk again until you can respect my deci-sions. I wish you a good day."

Charlotte tapped the END CALL button and threw her phone across the bed.

I shouldn't have answered. I should have known better. I should pull the covers over my head and cry myself back to sleep.

But for the first time in her eighteen years, Charlotte didn't.

She didn't cry.

She didn't allow her mother to ruin her birthday.

Instead, she kicked off her pretty flowered comforter and went to the slid-ing glass door that led to her balcony. Not caring that it was raining and the wind was crazily whipping the seashell chime she'd hung the day she'd moved in, Charlotte grabbed her soft pink bathrobe, wrapped it around herself, and stepped out onto the balcony.

Stretching her arms wide, Charlotte did what she'd done every morning since she'd arrived on Galveston Island—she embraced the vast expanse of gor-geous water that stretched before her as far as she could see.

Waves crashed against the seawall and the slanting rain impaired visibil-ity, but Charlotte loved every molecule of it. The water fed her soul, washing her clean of her mother's anger and negativity.

It's my eighteenth birthday and no one here knows it!

The thought didn't make Charlotte feel sad—quite the opposite, actually. The fact that she hadn't really made a friend yet wasn't a big deal. Charlotte always took her time making friends. She'd learned years ago that people could be cruel. Very cruel. Especially people who claimed to be her friend. And not having any friends meant she could do *exactly* what she wanted to do on this big, important, life-changing birthday.

Turning eighteen meant Charlotte would be able to complete her gender reassignment surgery *next summer break*!

"And that is a fantastic reason for me to celebrate today—by myself—doing exactly and only what I want to do."

She checked the clock. It was eight-thirty. Grandma Myrtie wouldn't call until around noon because, unlike her mother, her grandma understood her perfectly. She knew Charlotte loved to sleep in and wake slowly—and Grandma Myrtie respected that.

Charlotte stared out at the seething waves for another moment before hurrying into her tidy kitchenette and blending a quick smoothie. She pulled on her wetsuit and tied her long blond hair up in a high ponytail. Then she grabbed a cover-up, beach towel, and her bag and skipped lightly down the stairs.

She'd made it to her car when Kate, her next-door neighbor who was in her Intro to Marine Biology class, called from across the parking lot to her.

"Hey, Charlotte! You're not going to the beach, are you?" Kate eyed the beach bag and towel. "The hurricane's been downgraded to a tropical storm, but it's really not safe out there."

"Oh, I know," Charlotte replied cheerfully. "I'm not actually going *in* the water," she lied. "I'm just going for a quick jog."

"Suit yourself, but I say the school's gym and a dry, warm treadmill is a better choice."

"I hear ya! Thanks!" Charlotte dismissed her with a wave and a smile as she slid behind the wheel of the old Focus. "And *that* is exactly why it's good I don't have any friends. Yet. Friends are nosy. Acquaintances are not so nosy."

Charlotte pulled out of the parking lot and let her instincts guide her. She turned east onto Highway 87 because it felt like the right way to go, and began to meander along the seaside, happy that the impending storm made the usually heavy weekend traffic sparse.

She'd planned on parking and walking along the beach, listening for the sounds of singing in the waves, but decided to cross the bridge onto the Bolivar Peninsula instead. She hadn't explored much there yet, and Charlotte quickly fell in love with the little strip of rugged lowlands.

She'd gone quite a ways east when the sign for Cobb's Cove caught her eye, and she took a right, bumping along the narrow, sandy road until she came to a small, deserted beach parking lot where she parked. Grabbing her bag and her towel, Charlotte locked her car and then hurried toward the waves and the sound of beautiful voices that called seductively to her.

Mark

"Okay, breakfast is more than ready!" Eve called from the kitchen. "Mark, I do not care if that old man is still French-kissing that damn dog. He's been out there half an hour. Go get him. Now."

"I love it when Markey's in trouble," Matthew said without looking up from his laptop.

"Ditto, my bro!" Luke's laugh was tinged with cruelty as he and Matthew fist-bumped.

"Grow up. Both of you," Mark told them, then called to his sister. "I'll go out and get him." With one last frown aimed at his asshole brothers, Mark went out onto the porch.

The old man wasn't in sight, so Mark sighed in resignation and made his way slowly down the stairs to the garage. He liked Bowen. He also respected him for not betraying his grandson, and for being a tough old guy and not being intimidated by the four of them. He stopped at the garage door, and then realized that he couldn't get in that way without an opener, so he searched around and found the side door, which swung open easily.

"Mr. Bowen, sorry about rushing you, but Eve says breakfast is ready. She doesn't cook very often, so she gets pretty touchy about all of us sitting down at the same time to eat when she does. I know you don't want to leave Bugsy, but I'll come back out here with you afterward. Maybe we could even take her for a little walk if you feel up to—" Mark's words broke off as he realized the only thing in the garage was the sporty Miata and a bunch of woodworking equipment.

Mark backed out of the garage quickly, scanning the area nearby. With a terrible feeling of dread, he looked down and read the story in the sand.

The cane was there, discarded as superfluous. Near the cane were the tracks of a large, excited dog and a man who was clearly *not* injured or frail. They disappeared, side by side, into the sand and sea grass that stretched between the garage and the dunes that began several yards away.

Cursing under his breath, Mark sprinted back to the house.

"He's gone!"

Luke and Matthew looked up disbelievingly as Eve hurried out of the kitchen. She wiped her hands on a dish towel; her expression was a storm cloud.

"What did you say?" she asked ominously.

"Bowen. He's not in the garage. Neither is the dog. Their tracks lead off into the dunes."

Luke laughed sarcastically. "Well, I don't know what all the rush and fuss is about. The old bastard could barely walk."

Matthew closed his laptop and stood, stretching like a lazy cat. "Yeah, the biggest pain in the ass about this is going to be hauling his crippled ass back here. Old geezer is thick. Probably weighs two-ten."

"That fucking dog's a pain in the ass, too," Luke said. "I think it's time fire had a little talk with her. It'll be payback for Bowen running away."

"Running!" Matthew made a show of laughing and wiping his eyes. "Luke, you crack me up."

"Shut up. Both of you," Eve said. "Let's go get him." She paused. "Luke, Matthew, there's a bag of zip ties in the kitchen pantry. Get them. Grab some rags and rope, too."

"It's damn handy that old man has a stash of tie-'em-up crap," Luke said.

"Just do it," Eve said. "Come on, Mark."

Beside Eve, Mark descended the front porch stairs.

"They're wrong," Mark told his sister.

"No, I was wrong. Letting you handle Bowen was my mistake. You're too softhearted for this. I should have gone out there with him myself." Eve was obviously annoyed, but she touched her brother's shoulder reassuringly. "He won't be hard to find, and then I'll handle him from here on out."

"You're not understanding me," Mark said as he led her around the side of the garage to the abandoned cane and the tracks. Mark pointed down at the sand as Luke and Matthew jogged up to them. "He's not limping. He's not a frail old man. These tracks don't just say he walked away. They say he *ran*."

"Well I'll be damned," Luke said, peeking around Mark at the tracks. "Like Matthew and I said—the old bastard's a pain in the ass."

Eve looked at Mark and in her eyes he saw a hardness that before had been liquid, flowing around the fringes of her expressions. This morning it solidified, choking out the gentle, broken, compassionate sister he'd loved for as long as he could remember.

"We're going to get Bowen and bring him back here, and if we need to break his hip to get the old man to *stay* when we tell him to *stay,* then so be it. He brought this on himself."

Mark heard his brothers high-five each other, but his gaze didn't leave Eve's.

"I won't do that, Eve. He doesn't deserve it. I won't hurt that old man."

"I'm aware of that, Mark. I don't expect you to. That's why Luke and Matthew are coming with us. All I expect you to do is handle water. Bowen thinks he can run away from us on the beach when we control water? Let's show him how mistaken he is. You don't need to hurt him. You only need to slow him down. Make it rain, Mark. Now."

Mark bowed his head and reached for his element. It was a simple thing, especially right there on the beach. He was so close to the vastness of the ocean that he could feel it calling to him—feel it drawing him into it where he could finally lose himself—finally give in to the Frill that lurked just below the surface, circling, calling, anticipating . . .

"Mark! Snap out of it!" Eve's voice shredded his concentration and he blinked several times before he refocused on her face. "I didn't ask you to call a hurricane. Just some rain, that's all. It's really the least you can do."

"Okay, yeah, fine." Mark followed the connection with his element—not out to sea as he so longed to do—but up, up, into the atmosphere where he coaxed droplets to condense from vapor and then he made them become heavy enough to fall under the pull of gravity. Warm rain drifted lazily downward, caressing Mark's skin and causing polka-dot patterns in the sand.

Eve barely acknowledged him with a nod. Instead she smiled warmly at Matthew. "Now, air, please take those sweet, soft little raindrops and make them troublesome, *but if you start disappearing I'm going to be very angry with you.*"

Matthew took a step back from Eve's intensity. "Hey, no worries! Whipping up a little wind is no biggie."

"Then stop talking about it and do it," she said.

"Okay, okay. Sheesh, everyone's a critic," Matthew muttered. He lifted his face and his arms to the sky and shouted, "Blow, baby, blow!"

Wind responded instantly, blowing from the ocean in a growling rush of briny air—causing the otherwise tame droplets to slant, elongate, and pummel against them with enough force to be uncomfortable.

"Luke! Not now. Save it. We might need fire later and we don't have time to haul a case of Gatorade with us so you don't flame out," Eve snapped at her brother.

Mark glanced at Luke. Heat waves had begun to lift from his skin, evaporating the rain before it touched him, but at Eve's command he made an abrupt motion with his hand, and suddenly he was getting soaked like the rest of them.

"I fucking hate getting wet," Luke said. "Well, what the hell are we waiting for? To be totally water-fucking-logged? Let's go get the old man so we can dry out and eat our cold breakfast."

Mark moved forward as if he would take the lead, but Eve's sharp words halted him.

"No. All of you follow me. I'm not chancing any more screw-ups."

Mark said nothing. He fell into line last as Luke and Matthew jostled past, making mean, childish faces at him.

Why is this happening? Why is my sister changing from my best friend into some who . . . someone who . . .

And then it struck Mark like a tidal wave, drowning him in despair.

Eve is turning into someone who reminds me of Father, and not the father who cared for us and seemed to love us so much when we were children. Eve is turning into Rick Stewart, the mad, cruel man who broke us and stole our lives away.

As if jealous of the rain that slicked his skin, Mark's tears spilled down his cheeks while he ran behind his two brothers and the monster his sister was becoming.

28

EVE

Eve jogged, head down against the wind-whipped rain, and tried to get her temper under control. She didn't know what to do about Mark. He'd almost screwed everything up. Again. Just like in Missouri when he let Tate and Foster get away. It caused her pain, but it was becoming more and more clear to Eve that for the first time in their lives, she and Mark weren't on the same page.

She tried to convince herself that wasn't too terrible. Mark had always been softhearted, the kindest of all of them. Luke was a jerk. They all knew it. Like his element, it took nothing for him to combust. Matthew was undependable. His moods blew from good to complete asshole as quickly as the wind changed.

But Mark had always been different. She'd grown up using him as a feelings gauge. When she wondered if she should be sad about something, she turned to Mark. If he was very upset, well, then it was time for her to get sad. Mark felt things too deeply, and she'd been quick to protect him, especially after Father had changed.

Only now it was Mark who was changing, and Eve found she couldn't convince herself that wasn't terrible.

Why can't he understand that I'm doing all of this for us—so that we can be free? So what if that means eight teenagers are inconvenienced? The four of us have served our time. It's someone else's turn now.

Eve's legs were jelly. The sucking sand was hell to jog through, but it fueled her anger at Bowen. That old bastard was exactly what Luke and Matthew had labeled him—a pain in the ass. Well, she was going to deal with him from now on. She'd lock the old troublemaker in his room, without that damned dog, and as soon as Tate and Foster showed up she'd let Matthew and Luke handle the cleanup. Leaving Bowen behind to tell stories to the police was a mistake she wasn't going to make. Perhaps there should be a tragic accident that involved a candle and Bowen's house going up in flames *with* the old man and dog inside.

Mark wouldn't be able to handle that, so Mark simply wouldn't know about it.

Suddenly, someone grabbed the back of Eve's soggy shirt, causing her to almost fall back on her butt. She rounded on Luke, whose hot hand still had a hold of her.

"What the hell?" she snapped at him.

"Hey, open your ears! I told you to stop." Luke pulled her behind a big clump of sand and grass. Matthew and Mark jogged up to them, breathing heavily and sending the two of them questioning frowns. Luke jerked his chin in the direction they'd been heading. "Am I the only one of us who is actually looking while we run?"

"We don't have time for theatrics, Luke," Eve said, jerking her shirt from his grasp.

"It's Bowen. Just ahead. I don't think he saw us. He's talking to two kids. His stupid dog is there, too. Matthew, be sure you keep wind coming at our faces so that mutt doesn't scent us."

"Good eye, Luke," Eve said while her brother preened under her praise. "You three stay out of sight. I'm smaller than any of you. I'm going to get closer and check out what's going on."

Eve slipped around the far side of the mound of sea grass and sand. Crouching, she sprinted for another, smaller concealing dune closer to the people on the beach. She waited, catching her breath, and then, on her hands and knees, Eve crawled until she had a clear view of the beach.

Eve almost had to cover her mouth to smother a shout of victory. Retracing her path, she rushed back to her brothers, smiling with relief and pleasure.

"It seems Mark did a good thing letting Bowen get away. He's led us directly to Charlotte and Bastien."

"What?" Mark gasped before peeking carefully around the dune.

Eve let him get an eyeful before she spoke. "Take a good look. Those two kids are your salvation from the Frill and from Father."

Mark turned back to her, slumping against the sandy dune. "We're going to ruin their lives."

"No. We're going to teach them about their powers and give them an opportunity to use them," Eve corrected him. She reached out and took his hands, hating how cold they felt, wishing she could get through to him. "Mark, we're not going to hurt them, but we have to do this. If we don't it'll be the end of us."

"And we're not ending because you're soft," Luke said.

"It's three against one. You're outvoted, bro," Matthew said.

"Yeah, I get that. I'm part of this family and I'll help you so that we survive, but unlike the three of you, I won't like it, and I won't hurt them—any of them."

Eve read the hopelessness in Mark's eyes, and for once it didn't make her sad. It made her victorious. *I'll make it right with him later, after we're back on the island,* she told herself.

"Good. Okay, Bowen is going to be a problem, but remember we still need him to get to Tate and Foster," Eve said.

"But we don't need that damn dog," Luke said.

"True," Eve agreed. She caught Mark's gaze. "Hurting a dog isn't like hurting a person. Remember that, Mark."

"That old man loves her like she's a person," Mark said.

"Not our problem," Luke said.

"If we have to hurt a dog to show those kids and that old man that we mean business, then so be it," Eve said. When Mark opened his mouth Eve said brusquely, "It's the dog or Bowen. You choose."

Mark closed his mouth and didn't say anything.

Eve nodded. "So, use the dog. Matthew, be ready to get air involved. Mark, whatever Matthew does you should assume rain will be needed with him. This place looks deserted, but we can't chance being seen, and we already know the old man is a pain in the ass. Even if the kids come willingly with us, we're going to have to tie him up." She gestured at the zip ties and rope her brothers were holding. "No one needs to witness that. Be ready to shield us from watchers. Okay, follow my lead. Oh, and Mark—tell that tropical storm it's time to come to land."

Standing straight and tall, Eve strode out from behind their concealment with her brothers following her.

Bastien

"Am I on speaker? Can both of you hear me?"

"Yes, Josie. We can both hear you," Dickie replied, switching on his turn signal as he guided the Jeep onto Highway 87 East.

"And I'll take that snippet of silence as Bastien telling me he can hear me, too."

Dickie punched Bastien's shoulder and Bastien let out a grunt.

"Good," Josie continued. "Now, I told Richie last night, but he *obviously* didn't listen, that you two *cannot* surf today."

"We're not," Dickie grumbled, looking expectantly at Bastien.

"Yeah, no, just out for a drive, us."

"For some reason I don't believe you. Either of you." Josie sighed. "It's been downgraded to a tropical storm, but can intensify back to hurricane status in a blink. Come home, both of you. Bastien, you're staying with us until this storm passes. I don't want you out on the beach. It's not safe." Josie's concern was audible, and Bastien was glad he didn't have to lie to her face. "Promise me you'll turn around right now and come home."

"We promise, Josie," Bastien said, reaching over and ending the call.

"What the hell, man? You can't hang up on a woman, especially not my sister. Now she's definitely going to freak out on us."

"Here," Bastien jabbed his finger against the windshield as they neared the exit to Cobb's Cove. "Turn here."

"Jesus!" Dickie hissed, the Jeep fishtailing slightly as he abruptly turned onto the sandy road. "A little notice next time would be good."

But Bastien couldn't have given Dickie notice any more than he could have predicted that on his eighteenth birthday he'd be bumping along the road to a nearly deserted beach parking lot next to a guy who still hadn't figured out that his nickname stemmed from his dickhead personality.

Dickie pulled in a few car lengths away from the only other car in the lot. "You sure about this? Josie's right. The storm is one thing now but," he hiked his bony shoulders, "it could turn bad real quick. You can surf better than anyone I've seen, but . . ." Bastien followed Dickie's gaze out the open window, to the thrashing, white-capped swells. "Those waves look brutal."

"Don't fret about me, no. *Je nage comme les poissons.*" I swim like the fishes. With a click of his tongue, Bastien hopped out of the Jeep and unstrapped his surfboard from the roof rack.

"It doesn't make me feel any better when you switch languages like that," Dickie called out.

Bastien rested his board against the car and leaned in through the window.

"You know, I didn't much like you at first," Dickie said, his long, skinny fingers picking at the Jeep emblem on the steering wheel. "But I guess I do now."

"Aww, little Dickie's sweet on me," Bastien said with a wink.

Dickie extended his middle finger. "Fuck off."

The phone rang, blaring through the speakers. "It's Josie," Dickie said, reaching down to silence it.

"Tell your sister I said thanks. For everything."

Are you coming back? The unspoken question caught in the air between them.

"Nah," Dickie ran his hand along the nape of his neck. "You tell her next time you see her."

With a nod, Bastien tucked his board under his arm and slapped the roof of the Jeep. "I'll be seeing you, *podna.*"

"Be safe out there, Bastien," Dickie said, putting the Jeep into drive. "And make those waves your bitch!" With a final whoop and a few quick honks of the horn, Dickie peeled out of the parking lot.

Squinting against the wind, Bastien turned to face the ocean. Leaving Louisiana had been easy, so why was putting Dickie and Josie in the rearview so much harder? He barely knew them. Sand crunched between his teeth as his jaw tensed against a sudden memory.

"You'll be back! This is your home! The only place anyone will ever love you!"

What his mother had said as he'd collected his board and walked out the door, it was wrong. *She* was wrong.

He dropped his board a few yards from the ocean's wet stain on the shore and slipped off his shoes.

This city could be his home. People would love him here. But he couldn't stay. The ocean wouldn't let him. It had called him here, to this cove, the same way the indescribable wave-like crashing in his gut had called him to Galveston. It was the same feeling he'd had as a little boy, that his mother had called a *grisgris*—a curse, the moment in time that had ruined her life, his life, their lives, the moment that had called forth the slick and then the silence.

So Bastien had swallowed the feeling, the curse. He'd buried it down deep under self-hate and despair. He'd tried to hide his tie to the ocean and be a better son. But his mother saw the strangeness of him growing behind his eyes. She always saw it. He was the planned mistake that hadn't saved her marriage, and had instead left them cursed.

Twelve years later, he looked inward at that pebble of a feeling he'd covered up for so long, and saw that his curse was a blessing, a way out, a compass. And he'd followed it here.

Bastien waded out until the sudsy waves lapped against his shins. He spread his arms wide and tipped his chin to the sky as the steady push and pull of the ocean drove him deeper and deeper into the sand. Yes, this could be his home.

"You shouldn't be out here!"

Bastien's arms snapped down to his sides as he swiveled his head to follow the voice.

"Hello! Hi!"

Bastien squinted at the willowy young woman standing even farther from the shoreline than he was. It was *her*. Had he really been so lost in his thoughts that he'd missed her?

She waved her long, graceful arms to get his attention before cupping her hands around her mouth. "Sorry, but the ocean, it's really angry. You shouldn't be here."

Bastien splashed toward her, his legs reacting to the sight of her, the *ange*, fluttering those delicate wings of hers as she warned him to be wary of the only thing in life he didn't fear.

He slowed before reaching her, careful to not splash her pretty blue top that fit her slim body like a second skin.

"Oh," a warm smile curled her pink lips. "It's you."

Bastien's mouth hung open, his thoughts heavily clanking together like marbles. *Speak!*

"Neither should you."

Wind whipped strands of her fair, blond hair from her ponytail and she tucked them behind her ear. "Neither should I what?" Quizzically, she looked up at him, but not too far up.

Bastien's cheeks warmed as a quick look took in the length of her silky, ballerinaesqe legs. Refusing to repeat his past behavior, he snapped his gaze back to hers. "Be out here. With the ocean like this, *furieux, sauvage*."

"Savage," her lips parted gently as she took in the gray waves reaching like mountains across the shore break. "Yes, that's a good way to describe it." She paused, closing her eyes and bending down until the end of her ponytail fell into the water and splayed under the surface like threads of gold.

The way she listened to the water was the most beautiful thing Bastien had ever seen. Every nerve in his body, every tendril of his soul yearned to reach out to her.

Her eyelids fluttered open and she abruptly righted herself, her cheeks deepening to a bright coral reef pink. "Sorry, I'm not sure what came over me." She held on to the dripping end of her ponytail as she braced herself against a sudden gust of wind. "But you definitely shouldn't be here. I um, I have to be. I can't explain it exactly, but I do."

The water cooled and thickened to jam around his feet. They were coming. "I'm staying here, me."

The wind intensified, hurling sprays of salty water against them.

"It's getting worse." Her eyes seemed to darken, reflecting the same oyster gray as the roiling waves.

"Ouragan," hurricane. Bastien whispered as the first droplets of rain splattered against his shoulders.

Violent splashing pulled Bastien's attention from the darkening sky and ominous, curling waves to the shore behind him. A lean, scraggly beast sprinted toward them, its tongue flopped listlessly to the side as it splashed closer.

Bastien tensed, readying himself as the long-legged beauty skipped a few paces toward the animal and crouched down, her arms spread wide.

"No!" Bastien leaped forward as the two of them collided, the young woman falling back onto her butt in a splash of water and giggles.

"It's fine," she laughed, coming to her knees and wrapping her slender arms around the dog's lean neck. "She just wanted to say hello." She buried her face into the wet fur with a smacking kiss noise.

Bastien unclenched his fist and tentatively extended his hand. Growing up, he hadn't had a dog or any animal, so he wasn't certain if the scruffy dog would take to him. She pressed her cold nose against his fingers and, with a wag of her tail, licked the rain pooling in his palm.

A sharp whistle split the air, followed by a shout.

"Bugs-a-Million!" A gravelly voice called over the increasing wind and pelting rain. "Bugsy, ol' girl, get back here!"

The young woman waved to the man in the same graceful, fluttering way she had to Bastien as she hooked the fingers of her free hand under the big dog's collar. "She's no bother!" she shouted, leading the bouncing dog to its owner.

Bastien bit his lower lip, nodding at the shadows circling his feet before following her to shore.

"Really, it was nice having another visitor," the young woman was saying as she twirled one of the dog's floppy ears between her fingers.

"I appreciate you returning my girl to me, Miss . . ."

"Charlotte," her curtsey echoed the old Southern politeness and charm he hadn't realized he'd been missing. "And this is Bastien."

She remembers! Bastien silently cursed himself for not having enough sense to ask for her name.

The gentle creases around the old man's eyes deepened with a squint. "Well, I'll be goddamned. No wonder you two are out here acting like this is some regular ol' day when there's a big storm coming." He scratched the top of the dog's scruffy head. "And it's raining again. Damn." He peered down at his companion who looked up at him expectantly. "Not a good sign, ol' girl. Not a good sign at all. But goddammit, we found 'em. We still got it, Bugsy." Then he lifted his gaze to the two of them again. "My name is Linus Bowen. I live down the beach a couple miles. Do either of you have a phone? I need to make a call. Fast. It's an emergency. Then I need to talk to you kids. It's going to sound crazy, but—"

"Mr. Bowen!"

The old guy whipped around with the agility of a much younger man. A switch flipped inside the huge dog's head, sending it from a tongue-lolling sweetheart to a dangerous beast. She hugged Bowen's side, lips curled back in a growl as a petite black woman, flanked by three men, seemed to materialize from the rain and wind.

"Like I said before, you're a hard man to find."

29

CHARLOTTE

As soon as the four people appeared the change in Bugsy's demeanor reflected the tension that was visible in Bowen—and that had Charlotte instantly on guard.

"Kids," the old man positioned himself and the big dog between Bastien and her, and the four approaching interlopers while he spoke urgently under his voice to them. "Whose car is that in the parking lot?"

"Mine," Charlotte said.

"Good. You and the boy get out of here. Now. I'll handle them." Then Bowen started forward as if to cut the four off from getting too close. "Fine. You found me. I'll come back with you." As he spoke he motioned behind his back for Charlotte and Bastien to flee.

Charlotte looked at the handsome, dark-haired Cajun. Their eyes met.

"Something feels wrong," he said.

"I think so, too," Charlotte agreed.

"I don't like the old guy's odds," Bastien said.

"Then let's help even them." Charlotte folded her arms across her chest and stood her ground. From the corner of her eye she saw Bastien mirroring her.

Bowen glanced back at them and whispered, "Kids! Get out of here!"

"No, sir," Bastien said. "Not unless you come with us. It's not good to be out here in this storm."

"Aww, how sweet. And convenient. You've already made friends with Bastien and Charlotte. That makes everything so much easier," said the petite black woman with mean eyes.

"How do you know our names?" Charlotte stepped up beside Bugsy.

"Yeah, I'd like to know that, too," Bastien said, moving so that he stood on her other side.

"I see Bowen's already been filling your heads full of lies about us," said the woman.

"Eve, I just met these two kids. I haven't said anything to them except that they need to get the hell out of here, and that's not a lie. I don't lie. I've lived a long time and learned decades ago lies make things worse. So, you know I'm telling you the honest truth when I say this," the old man looked from Charlotte to Bastien. "You two need to get to that car and get out of here. These four aren't just after me. They're after you, too. And they're bad news."

"Shut it, old man. In one day you've been enough trouble for a lifetime," shouted one of the men. He had a strange shock of white hair that lifted from his head like it'd been poured from a Dairy Queen vanilla ice cream spout.

"That's not a polite way to talk to your elders," Bastien's voice deepened with anger.

"No one asked you, water boy," the man sneered.

"Luke! Enough!" snapped Eve before she refocused on Charlotte, Bastien, and Bowen. Charlotte watched the woman's face attempt to form a smile, but she thought it looked more like a grimace. "Okay, I'm going to make this fast because I'm really sick of this weather." She wiped a hand across her rain-soaked face. "Charlotte and Bastien, I'd like to introduce myself and my brothers to you. I am Eve Stewart, and these three are Luke, Matthew, and Mark Stewart." Each man nodded as she called his name, though the handsome, dark-haired Mark looked obviously uncomfortable. "We know your names because you're the reason we're here."

"Why?" Charlotte said.

"And how could you know I would be here? No one knows that," Bastien added.

Eve's smile looked genuine for the first time. "Oh, that's easy. We knew you'd be here because Mark drew you here with this storm. You see, Mark is special like you two are special. He also has a connection with water."

Charlotte felt as if the woman had punched her in the gut. *How did Eve know?*

"What do you mean, our connection to water?" Charlotte said.

"Oh, no need to be coy. Tell Bastien and Charlotte how well you understand them, Mark," Eve said.

Mark had been staring out at the angry ocean, but at Eve's words he pulled his gaze away and looked from Charlotte to Bastien. Charlotte thought she'd never seen such hopelessness in anyone's eyes before—ever. And that included her own reflection during the emptiest, most horrible times in her life.

"You've always loved water, especially the ocean. It started when you were children, probably about six years old."

Charlotte jerked in surprise and sensed Bastien reacting the same.

"You're most at peace in or on the water," Mark continued, speaking slowly and carefully so that he could be heard above the crashing waves and whining wind. "You even sense things about it, see things or hear things, that no one else does, and when you've tried to explain those things to friends or family, no one ever understands you."

"What else?" Bastien said.

"You were drawn here today, this morning, without understanding why, but you *had* to come here," Mark said.

"This is too weird," Charlotte said. "Look, if you have something to tell us, fine. I'll give you my phone number and maybe we can talk sometime, but not here. Not now."

"Your parents went to a lot of trouble to conceive both of you at a special clinic in Portland, Oregon. Did you know that?"

Eve's words made Bastien's body go rigid as Charlotte felt ice enter her blood. *Her mother and father had told her over and over about the fertility*

*treatments at the famous clinic in Portland, and how much the in vitro fertil-
ization had cost—like it had been Charlotte's fault her mother's uterus was unable to conceive a child.*

"Who exactly are you? What does Mr. Bowen have to do with this? And
what do you want?" Bastien's voice was flint.

"Your annoying questions have given me an excellent idea," Eve said.
"Bowen can help me explain all of this because *he doesn't lie.* So, tell them what
this has to do with you, old man."

Mr. Bowen ignored Eve and Mark, speaking only to Charlotte and Bastien. "My grandson, Tate, he's like you two, only he has a special connection
with air. His friend, Foster, has it, too. There are eight of you—four pairs.
Each pair is connected to an element. They're after me because my grandson
and Foster have managed to stay free of them and they're trying to trap the
two of them by grabbing me. Who are the four of them? Well, they're jackasses who are brainwashed goons for the biggest jackass of them all—the scientist who did this to you, Rick Stewart. Far as I can figure, he's crazy as a
damn bedbug."

"That's it, you old pain in the ass! I'm so done taking your shit!" Luke
started toward Bowen. His hands were raised, and Charlotte saw that *they were
glowing, like candle wicks, causing the rain falling on them to sizzle and turn to
steam!*

Mr. Bowen's big dog, who had been growling softly ever since the four had
made an appearance, stalked forward, teeth bared menacingly.

Luke's small, mean eyes glittered with excitement. He snarled at Bugsy
and stomped at her, obviously baiting the dog. And it worked. Barking furi-
ously, Bugs-a-Million lunged forward.

"Bugsy, no! Come back—" Bowen began. The big dog paused and turned
her head to look at her master.

Charlotte hadn't been able to take her eyes from Luke's burning hands,
so she saw everything—how Luke flicked his wrists, somehow throwing the
glowing flames at Bugsy!

The flames landed on the dog, lighting her fur instantly as Bugsy's growl
changed to howls of pain.

"No!" Bowen shouted. He ripped the sweatshirt from around his waist and sprinted to the dog, but as the fire caught more of her fur, Bugsy panicked and ran. "Bugsy! Come, girl! Come!" Bowen cried as he rushed after her.

No, please don't let that sweet dog burn to death! Charlotte was frozen with horror. She couldn't think. She only felt. Instinct flooded her as the beautiful, magical voices echoed from the ocean and filled her ears with words she suddenly understood, *"Put it out! Put it out! Put it out! Drown fire! Drown fire! Drown fire!"* The strange song blasted through her mind until Charlotte couldn't bear the pressure of it anymore, and the words exploded from the depths of her soul as she screamed them: *Put it out! Drown fire!*

From the seething ocean an enormous arm of water lifted. As if it was sentient, it crashed past the shoreline, lifted again, gaining energy and speed as it followed the panicked dog, passing Bowen and easily catching her, it poured over Bugsy, extinguishing every bit of the fire.

Charlotte didn't realize that she'd moved with the wave until her running feet tripped over a rough tuft of sea grass and she almost fell headfirst into the sand, but Bastien's strong hand was there, steadying her and helping her to her feet.

That's when it happened. The instant they touched. They were at the shoreline, just yards away from Bugsy and Bowen, but Charlotte wasn't looking at them. She only had eyes for the ocean and the beings of ethereal beauty she could finally see, just beneath the surface. The creatures, shimmering like the Northern Lights, were huge, but as graceful as hummingbirds and as delicate as butterflies as they circled and frolicked in the waves while they sang and sang and sang the wordless melody Charlotte had been listening to since she was a little girl.

"So beautiful! I—I can't believe how beautiful they are!" Mesmerized, she spoke to herself, as Charlotte was in a watery world of her own—until she realized Bastien was still holding her hand.

"You can see them!" he said, staring at her with eyes wide with shock.

Through their joined hands, Charlotte could feel him trembling. "I can." She spoke softly, reverently, as if they were in a fantastic library or otherworldly cathedral. And then she understood. "You can hear them, too!"

Bastien nodded, his eyes bright with tears. "I can! I have always been able to see them, but I've never heard them before now, this moment."

"And I've always heard them, but never seen them. Not until now."

"Don't they terrify you?"

Charlotte turned with Bastien to face Mark. He was standing beside them, his handsome face white with fear as he stared out at the waves.

"No," Charlotte answered automatically, and though she wanted to reach out to the man, she stopped herself and held tighter to Bastien's hand. "How could they terrify anyone? They're beautiful."

"They're beyond beautiful. They're *magique,*" Bastien said.

"Isn't this interesting?" Eve joined them. "I don't see anything or hear anything, but you water people obviously do. And what Bastien and Charlotte see *isn't* terrifying." Eve shot Mark a pointed look. "If I wasn't such a good sister, I'd say told ya so." Then she called over her shoulder to her other two brothers. "Matthew, tie up the old man. Luke, come here and give me a hand with these two."

Charlotte's gaze went to Bowen and Bugsy. The old man was on his knees beside his dog, running trembling hands over her singed, but apparently uninjured body.

"Why are you tying him up?" Charlotte felt as if she must be in a waking dream that was part fantasy, part nightmare. It was hard for her to focus on anything but the alluring sirens that were calling . . . calling . . . to her.

"Oh, don't worry about that. We're not going to hurt him. It'll just make things easier," Eve said. "Now it's time for you and Bastien to come with us."

"Huh? Where?" Charlotte struggled to think through the pull of the ocean.

"You're going to love it. It's an island all to ourselves. We'll go there and Mark will show you how to control your powers," Eve said.

"Powers?" Bastien sounded as foggy as Charlotte felt, and his gaze kept drifting out to the seething waves.

"Well, yes. Like commanding a wave to put out a dog fire. Nice trick," Eve said. "Only bigger and better."

"Wait, I need time to think about what's going on," Charlotte began. A gust of wind caught her hair, whipping it across her face, and she pulled her hand from Bastien's to clear her vision . . .

The singing stopped. The shimmering creatures dissolved into waves.

Charlotte's mind cleared.

"No. We're not going with you." Bastien's voice was flint.

"I'm with Bastien. If we have to pick a side, I'm taking Mr. Bowen's. As my grandma would say, setting his dog on fire was impolite, and that's about as bad as it gets if you're a Southern woman."

Eve shrugged her shoulders. "Have it your way. If you're on Bowen's side, we'll treat you like we treat him. Luke, tie them up."

Bastien and Charlotte moved together, backing slowly into the ocean, with Luke, hands alight, following them—though he hesitated at the water-line as the reaching waves hissed and steamed at his feet.

"Now this is truly a pain in the ass!" Eve snapped. Her face was twisted into a mask of anger and very deliberately, she stomped her foot—and the sandy ground under their feet shook.

Charlotte gasped in shock.

"Charlotte! Bastien! You kids get away! Get out in that water and swim!" Bowen shouted at them.

Charlotte could see that Matthew was closing on Bowen, who was standing in front of a soggy, singed, and panting Bugsy.

"Ready to swim?" Bastien spoke low, for her ears only.

She'd just begun to nod when everything changed. A voice boomed across the beach.

"Get the fuck away from my g-pa, you dickhead!"

Charlotte looked up the beach to see a couple—a very muscly, very pissed-off-looking guy and a pretty redhead—sprinting across the sand toward them.

"Isn't this your saying, Mark: when it rains it pours?" Eve spoke sarcastically, turning with her brother to face the two newcomers.

30

TATE

"Okay, look down that road as we drive by. See that big yellow house on stilts?" Tate lifted one hand from the wheel and pointed.

"Yeah, I see it," Foster said, peering around Tate.

"That's G-pa's house."

"Then why are we driving past it?"

"Because *we* aren't going in there. I am," Tate said. When Foster sucked air and opened her mouth to blast him, he held up his hand to stop her and tried to sound reasonable. "Think about it, Foster. It is the right plan. If they have both of us they get what they want, and we don't have any bargaining power at all."

"So instead you're going to give yourself up and then what?"

Grinning, Tate gave her a sideways leer and said, "Then you'll rescue me—as usual."

"No."

"Yes."

"Tate, *no.*"

"Foster, it's the only way. I'm going to pull off this highway in about a mile or so at a place called Cobb's Cove. There's a parking lot there where you can wait. It's walking distance down the beach to G-pa's property. I know this peninsula. I spent every summer vacation here. I'm going to sneak up to G-pa's house and check things out. If I can get him out of there, I will. If not, I'll come back to the cove and we can figure out what to do."

"And what if you get caught?"

"I won't get caught."

Foster snorted.

Tate held up the burner phone that was a twin of the one in Foster's pocket. "We have these. If I'm not back in an hour and you don't have a text from me, call me. If Eve answers, you know I'm in trouble."

"I don't like it."

"But it makes sense," Tate said.

"It's misogynistic. If I were a guy you wouldn't be telling me to stay behind."

"If you were a guy who wasn't familiar with G-pa's place, I would definitely be telling you to stay behind. Foster, you kick ass. There's no doubt about that. But do you know how to get into and out of G-pa's spare room upstairs?"

"Of course not," Foster said.

"I do. I used to sneak out all the time when we spent summers here with G-pa. Had to bribe Bugsy, but still." He reached across the center console and took Foster's hand, raising it to his lips. "Trust me, okay?"

Foster scrunched down in her seat, folding her arms around herself. Tate thought she looked like an adorable, pissed-off little girl, but he valued his life and would never, ever tell her that.

"There it is, Cobb's Cove drive." Tate braked and turned left. "Damn, almost didn't see it through all this rain."

"Yeah, it let up for a while, but it's definitely back now. Are you sure you don't want me to drop you off closer to your g-pa's house?"

"Nah, this is fine." They bumped down the road, slowing as it turned to a sandy parking lot that held only one other car. "Okay, you wait here, and—"

"Tate! Look!" Foster pointed down the beach, and Tate's eyes followed her finger.

All hell was breaking loose down there! Tate saw two kids backing into the crashing waves, while Eve, Luke, and Mark faced them down, and a few yards away Matthew was circling . . .

"G-pa and Bugsy! Hell no, they're not gonna mess with my g-pa!" Tate was out the door and moving so fast he didn't expect Foster to keep up with him, let alone stop him. But suddenly there she was, standing in front of his face, with her hands on her hips.

"Foster, it's G-pa!"

"I know." She put her hands on his chest and looked into his eyes. "You have to calm down, Tate. Remember what happened the last time we messed with air and didn't have ourselves under control?"

Tate nodded shakily, his eyes darting to the beach. "Okay, okay. I hear you."

"Breathe. Think. Do not let them get to you. And remember, I'm here. Right here with you. We're going to get your g-pa away from them. Together."

"Okay. You're right." Tate spoke more calmly as he focused more on Foster's green eyes than what was happening on the beach.

"Ready?" she asked.

"I think so," he said.

Foster tiptoed and kissed him softly. "How about now?"

"Now I know so." It was then that the sandy ground beneath them shook. Tate's eyes narrowed. "Okay, let's go be superheroes and save the day."

"Absolutely," Foster said.

Side by side, they sprinted to the beach.

Foster

Foster ran after Tate, silently praying that he kept a handle on his temper.

"Tate! Son!" His g-pa shouted. Matthew had been approaching the old man and the waterlogged, giant dog, but at the sound of Tate's voice the big dog's ears and tail went up, and with a happy bark, she dashed past Matthew and ran to meet Tate.

"Good girl! Good Bugsy! What happened to you, old girl? You look terrible." Tate crouched to greet the dog.

"Oof!"

Foster glanced down the beach in time to see Tate's million-year-old g-pa lower his head, sprint at the Matthew man, and like he was playing college ball, knock the younger man smack on his butt as he raced past him straight to Tate's side.

"G-pa!"

The old man pulled Tate into a fast bear hug, speaking urgently and quickly. "Eve's bad news. She's got the water kids Charlotte and Bastien over there with Luke, the second worst, and Mark, who doesn't want to hurt anyone. Matthew is a follower."

"Welcome, Tate and Foster." Eve strode away from the two strangers standing knee-deep in the roiling waves. Her brothers stiffened as she walked past, their heads swiveling between the sets of teens. "I'm so glad we're all together now."

"Hello, Eve," Foster pinned her fists to her hips and planted her feet in the sand. "You bitch."

"Is that any way for family to speak to each other?"

"I don't have any family. They're all dead, and I'm no part of whatever twisted thing you have going on."

"All dead? Oh no, my sister, our father is alive and well and wants very much for us to be reunited."

"A father doesn't kidnap his children," G-pa said with a disgusted shake of his head.

"We haven't kidnapped anyone, old man," Luke shouted.

"Fire boy, you're a jackass," G-pa spoke to him dismissively. "And I've listened to your lot scheme and plan for the past twenty-four hours. You're here to take these kids from their lives—to steal them away to fulfill some fantasy your *father* has brainwashed you into believing. That's not a family. That's a delusion."

Foster said nothing as she squinted against the wind and rain, her eyes following Bastien and Charlotte's slow retreat toward the heaving waves.

Wait! Foster's mouth formed the word, but it lodged in her throat. They should leave—sink beneath the storm and swim, swim, swim. Now she and Tate knew their names, had seen their faces. With Sabine's help, they would find them again.

"Mark! Stop them!" Eve's shout split the howling gusts.

Foster's focus shattered, her hands tingling as air currents flickered to life around her. She had to do something. She wouldn't be a spectator, not if it meant the Fucktastic Four would win.

A sharp blast of wind caught Eve and she turned, her features softening slightly as she closed her eyes and steadied herself. But there was something about the fullness of her cheeks; her wide-set, almond eyes; and the way she held her mouth that ghosted over Foster's subconscious, haunting her with a familiarity that made her step forward, closer to Eve, closer to . . .

Cora?

Foster's fists relaxed and the shimmering currents dissipated as she stared at a younger copy of the woman she called Mother.

Eve shifted, snapping her attention back to her brothers, and it was gone. Cora's soft lines cracked like dry earth, exhuming Eve—hard and mean and ruthless.

"Mark, wake the fuck up and do *something* right!" Luke sneered.

With a commanding sweep of his arms, Mark directed the churning seas, "Bring them back!"

The water rippled and flexed, lifting tongue-like from the sand as it lapped toward Eve, cradling Bastien and Charlotte. He clutched her against him as he rode the wave and pointed at the shore, at Foster. "Take us there, you!" The wave seized a moment as if weighing its options before changing course and heading toward her, Tate, Bugsy, and G-pa.

The wave slid closer, and water rushed around Foster's feet. *"Merci, ami."* Bastien bowed slightly as he and Charlotte stepped from the swell that had rolled out to present them.

The girl tripped and almost fell into Foster. Righting herself quickly, she brushed back a soggy, blond strand of hair and held her hand out as if she was at a cotillion.

"Charmed to meet you. I'm Charlotte and this is Bast—"

"Look around, Scarlet O'Hara. This is not the time for Southern charm."

"But we're glad we found the two of you," Tate added.

"Goddamnit. Bugsy found 'em. But Foster's right. Southern charm later. Let's get out of here now," G-pa said.

"Seriously?" Eve faced their group, her brothers tightening the defensive line behind her. "I know the four of you are *special*, but Jesus you're stupid. Or shall we all just have a tea party here and become, wait, how do you say it— BFFs?"

Foster swiped at the droplets clinging to her lashes. "Are we done yet with the tight-ass-bitch routine? I'm pretty fucking tired of standing in a hurricane."

"And you're crazy, you," Bastien muttered.

"He's right. You're insane. And we're going home. Now." Foster started to back away, and the group moved with her.

"So, are you all children and Foster is your mommy who makes decisions for you?" Eve's voice filled with sarcasm.

"You were going to tie Mr. Bowen up and drag him down the sand *after* you told that horrid fire person to burn up his dog. I don't need a mama to decide for me that I'm not going anywhere with you," Charlotte was the first to speak up.

"Foster and I are together on this. We want nothing to do with any of you," Tate said.

"Leave these kids alone and crawl back under whatever rock someone was stupid enough to lift off you," G-pa grumbled.

"Old man, I have had all I can take of your mouth!" Luke raised his hands and as they began to glow, he started forward.

Tate moved fast, shoving his grandpa and Bugsy behind him. The four kids stood side by side, blocking Luke.

Foster took half a step forward. Wind followed her, lifting her wild red hair ominously. "I will blow that little hand fire of yours up your ass if you try that shit with us." The sky above Foster darkened as air rotated around them, blowing out Luke's twin flames like candles on a birthday cake.

"Oooh, so angry! So passionate! Father's going to love dealing with you," Eve said.

"Too bad he won't get the chance," Foster replied.

"Oh, sister. That's just one of the many things you're wrong about." Then Eve lifted her foot and stomped. Hard.

The earth beneath them shivered as if they were standing on a plate of Jell-O, knocking Foster to her knees. Tate was there in an instant, taking her arm and helping her regain her feet.

"Get off me!" Foster jerked free. "I can handle her myself." Undiscovered rage coiled in her gut. Her father had sent the Four. He'd put her and Cora through the anguish of losing him and the panic of running from his sick creations, and for what? So he could send the children he deemed worthy of his love to capture the only one who truly knew him as father?

Foster understood how he saw her.

She wasn't deserving.

Message received.

Now she'd send a message of her own.

It started with her hair—the air lifting her long, wet strands as if gravity had stitched itself between the clouds. Currents blazed to life around her, snapping snake-like at the unrelenting rain as her arms lifted and her heels rose weightless from the sand.

"Cyclone," Bastien breathed, and Foster tilted her chin toward the heavens.

The clouds were cement, pouring a thick, gray funnel above her like ice cream. Foster's spine frosted and her feet settled against the earth.

Her hate would kill them.

Eve's laughter filled the angry wind. "That's right! Call the cyclone. Show us your power and tear up this pathetic excuse for a town."

Tate's hand slipped over Foster's. Gently prying open her clenched fist, he wove his fingers between hers. "Not with anger, Foster. That'll only bring more death—more sadness."

"Anger's never the way." G-pa's gruff voice sliced through the wind, opening a conduit directly to Foster's heart.

"Shut it, old man," Luke said.

"Yeah, you're just jealous that anger's doing all of this." Matthew's arm swept up at the malevolent funnel swirling above Foster. "Check it out, you fossil. *This* is real power."

"No. This isn't real power." Charlotte was suddenly there, standing beside Foster. "Anger's *not* the way because hate isn't the strongest emotion."

"That would be *amour*—love," Bastien said, stepping up beside Charlotte.

"No, that would be childish bullshit," Eve said. "But enough of this. Here's the truth, precious little Foster. It's your turn to act like a real daughter and be there for Father. At his side. Where he needs you and your powers."

"Be there for him? Or be complicit in his crimes and madness like you've been?" Foster shot back at her.

"You know nothing, child," Eve said.

At that moment Eve seemed to speak Cora's words and Foster's breath caught in her throat. As she stared at Eve, seeing the familiar stranger within her expression, Foster's anger snuffed.

"I know the difference between right and wrong—helping and enabling. I don't know what broke you, Eve, but I pity you," Foster said.

Eve's dark eyes flashed with something that might have been embarrassment, but it was gone too fast for Foster to truly name it. Then the older woman shrugged. "No matter. Being a good daughter is a learned behavior. Time for you to go to school, Foster."

Foster's grin split her face and had her laughing with amusement. "School? No thanks. Never liked it. I prefer to think for myself."

"That's enough. Matthew, Mark, Luke, back me up! *Time* to *end* this *now!*" With every other word she stomped her foot. The earth flinched and quivered in response.

Charlotte's wet fingers found Foster's. "What can we do?"

"I'll fry you crispy!" Luke lunged forward, flames shooting from his glowing hands.

Foster didn't hesitate. She leaned forward, anchored to the ground by Tate and Charlotte, and blew a calming, soothing exhale. Wind crashed into fire. Luke groaned, his feet digging trenches in the sand as his flames suffocated.

"It's love, right?" Charlotte shouted excitedly over Foster's breath.

Luke fell to his knees, and Matthew rushed to his side. They had moments, seconds to work out a way to stay free, to survive.

"Are you thinking what I'm thinking?" Foster asked.

Charlotte held her free hand out to Bastien. As he twined his fingers with hers, she cleared her throat. "I love being a girl!" The thrashing waves changed direction, pulsing closer to shore, closer to the Fucktastic Four as Charlotte turned to Bastien.

"*Liberté!*" he hollered. Salt water rushed forward and pushed Matthew, Mark, Luke, and Eve's feet out from under them. The Four splashed against the rapidly deepening water in a jumble of legs and arms and curses.

"And I love my grandma Myrtie!" Charlotte added. The ocean surged then, filling an invisible bowl and surrounding the Four in a bubble of good wishes and water.

"I love strawberries!" Tate winked at Foster, a small laugh twitching his lips as the Fucktastic Four beat against the skin of the slowly spinning circle.

Hand in hand, Foster led Tate, Charlotte, and Bastien to their creation. Beads of air shot from Eve's mouth as she floated, kicking and screaming. Compassion twitched through Foster as she met Eve's wild eyes.

Does who you love, love you back?

Foster wet her lips and took a deep breath. "I love my mother, my Cora. Now, Tate," she glanced at her Clark Kent, his shirt billowing behind him, a bit cape-like, in the strong gusts. "Let's make them fly." They lifted their joined hands and flicked their wrists as if shooing a bug. The rippling ball surged up, then out, out, out, a liquid meteor arching past the horizon to disappear against the clearing sky.

The change was instantaneous. The rain stopped. The wind faded to a warm caress, the clouds clearing to reveal the aquamarine sky. Foster staggered, and Tate caught her, hugging her tightly as he whispered against her ear, "We did it! We did it!"

Someone coughed and they turned to face Charlotte, Bastien, and the waterlogged G-pa and his Bugsy.

"What now?" asked Charlotte as her gaze went from Foster to Tate, and back to Foster again.

"Well, we'd like you to come home with us—to our Fortress of Sauvietude," Foster said, trying her best to sound friendly and reasonable and not psycho-killer-like.

"Yeah, it's a long trip home, but a really good story. Promise," Tate said.

"Are you *asking* or *telling* us to?" Bastien spoke up.

"Or *forcing*," Charlotte added.

"Asking." Foster shrugged, putting on a show of being unconcerned. "Unless you think you have a better shot on your own."

"What she is trying to say is that we can't promise the Fucktastic Four won't find us," Tate said. "We can't promise you'll be safe, but I give you my word that we think we have a better shot together than apart."

"You can believe them," Bowen said, resting his hand on his big dog's head. "They're like me. They don't lie."

Tate grinned at his g-pa before saying, "We'll never lie to you. Or evade any of your questions. Ever."

"But we're not perfect," Foster said. "And we don't have all the answers. Actually, we don't have many answers. But we're not about threats or kidnapping or any of that garbage."

Charlotte and Bastien shared a long look, then the girl returned her attention to Tate, Foster, and Bowen.

"Yes, I'll come with you," Charlotte said.

"*Oui.* I go with Charlotte, me." Bastien nodded.

"Great!" Tate said, with an enthusiastic bob of his head.

Foster chewed the inside of her cheek and shifted uncomfortably. Charlotte and Bastien had agreed, which was fantastic. Well, maybe not super fantastic. Who knew what kind of weird quirks the two of them had. But they would be safe. All of them. Together.

Charlotte dug the toe of her shoe into the sand. "Umm. How are we getting to this Sauvietude place?"

"And what is it?" Bastien asked, scrubbing his hand down his tanned bicep.

"Well, that's part of the long story." Tate's chipper ease reminded Foster of a museum docent, which wasn't too far off since they probably qualified for their own exhibit by now. "How about we hit the road and explain things as we go?"

When Charlotte and Bastien hesitated, Foster added, "Or you can hang around here and wait to see if the Fucktastic Four blow back to shore."

"No." Wet, blond strands brushed Charlotte's shoulders as she shook her head. "I don't believe I'd like to do that."

"All right then, let's get out of here," Tate said, taking Foster's hand.

As they sloughed through the wet sand back to the parking lot, Linus Bowen ruffled the singed fur on the top of Bugsy's head. "Good thing I'm a rich old man. Let's get ourselves onto my plane and take a little trip. This family's growing like fleas on an old dog." Bugsy barked once, and Bowen chuckled. "Oh, not you, ol' girl. You're too sweet for fleas. Gotta get these kids to their fortress, though. Life just gets more and more interesting, doesn't it, Bugsy? And I can't wait for what's coming next . . ."

The end . . . for now

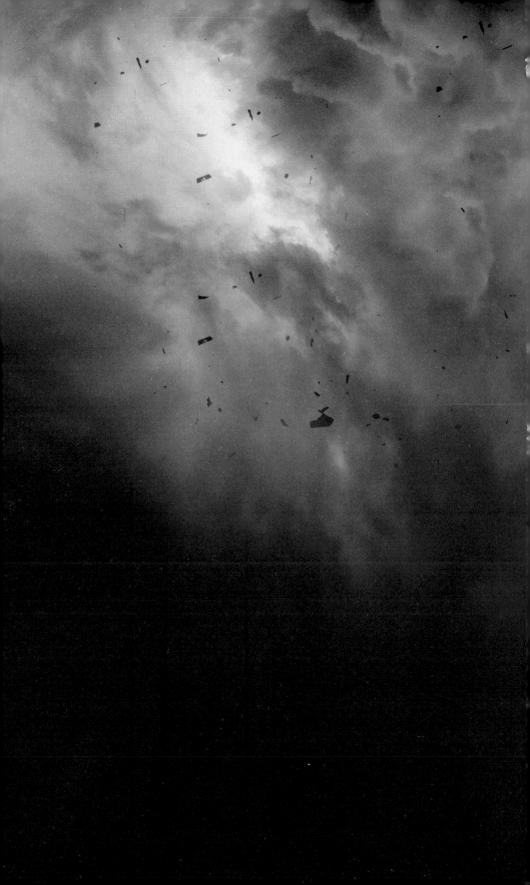